P9-DWY-250

plan B

sharon lee and steve miller

BAKER COUNTY LIBRARY
2400 RESORT
BAKER CITY, OREGON 97814

2003
50TH
ANNIVERSARY

ACE BOOKS, NEW YORK

If you purchased this book without a cover, you should be aware that this book is stolen property. It was reported as "unsold and destroyed" to the publisher, and neither the author nor the publisher has received any payment for this "stripped book."

This is a work of fiction. Names, characters, places, and incidents either are the product of the author's imagination or are used fictitiously, and any resemblance to actual persons, living or dead, business establishments, events, or locales is entirely coincidental.

PLAN B

An Ace Book / published by arrangement with
Meisha Merlin Publishing

PRINTING HISTORY
Meisha Merlin trade paperback edition / February 1999
Ace mass-market edition / May 2003

Copyright © 1998 by Sharon Lee and Steve Miller.
Liaden Universe registered ® 2000 by Sharon Lee and Steve Miller.
Cover art by Michael Herring.
Text design by Julie Rogers.

All rights reserved.
This book, or parts thereof, may not be reproduced in any form without permission. The scanning, uploading, and distribution of this book via the Internet or via any other means without the permission of the publisher is illegal and punishable by law. Please purchase only authorized electronic editions, and do not participate in or encourage electronic piracy of copyrighted materials. Your support of the author's rights is appreciated.

For information address: Meisha Merlin Publishing, Inc.,
PO Box 7, Decatur, Georgia 30031.

ISBN: 0-441-01053-9

ACE®
Ace Books are published by The Berkley Publishing Group,
a division of Penguin Group (USA) Inc.,
375 Hudson Street, New York, New York 10014.
ACE and the "A" design
are trademarks belonging to Penguin Group (USA) Inc.

PRINTED IN THE UNITED STATES OF AMERICA

10 9 8 7 6 5 4 3 2 1

PB Science Fiction
Lee, Sharon
Plan B

DISCARDED
BAKER CO. LIBRARY

BAKER COUNTY PUBLIC LIBRARY

3 7814 00224 6784

and totally entertained, I am

LOCAL CUSTOM
CONFLICT OF HONORS · AGENT OF CHANGE · CARPE DIEM

AND COMING IN AUGUST 2003
I DARE

**Praise for Sharon Lee and Steve Miller's novels
of the Liaden Universe® . . .**

"One of the never-failing joys of [*Local Custom*] is the crisp language, the well-turned phrases, the very exciting action, not to mention the confrontation of two vastly different cultures."
        —Anne McCaffrey, author of the Dragonriders of Pern series

"The stories have it all. Adventure, intrigue, romance. Loyal friendships and hidden treachery. The authors deftly weave plot elements that stretch across the known universe, while still remaining focused on the characters who drive the action."   —Patricia Bray, author of *Devlin's Luck*

"Sharon Lee and Steve Miller have imaginations matched only by the precision of their writing."
        —Gerry Boyle, author of *Cover Story*

"Lee and Miller strike space opera gold."
        —Robin Wayne Bailey, author of *Night's Angel*

"Val Con and Miri are the most romantic couple in SF!"
        —Susan Krinard, author of *Touch of the Wolf*

"The Liaden series is a satisfying blend of adventure, political intrigue, and romance. The authors do a wonderful job of portraying several different cultures, and the inevitable clashes that occur as Terrans, Liaden, Yxtrang, and Clutch Turtles interact. I highly recommend *Plan B,* and am anxiously awaiting the reissue of the first books, so I can share the Liaden universe with my friends."

        —*Science Fiction Romance*

continued . . .

"Lee and Miller have taken standard space adventure fare, added a touch of romance, and turned the whole into powerful stories."   —Melisa Michaels, author of *Cold Iron*

"I was mesmerized, awed, and totally entertained. Only rarely do I read a book that I literally can't put down, that draws me so deeply into the world created by the authors that I feel a part of it and don't want to let it go. It happened with [*Local Custom*]. I loved the action, the conflict of cultures, the characters, and the romance. But best of all, and what makes each story enduringly special to me, is the strong sense of honor that impels the actions of the main characters and is often the basis of the conflicts among them. The Liaden world is an admirable world."   —Mary Balogh, author of *More than a Mistress*

"The plot threads are intricately interwoven . . . The plotting is careful and well-balanced . . . the great excellence lies in the relationships."   —*Analog*

"You may never care about a cast of characters more or await their return with more anticipation."   —*SF Site*

"Full of action, exotic characters, plenty of plot, and even a touch of romance. Outstanding."   —*Booklist*

"Space opera isn't just ripsnortin' adventure, though Lee and Miller give us plenty of that. The thing about space opera is it's more that nifty science, the clash of customs, the evolution of ideas, interesting planets, cool tech, and new pioneers, it's also and above all about character . . . and one cares about the characters, about their further adventures, and their families' adventures, and even about the villains. The Liaden Universe stories are very good space opera."
      —Sherwood Smith, author of *Journey to Otherwhere*

"Ambitiously creating a complex emotional environment, Mr. Miller and Ms. Lee pique our curiosity with an equally complicated plot development."   —*Romantic Times*

"No other authors can compare to their skill at bringing characters to full and robust life, half convincing me that there is a time portal to the future, hidden up in Maine through which Sharon and Steve have been watching and recording the lives of the Liadens for years."
      —Jennifer Dunne, author of *Raven's Heart*

PB
Science
Fiction
LEE
(Sharon)

JUL 21 2009

For the Friends of Liad:
lisamia keshoc.
We are in your debt.

Here we stand: An old woman, a halfling boy, two babes; a contract, a ship, and a Tree.
Clan Korval.
How Jela would laugh.

—Excerpted from Cantra yos'Phelium's Log Book

LIAD

DEPARTMENT OF INTERIOR COMMAND HEADQUARTERS

There was time, but neither night nor day.

Time. Current time on twenty planets was counted along the digital displays in the long left wall. The light was impartial, unchanging. Shadowless.

In addition to the silent, steady chronometers, the room contained a desk upon which sat two screens—one large, one small—a keypad, some few files of hard copy, a stylus. Behind the desk was a chair; in the chair was a man.

Those who owed allegiance to the Department, to the Plan, addressed him as "Commander" or, formally, "Commander of Agents." That was enough.

Commander of Agents touched his keypad, advancing the file displayed upon the larger screen.

Blindfolded and questioned—if any would dare it—he could easily have recited the entire contents of the file. He perused it without reading it, as another might shuffle and deal hand after hand of Patience, mind wrestling a problem light-years beyond his busy fingers.

The immediate problem was threefold, the sections named thus: Clan Korval, Val Con yos'Phelium, Tyl Von sig'Alda.

Clan Korval. The Department of Interior had long been aware of the danger presented by Clan Korval, that maverick and most oddly successful of clans. The Department of Interior had taken measures—bold measures—in the past, with an eye toward nullifying Korval's menace. The culmination of these measures was the recruitment of Korval's young nadelm into the Department and the subsequent redesign of that same Val Con yos'Phelium into an Agent of Change.

That stroke, brilliant and necessary, had produced uncalculated results. Korval became aware of the Department. And, being Korval, measures—bold measures—had been taken. The Department found its name spoken in public places; long-stable funding sources came under scrutiny, several dummy accounts were unmasked and summarily closed by the Masters of the Accountants Guild, the funds returned to the Council of Clans.

Not satisfied with such unseemly commotion, Korval moved again—and more boldly yet. The clan vanished—ships, children, servants, and pets—all, all gone from Liad.

Not quite all.

Commander of Agents touched his keypad. One of the line direct remained upon Liad: Anthora, youngest of the adult yos'Galans, who had prudently moved to the ancient and formidable Jelaza Kazone, Korval's first base of planetary operation, and was living there retired. For now.

Commander of Agents advanced the file, eyes looking beyond screen and data. Korval was out *there* somewhere. Who knew what they might do? Or when?

The Commander considered the probability that they had gone entirely, leaving behind one too odd to understand her peril. Were Korval to abandon Liad and accept sanctuary from Terra, the balance long in favor of Liaden trade missions and Liaden expansion would be at risk. The children of yos'Galan were half-Terran. Mongrels. They might well go to kin.

The Commander was not one to feel qualms. The various actions against Korval, including fomenting revolution on the world of Korval's oldest trade partner, were necessary to reduce Korval's influence and bring about the true ascendancy of Liad.

The recent revolt had not been an entire success, for Korval's old ally and sometime bedmate had prevailed. Still, it would be a generation before the economy of the planet healed, and the political conflicts would take a dozen dozen relumma to settle.

More, there was rumor that one string not yet strung to the bow of the alliance was now gone. The Commander allowed himself a faint smile: fight them over and over, covertly, and even Korval must fall. They had almost been eliminated twice now.

The Commander blinked. This time, perhaps. On *his* watch.

This nearly open flight was unfortunate, and unexpected. That Korval searched for their missing delm-to-be was certain. To allow them to locate and reclaim Val Con yos'Phelium would be an error. A very serious error.

A most successful Agent, Val Con yos'Phelium. There was that in the madcap Korval genes that inspired its members to excellence, whatever course they might chart. Before the adjustment of his loyalties, Val Con yos'Phelium had ridden the mandate of his genes to a certain pinnacle of achievement: Scout Commander, First-In. A man of infinite resource, a pilot from a clan that bred for pilots; intelligent, flexible and—after suitable training—exquisitely deadly, he had among his armament the greatest of all an Agent's weapons, the Probability Loop.

The Loop allowed an Agent to calculate odds of mission success and personal survival. To some extent, it served as a predictor of coming action, and as a strategy program. There were, of course, certain other mandates implanted, as well as a self-destruct subroutine. These mandates and subroutines were provided to ensure that an Agent remained loyal to his mission, to the Department, and to the Plan. It should not be possible for an Agent of Change to break training.

And, yet, there was evidence—disturbingly strong evidence—that Val Con yos'Phelium, delm genetic of a clan that seemingly valued random action just slightly less than piloting skill, had broken training.

So. Agent of Change Tyl Von sig'Alda had been dispatched on the trail of a rumor, to seek Val Con yos'Phelium along the ways of an interdicted world, to offer transport to the home world, to debriefing and recalibration. Had the

Agent merely come against mischance, these things would be accepted. Had he suffered severe mischance, Agent sig'Alda was to bring his Commander a body, a skull, sections of vertebrae—*proof.* An Agent was no such thing to be carelessly left lying about the galaxy, after all. Especially no such Agent as Val Con yos'Phelium.

Commander of Agents came to the end of the file and closed it with a flick at the keypad. He leaned back in the chair which conformed to his body's shape, and briefly closed his eyes.

Agent sig'Alda had been gone some time. It was understood that ransacking a low-tech world for one man—or one corpse—might consume time. The Commander was prepared to wait some small time longer, before loosing another Agent to the search.

Commander of Agents opened his eyes, seeking the smaller second screen.

This screen showed a sector map. Marked plainly on the map was Interdicted World I-2796-893-44, where Tyl Von sig'Alda sought Val Con yos'Phelium. An amber light near the world marked the location of sig'Alda's ship, as reported by the concealed pin-beam locator beacon. Some time ago, the beacon had reported that it was on world and Commander of Agents had allowed himself hope.

Alas, the ship lifted very soon, thence to dawdle in orbit now several more days, so the scent that had enticed Agent sig'Alda to the planet's surface must have proved false.

Commander of Agents moved his eyes to the chronometered wall. He was due in conference very shortly, where another portion of the Department's Plan would be reviewed.

Korval's links with outside interests were being attended to, carefully. It was the Commander's thought that Korval had dwindled to the point of being too few to attend to their own security. Thus a test case. It would do Korval no good, should *Dutiful Passage* fall.

Hands on the armrests, the Commander pushed his chair back, glancing to the beacon screen—and freezing.

For the beacon's light was no longer the placid amber indicative of a stable position. It blazed green on the star map, its glow eclipsing the world called "Vandar" by its natives, the pre-Jump coil-charge smearing the telltale into a blur. Coordinates appeared at the bottom of the screen, the beacon phased from green to turquoise, then flared into nothing as it and the ship around it entered Jump.

Commander of Agents reached forth a hand and tapped a command into his keypad. The home system of the interdicted world melted from the screen, replaced by another map, this with a ship route limned in red.

Commander of Agents leaned back in his chair, and allowed himself to believe that all was well.

Tyl Von sig'Alda was Jumping for Waymart.

And from Waymart it was but two Jumps to Headquarters.

STANDARD YEAR 1393

VANDAR ORBIT AND JUMP

She was quick, canny, and careful, a former mer-
cenary master sergeant with the battle wisdom of a hundred
combat encounters behind her.

He was not without resources, trained first as a scout and
then as an Agent, but the knife nearly penetrated his guard,
so smoothly did she manage the thing. He snatched her wrist
as it snaked past, shifted balance for the throw—and ended
the move in an ignominious twisting breakaway as she broke
his grip and rode the attack forward.

She danced back to the metal wall, gray eyes intent, muscles coherent; poised, not stressed; the sweat bathing her face
the residue of physical exertion, rather than strain.

She let him regain stance, she allowed him time for orientation, time to conceive and launch an attack; uncommon
courtesy from so deadly a battle-mate. He feinted with a
move out of L'apeleka, saw the grin flit across her face even
as she shifted balance in proper response to the phrase.

He danced another half-phrase of the Clutch discipline,
choosing a subtle variant beyond her current level of attain-
ment. He was not really surprised when she moved smoothly
in response, timing perfect as a heartbeat. His mental Loop,
residue of his days as a full Agent of Change, indicated her

chance of besting him in this encounter was nearly seventeen percent—four times higher than it had been half a year ago.

She charged.

Training took over and his hands flashed out, faster than thought. The knife spun away as he caught both her wrists this time and took her with him into the somersault, both aware of the constraining walls.

She twisted and broke half free. He countered, snaking around and pinning her flat against the metal floor, one hand tight under her chin.

"Yield!" he demanded, trying not to see how easily his fingers encircled the fragile column of her throat.

She sighed slightly, considering him out of calm gray eyes. "Sure," she said. "What the hell."

He laughed, taking his hand from her throat and rolling away to prop hip and elbow against the cold deck. "Not quite the attitude I might expect from a seasoned mercenary."

"No sense gettin' killed," Miri said reasonably, grabbing his free hand and laying it over her breast. She squirmed a little, as if to settle more comfortably against the deck plates. "That's better."

"Fraternizing with the enemy?" inquired Val Con.

"Taking a little rest with my partner," she corrected him sternly. "Liadens and Terrans ain't enemies—they just don't get along too good."

He opened his green eyes very wide. "Don't we get along, Miri?"

"Yeah, but see," she said earnestly, reaching to touch his right cheek and the scar that marred the smooth golden skin, "we're crazy. And that's besides you being a scout and having this funny idea about how Liadens and Terrans and for-space-sake Yxtrang are all from the same stock."

"It is true," Val Con allowed, feeling her heartbeat through the breast nestled in his palm, "that scout training may have identified those characteristics that are classified as 'crazy' and honed them to a fine degree. However, the hypothesis of the common root of the three human races is from my father's studies." He smiled. "So you see that insanity is hereditary."

"Yeah, all you do is believe it." She stretched suddenly

and sat up, face abruptly serious. "Tell you what, boss: I think I'm cured."

He rolled over onto his back, crossed his arms behind his head and considered the other thing inside his head—a precious gift, balancing the Loop's distasteful, inevitable presence.

Legend said that lifemates had often been linked this way, soul to soul, not quite sharing thought, but rather sharing intent; joying in a knowledge of each other that went deeper than any kin-tie. That he and Miri should be so linked, now, when Liad's wizards were on the wane and lifemates were merely in love, was wonderful past belief.

"Boss?"

"Eh?" He started and smiled at the ripples in the song that was Miri in his head; smiled at the frown of concern on her face. "Forgive me, cha'trez. I was thinking." He stretched and sat up next to her. "I believe your estimation is correct, however: you certainly fight as if you are cured."

"Huh." She shook her head. "You need somebody around can really give you a workout."

"So? You very nearly had me. Twice," he added thoughtfully. "Miri."

"Yo."

"Where did you learn the response to that Clutch move?"

"The second one?" She shrugged. "Seemed the only logical way to go, given how you shifted . . ." Her shoulders dipped, upper body sketching the essence of the move. "Yeah . . ."

"Ah."

She glanced at him suspiciously. "Ah, is it? What's that supposed to mean?"

"Nothing, Miri," he said meekly; and grinned in shared joy when she laughed.

"So, partner, seeing as we both agree I'm cured, how 'bout you bust this tub outta orbit and we get a move on."

"It must certainly be my first wish to please my lady and my lifemate," Val Con said, coming to his feet and offering her a hand in graceful Liaden courtesy. "But I wonder if you can suggest where it is we should get a move on *to*?"

"Had to ask, didn't you?" She rose lightly, gripping his

fingers for the pleasure of contact rather than because she required assistance. "Let's go up front and get some tea." She led the way, hand stretched behind her to his as they moved through the narrow corridor to the control cabin.

"Family of yours is on the lam, right? When's this Plan B thing go outta force?"

He hesitated. Miri considered herself Terran, though she carried a Liaden house-badge among her dearest treasures, and had agreed, perhaps too hastily, to share life with a Liaden. She had not been raised to the tradition of clan-and-kin, and the first eight months of their mating had been spent on an Interdicted World, learning to survive and prosper in a culture alien to them both.

"Plan B," he began slowly, feeling his way along thoughts that seemed to shift nuance and urgency as he tried to convey them in Terran. "Plan B may be called into effect by delm or first speaker in the instance of—imminent catastrophic damage to the clan. It is thus not established lightly, nor do I think it—goes out of force—until the dangerous situation has been resolved. I believe this may be its first use."

"Imminent catastrophic damage to the clan," Miri repeated, gray eyes sharp on his face. "What's that mean? Who's the enemy? And how do we get past them and connect with your family?" She frowned, chewing her lower lip. "I take it you *want* to connect up?"

"I—yes." Such clear knowledge of his own will was still unsettling to him, who had only shaken off the mind-twisting Agent training with the help of Miri and the luck. "It is possible that the danger is the Department of Interior," he said. "After all"—he waved a slender hand at the neat little ship enclosing them—"the Department managed to locate us and send an Agent after, and we were most wonderfully lost."

"Much good it did them," Miri commented, meaning the Agent, dead at the Winterfair on the far-below surface.

"Much good it very nearly did us," Val Con retorted warmly, meaning the wound she'd taken and the Agent's too-near success in completing his mission.

"Yeah, well . . ." she shifted, reached to take his hand again. "You talked to your brother Shan, you said . . ." and

that made her uncomfortable, he could tell from the subtleties of her mind-heard song.

"I am not," he said gently, "an expert at speaking mind-to-
mind. In fact, the whole exchange must have been on Shan's
skill, without anything at all from me. I can't even bespeak
you, Miri, as closely as we are linked."

"Tried it, have you?" She grinned briefly. "But didn't your
brother tell you what kind of danger?"

"Just that Plan B was in effect . . ."

"Moontopple," Miri muttered and Val Con laughed even
as he shook his head.

"Things were rather confused at the time, recall. The
Agent was hunting me, you and I were separated, Shan was
talking inside my head—and very annoyed he was, too! We
hardly had time to set up a rendezvous before contact was
cut."

"So you did set up a meeting!" Approval lightened her
face. "Where?"

He took a deep breath and looked her steadily in the eyes.
"At the home of your family, Miri."

"My fam—" She stared at him, dropped his hand and
backed up, shock rattling the constancy of her song. The
back of her knees hit the edge of the co-pilot's chair and she
sat with a slight bump, eyes still wide on his face.

"Look, boss," she said finally, "I ain't got a family. My
mother's dead—died my second year in the merc. And if
Robertson *ain't* dead he oughta be, an' I don't wanna be the
one does the deed."

"Ah." Sorrow touched him: Clan-and-kin, indeed. He
perched on the arm of her chair. "The family I meant was
Clan Erob."

Her hand dropped to the pouch built into her wide belt.
"Clan Erob," she said huskily, "don't know me from Old
Dan Tucker. I *told* you that."

"Indeed you did. And I told you that Erob would not shun
you. You have—what? Twenty-eight Standards?"

She nodded, wariness very apparent.

"So," said Val Con briskly. "It is high time for you to be
made known to your clan and to make your bow to your

delm. Now that you are informed of your connection, you would be woefully rude to ignore these duties."

"And besides, you told your brother to meet you there, so that ends that. Might just as well go there, *first,*" Miri glared at him. "I just hope you know where it is, 'cause I sure don't."

"I know exactly where it is," Val Con said, taking her hand and smiling at her.

Miri sighed, though she did return the pressure of his fingers. "Why don't that surprise me?" she asked.

"No," Miri said flatly, teacup clenched tight in a hand gone suddenly cold.

"Cha'trez . . ."

"I said no!" She glared at him over the cup-rim. "This is your idea, Liaden, not mine. You wanna visit a buncha strangers and claim favors, *you* take sleep-learning to find out how!"

"I already know how," Val Con snapped. "And the case is, my lady, that you will be claiming not favor, but rightful place, based on kinship. Proof will be properly offered, in the form of—"

Miri slammed the cup down. "A piece of enamel-work my grandma most likely swiped from some poor sot in an alleyway somewhere, along with everything else in his pockets!"

". . . a gene test," Val Con finished, as if she hadn't spoken.

She took a hard breath against the upset in her stomach.

"Don't need to talk to get a gene test done. Comes to that, I can talk, some. You taught me Low Liaden. No reason why you can't teach me enough High so I don't embarrass you."

"Miri—" He sighed, raising a hand to stroke the errant lock of hair out of his eyes. Miri bit her lip, knowing as plain as if he'd spoken that he'd noticed her upset inside his head, just like she could see his frustration inside hers. And he'd figured out she was far more upset than she should be, given the request, given the partnership, given the love.

"It is not a question," he said now, "of shaming me. We are lifemates, Miri: I am honored to stand at your side. But there is this other thing, when one is lifemated—would you send me into battle without insuring that I knew the field as well as you?"

"Huh?" She shook her head. "Likely get you killed, holding back information. And I'd have to give you everything I had, 'cause you never know beforehand what's gonna be important."

"Exactly." He leaned forward, holding her eyes with his. "We speak of the same situation, cha'trez. Liadens . . . Liadens are very formal. Very—structured. There are six ways to ask forgiveness—six different postures, six distinct phrases, and six separate bows—and none of the six is what a Terran would call an *apology*. Apologies are—very rare." He pushed at his hair again, leaning back.

"You speak Low Liaden—adequately. You have some High Liaden from book-study—enough to get by, I think, if we merely work together on your accent. But language is such a small part of communication, Miri! It is as if I gave you pellets, but failed of giving you the gun."

She closed her eyes; opened them. "You studied this Code-thing, right?"

"Right." He was watching her, very wary. "I grew up in the culture; studied the Code through sleep-learning to correct my understanding of nuance; took what I had learned and shaped it in keeping with my own melant'i. Your melant'i is not mine, Miri. I cannot teach you how to present it. But your lifemate may counsel you on how best to guard it."

"Is there a book?" She was conscious of her breath—shortened and half-desperate—of blood pounding in her ears and sweat on her palms. "Can I study it out of a book, and then you and me can work on the accent?" *Does it have to, HAVE to be sleep-learning, gods?*

"The—book—is actually several volumes," Val Con said softly; "several large volumes. I used to stand on them to reach the top shelf in my uncle's study, when I was a child."

"Must've been an easier way up than that," Miri said, half-grinning.

"There was," he said repressively; "but I was forbidden to

climb the bookshelves. My uncle was quite clear on the point."

She laughed. "That uncle of yours had his share of trouble."

"It is true that Shan and I tended to embrace—inappropri-ate—necessities," he murmured; "but Nova was quite well-behaved as a child." A ripple of the shoulders. "Mostly."

Miri choked back another laugh. "What about the baby? Anthora? She as bad as the rest of you, or did your uncle get some sleep?"

"Ah, well, Anthora has always been Anthora, you see. Her necessities are often on another plane altogether." He tipped his head, green eyes very bright. "What distresses you, Miri?"

"I—" *Hell, hell, HELL and damnation!* Memory triggered and for an instant she was in the stifling cubicle in Surebleak Port, fourteen, brain-burned and reeling; and the tech was telling Liz, "I'm sorry, Commander. Doesn't look like she can take sleep-learning."

"Miri?" The fingers brushing her cheek were warm; out of the present, not the past. "Cha'trez, please."

"I can't." She swallowed; focused on his face. "*Can't,* boss, get it? Liz took me to a Learning Shop in Surebleak Port to tack on Trade before we left planet. Damn near killed me. Tech said—said I couldn't take it. Sleep-learning. Found out later that—defectives—can't take the—strain on their brains." She managed a wobbling grin. "I know I'm not sup-posed to tell you I'm stupid . . ."

"Nor are you defective." He stroked her cheek, her fore-head; lay his fingers lightly along her lips and then let them drop, eyes troubled. "Tell me, were you given a physical be-fore you took the program?"

She shook her head. "Just plugged in and left alone. It started to hurt—I remember screaming, trying to rip the wires out—"

He frowned. "Why not use the dead-man switch?"

"What dead-man switch?"

Anger, jolting as an electric shock—*his,* not hers; then his voice, very calmly. "A dead-man switch is required in all sleep-learning modules. Lack of the switch would cost a Learning Shop its license to operate."

Miri closed her eyes, suddenly very tired. "So, who checks licenses on Surebleak?"

Silence; then a sigh and the warmth of his fingers closing around hers. "Let us go to the 'doc, cha'trez."

She stood quietly at his shoulder while he made the inquiry, in Trade, so she could read it: MIRI ROBERTSON: PROGNOSIS FOR SLEEP LEARNING.

The autodoc took its time answering, lights flickering while it consulted its data banks. MIRI ROBERTSON WILL INSERT HER HAND INTO THE UNIT, it directed, a small slot opening to the right of the keypad.

Miri stuck her left hand in as far as it would go, felt the tingle; heard the chime and saw the words. MIRI ROBERTSON WILL WITHDRAW HER HAND.

The slot closed and the screen cleared. More lights flickered. Then: RECUPERATION NEARING COMPLETION. SLEEP-LEARNING ALLOWED FOR MAXIMUM THREE-HOUR SHIFTS, NOT EXCEEDING THREE SHIFTS PER DAY; MINIMUM BREAK SHIFTS TWO HOURS. SUPPLEMENTS SUGGESTED AFTER EACH LEARNING SHIFT TO INSURE RECUPERATION AT CURRENT SATISFACTORY RATE. DISPENSED BELOW.

"I suggest," said Val Con softly, "that you are better nourished than you were at fourteen. I also suggest that this module is properly tuned and equipped." He slipped the supplement pack out of the dispensary and handed it to her. "An Agent is too valuable to lose to brain-burn; a failed mission far too high a price to pay for faulty machinery."

She stared at him; turned to look at the module, complete with dead-man switch, open and ready to receive her.

"Three hours?" It seemed like three centuries.

"It is the most efficient block of time," Val Con said gravely, and stroked her hair. "Miri, I swear that you are in no danger."

She looked at him, remembering the pain and the burning and the terror. "It's really that important?" But of course it was that important. He was her partner. It was his responsibility to see she had what she needed to survive; what she needed for them both survive.

"OK," she said, and suddenly, desperately, reached up to kiss him. He hugged her tight.

"I will be watching," he murmured. "Malfunction triggers an alarm on the pilot's board. Use the switch, if you feel any discomfort."

"Right." She stepped back, stuck the vitamin pack in her pouch and went over to the module. She lay down and took a grip on the switch. Val Con lowered the lid.

The connectors slid out of the mattress and out of the canopy, stinging a little as they pierced her. Miri closed her eyes against the starless black overhead, and let the program take her.

A two-toned chime was going off insistently in her left ear, gradually gaining volume. Miri opened her eyes and sat up, blinking in bleared confusion at the nest-like unit, its black dome lid raised.

Right. Learning module.

She struggled out of the nest and took a couple of deep breaths, head clearing rapidly. Behind her the chiming changed from a two-note chiding to a one-note demand. Frowning, she turned, saw the slip of paper sticking out of the slot near the timer and yanked it free.

The chiming stopped.

Miri frowned at the paper. The words blurred out of focus; steadied: *Absorption rate 98% overall. Feedback accurate 99.8%. Self test consistent 98.4%.*

Miri shook her head, remembered the packet of vitamins in her pouch and went to get something to wash them down with.

Val Con was coming toward her as she entered the bridge and she froze, mind presenting a good dozen ways to address him; combinations of bows and salutations branching off into a veritable jungle of possibilities, none seeming more right than another. The combination for greeting a senior officer presented itself and she grabbed it, executing the bow in barely proper time.

"Sir," she said, remembering to straighten before speaking, and to speak with the inflection of respectful attention, "I have completed my session with the Instructor."

Both brows shot up before he returned her bow, briefly, and with subtle irony. Miri was dismayed; recalled that one might accept idiosyncrasies of style, so long as they did not cross the line of what one's own melant'i would tolerate.

"Ma'am," Val Con said, senior to junior, though with an undefinable under-inflection, which seemed to echo the irony of his bow, "I am delighted to find your time with the Instructor so fruitfully spent. However, I believe that the length and—intimacy—of our relationship might allow you use of my name."

"Yes, certainly . . ." But *that* combination did not arise and the more she scrambled to find a mode that would allow it, the more confusion rose. She lost the timing of the conversation, shattered cadence and art, was adrift in an echoing sea of inflection.

"Miri."

She looked up at him, helpless to choose from the endless and proliferating possibilities; unable to define herself, since she could find no way to define him.

His hand closed over hers. "Miri. Stop worrying at it, cha'trez. Let it find its level and settle."

The Terran words wrenched her out of confusion; she sagged against him, suddenly aware that she had been holding herself at full attention.

"I don't guess I learned how to just use somebody's name," she muttered.

He hugged her. "That's Low Liaden. 'Val Con-husband,' remember? Eh? And 'Val Con-love.' Much nicer to hear from you than 'sir.' I thought I was in black disgrace."

She snorted a laugh. "Worried you, too."

"Certainly."

She laughed again and pulled away, shoving the piece of paper under his nose.

"Came out of the machine. Any idea what it means?"

"Ah." He slipped it from her fingers; read it with a nod. "On many worlds it would mean that you are a genius, Miri. The module is set up to test gain and chart the student's recall. A defective person, for instance, would have been expelled from the program after the first test demonstrated that no learning had taken place. Those scores," he handed the paper back, "will have triggered an accelerated program."

"Genius?" She frowned at him, then at the paper.

"Genius." Val Con sighed gently; reached to tap the paper. "On Liad, these scores would gain you admittance to Scout Academy. Since you have also demonstrated ability to operate—and prosper—in a low-tech culture, you would likely be admitted to the middle class."

"I ain't a pilot," Miri protested, thinking that scouts were the best there was. Thinking that Val Con was a scout. Thinking that it had to be a glitch in the machine somewhere. Thinking . . .

"It can be arranged," Val Con was saying, "to have groundwork laid for piloting lessons while you are sleep-learning—a matter of appending the program to your study of the Code. It is only a preparatory program, of course, but I can teach you the math and the board-drills."

"Sure," Miri said, absently.

"Good. Would you like some tea?"

"Huh?" She shook out of her reverie, looked at the paper again—written in Liaden, she noticed, then, but was beyond being surprised. "Tea'd be fine, thanks. Gotta take my vitamins anyway."

"Yes." He went to the menu board and she followed. "I suggest you use the Rainbow tonight, cha'trez, to anchor today's learning. Tomorrow you should be able to do all three sessions."

"All three—!" She glared at his back and then sighed, recalling another bit of learning. "Guess if I'm gonna have this melant'i stuff to take care of, I'd better get the rules right." She took the cup out of his hand.

"Genius, huh?" She shook her head. "Tell you what, though, boss—I don't feel the least bit smart."

DELGADO

BJORNSON-BELLEVALE COLLEGE OF ART AND SCIENCES

". . . coffee, flapjacks and YOO-oo-OO!" The voice wavered unmelodically, though with evident sincerity, from edge-orbit across the general beam and into the tiny professorial office. The man at the desk glanced over his shoulder at the beam-set, frown flickering into a smile as he recognized Number Three-Fifty-Eight singing his way into port, if not into the heart of *Vail Runner's* satiric mistress, as he did precisely at the professor's midnight, every night.

"Speak to me, beautiful captain!" the singer urged against the background chatter of half-a-hundred ships, from port to the fringe of the third world out; and in blithe disregard of the possibility that there might be any number of beautiful captains within hearing.

"Sorry, Three-Five-Eight. Thought you were in the middle of breakfast." The woman's voice was cool, with an undercurrent of amusement, precisely as always. The professor smiled again and turned back to the screen and the thesis he was grading.

A singularly disappointing document, truth told; even though the author had not been one from whom he had hoped great things. However, one liked to know that a *little* learning had taken place, even in the least promising of scholars. Ah, well, they were but at the mid-term. Perhaps guidance might yet produce thought.

So thinking, he brought his wandering attention more firmly back to the thesis, seeking the most profitable means of providing guidance. Behind him, Three-Fifty-Eight pled his case with the cool-voiced lady, one tile in a familiar, comforting mosaic of voices. The professor listened with half-an-ear, then with even less, as the key to guidance presented itself and he gave it his full attention.

ATTENTION! ATTENTION!

It snarled across the familiar mosaic like an angry boot heel. The professor had already spun in his chair, dark eyes intense on the squat receiver as if he would see through it to the ship that carried so urgent a message.

> ATTENTION! ALL JUNTAVAS EMPLOYEES, SUPPORTERS, DEPENDENTS, ALLIES SHALL FROM RECEIPT OF THIS MESSAGE FORWARD RENDER ASSISTANCE, AID AND COMFORT TO SERGEANT MIRI ROBERTSON, CITIZEN OF TERRA; AND SCOUT COMMANDER VAL CON YOS'PHELIUM, CITIZEN OF LIAD; TOGETHER OR SINGLY; REDIRECTING, WHERE NECESSARY, YOUR OWN ACTIVITIES. REPEAT: AID AND COMFORT TO MIRI ROBERTSON AND/OR VAL CON YOS'PHELIUM IMPERATIVE, PRIORITY HIGHEST.
>
> MESSAGE REPEATS . . .

That quickly it was done, gone; leaving nothing but dead beam for a heartbeat—for two . . .

"What the hell was that!" The irrepressible Three-Fifty-Eight.

"Courier ship," snapped someone else and, "You should've seen that brother go! Third planet kick-off, skimmed in, dropped it and gone!"

Five days out. The professor eased out of his chair, went with wary, silent grace across the room to the little receiver, staring at it as if it had suddenly become something quite else.

"Scout Commander Val Con yos'Phelium," he whispered,

extending a hand to touch the power-off. "Scout Commander Val Con yos'Phelium . . ."

He turned, paced the length of the tiny office—five of his strides—and the width—five more—until he came again to the desk and the work awaiting him. A hand slipped into one pocket; emerged —and he stood staring down at the flat gleam of a ship's key, incongruous in his soft, scholar's palm.

Professors of cultural genetics did not as a rule own space-ships. He sighed and slipped the key away.

So deep a cover, constructed over so many years . . .

He shook his head, banishing the thought with the key and sat once again to his work, trying to recapture his previous mood of gentle instruction. Screen-light gleamed off his single ring—three stands of silver, twisted into a flat knot, worn on the smallest finger of his left hand. After a moment, he sighed again, leaned back in the chair and closed his eyes.

Scout Commander Val Con yos'Phelium . . .

LYTAXIN

APPROACHING EROB

House. She was sure that was the word. House.

Sleep-learning had reinforced her vocabulary, made her comfortable with sounds and meanings, and the recent social encounter at the landing field had almost convinced her she had all things Liaden by the scruff of the neck.

House.

It was huge.

Miri stopped on the crest of the gentle rise, staring up at the long expanse of velvet-lawned hill, and the u-shaped sweep of gray-and-black stone, several stories high. The house, that was. She looked at Val Con.

"Are you *sure*?"

He glanced away from his own study of the landscape, one brow quirking. "It does *seem* to be a clanhouse," he murmured; "but recall that I have never called upon Erob, either."

She took a deep breath. "It's as big as a hyatt," she told him, stating the obvious in as calm a voice as she could muster. "A *big* hyatt. Maybe we got the wrong directions. Maybe it is a hyatt, which ain't all that bad. We could maybe get a room if we got enough money, and call ahead."

Val Con grinned and stroked her cheek. "This is a frontier

world, cha'trez—the entire clan would live in one house, plus necessary staff, plus guesting rooms, contract-suites, administration, supplies."

"Recall that this is the capital-in-fact of the planet until they recover from the revolt—actually the center of the world in some ways even before." He lifted a shoulder. "I would say that they have no more space than they likely need, depending upon the size of the clan and the amount of administration they feel it necessary to perform."

"Gods." She looked at him, suddenly struck with a thought. "Is *your* house this big? The one you grew up in?"

"I grew up in Trealla Fantrol," he said softly; "yos'Galan's line house. It is very grand, of course, but not nearly so large as this. Korval has never ruled the world." He offered his hand, smiling.

After a moment, Miri dredged up a smile of her own, wove her fingers around his and went with him, toward the house.

The good thing about being on world was the smells. The breeze. The colors. The hand in hers. The quiet.

That was an odd one, Miri realized as they walked paths that had only recently been guard marches and troop routes. Quiet.

As many worlds as she'd been on, none of the planetfalls had been like this. Leisurely, and—aside from her own certainty of ruin at the end—calm. The weapons checks were habit, the vitamin dosages learning aids rather than war-prep, the entry to atmosphere a tourist's wonder of ocean, continents, and ice caps.

They'd come in as the cordon around the planet was being dismantled. Troop and guard ships alike had failed to notice them—as Val Con had prophesied—and there'd been no alerts, no threats, and no danger.

For three orbits Lytaxin had spun below them. The radio had told the tale pretty clearly: A stupid and bungled coup attempt followed by a dirty little war mostly confined to a single continent. The mercs had come quickly.

What they hadn't gotten from the radio they had soon

enough from Riaska ter'Meulen. Now *there* was a person who could talk. She'd limped out of the office of the little general aviation field, to Miri's eye unflapped by the sudden and unannounced appearance of their—of the Department of Interior's—vessel.

"Scouts," she'd said, nodding a rather unconventional kind of a bow at both of them. "How may I be of service? And how shall I register your visit?"

Val Con returned the nod with a formal bow. "Of your kindness, register the ship as *Fosterling,* out of Liad, piloted by Val Con yos'Phelium, Clan Korval. Business of the clan."

The woman made her own bow at that point and Miri's new-poured training kicked into gear. Val Con's bow, acknowledging what?—personal debt, personal respect?—to the clan of an ally or friend of his clan? And ter'Meulen's bow acknowledging . . . acceptance of respect and recognition of the—honor, was it, of being so acknowledged?

She walked with them across the airfield, discussing the war, her limp growing more evident with each step. She stopped them in front of an open hanger housing a vintage ground attack aircraft.

"Pilot of Korval, I expect you are well-placed to assist us. This is the official airfield defense craft. It and its kin were gifts of Korval, and before the war we had perhaps a double dozen of them. There were five here, but all save this one went off in The Long Raid. I understand that the contingent on the islands were destroyed by our side, and Erob's allies in the highlands used theirs until they were relieved by the mercenaries. The Long Raid was their idea, I gather—stuff enough fuel and strip enough weight to get them 'cross the ocean . . ."

Val Con listened, quiet, while Miri nodded at the good sense of the tactic. Sounded like the kind of thing Kindle would pull together.

"Many planes were shot down—where Clan Kenso got weapons like that I'd give the rest of my leg to know!—and so I have this . . ." She bowed toward the plane—fond respect, Miri thought.

"Parts are hard to come by, and while this one flies, and will continue in its duty, it would be good to have spare parts. If there might be a way—the patterns and the equipment that built them are on Liad, in your own shops."

Val Con bowed. "As time permits I shall speak to the first speaker."

Riaska ter'Meulen bowed. "I am grateful."

"Cars are yet in short supply," she said then. "May I call the House and have them send, or may I offer you service of my flitter?" A wave of a hand indicated a tiny craft—barely more than a cabin over a lift-fan.

Miri stirred, in no hurry to raise the house and seeing no need to deprive a wounded woman of transport.

"It's a fine day," she said to Riaska ter'Meulen, in the mode of equals, "and we've been long aboard. A walk will be welcome."

The woman bowed again, willing equality. "As you say. Allow me to point you on your way."

They stopped just short of the three low stairs leading to a sort of black stone dais and a front door that was all pieces of high-glaze tile forming a field of indigo, across which a crimson bird stooped toward a gold-limned mountain, far below. Miri felt the hairs lift at the back of her neck and her free hand touched her pouch, where a miniature of that very design rode, perfect in every detail.

She shook her head sharply and frowned, slanting a glance at her partner's face; saw him gazing with sharp interest to the left.

"You gonna ring the bell or not?" she demanded.

"In a moment." He set off across that soft, resilient lawn purposefully; fingers still firm and warm around hers.

And stopped in front of a tree.

It was a largish tree, Miri thought, with a pleasingly tree-like trunk and nice, broad, four-fingered leaves a shade greener and a shade less blue than the grass. Nuts or seed-pods hung in clusters here and there and the whole thing smelled good, in a kind of olfactory tree-ness.

Val Con loosed her hand, took another step toward the tree and bowed. Deeply. With the stylized hand-sign that offered instant, willing, and unquestioning service.

"I bring thee greeting, child of Jela's hope," he said in the High Tongue, but in a dialect beyond any of those Miri had studied in her crash-course sleep-learning. She thought it might be related to the mode used by the most junior servant to the ultimate authority—and then thought that was crazy.

"When last this one visited the homeworld," Val Con was telling the tree, "thy elder kin yet flourished, grew, and nurtured. The charge is kept and the guard continues. When next this one is upon the homeworld, thy name shall be whispered to the elder's leaves."

He stood for a moment or two then, head bowed, maybe listening to the little rustling sounds the breeze made against the leaves. Then he bowed again, like he was going to ask a favor.

"This one has not had grace of Jela's children in some years, and this one's lady has yet to know the elder. In need, this one asks the boon of two fruit, and one leaf."

He stepped forward then, reaching high; and pulled two nuts free from the lowest cluster. He plucked a leaf from the same branch and stepped back, bowing thanks.

Grinning, then, he cracked a nut and handed it to her; cracked open the second and pulled the shell apart, revealing a plump pink kernel.

"These are good," he said, back in Terran. "I ate quite a number of them when I was a child, to the gardener's dismay."

Miri pulled her own nut apart, blinking in surprise at the aroma. She paused in the act of fishing the meat out and looked at her partner.

"It's a nice tree, boss. Does it talk back?"

"Eh?" He blinked, then laughed. "Ah, I had forgotten . . . There is a very old Tree on Liad that my clan is—involved with. A long story. The name of that Tree is Jelaza Kazone. This tree here is a seedling of that, so it behooves me to pay courtesy, wouldn't you say?"

"Um." Miri nibbled the kernel, finding it delicious. "How do you know this one's related to yours?"

"There is only one Jelaza Kazone," Val Con murmured. "And Korval does occasionally seal—certain—contracts with the gift of a seedling."

"Right." The nut was gone. Miri sighed in real regret and looked up as Val Con handed her the leaf.

"Wear this in your belt, cha'trez. Are you done? Good. Let us ring the bell."

The doorkeeper was young, narrow-shouldered and too thin; the fragile bones almost showing through the translucent golden skin. His hair was pale red, shading toward blond, and tumbling over a high forehead, not quite hiding the bruises at both temples, where the combat helmet had been too tight. The blue eyes were wary, with a darker shadow, lurking far back.

"Delm Erob?" he repeated, looking from Val Con to her and back again. And seeing, Miri knew from the slight change of expression, two soldiers, coming where they shouldn't be, asking for somebody they had no business to see.

"The delm is quite busy," he said now, speaking the High Tongue in the mid-mode reserved for strangers whose melant'i was yet unclear. "If you will acquaint me with your difficulty, sir—ma'am—perhaps I may direct you to the proper person."

"It is essential," Val Con said, his own mode shifting subtly, so that he spoke from senior to junior, "that we speak to Delm Erob with all speed, young sir."

The boy's cheeks flushed darker gold, but he let no hint of that spurt of temper enter his voice. "I must insist you acquaint me more particularly with your mission, sir. If you are separated from your unit—if you have not received proper pay—if you have missed your transport—none of these difficulties will be addressed by Delm Erob, though Clan Erob is able to solve any or all for you. I merely require adequate information."

Not too bad, Miri thought, for a kid who was obviously out on his feet and at the tail end of seeing and doing a bunch of stuff he'd probably rather never have known about. The blue eyes shifted to her and she gave him a grin of encouragement before the sleep-learning kicked in and let her know that was a mistake. The kid frowned, eyes suddenly hard.

"Have you been in our garden?" he demanded, mode shifting fast toward belligerence, courtesy forgotten in outrage. "Have you defaced our tree?"

Miri came to full attention, eyes tight on his. "We have certainly not defaced your tree!" she snapped, in a mode very close to the voice she used to chew out a soldier who'd been particularly stupid. "We asked grace for the leaf and it was freely given."

The boy's face altered amazingly, shifting from outrage to shock to a sudden dawning dread. He touched his tongue to his lips and brought his eyes back to Val Con.

"We do," Val Con said, gently, and still only in the mode of senior to junior, though he could have done much worse to the kid than that, "very much desire to speak with Delm Erob. Now, if possible. You may say that the Second Speaker of Clan Korval is calling, regarding a daughter of your House."

The kid had gone to get his boss, leaving the two of them to kick their heels in what sleep-learning suggested was a formal reception parlor.

Miri pictured him running down the long hallway the minute the door was shut and grinned as she glanced around, wondering what this room had over the one at the front of the house they'd almost stopped in. The kid had actually crossed the threshold of that room, and Miri got a glimpse of white paneled walls and uncomfortable looking furniture before he apparently thought better of it and stepped back with a slight bow and a murmured, "Follow me, please."

So now, the Yellow Salon, and another kid, a little younger than the first, bringing wine and glasses and a porcelain tray of cakes. She kept her eyes averted, after one disconcertingly bright blue glance that seemed more interested in Val Con than in her, and bowed real pretty, asking if anything else was required in a voice that said she hoped not.

"Thank you," Val Con said gravely. "The solicitude of the House gives gladness."

"Sir." The kid bowed again and escaped, forgetting to wait for the door to fully close before she ran.

Miri grinned again, slid her hands in her belt and wandered over to look out the window, squinting a little against the sun.

"There's your tree, boss."

"So?" He came over, shoulder companionably touching hers as he took in the view. "But that is not my Tree, Miri. That is Erob's tree. Mine is much older—and taller."

"Sounds like a quibble to me," she said. "If this one's a seedling off yours and yours is the only one there is, besides its own seedlings . . ." She stopped, cheeks heating in an unaccustomed blush.

Val Con laughed.

"Ah. Clan becomes discovered."

"Real funny . . ." she began, and then cut off as the door clicked.

Val Con went silently toward the center of the room, Miri half-a-pace behind his right shoulder.

The woman who entered the salon had not run full-tilt down the hallway, but she hadn't dallied, either. She was gray-haired, gray-eyed and golden skinned, wire-thin and charged with energy. Two heavy lines were grooved horizontally across her high forehead; more lines ran starkly from nose to mouth. Still more lines radiated from the corners of her eyes, puckered now as she stared against the sun. She was dressed simply, in what sleep-learning told Miri was house-tunic, and tight trousers tucked neatly into a pair of buff-colored short-boots.

All business, she marched across the buttery carpet, stopped a precise four paces before Val Con and bowed crisply, hand over heart.

"Emrith Tiazan," she said in a low, clear voice, "Delm Erob."

Val Con made his own bow, more fluid than hers, though as deep. "Val Con yos'Phelium, Clan Korval."

Miri tensed—but the old eyes stayed on Val Con.

"Yes," she said. "You have your father's look."

Val Con bowed again, slightly—and with irony, Miri thought.

Emrith Tiazan might have thought so, too; she lifted a sharp-bladed shoulder, and let it fall. Miri again tensed to make her own bow, but the old woman seemed intent on ignoring her.

"I'll tell you plain, Korval, before we sit to tea and cake and behaving as though we're civilized—it's no joy to see you at this time, tree-kin though we be. We're just through with a matter that will heal in a generation or two—if all goes well and no one breeds another hothead like Kel Bar Rentava. I am aware that Erob owes a contract-wife this term, but while plain speaking's in force I'll tell you that the one we'd settled on went the soulroad in the war." The old face shifted then, all the lines tightening, but her voice stayed smooth.

"They shot her down—Clan Kenso. She was the very best we had, and they shot her down. Her ship crashed in the rock plain, east of here. I expect we have all the pieces, by now."

She closed her eyes briefly; lifted her shoulder again. "I'll have nothing of such excellence to offer Korval until Alys comes to her growth—nine years, perhaps. Alys should do very well—but she'll be no Kea Tiazan."

There was a silence.

Miri's mind raced, but nothing from her own experience or from the sleep-learned stuff helped her make sense of this one. The old lady was clearly at the end of her rope, worn to skin, bone, and character. Her mind might even be wandering, though Miri doubted that. It might have been that Val Con's clan and Clan Erob had sealed an alliance with a marriage, when this lady had been a young delm . . .

"Forgive me," Emrith Tiazan was saying to Val Con, "if my frankness offends. I've no time for wasteful courtesies and it is certainly not necessary for Erob to stand upon ceremony with our old ally, Korval. We have always understood each other very well."

"In this instance, however," Val Con said neutrally, "understanding may have fallen short. I assign no blame, nor does frankness offend." He reached out to capture Miri around the wrist and drew her lightly forward to stand at his side. "I present my lifemate, Miri Robertson Tiazan, Lady yos'Phelium."

The gray eyes in their golden net of wrinkles went wide, then narrowed as they swept Miri from face to feet. The glance scathed, lingering longest on the leaf before whipping back to Val Con.

"So! You discover a houseless favorite and you *dare* bring her to *me*? I shall acknowledge her, shall I, and give her place among the clans? Korval presumes—and presumes too far. I will remind you that you *guest* with Erob. Your whim is not law here!"

That was enough. Miri moved, deliberately turning her flank on the old lady and her rage.

"I tell you what, boss," she said, in her flattest, ugliest Terran accent—one-hundred-percent Surebleak. "I ain't about to join this outfit, genes or no genes."

"Ah," said Val Con.

"*What* did you say?" demanded Emrith Tiazan, in Terran, though Terran slurred and softened and pronounced like Liaden.

"I *said*," Miri snapped, in the stiffest mode she could call to mind from the High Tongue, "that it is not the place of a high commander to reprimand another commander who is come to parlay."

For the space of two heartbeats, Emrith Tiazan stood frozen, and then she bowed, very gently.

"Forgive me—madam," she said, the High Tongue carefully conveying equality of rank. "You spoke of genes. I desire further information upon the subject as you believe it to concern yourself and—this outfit." She paused. "If you please."

Miri hesitated, more than half determined to walk out the door and down that long hallway and out into the sunshine. *Ought to be able to find the merc camp without too much trouble,* she thought; *get a hot meal and a place to bunk . . .*

"Miri," Val Con said softly. "Will you show Delm Erob your heirloom?"

Damn him, she thought; and then sighed and worked the catch on her belt-pouch. She fingered the disk free and held it out to the old lady, belatedly remembering to bow.

Emrith Tiazan glanced briefly at the shield, then turned to the obverse, frowning at the engraved genealogy. She looked back at Miri.

"How came you by this?"

"I have it from my mother," Miri said, matching the other's mild tone; "who had it from hers."

"So." The old lady looked at Val Con. "This appears genuine."

He lifted a brow. "Many clans possess—protocols—for determining authenticity."

She stared at him. "Indeed. You will excuse me for a moment." She turned and marched out of the room without waiting for their permission.

The door had barely closed when Miri swung around. "What is this? How come she thinks you came here for a contract-wife? If you're pulling one—*one*—of your damned Liaden tricks, that old lady ain't gonna have to bother taking you apart, 'cause I'll do it for her, you understand me?"

"Yes, Miri," he said meekly, but for once meekness failed to gain her smile. She stood glaring, poised on the balls of her feet, a trained fighter, more than half-ready to fight.

Val Con took her hand, led her to the couch by the refreshment table and sat down. "Miri." He tugged gently at her, patting the cushion beside him.

For a moment he thought she'd refuse, yank her hand free and stomp away, as he had been certain she would earlier, and he with no choice but to follow his lifemate . . .

"Hell." She flumped down next to him and dropped her head on his shoulder. "You're more trouble than you're worth, you know?"

"Shan has often expressed that view," he said, sighing in mock remorse. "The two who know me best cannot both be in error."

She snorted a half-laugh; stirred and sat up. "That kid who died—Kea? She was a pilot."

"So are you."

"Like hell—" The door clicked and she swallowed the rest of that argument.

Emrith Tiazan stopped before the couch and held the disk out to Miri, bowing with careful equality. "This has tested genuine." She straightened and looked at Val Con. "Genes, you believe?"

"I have no doubt," he said calmly. "You will, of course, wish to attain your own surety."

"Of course." She went across the room to the desk comm and touched a button. In a very short while, the door opened to admit the young doorkeeper. He flicked a nervous glance at the couch, then bowed deeply to Emrith Tiazan.

"My delm desires?"

"You will go to the older storehouse and find in Room East 14 a large package stasis-locked and wrapped in blue silk. Bring it here. You will bid Win Den tel'Vosti attend me here. You will likewise bid the senior medical technician, adding that she shall bring her sampling kit."

The boy touched his tongue to his lips, bowed, turned—

"An Der."

He glanced back over his shoulder. "Yes, Aunt?"

"You will speak to no one, excepting tel'Vosti and the senior med. You will go to the storeroom alone and bring what I require away with your own hands."

The boy bowed again. "I hear," he said—and ran.

"Well, Emrith?"

The old man leaned on his stick in the center of the room. "To what do I owe this interruption of my studies?"

"Studies!" The delm stared at him for a moment, then moved a hand, directing his attention to the couch. "I make you known to Val Con yos'Phelium, Second Speaker for Clan Korval. Korval, my kinsman, Win Den tel'Vosti, thodelm."

"So." The brown eyes watched with seeming amusement as Val Con stood and made his bow.

"My Lord tel'Vosti."

"My Lord yos'Phelium." The return bow was more complete than Miri would have expected, given the cane. "Your father was a rare one for Counterchance."

"So my uncle has told me, sir."

"Er Thom yos'Galan? Now *there* was a demon for the game! Very good he was—a thoughtful, subtle player, no shame. We came even, the times we played. But Daav . . . I believe I may yet owe him a cantra. Perhaps two. I'll consult my account books. Do you play?"

"A bit, sir, but not to match my uncle."

"Pity." The brown eyes sharpened. "You'll want to have that wound looked after, of course, before you meet the House."

Wound? What wo—Sleep learning surfaced and Miri gulped against the sudden *understanding* of what it meant, to be a Liaden with your face scarred. . . .

"Thank you, sir," Val Con was saying calmly. "It's healed cleanly."

"*Win Den.*" Emrith Tiazan began, but tel'Vosti had come to attention, as if he were a corps captain facing another, and half-sketched a salute.

"It is your campaign, sir."

"Win Den." This time his delm's voice could not be ignored. She moved her hand. "I am told that this lady is Miri Robertson Tiazan."

Miri came to her feet and bowed into those amused brown eyes.

"Well, and why not?" said the old gentleman, returning the bow with a certain flair.

"Lady yos'Phelium," Val Con murmured in the room's sudden stillness and tel'Vosti straightened with a laugh.

"Aha! A man who wishes to be absolute of his assets! My felicitations, sir! Perhaps you are not so poor a player of the game as you would have me believe." He glanced back at Miri.

"You are a soldier?" he asked, in the almost-friendly mode of Comrade.

"I was," Miri said, allowing him the mode, though not without a few mental reservations. "I retired a year or two ago."

"Indeed? At what rank?"

She eyed him warily, wondering where this line of questioning was going; wondering, with a sudden spurt of panic, if he was trying to figure her melant'i and if it was going to come up to par. "Master sergeant."

"Master sergeant." He said it like a caress. "And your age is?"

"Twenty-eight Standards." She considered him, the lurking amusement, the straight shoulders, the cane, the mane of pinkish hair. "More or less."

He laughed and glanced at Emrith Tiazan, who stood, grim-faced and silent, near the desk.

"So you tell me you retired two years ago, with the rank of master sergeant. A private troop, perhaps? Industrial?"

"No," Miri had to tell him, against a building wave of dread. "Mercenary unit." She mustered enough nerve to glare into his perpetual amusement. "I was with the Gyrfalks before I retired. I began in Lizardi's Lunatics, which is how I came to be a sergeant in the first place. We got into a spot of trouble, command-chain broke down . . ."

"So you were made field sergeant." tel'Vosti tipped his head. "But your rank was upheld, once the—trouble—was past. And the Gyrfalks raised the stake by a star."

Suddenly, amazingly, he bowed. "A Master of mercenary sergeants by the time you attained twenty-five Standards! A significant feat, Lady yos'Phelium, for I have seen the Gyrfalks in action. Their conduct is always professional and they are most resourceful. Their services do not come cheap—am I correct, Emrith?—but they are worth their weight in cantra, each of them. Korval does well to guard his assets."

The door clicked, and opened to admit the wide-eyed doorman, barely seen behind the flat crate he carried against his chest. After him came a stern dark-haired woman in a crisp coverall: the senior med tech.

"Great," Miri whispered to Val Con, as tel'Vosti and the delm turned away to deal with the new arrivals. "Now maybe we can get this over and get outta here."

The crate had been placed against the desk, and the blue silk drawn away. Emrith Tiazan knelt before it and with her own hands loosened the seals. An Der helped her rise, a solicitous hand at her elbow, a ready arm by her waist.

She shook him off and stepped back. "Open it," she said harshly, and the boy bent to comply.

Val Con drifted forward, Miri at his side. They stopped to the right of Win Den tel'Vosti, who stood with both hands covering the knob of his cane, no amusement at all in his face. The med tech had shrugged and gone over to the couch, perching on the wide arm and watching the proceedings with a sort of distant interest.

An Der wrestled the cover loose and stepped away.

The med tech drew a noisy breath in through her teeth.

Nobody else moved at all, and Miri frowned, wondering why an old mirror should be the focus of such tension, such expect—

"Oh, shit," she breathed, and moved away from Val Con's side, staring at the reflection that didn't move—didn't move because it was a painting—a portrait, not a mirror. A portrait of a woman in flying leathers and loose-laced white shirt, arms crossed under slight breasts, legs braced wide, gray eyes direct in a willful, intelligent face, and the copper-colored hair done in a single long braid, wrapped three times around her head.

"Miri Tiazan," Emrith Tiazan said, voice still strained. "Who left the clan in disgrace."

"Who put the clan in disgrace by leaving," tel'Vosti corrected. "Be precise, Emrith."

"It is disgrace to ignore the delm's order!"

"But she never did ignore it—as you well know. She merely asked leave to postpone contract wedding until love's seed should bear fruit. Tamishon was in no great hurry, being content to know the contract was valid and eventually would be fulfilled. Four month's delay was no cause to abort the babe." He turned to Miri and bowed slightly, indicating fuller information forthcoming.

"The lad was dead, you see—she'd get no other child from him. And Baan Tiazan was a tyrant who ruled both his daughters hard, eh, Emrith?" He moved his shoulders when she gave no answer, amusement back in his eyes.

"She was not always dutiful, understand—that would be unlike her name. But she acquiesced in the large things, and made shift to come the sophisticate, in company."

Miri shook herself. "She ran away to have her kid," she finished, in Terran, too shaken to sort through sleep-learned modes. "She crashed on Surebleak and couldn't get home . . ."

"Is that what came of her?" tel'Vosti asked softly. His Terran was better than the delm's. "We had wondered."

She shook herself again, ran the Rainbow, fast, to get distance from the shock of the picture and the tension focused now on her. "I'm guessing," she told tel'Vosti. "She's dressed like a pilot—and there ain't any reason to choose Surebleak, when you got the whole galaxy ahead."

"So," he said, and looked ready to say more.

"There will be a gene test," Emrith Tiazan snapped. "Med Tech, attend your duty!"

The tech came to her feet, looking open-mouthed from the picture to Miri. She looked finally at the old lady and bowed, rearranging her face into an expression of cool interest.

"As you say," she murmured, and drew a flat kit from her utility pocket. "If the young lady will attend me here . . ."

The blue dress felt nice.

It looked nice, too, Miri decided. In fact, she looked amazingly respectable for a woman who had lately been a mercenary master sergeant, a bodyguard, a fugitive from justice, a woman of all work, and a singer.

Whether she looked respectable enough to please the circus gathering in the reception room below was something she'd find out far too soon.

She took one last turn before the mirror, admiring the way the bluestone necklace lay just right against her throat. She was wearing her hair loose, held back with a set of deceptively simple silver combs. Central stores, located in the cavernous belowstairs had provided dress and combs. The necklace and matching ring were hers, gifts from Val Con, from a time when gifts from Val Con were potentially deadly.

"Very elegant," she told her reflection, and bowed pleasure at making acquaintance, remembering to include the hand-gesture one used toward newly-met kin.

"Gods," she said, and came slowly erect, as if the woman in the mirror might jump her. "Oh, gods, Robertson, what the hell have you gotten yourself into?"

Val Con's dressing room—the "apartment" set aside for their use was bigger than Zhena Trelu's whole house, back on Vandar—was on the opposite side of the bedroom. There were three other rooms—a parlor, an office and a bookroom, plus a bathroom the size of Lytaxin spaceport and a balcony that looked out over the East Garden.

A huge bed commanded the bedroom. Flowering vines grew up two of the posts and all over the canopy, dripping long tendrils like flowering curtains around the sides. Miri shook her head. Liadens . . . A whole room just to dress in, a garden growing in the bedroom, and a bunch of other stuff, here and there, apparently just done for pretty. She bit her lip, recalling the apartments she'd lived in as a kid, an endless succession of rats, peeling synth-lam walls and near-paneless windows leaking Surebleak's frigid winter winds.

"Forget it, Robertson," she whispered; "you ain't going back there. Never going back there."

The bed-flowers were pale blue with soft white stripes, lightly and agreeably perfumed. On impulse, she pulled one free and tucked it behind an ear as she continued across the cream-and-blue carpet to Val Con's dressing room.

He caught her eyes in the mirror as the door opened, and smiled.

"Cha'trez."

She tried to smile back—saw her reflection's mouth wobble and then straighten in distress as the big gray eyes got bigger, taking in the ruffled white shirt, the rich dark trousers, the green ear-drop and finger-ring—all the accouterments of a Liaden gentlemen about to attend a formal dinner.

Val Con spun, eyes and face serious.

"Miri? What is wrong?"

"I—" she shook her head and managed to dredge up a half-convincing grin. "You look like a Liaden, boss."

"Ah." His face relaxed and he came across to her, lifting a hand to touch her hair. "But, you see, I am a Liaden, which no doubt accounts for it."

"That's probably it," she agreed and sighed. "You ready to go face the lions?"

One brow rose. "Clan Erob? Hardly lions."

"Yeah, and suppose that gene test comes out negative? *You're* OK, but I ain't the kind Erob usually has to supper."

JUL 21 2009

BAKER COUNTY LIBRARY
2400 RESORT

"And the portrait of Miri-eklykt'i?" He touched the flower behind her ear with a gentle forefinger.

Miri sighed, recalling with a certain queasy vividness the face of the woman in the old painting. The resemblance was spooky enough if she *was* that one's granddaughter . . .

"I don't guess coincidence'll cover it, huh?"

"It seems unlikely in the extreme." He touched the flower again, then drew it from its resting-place.

"Not," he murmured, "for this sort of dinner."

"Huh?" Miri followed him into the bedroom. "It's against the law to wear flowers to dinner?"

"This particular flower," said Val Con, placing it gently in a cut crystal water glass, "is an aphrodisiac."

She blinked at him; blinked at the canopy. "And they've got 'em growing all over the bed?"

"What better place?"

"Right." She closed her eyes, willing tense muscles to relax.

"Miri?"

She looked at the pattern of him inside her head—bright and clear and beloved—then opened her eyes and grinned wryly at the proper Liaden gentleman before her.

"Tell you what, boss: This whole masquerade's gonna come crashing down over something as stupid as that flower. If you hadn't been here to tell me before I went on down, I could've blown everything." *Everything,* she thought: His melant'i; the melant'i of Line yos'Phelium; her own insignificant amount—all gone. Because of a flower.

"I ain't up for this," she said suddenly, feeling the panic boiling in her stomach. "Look, boss, I'm a soldier, not an actor—and nobody down there's gonna believe for one minute that I'm Lady yos'Phelium. Let's see if we can't catch the old lady and tell her we made a mistake, OK? All the mercs in the city right now, there's bound to be somebody around who owes me dinner—"

"Miri—" That quick he was across the room, arms around her tight, cheek against hers. "It is not a masquerade, cha'trez. It is truth. We are lifemates. And a portion of our shared melant'i involves standing as lady and lord to Line yos'Phelium." He laughed softly. "For our sins."

She choked a half-laugh and pushed her face into his shoulder. "I'm gonna wreck your melant'i."

"No." He kissed her ear. "My lifemate is a lady of intelligence, wit, and courage. How else could it be, but that her melant'i supports and enhances my own? And together—" He slipped his hand under her chin and tipped her face so she could see the bright green eyes, awash in mischief. "*Together,* cha'trez, we are"—he put his mouth next to her ear and breathed—"*hell on wheels.*"

"You—" She laughed and hugged him hard before stepping away and taking his hand. "All right, let's go meet the family."

She stopped him at the hall door, though, struck by one more detail.

"We gonna let on I don't know your family from sliced bread? I don't think even tel'Vosti'd like a lifemating where I ain't met your First Speaker, much less you got her permission."

"A valid point," Val Con murmured and tipped his head, staring hard at nothing, with his brows pulled slightly together.

"Line yos'Phelium," he said after a bit, "presently includes Kareen, my father's sister; her son Pat Rin, and his heir, Quin. My father is Daav yos'Phelium, who is eklykt'i. His lifemate, my mother, was Aelliana Caylon. She is dead. I was fostered into the household of my father's cha'leket, Er Thom yos'Galan, and his lifemate, Anne Davis. They, also, have died. Shan is Lord yos'Galan, Nova is First Speaker, Anthora is—Anthora." He paused.

"yos'Galan children are Padi, who is Shan's heir, and Syl Vor, who is Nova's. Korval's seat is Jelaza Kazone; yos'Galan's Line House is Trealla Fantrol. We are located to the north of Solcintra City. The ship of which Shan is captain and master trader is *Dutiful Passage.*"

Miri considered him. "That's it?"

"Yes."

"Nothing else?" she persisted. "I don't wanna trip up."

"This should be sufficient to see us through dinner," Val Con said softly. "It is scarcely to be expected that a new bride will have complete intimacy of her lifemate's clan."

"Great." She shook her head as he opened the door and bowed her through ahead of him. "All right, Liaden. Just remember—it's your neck we're gambling with."

She'd never seen so many redheads in one place.

The reception room was jammed with them, male and female; old, young and in-between, with hair shading from the lightest strawberry blonde through orange, mere-red, auburn and a particularly striking mahogany.

Hand resting on Val Con's arm, Miri considered the crowd, noting the eyes that slid toward them and slid away—and also something else.

"You're *tall*!" she blurted, remembering at least to whisper, though there was no one directly beside them.

One eyebrow slid upward. "A little above middle height," Val Con acknowledged, lips twitching. "For a Liaden."

He glanced across the room to where Emrith Tiazan stood talking to tel'Vosti and a youngish woman with carroty hair piled high on her head. "We to the delm, now, cha'trez, to make our bows."

And to hear the results of the gene test. She sternly put down the rebellion in her stomach and walked head up at his side, fingers curled lightly around his wrist, trying to act like she didn't notice the way conversation ebbed at their approach and picked up again, once they were past.

"Is this a good idea?" she muttered out of the side of her mouth.

"No, of course not," Val Con muttered back and she almost laughed.

Emrith Tiazan's face saved her—half-relieved and half-approving, as if she'd expected them to show up for dinner in leathers. Miri felt a spurt of sympathy as she bowed respect for the host, Val Con bowing at the same instant.

"Ma'am," he said, soft voice pitched so that it carried across the still sea of redheads, "we offer thanks for the grace and care the House has shown us."

"It is the House's honor," the old woman said into the silence, "to guest its ancient ally and friend." She looked up across the room then, and raised her voice, though it wasn't necessary.

"Hear me, my children, for I tell you of wonder and joy. Come to us only today is Miri Robertson, who is of Erob by Tiazan, this without doubt." She looked hard at Miri out of stern gray eyes.

"Turn," she ordered, still loud enough for the whole room to hear, "Miri Robertson Tiazan, that your cousins may see your face and rejoice."

Sure. She squared her shoulders and turned, looking out over the mob and seeing precious little rejoicing—unless you counted an orange-haired somebody around eight or ten— she wasn't too good at guessing ages that young—who was grinning fit to split her face.

"See also Val Con yos'Phelium," Emrith Tiazan continued behind her, "Thodelm and Second Speaker of Clan Korval, our oldest and most honored ally. It is through Korval that we rediscover our kinswoman." There was something of a stir at that and a bigger one when Val Con turned around to face them.

"It is further told the clan that Miri Robertson Tiazan and Val Con yos'Phelium have each seen the face of the other's heart and, having seen, joined hands and hearts and lives together."

Sleep-learning kept Miri from a gulp; years of dicing and playing cards for kynak and money kept her face straight. *Damn,* she thought, *put that way it sounds all mystic and misty and stuff, when it's just him and me holding together and doing what needs doing . . .*

The carrot-top who'd been talking to Emrith Tiazan and tel'Vosti came forward and bowed, thin face earnest.

"Line Tiazan acknowledges Miri Robertson Tiazan and welcomes her with joy."

Miri returned the bow, hand automatically signing recognition of kinship. "Lady Tiazan, I am honored."

tel'Vosti stepped up next, bowing all courtly over his cane. "Line tel'Vosti sees Miri Robertson Tiazan with delight, welcomes her with honesty and acknowledges her with anticipation."

She almost grinned at him, but sleep-learning kicked in, and pattern recognition with it, adding up all the things the

Code didn't say, like that Liaden society was controlled, yeah, and formal, sure, and all those pretty words and modes and gestures were the weapons you used to survive in an unending, cut-throat competition. Melant'i and Balance. Face or no face. And here was tel'Vosti, who had lived a long lifetime immersed in well-bred in-fighting, giving her a non-standard greeting, there in front of delm and everybody. Tweaking her, he was. Trying her, to see what she'd do.

She bowed, timing it to centimeter and millisecond. "My Lord tel'Vosti." High Tongue Equal, that was the mode; it leaned on Val Con's melant'i, but that was fine, since he was thodelm just like tel'Vosti, and the whole room had just heard the delm say she was a thodelm's lifemate. "I see you with appreciation, hear you with understanding, and acknowledge you with trepidation."

The brown eyes gleamed; the rest of his face remained merely polite. No way to tell if she'd scored points. She didn't think she had. But she didn't think she'd lost any either. Even was OK; tel'Vosti'd said it himself, when he'd been talking about Val Con's uncle. Inside her head Val Con's pattern held steady, inscrutable as a mandala.

The delm stepped forward, indicating Thodelm Tiazan with a backhanded wave. "Your cousin Bendara, daughter of your late cousin Cel Met Tiazan."

The carrot-top gave a little bow, barely more than a heavy nod of the head. "Cousin Miri."

Miri gave the bow back, "Cousin Bendara," straightened and felt Val Con shift, oh-so-slightly, at her side. She directed Bendara's attention his way with a copy of the delm's backhanded gesture. "One's lifemate, Val Con yos'Phelium."

Bendara bowed again, a shade deeper than equality of rank demanded, as if maybe Val Con had more time in grade. "My Lord yos'Phelium."

"My Lady Tiazan." His voice was soft as always. She couldn't see his bow.

The delm waved for her attention again, this time for a man of late middle years, hair aggressively red, hazel eyes hooded.

"Your cousin Dil Nem, son of your late uncle Kern Tiazan."

Again the heavy nod, the exchange of names; the pass on to Val Con.

"Your cousin Ilvin, daughter of your cousin Jen Sar Tiazan, who is from clan at present."

"Your cousin Kol Vus . . ."

"Your cousin . . ."

Miri lost count, very likely lost names, after the first dozen or so. Her head was beginning to ache with all the cool, polite faces and she started to want a slug of kynak. She gritted her teeth and bowed kinship to tel'Vosti, damn him: "Your uncle, Win Den tel'Vosti, son of Randa Tiazan and Pel Jim tel'Vosti."

There was another blur of names and faces after him; the next she took clear note of was the last.

"Your cousin Alys, daughter of your cousin Makina Tiazan, who is from clan at this moment."

Alys, who would be "very well," but never a Kea Tiazan. Alys, who they were going to offer as a contract-wife to Val Con, when she came of age.

She made her bow, very serious, and stood tall, all three and a half feet of her, curly, orange-y hair held down by the brute strength of three formidable-looking combs. The brown eyes shone with something past curiosity or even friendliness and Miri caught her breath. She'd seen that look on recruits, sometimes, the ones who fancied themselves "in love" with the commander.

"Cousin Miri," she piped up, "I'm happy to see you."

Oh, hell. Like she didn't have enough trouble without an elf hooking onto her. Miri returned the bow with matching dignity.

"Cousin Alys, I am happy to see you." She made the backhand wave toward Val Con and repeated the weary formula for the last time, moving the kid along. She wanted that drink bad, she thought, and looked up to find Emrith Tiazan watching her, something like approval in the lines of her face.

"Appropriately done," the old lady said. "We now go in to dinner. Win Den, attend me, by your grace."

tel'Vosti stepped forward and offered his arm, which she took, allowing him to lead her down the room toward the door at the opposite end. The mob of redheads made room for them to pass, but nobody followed.

"Us now, cha'trez." Val Con's voice was soft in her ear as he took her arm. "You did admirably."

"Easy for you to say," she muttered. "I'd rather sing for my supper, though. Any day."

"I need a drink."

Miri leaned against the wall just inside their private parlor, eyes closed against the scented darkness. Dinner had been horrible. Her place had been set with an arsenal of forks and tongs and spoons and knives, all of which, sleep-learning told her implacably, had a specific use. She'd fair busted her head while she'd waited for the first course, trying to remember the long list of foods that could and should be addressed with each implement.

Then the first course was served and she'd broken out in an ice-cold sweat as dish after unidentifiable dish went by. She'd snuck a look to see what Val Con was having; took a little of that and nibbled while she tried to do her conversational duty to the woman on her left. She'd left the wine strictly alone, terrified at getting even a little fuddled with all those new cousins watching and keeping score.

"A drink," she said firmly. "A *big* drink."

"Certainly," Val Con murmured in her ear. He slipped a hand beneath her elbow. "Come sit on the couch, cha'trez . . . There. Red wine? White? Jade? Canary? I believe—yes, there is misravot, if you would prefer . . ."

Miri sighed, leaned back in the cushions and finally opened her eyes. Val Con had lit the low-lights—the ceiling sparkled with starring pinpoints; the carpet glittered like new snow.

"What do I know about wine? You pick."

"All right," he said, and poured pale green wine into two crystal cups. He brought them to the couch and handed her one, raising his own in salute.

"To Lady yos'Phelium, my love."

She laughed and shook her head. "Why not to Lord yos'Phelium?"

"Lord yos'Phelium was not courageous, nor did he comport himself with anything but mediocrity." He touched her cheek. "Miri, you are a treasure."

"If you say so," she said dubiously and sipped her wine. "I think it's pretty brave, myself, to trust everything to somebody who don't even know what fork to use—" She shook her head. "Who knows what fork to use," she corrected herself, "if there'd been a clue to what the food was!"

"Ah, I had wondered why you ate so little . . ." He tipped his head. "You must not let it burden you," he said softly. "You imagine my melant'i is so fragile it will shatter at your slightest error. Instead, it has—resilience—and certainly strength enough to withstand my lifemate's mistaking a fork—or even using a fork instead of tongs!" He tasted his wine, suddenly serious.

"In all matters of importance—in your conduct toward your delm and the head of your line; in your answer to tel'Vosti—you were above reproach. If in less vital matters you err, or simply choose to disregard the Code, then it is—a nothing. People will say, if they say at all: 'Ah, she is an original.' Which is no bad thing."

"An original?" She frowned and shook her head.

Val Con sighed. "It is one of the reasons I insisted you learn the Code from the source, rather than from my tutoring," he said slowly. "Each individual takes the Code and—shapes it—according to his own character and necessity. Now, I have, perhaps, taken too much from my uncle's tutelage—or learned too young, as Shan would have it—so my manner tends toward coolness and extreme precision." He sipped wine, brows drawn.

"Shan is an original," he murmured: "his manners are appalling, but his *manner* pleases. Anthora follows his style. Pat Rin is very correct, but easy, so the correctness seems joined to and flowing from his melant'i. Nova—" he shook his head, smiling with a touch of wistfulness. "I once overheard someone say he would rather meet an angry lyr-cat unarmed, than Nova and I in a reception line."

Miri laughed.

Val Con leaned over and kissed her.

"Mmmm," she said and shivered delightedly as warm, knowing fingers stroked down the line of her throat.

"You find me too Liaden, Miri?" Val Con's voice was husky in her ear, his cheek soft against hers.

She breathed in the scent of him and let the breath go in a half-gasping laugh as desire broke over her. "The clothes threw me," she murmured. "Why don't you take 'em off?"

He laughed gently, took her wineglass and bent to put it aside, his weight pushing her into the cushions. Then his lips were back, demanding full attention, while his hands stroked and teased and finally found the fastenings of the dress and loosed them.

She tried to return the favor, reaching to open the fine white shirt, but he eluded her hands, keeping her pinned and all but helpless while he slipped the dress down over her shoulders and a bit further, nuzzling her throat, kissing her breasts, her belly . . .

The dress was gone. She reached again to help him out of the shirt, aching to feel his skin against hers—and was fended off with a breathless laugh: "Ah, not so greedy, cha'trez . . ."

Mouth and hands engaged her full attention once more, the soft fabrics of trousers and shirt stroking against her nakedness alternately frustrating and exhilarating.

At some point, he picked her up and lay her down again on that high, wide bed, and was gone for a moment, returning with his hand full of bed-flowers.

He covered her in them, laughing; crushed one in long fingers and stroked the fragrance across her breasts. She shivered and laughed and twisted, pulling him down and mock wrestling, desperate to have him, with an urgency the flower-scent fed.

He laughed, fingers and lips teasing; but allowed the shirt—and at once allowed everything, abandoning the role of command as she bit and kissed and stroked and the flowers were crushed beneath them and gave up their seductive odor.

She lay across his chest, teasing, nearly lazy against the flower's urgency. Val Con's eyes were half-closed, his face blurred with desire, hands stroking, beginning to insist. But he wasn't in control now, she was. She rubbed against him, felt his hips move and laughed as she kissed his ear.

"So greedy, Val Con . . ."

A laugh—or a soft groan. "Miri . . ."

She closed her eyes, concentrating on the feel of him, on the warmth, on how well their bodies fit, on the desire barely restrained, soon to be loosed.

She looked at the pattern of him inside her head.

And—*reached out,* very softly, to stroke it and breathe on it and—kiss it—and love it and desire it and—

Beneath her, Val Con went utterly still. Miri opened her eyes.

"Cha'trez . . ." He touched her face, his eyes wide and shocked-looking, as if he'd been suddenly wakened. "Miri, what are you doing?"

She looked at him through slitted eyes, still more than half cuddling the pattern of him—the *him* of him—against her, feeling the love flow from her; feeling it return, enriched and expanded.

"Loving you," she managed. Then, as the distress in his eyes began to resonate in his pattern. "Should I stop?"

"No." His hands closed hard around her waist and he rolled, spilling her over into the crushed flowers and him hard and urgent atop her. "Never stop."

It was bodies, then, and lust and the flowers and finally two voices crying out as one in joy and wonder.

They were still tangled around each other when the timer shut the room lights down. Both were fast asleep.

DUTIFUL PASSAGE

IN ORBIT

"Once more," First Mate Priscilla Mendoza called, "sequence twelve . . . *now!*"

Inside the lifeboat the pilot hit the sequence. Outside, the laser turrets swiveled, left, right, up, down, extended and finally withdrew into their shielding.

"Great!" she said. "Shut her down, Seth; we're meshed."

The little ship obediently powered down and the pilot slipped out of the slot, slamming the hatch.

"Last one," he said. "Time to take on the Yxtrang."

Priscilla blinked up at him—long, rat-faced, laconic Seth, matter-of-factly installing laser cannons on lifeboats.

"Is that what you think we're going to do?" she asked. "Go to war with the Yxtrang?"

Seth shrugged, bending over to gather up his toolkit. "Can't think of anybody else'll fire on escape pods," he said calmly. "Terrans won't. Liadens won't—pay all that weirgild?" He grinned, a surprise of white teeth in his narrow face. "Never met a Liaden crazy enough to bankrupt himself on a sure thing."

Priscilla smiled back and slung her tool bag over her shoulder. "So it's the Yxtrang, by process of elimination?"

"Seems reasonable," Seth said, ambling at her side down

the service hall to Bay Four. "Either that, or Shan wants an ace up his sleeve." He shrugged. "Never known Shan to make a bad play, where the ship was concerned. I'll follow him on this one."

Priscilla stopped and looked directly into his eyes—mud brown and smallish—Healer sense tuned to read every nuance of his emotive pattern.

"Seth, it's not Yxtrang. But it could still be very dangerous. People who well *might* fire on an escape pod, and Balance be damned. We don't know that they will, but we aren't at all convinced that they won't." She paused and packed the next words heavily, timing them to his inner resonance. "Be certain, Seth. There's still time for you to ship down—no blame."

He stared back into her eyes, more than half-tranced.

"Shan found me in a backworld dive," he said, so softly she strained to hear. "I was scraping out a living running in-system ore boats and garbage scows. Drinking too much, doing too much smoke. Lost my family in an Yxtrang raid—wife, kids, parents. Went off my head, I guess. Came to, eventually—no money, no job, and no friends. Shan needed pilots—'Always need a good pilot,' he said—gods, I can still see him coming into that dive—skinny, shoulders not filled yet, cutting deals like a pro—sixteen, maybe seventeen Standards—with that white hair and a kid's face and those eyes. Never seen eyes like that . . ." He blinked; shook his head and Priscilla let him break the trance.

He sighed. "Shan got me out of there—out of *all* of there. Gave me a chance. 'My man,' is what he told the port guard. 'That's my man, sir; and he's wanted at his post.'" He nodded sharply and turned away, heading doggedly down the hall.

"If it's Yxtrang or if it's something worse," he said as Priscilla fell in beside him, "I reckon I can man my post."

Shan looked up as she entered his office, smiled wanly and returned to the screen. Priscilla crossed to the bar and poured two glasses of wine—red, for him; white, for her—and carried them back to the desk. She slid into the chair opposite and waited, holding the glass and running through a low-level exercise to restore tranquility.

"Thank you, Priscilla." He picked up his own glass, waved it in ironic salute and took a healthy drink.

"You're welcome," she murmured, reading the worry and the exhaustion and the sparking nervous energy overlaying his emotive grid. "The First Mate reports all lifeships armed. Field tests remain to be done, but everything reads fine on the circuits." She sipped wine. "Seth Johnson chooses to remain with his captain."

Shan sighed. "Seth Johnson is a sentimental fool," he said, and nodded at the screen. "We have a match."

"So soon?"

"Amazing, isn't it? With so many gene-maps in the galaxy?" He grinned tiredly. "I played a hunch—that notation on Sergeant Robertson's birth certificate—*mutated within acceptable limits*—you recall?"

She nodded. "You thought that might mean 'partly Liaden.'"

"And my thought has proved correct—I tell you, Priscilla, I'm not a master of trade for nothing! Though you would consider that a scout might more fully communicate—but I digress. How unusual." He took another swallow of wine and waved at the screen. "Miri Robertson's gene-map matches that of Line Tiazan." He eyed her expectantly.

She sipped her wine, knowing that her temple training had taught her more than enough patience to wait out one of Shan's rare silences.

"You disappoint me. Don't you have the least wish to know who the devil Tiazan is and where we'll be meeting my wretched brother?"

"But I was certain you were about to tell me."

"Unkind, Priscilla. I can't think why I lifemated you."

"Because I let you talk as much as you want."

"Do you? How odd. Especially as I have the distinct impression that I'm talking less than I ever have. But, I perceive you a-quiver with curiosity and hasten to explain."

He set his glass aside with a flourish and sat up straighter in the chair, humor vanishing from face and emotive grid.

"Tiazan is First Line of Clan Erob," he said; "which has its

seat upon Lytaxin. So to go to 'Miri's people' as directed by
my brother and delm-to-be, we need merely go to Lytaxin.
Very simple, once one has the proper information. What as-
tonishes me particularly is that for once in his life Val Con
seems to have done exactly as he ought."

Priscilla blinked. "He has?"

"As I said, astonishing. Though, to be just, Val Con *often*
does as he ought. Of course, he just as often does precisely as
he pleases. I expect there's a deliberate pattern involved, calculated to a hair's breadth to appear random. One afternoon
when I'm bored I'll feed the parameters to the tactical computers and see what they make of it. But to continue! Erob is
Korval's most ancient ally. The family diaries speak of Rool
Tiazan and his lifemate, leaders of the dramliz, who chose to
evacuate the Old World on the ship piloted by Cantra
yos'Phelium."

Priscilla allowed a wisp of inquiry to escape her and Shan
nodded.

"Rool Tiazan had read the luck, you see—and the luck
sent him to Cantra yos'Phelium."

"Rool Tiazan was a full wizard, then," Priscilla murmured.
"He had the Sight."

"Apparently so, since *Quick Passage* and her passengers
eventually came safe to Liad."

"And all that time since the ship came to Liad, Korval and
Erob have been allies?"

"Actually a bit longer than that," Shan said. "Cantra's log
indicates that she and Jela—her partner before she took on
the revered yos'Galan ancestor—had known Rool Tiazan
and his lady some time prior to the evacuation. If it comes to
that—recall that I promised to amaze, Priscilla!—we're a bit
more than allies. More accurate to say cousins—or half-clan,
there's a word! Ever since the ship landed on Liad, Tiazan
and Korval have been sticking to an arrangement—actually a
protocol, all properly signed and sealed—a schedule of a
contract-marriage every three generations, with the child
going, in unfailing sequence: Erob, Korval, Erob, Korval . . ."

Priscilla frowned. "You said Tiazan and Korval—"

"So I did, and so it was. Korval seems to have sent equally

from yos'Phelium and yos'Galan, but Erob seems only to
have sent from Tiazan, never from the subordinate Line. In
any wise, the schedule demanded a contract wedding this
generation. yos'Galan was sent last time, and the child came
to Korval."

"And Val Con knew all this?" Priscilla demanded.

Shan shrugged and reached for his glass. "Now that's a
different question. Unless he's knocked his head rather
sharply, he certainly recalls our long association with Erob.
That a mating was mandated and that yos'Phelium must
send—I doubt he did know that. I only know it because when
I was First Speaker in Trust, I received a note from Great-
great-great Aunt Wayr yos'Phelium, dated one hundred ten
Standard years ago." He sighed. "I sent it forward a little
time more, to Val Con's thirty-fifth Name Day: a puzzle for
him to solve on the day he becomes delm."

"But Miri Robertson is Line Tiazan, and she and Val Con
are *lifemates* . . ."

Shan nodded. "The child of a contract-marriage would
have gone to Erob. But the children of a lifemating will come
to the clan sheltering both partners."

"And Val Con will not leave Korval for another clan." She
made it a half-question, and Shan answered with unwar-
ranted soberness.

"Val Con is Korval Himself—the one who will be delm.
He *can't* leave. There's no clan in the Book who would have
him." He sighed. "Korval has this certain—reputation. Even
among our allies." He stared into the dregs of his glass, then
all at once seemed to shake himself and looked over to her
with a wry smile.

"It's been a long day, Priscilla. Will you join me for a nap?"

"Certainly." She came gracefully to her feet, despite the
weariness that grated behind her eyes and pulled at her back.
"Ken Rik has shift-authority and will call if there's a problem."

"Wonderful," Shan muttered, stepping aside to let her pro-
cede him into their private quarters. "I always wanted to be
captain of a military vessel, Priscilla. Remind me to give my
brother a very sound shaking, when we finally catch up with
him."

"Yes, dear," she said placidly and turned to give him a hug.

Val Con struck the last note, held it and looked over to Alys Tiazan, standing alert by the audio unit. He nodded and she pressed a key, ending the recording. Val Con lifted his hands from the keyboard and smiled.

"I thank you, Miss Alys. Your assistance was invaluable."

"You are kind to say it," she responded, very properly indeed, for one rising ten Standards, and then dimpled. "But you had much better have had me than Kol Vus, you know. He fidgets awfully!"

"Then I was doubly fortunate to encounter you," Val Con said gravely, touching the omnichora's power-plate. "Shall we play the tape back, do you think? It would not do to give Kol Vus a muddy recording, when he has been so gracious in accommodating me."

"But he must do that, mustn't he?" Alys said, with the cool matter-of-factness of childhood. "After all, you are Korval."

"So I am, but I am also a guest in your house. Allow me to possess some address, I beg."

That bought a bright glissade of laughter, after which she considered him for a moment more soberly, face intent and looking, so he fancied, very much as Miri had, at ten.

"I don't think you're the least frightening," she stated at last and Val Con inclined his head.

"You relieve me."

"Now you sound like Uncle Win Den," Alys told him severely, and bent to the audio unit, pressing three keys in sequence.

Music swelled out of the tiny unit, filling the room to the walls.

The name of the piece was *Toccata and Fugue in D Minor* and it had been written many years before Terrans achieved the stars by a man named Johann Sebastian Bach. It had been Anne Davis' favorite piece of music, and for this present purpose Val Con had striven to play it in precisely her style.

The role of Clan Radio Tech Kol Vus Tiazan in the project was to seal the brief recording to Lytaxin's perimeter beacons. Ninety seconds, Val Con thought, would surely be long enough for Shan to descry their mother's favorite and read into it verification that Val Con awaited him on world.

The music-fragment ended, snapped off clean at 90 seconds, and Val Con again inclined his head.

"I believe that will serve the purpose quite well. May I discommode you further, Miss Alys?"

"You would like me to take this down to Kol Vus?" she asked, rising and sliding the unit's carry strap over her shoulder. "That's no trouble. I need to pass the comm room on the way to my tutor." She hesitated. "You play very nicely. I would be happy to hear more, if time allows it during your guesting."

His touch on the omnichora was god-gift, honed by years of study. He could easily have been a master musician—a *maestro,* according to Anne, who had taught him his scales. But he was Korval: Stranger passions claimed precedence.

He smiled at the child before him, her hair a riot of orange curls, her eyes an intelligent, sparkling brown.

"I would be honored to play for you, Miss Alys. Only name a time."

She tipped her head, apparently consulting some inner schedule. "Tomorrow?" she said eventually. "In the hour before Prime?"

"Done," he said gravely, and bowed as one accepting a treasure.

She did not, as he expected, erupt into giggles at this, but returned the bow most creditably, murmuring an exquisitely proper "The pleasure is mine."

She straightened, then, adjusted the strap across her shoulder and smiled. "I have to go before my tutor tells Aunt Emrith I've been late again."

"Please do not allow me to be the cause of such distress to the House," Val Con said, and that *did* draw a giggle, cut off as she slipped out the door and pulled it closed behind her.

He stood alone in the music room, considering his options. Miri was closeted with Erob's Historian, filling details in the lives of Miri-eklykt'i and Katalina Tayzin —an interview that promised to be both lengthy and productive of an uneasy temper in one's lifemate.

His duty plainly lay in the direction of Erob. Some explanations must, in courtesy, be made to the delm of Korval's oldest ally, and yet . . .

Music tingled in his fingertips, awakened by his brief playing for the beacon. Surely, he might steal ten minutes to set the rest of the music free?

Slowly, knowing that duty called him elsewhere, yet unable to resist the lure of a concert-quality instrument perfectly set in a room tuned for its unique voice, he went to the omnichora, sat on the bench and pressed the power plate.

The wall he faced over the omnichora was mirrored.

Val Con sighed, recalling the revulsion on several faces last night, despite the courtesy due a guest; wondering if he should have followed tel'Vosti's hint and had the scar canceled.

The scar was there for a reason, after all; he might have had the autodoc erase the wretched thing anytime during their voyage from Vandar. He had chosen to allow it to remain, a constant and sometimes painful reminder of the wages of foolishness.

"No more than you traded for, young sir." He heard Uncle Er Thom's dry reproval in his mind's ear, and half-smiled in agreement.

It would be another matter entirely, he told himself, fingers adjusting stops and frequencies, had the cut failed to heal—or if

one's lifemate objected to the mar. But the wound was clean, as
he had told tel'Vosti, and Miri made no objection.

"No call," Uncle Er Thom's voice instructed him from memory, "to concern yourself with the comfort of non-kin. Korval
acts upon its own necessities. Let others mind their melant'i."

"Yes, uncle," he murmured, and touched the keyboard,
softly playing the cool and logical line of his uncle's musical
signature, that the boy Val Con had composed many years ago.
His ear caught a possibility in the old theme and he played on
half-aware, letting his fingers find what they might.

Let others mind their own melant'i. An old lesson, that;
among the first. One kept one's own care close, for clan, for
servants, for kin . . . Val Con's fingers faltered on the keys.

Shan would be here—soon.

Shan was his cha'leket, the brother of his heart. Shan might
well mind the scar. Might well mind other things, truth told;
things that would distress one who had helped a green-eyed
fosterling grow. That would surely distress one who was a
Healer and able to see what was now that fosterling's soul.

The Department of Interior . . . the Department of Interior
had done much damage, severed memories, stolen home,
love, music, mother—". . . our mother," Shan's voice said
from years gone. "Your mother's gone, but you can share
mine, all right?"

Our mother . . . Anne Davis: chestnut hair, merry dark eyes,
clever hands, scented with bound books and flowers; wide-
hipped and full-breasted, as many Terran women; full with
laughter and passion and more than enough love for the children of the house—her own three and the child of her lifemate's cha'leket. She had taught him to play the 'chora, taught
him his letters—Terran and Trade—wiped tears, comforted
child-woes and halfling griefs, shared out justice and kisses, re-
joiced with him when he was accepted to Scout Academy—

And the Department of Interior had stolen her.

"My kinswoman . . ." He recalled his own voice, telling
Miri—a Miri nearly lost, gods; wary-faced and distrusting, as
she had very good cause to be. "My *kinswoman*—" without
feeling, without even such a memory as flashed now, of big,
warm hands holding his, shaping tiny fingers above the keyboard.

His right hand dandled True Scale as his left rose to adjust stops. Both hands centered above the keyboard, and at once came down, with sure authority, sweeping headlong into the *Toccata.*

It allowed much, as great music does, endless opportunity for variation and lessons from one's own fingers being among the chiefest of its joys. But their mother had loved it for its own sake, as well, and he played it that way now, as he had for Shan, while memories, suppressed and twisted and made strange—repulsive—by intent of his enemies, loosened and flowed and touched him true, until he closed his eyes and gave himself to the music and the remembering and didn't even know if he wept.

The music reached a natural end, as music will, and his fingers went still upon the keys. After a moment, it occurred to him that he was no longer alone in Erob's music room and he opened his eyes.

"Hi," she said from her perch on the polished curve of a listening-stool. Her hair was braided today; he saw the copper length of it gleaming down her back in the mirror. She was dressed in a rich yellow shirt and soft trousers the color of Shan's favorite wine—proper attire for an extended session with the clan historian. She leaned forward, eyes intent. "You OK?"

"I believe so." He took a breath and smiled. "Yes."

"Good." She shifted on the stool. "Came to tell you that I got a break from the question-and-answer bit. Historian says he'll see me for more after lunch. Not bloody likely, 'cause I already got a headache with remembering stuff that happened when I was three years old and would've sworn yesterday that I didn't know anything about." She stood abruptly.

"I'm going down to the merc camp and see if I can't find the 'falks—maybe Jase." She bit her lip, and he listened to the song of her that played inside his head, hearing the thin notes of exhaustion, and a certain wistful sadness.

"I know you don't think much of Jase," Miri was saying; "and you got no call to love the Gyrfalks. Folks here seem to appreciate them a bit though"—she chewed her lip again, and the chords of her song strengthened and clarified—"but you're welcome to walk that way with me, if you want to."

"I want to," said Val Con, touching the 'chora's power-down and standing. He smiled at her, relieved to see her return smile burn away the wariness in her eyes. "Thank you for inviting me."

"When do you think your brother'll get here?"

Val Con laughed softly. "Weary of being clan-bound so soon, Miri?"

She'd been squinting up into the bright sky, as if she might see the *Passage*; now she transferred the squint to him.

"Means you don't know," she surmised. "This mind reading stuff don't seem very efficient."

"Alas. I was offered use of the House's pin-beam so that an answer to *when?* might be achieved quickly. Unfortunately, one must know the position of the beam's target, and Shan has all the galaxy at his beck—and hyperspace, as well."

"Pin-beams're expensive," Miri commented.

"Erob may not consider it so, weighed in balance."

"That eager to get rid of us, huh?" She shook her head at him, mock stern. "You got some reputation among the home-folks, Liaden. And to think I was worried about wrecking your melant'i."

He laughed and swept a sudden bow—from lesser to greater, as she read it. "Had I not said that it was your own melant'i would carry us?"

She grinned and took his hand, and they walked across the fragrant, sun-warmed grass.

"Talked to tel'Vosti a bit while I was waiting for the historian to show," she said, slanting an idle glance at his face. "Said he knew your father real well."

The pattern of him inside her head flashed and tightened. "So, it seems that all of Erob knew my father," he snapped.

"Huh?" She stopped, yanking him to a halt, and frowned up into his face. "There something wrong with that?"

His pattern snarled and an acid wash of frustrated pain cramped her belly, so that she dropped his hand and half-cried out in astonishment.

"Miri!" His hands were around her waist, easing her down to sit on the grass. "Cha'trez?"

Worry was added to the emotional hash, mixing badly with the pain and the anger.

"You're hurting me," she gasped, eyes closed as she groped for him inside her head. "Stop it, boss—the pattern . . ."

Shock turned her icy, and the next instant she was the eye of a color-storm—*redyelloworangegreenblueviolet*—as the Rainbow whipped 'round her, and some unknown inner sense registered the near sound of a door opening—and closing.

Stillness, within and without.

"Gods." She let out a shuddering breath, tipping forward in controlled collapse until her forehead touched her knee. "Gods, gods, gods." She sat up and opened her eyes.

Val Con sat cross-legged before her, hands loosely cupping his knees. "Is the pain gone, Miri?" His voice was as calm as his pattern.

"Gone," she agreed and licked her lips. "What *was* that?"

Puzzlement shadowed his eyes. "I am without information. If you could describe the phenomenon, we might achieve understanding."

"Right." She frowned. "Told you that tel'Vosti had known your father, and you got pissed—saw your pattern—cramp up, kinda. And when I asked you what was wrong with that I was all of a sudden furious—frustrated—like I'd been banging my head against the same brick wall for years and wasn't any closer to busting through . . ." She sighed and reached over to take his hand, looking into his eyes worriedly.

"Seems like I must've gotten it straight from you, somehow," she said slowly. "Wasn't really that the *pattern* was hurting me."

"Ah." His fingers tightened around hers. "And you have never experienced this before?"

"No . . ." She shifted a little, thinking. "But I never did anything like I did last night before, either—just reaching out and *touching* the pattern. Never occurred to me. Maybe I got—sensitized—or something."

There was a small silence before he said, "Or perhaps Priscilla, who is after all dramliza, might have done—something—to me by way of insuring that I might hear Shan."

Miri blinked thoughtfully. "Something to that, ain't there? You can't tell—naw, I guess not."

"I—felt—despair and distress coming from you at the Winterfair," Val Con said softly. "But it was clearly emanating from *you*. I did not experience your emotions as my own." A faint wisp of something like hunger escaped him and Miri chuckled, squeezing his hand.

"Just as well—but you're talking emergency situation. Maybe that's the tip-off. Some kind of emergency hooked up with your father?"

Val Con sighed and lifted a hand to stroke the hair out of his eyes. "Only that he lost his lifemate—my mother—to assassins and, after taking Delm's Counsel, left his clan and his heir in the hands of his brother Er Thom, and went off into the wide galaxy, seeking Balance."

"And never sent word back," Miri finished, and shook her head. "Bad business, tel'Vosti said."

"tel'Vosti is more correct than he knows," Val Con murmured. "The options revealed by Delm's Counsel were a war with the Terran Party, who had employed the assassin . . ."

"Which would mean a war with Terra." Miri frowned. "Bad choice."

"My father thought so, as well. So he took the second option, which was slower, and less sure, but, if it worked, more fruitful." He sighed. "Or so it says in Korval's Diaries. The plan itself is not detailed." He glanced away; caught her eyes again.

"Tradition is, should an individual be estranged for twelve years, he is considered dead to the clan and the date of his desertion recorded as a date of death. Traditionally, the head of line announces the death and makes the notation."

Miri touched his cheek. "You didn't do that."

"Daav yos'Phelium is eklykt'i," Val Con said, coming smoothly to his feet and offering her his hand. "Momentarily beyond the clan. Korval's records show nothing else."

Jason Carmody walked down East Axis, an island of blonde quiet among the noisy, purposeful bustle going on all around.

Every so often, Jase turned aside to talk to this one or that; on two occasions he ducked inside half-dismantled tech-sheds to supervise some particularly tricksy bit of equipment balancing. Merc Center would be stripped down to dirt by this time tomorrow. Dawn the day after would find only torn meadowlands and a network of synthphalt service roads, already crumbling back to sand.

Jase ducked out into the sunlight and stood, techs and troops flowing around him like a dusty leather river, staring at nothing in particular and gently stroking his beard.

Eight days to Fendor, if the transport was on time. It had been known to happen. More often it wasn't, but the Gyrfalks had another contract pending, so they'd paid a premium for a guaranteed pick-up. Sometimes that worked. In the meantime, Suzuki and the spec-team were on their way to negotiations, leaving Jason, the tyros, and the low-ranks to break camp and tidy up.

Jase sighed and shook his massive frame into motion, going with the flow down East Axis until it intersected with Command Way, where he turned off, heading for his quarters.

"Jase!" The voice from behind was familiar, but not urgently so. Jason checked his stride unwillingly, half-minded to go on.

"Jase!" the voice persisted. "Jason Carmody!"

He sighed and turned, hoping the problem wasn't going to be too time-consuming and scanning the scurrying crowd, looking for a face to match the voice.

"Jason."

She was a mere four of his paces before him, a red-haired Liaden woman in a yellow shirt and burgundy trousers, comfortable boots, belt, pouch, no apparent gun. Her hair was single-braided and fell below the holsterless belt. A man stood at her right shoulder. Jase flicked him a look, established that he was Liaden, too—scar across the right cheek, dark hair, no gun—before bowing to the woman.

"Yes, ma'am," he said in respectful Trade, cudgeling his brain to recall which of Clan Erob she precisely was. "What can I do for you?"

The woman blinked, flashed a quick glance at her companion and drifted a step closer. Something in the way she moved sparked a flicker of deeper recognition, gone even as he fumbled for it.

"What the hell's the matter with you, Jason?" she demanded in Terran. "Tell me I can come back anytime I want, then forget what I look like inside of a year?"

"*Redhead*?" Jason very nearly goggled, at last seeing past the disguise of rich clothes to the lithe, familiar body, the sharp face and dark gray eyes. He fell to his knees, which put him only a head or so taller than she, and flung his arms wide.

"Gods love us all, my darlin'!" he cried. "Come and give Jason a kiss!"

"Yes, but darlin'," Jason was saying, handing kynak all around in the privacy of his quarters, "if you and Tough Guy was comin' to Lytaxin anyway, why not just come with us in the first case? We'd have saved you a good bit of time."

Miri lifted a shoulder and flashed a grin at her partner, who was perched on the arm of her chair. "Had a spot of trouble to clear up first."

"Spot o'trouble, indeed!" Jase sprawled on the thick rug, taking up most of the available floor space, and braced his wide shoulders against the side of a wooden chest, the delicate hand carvings just visible through the mars of rough travel. He waved a massive hand in Val Con's direction. "You didn't have that facial decoration last time I saw you, did you, my lad?"

Val Con considered him out of bland green eyes. "No."

"Wouldn't've thought there was much out there fast enough to touch you," Jason persisted. "Polesta still ain't recovered from that little love tap you gave her. Actually heard her say 'please' to the muster-clerk this morning. Enough to give a man religion."

Miri laughed. "Make a soldier outta her yet. How'd the campaign go? When you shipping out?"

"The angels won," Jase said comfortably; "and the employer was prompt with regard to the fee. Paid in full, yes, indeed, and due to ship out tomorrow."

"Tomorrow?" Miri's shoulders sagged; and Val Con shifted slightly to press against her.

"Now, now, my small, take heart. You know what trans-

port pilots are: why book three runs when six're offered?
They're bound to make at least two on time."

She laughed and sipped a little of her drink, laugh turning
to a gasp and half-choke.

"A little out of the way of it, darlin'?"

She managed a grin and shook her head. "Been drinking
wine lately. 'When on Maris . . . ' "

" 'Drink what they offer'," Jase finished and knocked back
a quarter of his glass. "Only too true. About this other thing,
though; you know we're not throwing you to the beasties.
Sign back up where you belong and there's a place on the
transport with your name on it. Suzuki and me're still wanting to give you that lieutenant's badge . . ."

"Yeah, well . . ." She sighed, not daring to look at Val
Con. "Thing is, we just got here yesterday and there's some
stuff I still gotta do, being as they're my clan and all . . ."

Jason stopped with his glass halfway to his mouth. "Who's
your clan, Redhead?"

"Umm—people up at the house."

"What!" Jase sat up straight, hitting his head a solid *whack*
on the overhanging chest-top. "What house—the big house?
Erob's house?"

She looked at him doubtfully. "Yeah."

Jase slapped his thigh. "I *knew* they were right 'uns! The
old lady with the ring—damn me if I didn't think she was familiar the first time I saw her!" He suddenly seemed to do a
double take. "That is *your* clan, Redhead? Eh? Not your partner's?"

"My clan," Val Con told him softly, "has its seat upon
Liad."

"Mine," Miri said, half-grinning. "Late-breaking news, appalling everybody from the delm down, except maybe Alys
and tel'Vosti."

"The General? You could easily do worse by way of rela-
tives. The General's worth all four of my uncles—with a
grand-dame thrown in! And young Alys shoots like a
trooper. I wish I had a tyro as sharp with a yessir as she is!"
He slid back down against the chest and had another slug of
kynak.

"But you haven't said what you've been about, my small, besides the clearing up of business."

"Well, let's see . . . Got into it a bit with the Juntavas—their mistake, really—but I guess that's all straightened out by now. Spent some time, ummm," here she glanced at Val Con for a moment, "out of touch, sort of. Little bit of action there. Worked some odd jobs, did some singing and celebrating . . ."

"Directed the defense that turned an enemy invasion into a rout," Val Con's quiet voice picked up; "without loss to home guard. Learned High and Low Liaden, mastered the salient points of The Liaden Code of Proper Conduct, began the study of the opening equations and board-drills, sufficient to attain the level of provisional pilot, third class."

There was a small silence, during which Miri tried to decide whether to break Val Con's arm or only his jaw, then Jason cleared his throat.

"That right?" He shook his massive head. "Busy, my small—and here I was afraid you'd fall into trouble, what with having idle time on your hands." He looked at Val Con.

"You're a pilot, are you?"

"Master level, yes."

"And you been teaching Redhead piloting." He stared off into the far corner of the ceiling for a moment, then looked back at Val Con. "Your opinion, as a Master level pilot, is that Redhead is capable of attaining what class?"

There was a small pause. "Second class, easily," Val Con said. "If she chooses to apply herself, first class is certainly within her reach. Master—" He moved his shoulders. "It is too soon to know."

"Well," said Jase and finished off his drink. His eyes came back to Miri with something like wonder. "Your partner telling it square, darlin'?"

"Yeah," she said, throwing a glower at Val Con, who lifted an eyebrow. "Yeah, he's got it right."

"Well," Jase said again. "Might have to make that a captain's badge." He held up a hand. "Suzuki has to OK it, too—you know the drill. Learning how to pilot, tacking on both brands of Liaden . . ." He sat up straight, carefully avoiding the chest lid.

"I know Tough Guy's your partner. If you want to talk further on it, I can commit the 'falks to a pilot's slot at a rank comparable to his grade in—?"

Miri grinned wickedly. "He's a scout," she said, feeling Val Con shift sharply beside her. "Scout Commander, First-In."

"Ooof!" said Jason—and laughed. "You don't brag on yourself, do you, my son?"

"One does," Val Con told him, "what one does."

"Right you are." He laughed again. "Scout Commander . . . but you look to be at liberty, if I might say so. If you want work as a pilot, or if there's something else, the unit could only profit."

"I—" Val Con hesitated, alive to the sudden note of longing in the sense of Miri within him. He glanced down into her eyes. "There are discussions to be made," he said, and she nodded, wistfully.

"It sounds good," she told Jase truthfully. "And I want it—but him and me still got some stuff to clear up. You're going back to Headquarters, right?"

"For a time—there's a new contract on the burner, though, so it looks to be a jump-in/jump-out. Suzuki's gone to start the talk—which I assume you knew, since you didn't ask for her."

"Heard it on the chatter when we were coming in." Miri nodded. "I'll leave a message, after this other stuff gets settled." Val Con stirred slightly. "Or, at least, after we got a better idea of what's happening." She sighed and looked up at him. He lifted a light hand to her cheek.

"Know you can't hold an offer like that forever—" she said to Jase's suddenly speculative eyes.

"Never mind it, my small. If you decide you want us, believe that we want you! Anytime, anywhere, any terms. Why, I'll even give you my slot—"

Miri laughed and came to her feet. "Gods, look at the time!" she said, flicking a slender hand toward the window and the reaching orange rays of sundown. "We're gonna be late for dinner, boss."

"Alas," Val Con said, standing. He bowed slightly to the

towering Aus. "Honor attended the asking," he said stiffly. "My thanks to you and your troop."

"That's all right, son. I know quality when I see quality—not quite as thick as that!" Jase laughed and loomed to his feet. "Walk you to the access road. Pretty planet. Pretty sunsets."

The three of them stopped at the place where East Gate had been earlier that afternoon, and Jase bent nearly double to hug Miri and plant a kiss firmly on her mouth.

"Take care of yourself, my small."

"You too, Jase. Best to Suzuki. Tell her . . ."

The message was swallowed in the sudden appalling uproar—a banshee wail from the lone communication pole still upright beside the comm shack—and startled beeps from a half-a-hundred personal communits.

"Air attack—popped up over the mountains—reentry speed—" Miri could barely hear the words pouring from Jason's communit against the siren's wail and the new sound, a sound like a thousand thunderstorms, all letting loose at once.

"Bastards tricked us! Pull everyone . . ." Jason cut off in the middle of issuing orders to stare.

In the sky: A formation of deadly shapes, black against sunset orange. As they watched, one peeled off—another—a third, toward the distant city and the closer town.

"Oh, shit," breathed Jason. "Redhead—"

Redhead was already gone, moving flat out down the synthphalt toward Erob's house, her partner a fleet dark shadow at her side.

Warning to the civilians in hand, Jason whirled, bellowing to his troops.

"Yxtrang coming in! Blood war!"

14TH CONQUEST CORPS

LYTAXIN

Alone and weaponless, he held the planet.

It was an accident and one that would cost *someone* a stripe or two, though not himself, who had neither stripe nor rank to lose. The moment was laden with irony, had one taste for it—that Nelirikk No-Troop should be first Yxtrang upon this world, before even the General.

Having devoted most of ten Cycles to acquiring a taste for irony, Nelirikk embraced the moment and looked about him.

The world was beautiful and lush—exactly the sort of place Liadens usually chose to colonize. The wind—warm, yet edged now with evening-chill—brushed against his clean-shaven face, treating him to natural odors for the first time in—ah? those same ten Cycles! The noises behind him were those of war, but not yet the smells.

"Try now! Try again!" came the order from the ship.

Nelirikk rotated, put his foot back onto the landing chute, and with a swing of the solid metal mallet struck the recalcitrant holding lug. The mallet's head bounced uselessly on the first strike, and the second—but the third strike was true, and the offending lug shot free and rolled away into the crushed field grass.

Automatics took over then, and Nelirikk bounded away in

time to avoid being run over by the command cars coming
hastily to life in the chute.

He ran farther, perhaps, than was required—and then a
few steps more.

Behind him: sounds of motors, of shouting, of feet, hitting
the metal plank in troop rhythm. Before him: free growing
plants, high-flying birds, and flowers. Nelirikk filled his
lungs with fragrant air; sighed it out grudgingly.

A small gray animal poked its head out of the high grass
just beyond Nelirikk's grasp, ears perked, eyes bright. It
jerked abruptly upright; showing front paws very hand-like,
and in a nose-twitch was gone. Two soldiers hit the grass
from the landing tube, took aim instantly—and held fire
pending orders. Nelirikk breathed a second sigh—and was
instantly aware of this new irony, that a no-troop attached to
an invasion force pledged to slay thousands of sentients
should feel relief at the escape of a squirrel.

Someone shouted then and Nelirikk jumped aside, saluting
the General's car, as even a no-troop must, then melted
away, alone of the crowd without duty or orders, to watch as
the troops and vehicles of the 14th Conquest Corps turned
the pretty land into Field Headquarters.

The General's word brought him to the war room, a grim-
faced Captain Kagan as his guard. Nelirikk's greedy eyes
sought this screen, that, taking information in rapidly and indiscriminately.

So—there was no capital ship arrayed against them in
space, though there was strong resistance on the coasts of
this continent and heavier fighting on the other continent,
where they had inadvertently landed in the midst of mercenaries preparing to leave. Locally—

"This is the man, General."

The General looked at Nelirikk, perhaps recognized him.
Nelirikk stood at silent attention, face expressionless, hungry
eyes hooded.

There were three men under guard behind the General.
Two were corporals Nelirikk had dealt with recently; the
other was an officer he didn't recognize.

"No-Troop." The General demanded his attention. "Describe to me the situation you encountered at landfall."

"Sir." He brought his fist up in salute. "I was strapped in at the advance station. The ship touched down and the landing chute began its extension, however the lead vehicle—your command car—did not move. The chute completed its extension, but the column remained still.

"Under orders, I investigated the situation and discovered that the explosive lugs had failed to fire and that the metal retaining lugs prevented your car from moving. I reported and was ordered to remove the impediment. I pointed out that disarming the explosive devices would prevent potential injury to the craft and your car. They were disarmed, I knocked out the metal lugs with a mallet, and the invasion proceeded."

The General stabbed a finger at the first corporal.

"You—what was your role?"

"Sir. I set and checked the retaining lugs in orbit. All was well. Sir."

"And you?"

The second corporal was visibly sweating, her youth perhaps preventing soldierly performance.

"Sir. I—my duty was to set the power cords to the explosive lugs, as ordered by Over-Technician Akrant. They checked out correctly on Test Circuit B." She choked. "Sir."

"Akrant, your report?"

The Over-Technician answered easily enough—too easily, Nelirikk thought.

"All tested according to spec, General, and was rechecked. It wasn't until we set down that I discovered that Corporal Dikl had utilized reserve circuits which required pilot intervention to operate in atmosphere."

Corporal Dikl broke into a fresh sweat, her eyes showing a bit of white around the edges.

Nelirikk, hearing as the General no doubt heard, could have advised her not to worry, but a no-troop speaks when a no-troop is spoken to, and at no other time. Nelirikk turned his attention to the proliferation of information about him.

The air power charts showed the largest aircraft concentrations on the coast. The nearest to Field Headquarters was a small base, doubtless related to the—yes; a town and a large holding were equidistant from the field. Which meant it most likely held civilian craft—easy pickings. Another screen showed the numbers of the dropjets sent to secure it, and the transport bringing in a hundred of the deadly Spraghentz— the infantry-support aircraft—that would occupy it.

Other screens—uplinks and downlinks—were coming on line now: locations of ships in orbit, radar and other scans, visual searches, live transmissions from the front.

"No, sir, " said Corporal Dikl, with unsoldierly fervor, "I was working from training manuals. I'd never done the procedure before."

Nelirikk squinted his eyes slightly, focusing on a screen across the room showing the view from the combat camera of an interceptor. He found the cue number, checked the screens.

Bomb and strafing run. That same small airfield, on automatic target. The plane lifted and—Nelirikk's heart climbed into his throat. He blinked, checked the vision screen against the radar scans, but it had moved to the next scan—looked back at the radar screen.

It wasn't there.

He sighed. His once-exemplary eyesight was failing and had played him a shabby trick. As if such a ship would be found among a small field of backward civilian craft.

"On Akrant's orders?" the General demanded of the corporal. Nelirikk sniffed. Now, *there* was a dead career. Called without rank twice by the General during Inquiry? Might as well begin tearing off the stripes and swallowing the badges.

Again the camera-screen showed the tiny airfield, this time from the vantage of a low-level run. And there, among the tall trees and with a slight hill behind it, was a thing of awful beauty.

The beauty lay in the deadly, competent lines.

The awfulness—was it that such a ship should die—if die it must—fighting, rather than destroyed ignominiously upon the ground? Or was it that he was reminded all at once of his own ship—the *Command's* ship. Always the Command's ship, for a troop owns nothing but his rank and his booty.

Duty turned him toward the Captain.

Thought stopped him.

He was Nelirikk No-Troop, permitted to speak when spoken to. He had been given leave by his assigned commander to speak to the Inquiry. Speaking without permission would cost—

The missiles were launched: they struck and crumbled a building. The view in the screen slipped as the plane turned and set up for the next run. The radar cross-scans showed no sign, the computer listeners heard no slightest whisper, the metallics—

And what *would* it cost him? He'd had ten Cycles of shame.

Decisively, he sought the Captain's eyes; signed for permission to speak.

The Captain's face clouded. He deliberately looked away. Nelirikk glanced back at the screen. Someone—an air controller—had finally sighted the beautiful ship. It sat in a visual freeze-frame as the computer made analysis, the null-image of the comparative radar etched over it.

The view from the field showed an aircraft rising in opposition. An antique by its look and in the air only by the grace of the Gods of Irony. Impossibly, it wavered into the horizontal—*fired,* by Jela! on the rushing dropjet—and was lost to view.

And there, in the corner screen, the spire of that—other— ship!

The screen froze again, as if someone lacking proper information was trying to figure out—

Nelirikk broke position, took three hasty strides toward the Controller.

"Hit that ship! Do it now!" he demanded.

There was instant silence in the room. The General turned to stare. Captain Kagan's weapon was in hand.

The screen showed the ship again, and the silly, great-hearted antique, as well, rushing headlong against the cream of Yxtrang fighters. The camera showed it circling slightly as if to protect that ship—and the closing fighters lost one of their number as the antique apparently unleashed all of its weapons at once before it was shredded into smoke. But its mission had been accomplished: the attack was diverted away from the beautiful ship.

"Hit that ship now!"

"No-Troop. Explain yourself!" Kagan's voice was grim.

On the screen, the first pair of Yxtrang fighters leveled out before the camera plane, began a sweeping turn—

Glare! Glare!

TRANSMISSION LOST

Freeze-screen came back up, picture telescoping in on the deadly ship sitting there beneath the trees, the shielding hill behind it.

Nelirikk looked at the gun, looked back at the screen.

"Scout ship," he said, calmly. "That's a Liaden Scout ship, Captain. If it's not destroyed immediately it could take out a battleship!"

"Control! ID that ship!" The General at least had ears.

"Sir. No ID on record. We've never captured or seen one—"

"*I've* seen one," Nelirikk spoke before the General, against best health. "Take it now, before it's fully activated!"

"Control!" ordered the General. "Get another flight in there. Take it out."

"You'll need something bigger. Call the transports back before they get in range—" Nelirikk heard his traitor voice correcting, apparently determined to have him shot. "It's space-based—coil-fields, power magnetics—"

"Silence!"

Nelirikk fell silent; heard the mistaken order relayed.

"No-Troop will remain silent!" snarled the General. "You, Controller, will keep me informed."

Nelirikk watched the camera screen, heard as if from another galaxy the demotions behind him: the corporals busted a level each, retaining rank but losing pay and time in grade. The over-tech was now a life private in grocery supply, proper punishment for a stupid error. To trust to training-manual performance for a thing of such importance!

The camera screen came up, showing four planes ahead of

the camera plane. Munitions tumbled away, heading for the pretty ship—

Glare! Glare! GLARE! And a wildly swinging picture, smoke on the fringes—

TRANSMISSION LOST

"General, Flight 15 is not transmitting and does not show on scans." The controller's voice was level, soldierly, merely imparting the facts.

The General's voice bordered on frenzied. "I want the *Barakhan.* Now. No one will mention No-Troop's insolence or this occurrence outside of this room."

For several moments there was nothing to see, and then a new camera—from quite a distance—hazarded a look-see and then was gone: the flash of an energy weapon was unmistakable.

"Sir, *Barakhan* is in position and has acquired the target."

The camera screen came up once more and Nelirikk watched as the horrific fires of proud *Barakhan,* dimmed only slightly by atmosphere, punched through to the scout ship, leaving bright, dancing shadows behind his eyelids. He saw, incredibly, the small ship fire back, the first wave of the battleship's energy deflected up and away by some tremendous effort of shielding.

Now the small ship could be seen from a more distant camera, firing in several directions as the General raised his voice.

"Bring all available batteries to bear, transports . . ."

And that quickly it was both too late and all over, for the Liaden ship had launched missiles and beam hard on target in the moments before it exploded, leaving a smoking crater in its stead.

He had no doubt of it even before the stunned com tech relayed the word. "General—the Spraghentz—the transport is gone!"

Nelirikk blinked—once, twice. "Honored foe," he thought treasonously, for Liadens were never such, "we salute you."

The General turned from the screen and folded his hands

upon the table. "No-Troop will report to Security with Captain Kagan," he stated. "Now."

Stars like fists of ice above the rocks and trees.

Nelirikk sat with his back against a boulder, rifle and pack to hand, and stared at the stars until his eyes teared, ringing each bright dot with rainbows.

Ah, Jela, to be once more upon a world!

This, *this* was what they'd trained him for, from the time they'd plucked him from among his fellows in boot camp. They'd trained him for exploration, made him something other than a mere troop, that the Troop and the Command might be served more fully. Training . . .

He closed his eyes, abandoning himself, here, under the free stars, to memories he had not dared recall in ten full Cycles.

Training, yes: piloting, scouting, weapons—not only the soldier's carbine and grace blade, but also other, more subtle things. They'd trained him to operate—to make judgment and form appropriate response—without recourse to superiors, regulations, subordinates, or comrades. Trained him to make decisions. Trained him to impart information. Trained him, even, to command.

They'd made him a misfit, that they had. A troop with a voice of command. A commander with imagination. They'd made him a misfit and sent him alone to the stars, to find out—to report back. And when he returned from his most important mission with urgent information? Why, then they'd made him a no-troop, and buried his report so thoroughly that not even a description of the ship had survived.

Nelirikk sighed.

His mess orders had last—and quite recently—changed hands in an all-night betting game of the officers. Rumor was that Captain Kagan had lost one of the bouts of small-skills, and thus won the housing of the no-troop. Nelirikk had not been assigned to Captain Kagan's command, nor had he been given duties within the Troop. He had merely been relieved of the chit entitling him to eat from Captain Bestu's supplies and given another with Kagan's account number on it. To have that same no-troop call a General's attention upon himself had done Captain Kagan's credit no good at all.

Nelirikk opened his eyes and stared wearily up at the stars. In a moment, he straightened, ran through a mind-clearing exercise he'd learned with the rest of his age-mates in the creche.

The General, now . . .

Security had taken him to a room that held no sign of the devices most usually employed to punish the recalcitrant. Neck-hairs prickling, Nelirikk glanced around him, locating at least three grills and two lights that most likely held microphones and cameras. Three chairs, two computer terminals, a table upon which sat a carafe of water and three glasses—unthinkable courtesies for a rogue no-troop. Nelirikk was suddenly very tired.

Without orders he should not sit.

He sat.

No voice from a hidden loudspeaker ordered him up.

Security would have his records and files, Nelirikk considered, and would know his training and abilities—

Would know that he was not to be trusted, though some chance cruelty of the High Command dictated that he should be made to continue living, rather than receive the simple back-of-the-head execution Security itself had recommended. Security would have the file that said Nelirikk Explorer was hereinafter and forever Nelirikk No-Troop, shamed and shunned—the only living Yxtrang to have been captured by a Liaden.

Caught in a trap—tricked, as Liaden scouts had been tricking Yxtrang for untold years—and then *let go,* to return to his commander and report, half-dazzled by the possibilities he glimpsed within the information the scout had—knowingly?—given. He'd described the ship . . .

So they'd taken his report, ignored it, isolated him from the small cadre of Yxtrang explorers, made him a no-troop and forgot him.

And now he was here, a rogue no-troop, apparently so weary of his dutiless life that he interfered with command level action in the General's own war room! An explorer might possibly have done so, without punishment.

If there were any explorers left. He'd searched for traces of the unit, using stolen computer time and unauthorized glimpses of ship movements through distant portholes—to no purpose. His terror was that they had disbanded the explorers, and made him no-troop in a far different way.

"*Hup!*"

He came to his feet, at attention. The General stood before him, comrade close, eyes full of calculation, the tattoos of rank and achievement not quite disguising the unnatural ruddiness of his face.

"You retain your alertness, No-Troop."

"A soldier survives through alertness, sir."

The eyes narrowed.

"I have reviewed your records," the General said, "and I understand how you might have been able to identify a ship unknown to our scanning program. I understand how you might react without permission and assume compliance. I understand, also, that you have disturbed the organization of my war room."

A statement of facts required no reply. Nelirikk continued to look eye-to-eye with the planetary commander.

"What do you say of your insolence, Nelirikk No-Troop?" the General demanded. Nelirikk avoided the sigh.

"Sir. I sought to serve the Troop, and gave warning of clear danger. Pilots are not to be wasted—"

"Silence!" roared the General. "Do not consider yourself a pilot, No-Troop. That honor was long-ago forbidden you."

He turned abruptly, jabbing a finger toward the table and the computers. "Sit."

The General took the second chair, tapped in a request and leaned back as the battle-site filled the screen.

"Now, No-Troop, why do you think such a ship would be on this planet? Why did it remain grounded rather than rising to the fight? Mere Liaden cowardice?"

The urge to look wonderingly at the General was strong; Nelirikk instead stared at the screen, restructuring the logic chain he had formed in the war room.

"I have given this matter thought, sir. However, I have little information about the current military situation—"

"You need none. Speak to this case!"

Nelirikk did sigh, very quietly.

"Yes, sir. In this case several possibilities exist." Unconsciously, he moved into the lecture technique he'd learned for briefing fellow explorers.

"One possibility is that the ship was under repair and unable to lift. Supporting information is sparse—no repair machinery was observed about the craft. Another possibility is that a junior officer during the commander's absence manned the ship. We then have a reason for the delay in firing, and also for the failure to lift and engage."

The General gave a mildly approving click.

"Another possibility," Nelirikk continued, "is that the ship was unmanned and computerized self-defense functions were in force. Or that the crew was aboard and deliberately sought to escape notice so that a later strike at a capital ship might be launched. My assumption is that *Barakhan* took damage from that last bolt—"

"An invalid assumption, No-Troop. So small a ship, and firing through atmosphere, to touch *Barakhan*?" The General waved a hand in negation.

"I saw the ship fire when the particle-beams began the attack. A charged beam could well use the same path to—"

"I am not interested in traitorous assumptions!" the General snarled. "I asked you for whys."

Nelirikk stared at the screen—at the crater where the pretty ship had been—until the view changed to a map of the surrounding area.

"Sir. It is possible that the ship was ordered to remain grounded in order to defend an important center or person." He pointed.

"I propose that the town, the nearby command base, or the remaining mercenary troops are of special importance. That small plane, trying so bravely to hinder our jets—it may be that by luck we were attacking the escape ship of an important person."

Nelirikk paused, staring at the screen.

"Recall that by drawing fire the ship has taken out a number of our drop fighters and has forced a demonstration of our overhead strength. A scout might trade his ship for such information. For this possibility, I assume standard invasion policy has been followed and the planetary satellite net has been destroyed."

The General was eyeing him, displeasure apparent. "You insist on this scout, do you?"

"If all Liaden ships of that size were as powerful, sir, I believe Liadens would even now be pursuing us across the galaxy."

"Fool!" The General's fist rose, but, remarkably, no blow landed. He twisted in his chair, frowning heavily at the screen. "Hear yourself—naming Liadens—*Liadens*!—brave, assigning soldierly virtue to a race long known to be weak and honorless—*animals,* No-Troop. You entertain the possibility that the 14th Conquest Corps might be routed by *animals.*"

Nelirikk said nothing.

The General shut down the display. "We have discovered maps and a short-range radio transceiver in a captured enemy vehicle. I understand from your records that you are fluent in the language of Liaden animals and can read their scratchings as well."

The General rose, walked to the brown-gray wall and back.

"You will be outfitted for a special mission. You are to infiltrate the area bounded by a triangle of this airfield, this town, and this command center. You will be given the transceiver and the maps I spoke of, as well as a recall signaler. I will issue a weapon from my office. Security will issue a kit and a blade."

He came to Nelirikk's chair.

"We make use of your training and inclinations, No-Troop," he commented; "and allow you to avoid fighting."

Nelirikk sat quietly, refusing to show any reaction to an insult that would have demanded blood to balance—ten Cycles ago.

The General's lips pursed, as if he would spit; then:

"Let me be clear: You are to gather information—which you will note on the map. You are to return to the pick-up point no later than the tenth planetary dawn after you are released. This is a combat order."

Nelirikk straightened, unable to control the quickening of

his heartbeat. A combat order! Was he reinstated, then—once more a part of the Troop?

"Be sure you understand your orders entirely, No-Troop," the General advised him. "Deviate from them and you will be shot. Not even a Heroic Explorer's Starburst certificate in your file can protect you from proper punishment if you fail a combat command!"

Ten Cycles of keeping his face quiet served him well. But the blow was severe. Odd, that so sudden a burst of hope should leave such agony in its wake.

On the hillside, under the hard, beautiful stars, Nelirikk stirred and came out of his thoughts. The shattered hope of reinstatement had faded in the resolution of a mystery ten Cycles old. Almost, he was content. For he knew at last why they had not executed him.

The General had thought he'd known—had thought Nelirikk used the protection of a Hero's status to wreak havoc in the war room and flaunt command. The General had not taken into account the slowness with which such news trickles down through the levels, from the High Command to the soldier. Even the announcement of so signal an honor might take a Cycle or two, depending on battles and tours of duty. Nelirikk smiled at the sky: Heroic Explorer's Starburst!

It would have been awarded for the odd moon, of course. Strangely dense, with an atmosphere capable of supporting Yxtrang or Liadens, green-blue bushes and a storm-driven climate that brought daily rain to every spot on the surface.

He was a Hero, though his face bore no trace of the honor; and, like all Heroes, his name must now be listed on the Great Board at Temp Headquarters.

The Command preferred Heroes to die in battle—preferably in great victories.

As Lytaxin was likely to become.

Nelirikk picked up the pack and the long-arm, though he had no illusions regarding either. He rose easily to his lean height, smiled again at the stars and looked around at the velvet night.

A pretty planet. To die in open air would be a boon.

LIAD: DEPARTMENT OF INTERIOR

COMMAND HEADQUARTERS

Commander of Agents stared at the beacon screen, which informed him that Tyl Von sig'Alda's ship tarried yet about the planet of Waymart.

Days, about a minor Terran world offering nothing that an Agent in fulfillment of his mission might require?

He thought not.

Alas, other thoughts proliferated, chiefest among them that Val Con yos'Phelium had overpowered his brother Agent during Jump—and yet why simply *hang* there, when Waymart's sole charm was that it offered so much possibility in the matter of Jump points?

Commander of Agents frowned. Were he Val Con yos'Phelium—and not inclined toward a debriefing—he would make all haste to fling his vessel into Jump, thence to plan and make such arrangements as he might for re-entry into normal space.

Perhaps yos'Phelium had escaped to the planet's surface? But there was no record of the ship having done other than held this middling, dawdling orbit for several days. A painstaking reading of back files discovered no harm the vessel might have taken.

The thing made no sense.

Commander of Agents disliked nonsense—intensely.

Eyes on the beacon screen, he considered whether it was more prudent to dispatch a second Agent to Waymart, or a team of lesser operatives, such as he'd already dispatched to Lufkit, where Agent yos'Phelium's break from discipline had first manifested.

He had settled upon sending the team and indeed moved his hand somewhat toward the toggle that would summon his second to him when the beacon screen flashed. The amber light that denoted sig'Alda's ship and its conditions flared bright, began blinking, and brought up windows full of warnings: system overload, weapons released, coils overcharged, Jump coil engaged, ERROR, ERROR ERROR—

Commander of Agents flung out a hand as if to make adjustments, to resolve the problem, to disengage the coils— too late.

Commander of Agents blinked, then leaned closer to read the message at the bottom of the black screen.

NO SIGNAL. TRANSMITTER DESTROYED.

SHALTREN

JUNTAVAS HEADQUARTERS

Sambra Reallen, Chairman Pro Tem of the Juntavas,
folded her hands upon the desk and looked up at her two
large visitors.

"I regret that our actions on your behalf have as yet produced neither Scout Commander yos'Phelium nor Sergeant
Robertson, Aged Ones. I would remind you— with respect—
that the universe is wide."

"Indeed it is," rumbled the largest, who called himself
Edger. "Yet I had anticipated speedy reaction from our kin.
News of our search should most surely have reached them by
now. Yet we have no word. No whisper of possibility. It distresses me, Sambra Reallen. I begin to believe our kin are
perhaps lost more deeply."

She drew a breath, careful not to let a start of alarm betray
her. Had she not been present when these two beings destroyed both her predecessor and his weapon, and that with a
mere three notes of alien song? What might they not be
moved to, did they come to believe these claimkin of theirs
dead?

"I think there no reason to consider them so profoundly
beyond us," she said, keeping her voice level with an effort
of will that started sweat beading in her armpits. "Merely,

they may have gone to ground on one of the lower tech worlds, where word of our search would not travel so quickly. Eventually, they must leave their safe place. And when they do, they will make themselves known to us."

"And yet," said the second turtle, with a diffidence that sat oddly upon one so large, "why should they so?"

Both Edger and the Juntava stared at him, at which he ducked his head, moving his three-fingered hand in a gesture of—apology, thought Sambra Reallen. Or possibly of obeisance to Edger, who was larger-shelled and therefore in a position of command.

Edger moved his own hand. "You have asked. Can you answer?"

The smaller—Sheather, his name was—raised his head. "T'carais, I can."

"Do so."

"Yes, T'carais. Consider that our sister and our brother are masters of survival, though pursuit of art renders them no strangers to violence." He stopped and Sambra Reallen leaned forward, impatient for once of the mannerisms of long-lived Clutch-turtles, who might take as much as twenty human minutes for a pause of courtesy.

"Go on," she urged and there was an edge along her voice, so that Sheather looked at her out of his great eyes, then inclined his head.

"You are correct. I ask forgiveness, that I am careless of your time."

She waved a hand. "Granted. But say on—why shall your kin hide from us?"

"Why," said Sheather, blinking his eyes solemnly, "only because when last our kin had treat with yours, the Juntavas did their most to slay them. Neither our brother nor our sister is such a fool that they would willingly place themselves into the hands of a known enemy."

"Hah!" She sat back, staring at him and feeling dread like ice in the pit of her belly. For he was correct. Val Con yos'Phelium—a Commander of Scouts, no less!—and Mercenary Sergeant Miri Robertson had no cause to love the Juntavas, and many reasons to avoid them. The message the courier ships carried was, perforce, brief, and offered no reasons for the abrupt change of Juntavas policy with regard to the Turtles' kin. Who would of mortal necessity be compelled to consider the message a sham—or bait—and thus exert themselves doubly to avoid anything even remotely attached to the Juntavas.

Edger was looking at her. "Do you agree with my brother's summation, Sambra Reallen?"

She took a breath and met his eyes with what calm she could, who faced a being that could destroy her with a note. "Aged One, I do."

"So." He appeared to consider for a moment, then inclined his great head. "We shall go now, Sambra Reallen, to consider between us what might now be done to retrieve our brother and sister. Do you the same, of your kindness, and let us come to you again in three days' time to compare thoughts and perhaps build a more worthy plan of action."

They were not going to kill her out of hand? Relief left her giddy, yet she summoned the strength to stand, to bow. "Aged One, I shall be most happy to speak with you, three days hence."

"So it shall be," said Edger, turning ponderously toward the door. "I thank you for the gift of your time."

"It is freely given," she managed, though her legs shook with the strain of standing. It took them a few minutes to navigate the door. When they finally passed beyond the entry-eye, the door slid shut on its track and she collapsed onto her chair, uncertain whether to laugh, scream, or cry.

"It comes to me," Edger murmured into the soft silence of their evening habitation, "that you have thought more widely yet upon our sister Miri Robertson. Is it so, young brother?"

Sheather lay his hand flat, feeling the tiny rug fibers prick his palm. So many small bits of fluff, united in will to become a carpet!

"It is so," he answered softly, and raised his eyes from the study of the rug. "In truth, elder brother, there is little else with which I may occupy myself, here in this time and place. We have set motion upon certain projects with regard to our brother and sister. And now we wait. At home, waiting is put to use, for the benefit of the clan. But here, there are no knives awaiting sheaths. There are no young to instruct or any elder requiring my aid. So, indeed, I have thought much upon our sister, and studied what I might of her history."

This was rather a lengthy speech for Sheather, who was the most retiring of Edger's many brothers. However, Edger merely inclined his head.

"Ah," he said. "I would hear the tale of your study, if you would honor me, brother."

There followed a pause, of middling length for Clutch, then Sheather spoke again.

"Miri Robertson, Mercenary Soldier Retired, Personal Bodyguard Retired, Have Weapon Will Travel."

Edger moved his hand in acknowledgment. It was not so ill a name, for one yet young. A Clutch person who had seen his first Standard century might easily and without dishonor tend a lesser. Spoken fully, Edger's own name consumed several hours. Edger had seen seven Standard centuries, start to finish, and his name was not yet complete. It was the tragedy of humans, that so many died before attaining even a tenth part of their name.

"I placed my attention," said Sheather, "upon that portion of our sister's name 'Mercenary Soldier Retired.' I discover that there is a database, elder brother, containing the active rolls of every unit of mercenary soldier registered with Command upon the planet Fendor. It is accessible from yon device." He nodded across the room to the terminal built into the far wall.

"From this database I find that our sister holds the esteem of Suzuki Rialto, Senior Commander, Gyrfalk Unit and Jason Randolph Carmody, Junior Commander, Gyrfalk Unit, though she no longer holds herself at their word." Sheather hesitated.

"I comprehend that the bond between our sister and these commanders of gyrfalks is that of kin, T'carais."

"Ah." Edger felt a flutter of what might have been called excitement. "And your studies led you to believe that Miri Robertson may have called upon her kin to shelter herself and our brother."

"So they did," Sheather acknowledged. "However, I felt

my understanding to be yet imperfect and set myself the task of tracing our sister through the ranks of mercenary soldiers, in an effort to identify others of her kindred."

"And has our sister other kin among the mercenary soldiers, younger brother?"

"One other," Sheather said, and closed his eyes for a minute or six. Upon opening them, he resumed.

"This other is an elder, brother. She has known our sister since our sister was an eggling and stood as sibling to our sister's mother. I believe, if our sister were indeed to seek shelter from her soldier-kin, she would seek it first from this elder."

Edger considered this for a time, eyes slitted in the dimness. Across from him on the floor, Sheather sat respectfully silent, studying the weave of the carpet.

"It is well-reasoned," Edger announced in the fullness of time. "Surely even so masterful an artist as our sister must seek an elder's wisdom in the face of such difficulties as the Juntavas offered. An elder of quiet renown, based perhaps upon a backworld . . . such might offer greater immediate safety than the kin of our brother, who live busy and open upon Liad."

"These were my thoughts as well," said Sheather. "Most especially might they seek this elder, should one or both be in need of healing." He held up a hand. "I heard the Juntavas say that neither was harmed, my brother. I heard the recording of our kin, stating the same. Yet my heart whispers that the Juntavas have lied to us many times. And how easy to compel our kin to lie, as well! Merely threaten either with further harm, did they not speak what was required. I think we may not assume our kin were unharmed, merely upon the word of the Juntavas."

"You speak wisely," Edger said. "Have you the name of this elder? Her location?"

"Her name is Angela Lizardi, Senior Commander Retired, Lunatic Unit Inactive. She makes her home upon the world called Lufkit."

LUFKIT

358 EPLING STREET

The doorchime sounded loud in the cluttered room. Frowning, Liz lowered her book and raised her head, listening to the tinny echoes fade and die. She listened a moment longer, then bent again to her book.

The doorchime sounded.

Taking her time about it, she slipped a marker into the book, laid it atop several other bound volumes on the table beside her and levered out of the chair.

The echoes of the third chime were still fresh when she pulled open the front door to look out. And down.

Large violet eyes thickly fringed with dark gold lashes looked up at her.

"Angela Lizardi?" The voice was as lovely as the eyes, low and seductively accented.

Liz nodded.

"I hope you will forgive this imposition," said her caller, apparently oblivious to Liz's lack of cordiality. "I am come on behalf of Miri Robertson. You are her friend. I thought you might consent to—help."

Liz frowned and took a moment to consider the rest of the face: high cheeks, pointed chin, biggish mouth, complexion carrying the faintest blush of Liaden gold. The shoulder-length hair was a richer gold, but not as dark as the long lashes.

She pulled the door wider and stepped back. "Come in," she said, and it sounded like a command in her own ears.

Her caller seemed to find nothing amiss in her manner; she stepped inside and waited patiently while Liz locked the door, then followed her back to the main room.

Liz sat in her chair and the little woman stood before her, putting her forcefully in mind of the last person to stand there. "Redhead's Liaden," she called him in her head, since he hadn't told her any name. Liz very nearly snorted. Liadens.

"Well," she snapped at this one, "you got my name. Let's have yours."

"I am Nova yos'Galan," the woman said readily, and it seemed she was on the verge of something else, but stopped herself. Liz saw her right hand move, thumb rubbing over the ring on her second finger.

"And you're here on behalf of Redhead," she prompted.

"On behalf of Redhead," the other repeated slowly, and moved her head, sharply. "Miri Robertson. And also on behalf of her lifemate."

Liz blinked. "Redhead ain't married," she said flatly. "Not her style."

"Her partner, then," the golden woman persisted. "A dark man—green eyes . . ." She reached into a sleeve-pocket, offered a rectangle of doubled plastic.

Liz took it; sighed at the hologram it enclosed. Well, at least she'd find out his name.

"Or her friend," the Liaden was saying, softly, almost pleadingly. "They were together . . ."

"He was here," Liz admitted at last, looking from the picture to her visitor and back again. Even given the difference in coloring, the resemblance was striking. She handed the 'gram back.

"Relative of yours, is it?"

"My brother," Nova said softly. "He was here some time ago, I think. Perhaps as much as a Standard?"

"No more'n six, eight months." She shrugged. "Redhead

sent him by to collect something. Her partner, is what she told me."

"So." The word was a hiss of satisfaction. "They were pursued at that time, though I am not certain of the nature of the trouble. It is known that they left planet, traveling together; that they disappeared together . . ."

"Then you know more than I do," Liz said. "Last I heard, he thought they'd be able to outrun whatever mess they were in. Said when Redhead left he was going with her. Glad to hear they got off Lufkit. He seemed sound enough, and Redhead's no slack." She frowned. "But you're saying they didn't get wide of it."

"No. I am saying that they are presently—missing. They are not in places one would expect; they have not contacted appropriate persons. My brother has sent no word to his clan, or to—others."

Liz straightened in her chair. "That means they're dead." It was suddenly hard to breathe, thinking of Miri dead.

"No," said Nova yos'Galan again; "only that they are missing. There are indications that they may be missing for good cause. That they dare not send messages." She took a breath. "I must ask a question of you, Angela Lizardi. Forgive the necessity."

"OK," said Liz, still trying to figure what kind of trouble was *that* much trouble, and where the girl would go to ground.

"It is in my mind," Nova murmured, "that Miri Robertson is Liaden. My eldest brother tells me that it sometimes does happen that a half-blooded—even a full-blooded—Liaden will be born on—an outworld. Will have papers stamped 'Mutated within acceptable limits.' "

Liz sat very still, staring at the lovely face before her, while her mind's eye conjured up another face: Katy's face; worn to fine, supple gold, stretched over a fragile bone frame.

"Redhead's part Liaden," she said slowly. "Robertson was Terran, no question. Katy could've been half-Liaden, could've been full—she never said and I never asked. Don't even know for sure if she told the kid. Not the kind of thing you tell your kid, if you figured her to be stuck on Surebleak for the rest of her life."

"But Miri Robertson *left* Surebleak!" Nova snapped. "Do you know the name of the clan? Katalina Tayzin? There is no such name within the clans, though a few might be possible, given accent, vowel shifts . . ."

Liz hesitated; thought again of Redhead dead. "Something," she said, grudgingly. "Katy had a thing . . ." She closed her eyes, reaching for the memory. "Gaudy thing," she muttered. "Flat disk. Enamel work. Fine stuff—that's what I know now. Probably Liaden. Liadens do that kind of work—so fine you can hardly see the wires holding in the colors. Lots of colors . . ." She shook her head. "Never did make any sense of it."

"It looked like this?" Nova held her ring out, room lights skidding off bronze scales and green leaves. Liz narrowed her eyes.

"Like that," she allowed. "Different design, but that's the idea."

"Ah." The Liaden woman nodded as if to herself. "Then Miri Robertson is descended from one in the line direct. The search becomes simpler."

"That a fact."

Nova glanced up sharply. "Do you recall the design of this disk your friend had, Angela Lizardi? If—"

"I'd know it if I saw it again," Liz said lazily, watching through half-slitted eyes. "What're you gonna do now?"

"Run a search across all clans, specifying disappearances of those in the line direct within the last—sixty—Standards. That done, I shall try to match 'Tayzin' and, if the luck is willing, my brother shall be found."

"Not exactly encouraging." Liz stood. "OK, let's go."

Nova stared. "Angela Lizardi, I regret—"

"Don't have to. Redhead's my kin, near as I have any kin, and she's in trouble. Seems to me you're just a little more concerned with recovering this brother of yours than you are about what happened to her. Come here snatching at vapor-trails, thinking the thing's solved because you got a wisp of something to start a computer scan with—" She shook her head. "Seems like I got a responsibility to go along and assist the campaign, if you know what I mean. Make sure Redhead gets a fair shake, if and when we turn the pair of 'em up."

"It may be dangerous," Nova said flatly.

Liz shrugged. "I ain't out of practice with a gun, and I figure I still know a trick or two, hand-to-hand." She looked down into her visitor's lovely, cold face. "*Eldema,* your brother called me. That's 'first speaker,' right?"

Nova nodded.

"So, if one of my clan's missing and likely in some kind of jam, then I got a clear-cut obligation, don't I? As First Speaker?"

A pause, followed by a sigh.

"That is exactly correct, Angela Lizardi. The obligations of First Speaker are quite clear." Another sigh, and a glance at the watch she wore strapped to her wrist. "When can you be ready to leave?"

"Just let me get my kit," said Liz.

LUFKIT SPACEPORT

Their footsteps echoed off the floor and rever-
berated in the corrugated metal walls of the service tunnel.
Liz walked one step behind Nova yos'Galan, duffel slung
over her right shoulder and service pistol on her belt, scanning over the little blonde's head into the metallic dimness
ahead.

The corridor bent and straightened in an abrupt dogleg,
showing Liz the end of the tunnel and the vapor glow of port
lighting against the blue-black drop of night.

Nova yos'Galan continued her rapid, steady pace; stepped
over the edge of the tunnel into the yard and turned to the
left, Liz just behind.

There wasn't much doubt where they were headed; only
one ship sat on a pad in this part of the yard—a sleek little
scooter, the unfamiliar lines of which were lit by the honed
brightness of a labor-spot, which also picked out several
crimson coveralls.

"Thought you said you were ready to lift," Liz hissed.
"Looks like the maintenance crew ain't done yet."

The Liaden woman flung one sharp glance over her shoulder. "Maintenance crew! That's a hotpad!"

And she was gone, running toward the spot and the three red-covered figures.

Liz blinked and swore and jumped after her. She'd figured the Liaden woman was in a hurry, but to go to the expense of a hotpad—a guaranteed short-order lift-off, anytime 'round the clock; and an assurance that no port maintenance crew would do anything but steer wide of the area—!

Ahead, Nova yos'Galan had checked; Liz came even with her. "Could be just a mistake," she muttered, but her gut didn't believe it, and her head was working the moves, given the three in sight; wondering how many were out of sight, around the other side; wondering if they were the fighting kind or the running kind. The Liaden woman didn't even spare her a glance.

One of the coveralls turned, started, yelled, hand snatching at belt. The shot sang past Liz's ear as the three of them bolted, fanning wide.

"I've got left," Nova snapped and Liz was spinning, target marked; gun out and up; spitting—once—and she kept moving, swinging back toward center, crouching, gun ready. A shot chewed gravel at her feet and her answer jerked the man's head up and back before he slammed flat and stopped moving at all.

The third coverall was down, Liz saw, straightening slowly: a huddle of blurred red in the leakage from the spot. Nova was running toward the ship.

The fourth one broke from behind the ship just as she came level with the spot.

Small, slim—Liaden, most likely; Liz thought, holding her fire—sprinting for the tunnel, no weapon out, no backward look.

Liz straightened. Scared stupid, she judged; might as well let her go.

By the spotlight, Nova yos'Galan spun, knees flexed, gun up and steady in a two-hand grip, picture-book perfect.

The slim runner was halfway to the tunnel, arms pumping.

A pellet pistol spat, once, and the runner stumbled, staggered another step forward.

The pistol spoke again—and the runner fell, arms flailing.

Liz swallowed her yell; took a breath against the bile rising in her throat and walked, slowly, toward the spot.

Strapped into the co-pilot's seat, she stared at the perfect, golden profile; at the shapely hands, steady and certain over the unfamiliar board. Murder. Nothing but a senseless killing, no matter that Liadens rarely took prisoners. *Wouldn't done any harm to let that kid go,* Liz started to say, and forced the words back down her own gullet. Not her business.

Nova flipped a toggle. "Tower, this is KV5625, Solcintra. Lift initiates in five seconds. Out."

"Tower here, KV5625. I—umm—"

Liz kept the grin from reaching her face with an effort, trying to remember if she'd ever heard a pilot give the Tower clearance before.

"Is that a clear?" snapped Nova.

"I—yes," Tower managed, with belated decisiveness. "You're clear to lift, KV5625. Tower out."

"Recorded. KV5625 out." The toggle flicked off and quick golden fingers danced over the board, green go-lights glowing to life under the magic touch. Liz heard the teeth-aching screech as the magnetics kicked in; felt the pressure start— and was suddenly slammed back into her seat, shockstraps jerking tight.

"Ooof!"

Violet eyes flicked over her and the acceleration eased slightly. Liz took a hard breath against the pounding of her heart.

"You make that brother of yours look like a ray of sunshine," she snarled, and saw again the runner falling, shot in the back, and the woman next to her calmly holstering her gun and turning to inspect the hull for damage.

Nova yos'Galan barely smiled. "Only wait until you meet my elder brother," she said, hands flashing over the board. There was the barest shudder as the ship switched from magnetics to full power. "He takes an hour to say yes—and two to say no."

"Terrific," muttered Liz and tried to find a comfortable

way to sit in the too-small chair. She gave it up about the
time they achieved orbit and the power scaled down to maintenance; glanced over at the pilot's station and took a deep,
careful breath.

Nova yos'Galan sat rigid in her chair, fists clenched on the
armrests, eyes screwed shut, lips pinched to a thin, pale gash.
She was shaking. Hard.

Liz cleared her throat. "You get hit?" she asked, knowing,
knowing that there was no way—

Nova started, eyes opening and closing immediately, as if
the sight of the pilot's board was too much for her to bear.
She took a long, ragged breath and leaned woodenly back in
the chair.

"I have never—killed—anyone before," she said, and tried
another breath.

"Aah, hell . . ." Liz thought about that one, suddenly seeing the runner's death in a very different light. She unhooked
the shockwebbing and pulled the flask out of her pouch; tele-
scoped the lid to full extension and poured a healthy slug.

"Here you go."

Violet eyes slitted. Liz pushed the cup toward her, encour-
agingly. Nova closed her eyes.

Liz sighed. "When Redhead—Miri—had her first action,"
she said, keeping her voice conversational; "she had a slug
outta here."

The eyes opened again; locked on the cup. "Did it help?"

"The shakes," said Liz, easily. "It helps with the shakes,
girl. Ain't nothing except experience helps with the other."

One slim hand left the armrest, unclenched and took the
cup. Liz nodded.

"You want to knock it back quick," she advised. "Don't go
sipping at it like it's some fancy, hundred-year-old brandy.
All it is is kynak. Go."

Obediently, Nova lifted the cup and threw it down her
throat like medicine.

"Ah!" Tears started to her eyes, ran down her cheeks; she
choked and Liz pounded her on the back, retrieving her cup
in the process.

"Drunk like a merc!" she said cheerily and shook her head,
abruptly more serious.

"Thing to remember is you don't have to kill everybody on the field," she said, keeping her voice easy, without judgement or condemnation. "Wasn't any real reason to kill that last one. She was just running to get away."

Nova shook her head, unlatched the webbing and sighed. "You do not understand."

"So explain it," Liz invited, still easy in the voice.

Nova sighed. "There is danger," she said. "I told you that there was danger. My brother—there are—persons—hunting him. These—they fired on the First Speaker. It is the First Speaker's duty to survive, to serve the clan."

Liz stared. "First Speaker? Girl, I'm no First Speaker— that was just what Redhead's Liaden—"

"*I* am First Speaker," Nova said, flatly; "of Clan Korval. I could not take the risk."

Liz thought about that one, too, as she unscrewed the flask and had herself a shot, and finally shook her head.

"I can see where you might think that. But you're saying this brother of yours has got trouble of his own—in addition to the trouble him and Redhead were trying to lose?"

Nova sighed again, and leaned forward to stare at the piloting readout. "Circumstances are not quite clear, Angela Lizardi." She glanced over, violet eyes bland and beautiful. "I have several matters to discuss with my brother, when I see him again."

"Yeah," said Liz, thoughtfully; "I can see that, too."

DUTIFUL PASSAGE

JUMP

A certain awkward pride suffused the ship. Shan
felt it as an electric undercurrent as he approached the tower.

The ship's mood disturbed him. Barely three hours ago
they'd been escorted to their Jump point by Portmaster
Vinikov's hastily cobbled armada, and the crew—his crew of
mannerly merchanters!—was inebriated with the glory of it.

He'd called battle stations; and it had become immediately
and painfully apparent that there wasn't a ship in-system that
outgunned *Dutiful Passage*. Indeed, the ten military ships
comprising their escort were badly outclassed: the *Passage* had
three battle pods in reserve, with the others triple-targeted.
They could have broken the system defenses, held the planet
hostage.

Portmaster Vinikov and her fleet had held position until
the *Passage* Jumped.

If he decided to turn rogue . . .

Shan shivered.

The problem was power.

Suddenly the crew was aware of the ship's power. Suddenly, they had an inkling of Korval's strength.

As would Korval's enemies, of course, for such an escort
could hardly go unremarked. Within days the galaxy would

know that *Dutiful Passage* had pulled away from Krisko, the Tree-and-Dragon at every name-point, and transmitting not the neutral ID of a freighter, but the strident warn-away of a battleship.

I dare: Korval's motto.

Octavia Vinikov knew the motto; knew a thread or two of Korval history.

Octavia Vinikov had seen her old drinking friend and chess partner leave dock commanding a warship, and acted as a portmaster must, to ensure the safety of the port; though she must have known, canny tactician that she was, that her armada could never withstand an attack from the *Passage*.

Shan sighed. "Gods defend the innocent," he murmured, and pushed his palm against the comm-room door.

"Innocent? Who's innocent?" demanded the familiar voice of Senior Radio Technician Rusty Morgenstern.

Shan managed a wan smile. "We're all innocent, my friend," he said and nodded at the console Rusty sat before. "How fares the new set-up?"

"Almost done. Would've been done, if we hadn't got a lot of last minute stuff in code because of the farewell parade." Rusty grinned, soft, round face glowing with martial importance before he bethought himself of something else and rummaged briefly on the console's ledge.

"Got a couple here for you—"

He held out a sealed envelope with a holostripe across the seal.

Shan lifted his eyebrows.

"It came out in code after I decoded it," Rusty explained, suddenly diffident; "so I thought I ought to . . ."

"Of course." Shan took the package and weighed it idly in his hand. "From now on anything like that should be routed directly to me on the—"

Rusty nodded seriously.

"I tried that, but Priscilla said you were almost at the door."

"I see. And did Priscilla tell you anything else?"

"Just that I should double check all outgoing channels and be sure we've got Tree-and-Dragon on primary and back-up, and to do the same for the lifeboat comms when I get the chance."

Shan shook his head ruefully. "I see I could have saved the steps."

"Naw, one of us had to see the other. Need your signature on this."

Shan looked dumbly at the official-looking orange card: Korval's sigil was printed at the top; at the bottom were the words "Code Confirmation."

He looked at Rusty and caught the thrill of the other man's fear.

"It's in the book, Captain," he said carefully. "I'm sorry . . ."

"Yes, it is, isn't it, Radio Tech?" Shan bent and scrawled his name. He handed the card back with a straight look into worried brown eyes. "I'm sorry, too."

Rusty nodded, countersigned the card, carefully peeled back from front, and held out the second copy.

Shan tucked the card away, hoping he'd remember to file it at some point, then stuffed the envelope in the same pocket.

"Thank you, old friend. Carry on."

He left then, weaving a brief tapestry of good will to chase away Rusty's fear.

The first disk held the information he'd been expecting from their agent in-system: an up-to-the-minute listing of the locations and schedules of those Korval and Korval-allied ships still on regular trade runs, plus the first and second choice fall-back points of each.

To obtain more than that would require Nova's First Speaker's key.

Just as well, Shan thought with uncharacteristic grimness. *Better that I don't know it all.* He extended a long arm and activated his link with the first mate's station on the bridge.

"Priscilla, I'm sending up some information to go under Captain's Seal. Do take a moment to glance at it and memorize three or four coords from the bottom half of the list."

"Yes, Captain. I'll take it at number four."

He copied the information to her terminal and memorized two new coords himself. He already knew the others.

That done, he moved to the second disk.

He laughed aloud when the code formed on the screen: "Poor Rusty!"

Of course the key wasn't filed in the ship's codebook—how could it be? It was built on the constantly changing situations of four different correspondence chess games.

Shan tapped in the algebraic codes of the last move in each game.

Na5xBb2. 0-0-0+. d5xe4. g6.

He paused with his finger on go, considering the last notation. That pawn chain was an awfully tempting target and would take—

"Fool!" he snarled under his breath and smacked *go* with such force that the terminal beeped in protest. Flutter-witted Shan—trust him to worry about the outcome of a chess game with Plan B in effect!

He ran the codebook command and glared at the reformed screen. The decoded message was blunt. Adrenaline surged and he hit the direct line to the cargo master's office.

"Man the reserve bridge," he snapped as soon as the line came open. "I'll be with you momentarily."

There was one heartbeat of startled silence. "Yes, Captain," said Ken Rik, and the line went dead.

The next call was to the first mate's station.

"This is the Captain. Do me the kindness of calling battle stations—yellow alert. When you have 80 percent compliance, go to red."

"Shan, we're in Jump."

"Indeed we are. Call battle stations. And put Gordy in charge of . . ." He glanced at the ship's master plan posted above his desk. "Put Gordy in charge of courier boat thirteen. Now."

The sounding of battle stations nearly drowned out his next words, which were, "Always remember that I love you, Priscilla."

The headset of the light duty pressure suit Shan wore brought him the harsh sound of breathing. Deeper inside weapon pod six, Cargo Master Ken Rik yo'Lanna wore a heavy duty suit against the possibility of booby traps or contamination.

"Fingernails," Ken Rik muttered, fury and terror making an interesting counterpoint to the bloodlust in his voice. "One an hour, and then the toenails—with my own set of grab calipers, I swear it. Just promise me the opportunity—gods! Three more, Shan! I'll peel his face with a diamond-dust plane . . ."

"Do you have that, Priscilla?" Shan murmured into his link with the bridge. "Three more. These in sub-bay six. What's our count now?"

"Fourteen." Her voice was cool in his ear, soothing Healer nerves rubbed raw with Ken Rik's emotions. "The computer builds a pattern suggestion. It—"

"Another!" Ken Rik snapped. "This one's bad. Active. Rigged into the Jump scans."

"Location?"

"Access panel between sub-bay six and the emergency power module. There's a thin wire running off it through the panel edge. I can—"

"*Don't touch!*" Priscilla cried, Command Mode freezing even Shan for a moment.

"As you say, Lady. As you say." The old cargo master's voice held a note of near hysteria.

"Ken Rik, that is not to be touched," Priscilla said, very carefully—very gently. "I have a feeling . . ."

Shan shivered, though this was not the first time Priscilla's wizardly powers had saved a life.

"A feeling?" he ventured.

He heard the buzz of an open line, but it was nearly a minute before she spoke.

"Intent," she said finally. "That one has malicious intent behind it. I—"

"They all have malicious intent!" Ken Rik broke in, but Shan had already gotten his lifemate's meaning. The other devices had been set as—devices, hardware necessary to accomplish a goal. What Priscilla sensed around this latest trap was the lingering taste of anticipation and desire.

Whoever had set that booby trap had *wanted* them to die.

"Yes, friend," Priscilla was telling Ken Rik; "but you cannot see the pattern I have here on the screen. There's a density and—"

"Spare me the obvious, girl," Ken Rik snapped. "It's a spiral, any fool can see that! And as it spirals in toward the power storage and capacitor banks it gets more and more dangerous. We dare not make one mistake in disarming them. We dare not believe we might even find them all! I haven't begun to look in the firing heads . . ."

Out of view of everyone, Shan nodded. Someone had carefully planned the death of the *Passage*. Planned it to be mysterious and untraceable—an explosion in Jump, confined to the Jump locus-matrix—not much chance of survivors from that!

"Ken Rik, mark your place, leave the access panels open and come to me here." He hadn't intended his tone to be so sharp, or the order so abrupt.

"At once, Captain." Relief washed some of Ken Rik's terror away, but Shan scarcely noticed.

"Priscilla, cut pod six to minimum power. Shift as many of the crew as possible to the opposite side of the ship. Discounting Ken Rik and myself, you have eight full pilots. Keep three with you, send one to the inner bridge, and station two outside my quarters, to be given access to the captain's controls, should necessity arise. You will have Gordy go to Storage Unit 117-A and remove what he finds there to the courier boat. Once back at the boat he is to go to internal power and be at battle stations with the other pilot.

"And, Priscilla—please be good enough to pull and cross link every file we have on the theoretical and practical aspects of the mathematics of Jump."

"The situation," Shan said carefully, "is quite awkward."

He glanced up into the split-screen where nine serious faces watched him, even as he watched them: Gordy, his foster-son—and Priscilla's—tight-lipped and gray-faced beside the large eyes and dark face of Thrina Makami; Vilobar, mustache shiny with sweat; Seth, laconic as always; Priscilla . . .

It was hard not to watch Priscilla. He would have rather been on the bridge, where he could take comfort from her presence, but the melant'i of the situation was plain. Resources needed to be spread out as much as possible. Both ship and crew had a better chance if at least one pilot survived—

"Weapons pod six has been—mined. Booby-trapped. Sabotaged while in storage."

There was a brief outburst of anger and fear; Shan raised his hand and quieted the noise.

"Who? It doesn't matter for the moment. How? Apparently under the guise of maintenance the proper fittings were from time to time replaced with fittings containing built-in bombs. How did we know? I received a coded pinbeam from—an impeccable source. Claiming the pod seems to have set a number of rumors into motion, not the least of which is that the galaxy should soon hear of the destruction of a major Liaden trade vessel under mysterious circumstances.

"As far as we are able to determine, there are more than fifteen explosive devices on board, all designed to do some damage, several designed to do maximum damage. The difficulty is that the devices have a variety of timers and triggers associated with them—at least one appears to be Jump-activated—and we very probably have not seen all the devices. Master Ken Rik believes the chance of finding and disabling all these traps before Jump-end is vanishingly low."

He looked at each of the nine serious faces in turn. No one seemed unduly distressed. He glanced down at his hands, big, brown, clever hands, folded quietly, the Master Trader's amethyst shining like a small purple sun in the light of the instrument panel. He looked back at the screen.

"In normal space I would merely reset shields and take the calculated risk that we would be far enough away from the thing when it exploded—or use it for target practice if it didn't.

"Here, we have a different situation. We are, as you all know, in Jump, and cannot maneuver. On the other hand, the physical laws regulating Jump suggest that an explosion in the connected pod will release the energy therein which will then duly fill up the Jump locus-matrix with itself, the total energy/mass equivalency of the system not being altered. Does anyone disagree?"

Nine dismayed faces reflected agreement.

Shan sighed.

"The captain sees no immediate clear answer either. I suggest each command location consider alternatives for the next twelve minutes, on my mark. We shall then reconvene. Pilots, I give you my mark . . . three - two - one - now!"

"Pogo stick!" Vilobar protested, smoothing his mustache nervously. "I can't see how—"

"No arguments," Shan directed. "We're taking ideas now."

"No, but the springs—if rocket thrust won't work maybe springs will!" Gordy pelted on, overriding both the older pilot and the captain. "Put them in the connecting passage, compressed, attached to the support arm. Cut the connections—the springs will uncompress and push the pod away. Then we retract the support arm . . ."

". . . use the pod's own screens, if we can trust them. Once we achieve separation it depends on philosophy. Will energy flow through the whole system, or does loss of physical congruency stop energy flow?"

Seth looked up from his scrawled notes, and gave a wry grin. "If it works we'll give the philosophers and physicists plenty to argue about."

". . . cut the entire pod mount away, if we must," Ren Zel said rapidly. "The power expenditure is within tolerances, as is the weakening of overall ship structure. We'd likely lose the cutting team . . ." He glanced up, eyes bleak in a politely expressionless Liaden face. "Necessity, Captain."

This, too, Shan limited to twelve minutes; there really was not enough time to decide how much time there was.

Shan stared at a screen filled with a growing forest of landing struts, braces, jacked platforms, and the occasional shadow that was one of the volunteers, making fine adjustments, doing the best they could to get even pressure.

Ken Rik had charge of the volunteer team. There had to be a pilot in it, and an old first classer, Ken Rik had said with a sobering lack of his usual vitriol, would be less missed by ship and crew—if something went awry—than a master pilot. Even a master pilot who was a thorough young idiot.

Shan watched and waited. On his second screen he saw Priscilla, likewise waiting, and was surprised by a surge of longing so intense his eyes teared. He was going to have to do something soon about adjusting priorities; this keeping the ship's first and second officer apart for security considerations didn't have the feel of a long-term working solution.

"That's the last," Ken Rik announced from within the pod, still in that disturbingly calm tone. "We're coming out now, Captain."

"Fine," Shan said. "Each of you count off as you come into the hall. We don't want to leave anyone in there with that thing."

He touched a key, bringing up an image of the pod's base-wall, and increased magnification until the painted markers loomed—one mark every half-meter, to allow measurement of a movement the instruments could not detect in Jump. Movement that could not happen in Jump.

According to one theory.

Shan sighed. He'd calculated that they would achieve a separation rate of just under one half meter per second, under normal conditions. Who knew how fast the rate would be in Jump, where there was neither speed, nor distance, nor direction—assuming Gordy's "pogo stick" worked at all?

"Five." Rusty's voice in the count-off reflected nothing but exhaustion and Shan felt a burst of affectionate sympathy for the pudgy radio tech. Then it was Ken Rik, signaling into the camera, speaking over the com.

"Everyone clear, Captain. Give us twelve seconds to clear the hall . . ."

"You have forty-eight, starting with my mark. Three - two - one . . . mark. Priscilla?"

"On it, Captain. At minus twelve seconds we start power-down. The pod sequencer will cut the meteor shield for twenty-four seconds, after which collision shields come up."

"Effectively sealing the ship off at pod six access hall

while pod six tumbles down to hell. We hope." He shook his head, noted Ken Rik's all clear—twenty-two seconds—and glanced back to screen two.

"Please allow the ship's log to show that Gordon Arbuthnot is confirmed this day as pilot third class and entered as a candidate for provisional second class."

The crew, on battle stations, got a twenty-four second warning, for what it was worth.

The *Passage* gave a slight even a familiar—shrug as the external pod clamps were withdrawn. Nothing changed on the screens.

Twelve seconds. Nine. Six. Three. Two. One. *Shrug* . . . the internal pod clamps withdrew—

His prime screen showed dozens of landing struts flexing, jack stands kicking sideways, platforms shaking—and there was the tiniest of lurches, as the third screen showed the markings on the basewall: one half meter . . . one meter . . . more . . .

The monitor showed a half-second blur as the pod twisted under the uneven push.

And then there was gray. Jump gray. No pod. No basewall. No hastily painted measurements. Gray.

Priscilla was looking at him from screen two.

"Instruments have lost the pod, Captain. No reading from docking radar, Jump-matrix screen shows no change. Meteor shield goes up in six seconds . . . we've got a report from inertial guidance comp: point-two-five meter per second adjustment."

So. For good or for ill. Whatever they had done was done, and the outcome was upon the knees of the gods. Shan reached for the controls and shut down the grayed screens.

"Thank you, Priscilla. I suggest we meet in our cabin for lunch. We have six hours to Jump-break and I will spend at least one with you."

EROB'S COMBAT PRACTICE GROUNDS

In the distance was the tree, gift of Korval. Beyond that, the house, and well beyond that, the foothills and small mountain range named Dragon's Back. Somewhere there, on the lower of the mountain humps, was another gift of Korval.

This was a tower. Called Dragon's Tooth for reasons none could give, it currently housed three spotters, a circumstance that had charged Win Den tel'Vosti with glee.

"A fine use we make of Korval's contract-suite, eh! Well enough, niece Miri, that you come to us lifemated, else you and your term-husband would have taken residence in Dragon's Tooth, and nothing either might do to prevent it!"

"Pretty far to walk for breakfast," Miri commented, which observation tel'Vosti was pleased to greet with laughter.

On the other side of the Dragon's Back was rough country indeed, and beyond that occasional farms and forestry plantations. The Yxtrang had not penetrated there as yet and the spotters in the Dragon's Tooth were looking down at and beyond the tree, and Erob's House. Using a good telescope they kept watch on movements close to the coast, ignoring the fields below the house itself, where only those expected yet trod. The mists of morning made the observer's job difficult, the Yxtrang destruction of most of the satellites in orbit made it vitally necessary.

"Heh up!" Miri's voice echoed over the grounds and the members of Unit 1, Lytaxin Combined Forces, fell back from defending and attacking positions and turned to face their captain.

"Rotation!" Miri commanded, and those who had been defenders last round moved left to pair off with a new partner.

"Ain't proper training if they just work with one partner," Miri had said at the beginning. "We'll keep shifting 'em around, make 'em learn as much as they can; force 'em to be flexible. Maybe . . ."

Maybe, Val Con thought now, drifting along the line with seeming randomness in his role as the captain's second, *just maybe some of them would survive.*

Survival, of course, was problematical for all, though a measure of luck had attended the deployment of the Yxtrang invasion force. The majority of invaders had landed nearer the coast, with a mere battalion or so landing within striking distance of Erob's lands, though the Loop assured Val Con that a battalion of battle-hardened Yxtrang was likely sufficient to the task of overcoming the remnants of the mercenary units and Unit 1, Lytaxin Combined Forces.

Miri had nicknamed her command the "Lytaxin Irregulars," which was a comment after all on the state of most of the defending forces facing Lytaxin's tidy little difficulty. Aside from one of Jason's crack units, even the named and recognized forces were amalgams and hastily restaffed shadows of standing merc units. Val Con sighed, hid the Loop's predictions away in a corner of his mind, and came to attention with the rest of the troop on Miri's command.

"Partners A, C, E," Miri shouted. "Defend!"

His assignment this drill was the overseeing and correction of the attackers, speaking with the captain's authority and his own expertise in hand-to-hand technique. It was an assignment like most of the others he carried within the troop where he held no rank other than that of scout—and of Miri's partner.

The field was silent, awaiting the captain's next order. Val Con closed his eyes, recalling the Yxtrang landing.

He and Miri had been running to warn the Erob when the flight of attack craft circling overhead drove them to cover. The attackers dove toward the airfield, which sustained several passes before ter'Meulen's plane had risen in challenge. By then, the biggest roar in the sky had been the approach of the troop and transport ship.

Stupidly, the Yxtrang had attempted to take *Fosterling* out with a strafing run. The awesome fall of wreckage from the sky had been the result of that error—and the local keep's salvation.

Then came thunder from the sky and thunder from the ground as *Fosterling* replied to an attack from a space-based enemy. Valiant vessel—and all, eventually for naught. His ship was gone. Clonak ter'Meulen's heir was gone. The remnant of Erob's air fleet was gone. And he, a pilot of Korval, was grounded, charged with training children in the arts of death.

"Heh, go!" Miri commanded and the field went from absolute stillness to frenzied motion. Several pairs did absolutely the wrong thing. Miri headed for Trianna and Ilvin, as Val Con cut off An Der's charge with a sharp "Hold!"

"An overhead approach is acceptable for machete or broadsword," he told the boy's bruised blue eyes. "It is an inefficient technique for survival blade, in that it leaves the attacker vulnerable to a fighter with longer reach. Given the likelihood that the opponent you may eventually face with this blade will be considerably larger than you, the proper thrust is low, to surprise and injure, while making of yourself the smallest possible target. Then, an upthrust to chest or throat—thus." He demonstrated the sequence against an imaginary giant, reversed the blade and stepped aside. "The drill, if you please. Use your brain; terror wins no battles."

The boy took the weapon, bowed as student to honored instructor, and again faced his partner. Val Con watched them execute a far more reasoned drill and then moved down-line, pausing as necessary to correct, demonstrate, encourage.

"Heh, up!" The command rang out and all movement stopped.

"Drill done!" Miri called. "Return knives to Kol Vus. All at liberty until mess-call."

Val Con felt his shoulders sag in relief. It was amazingly tiring, this training of children and the Housebound. He began to walk toward Miri, and saw Emrith Tiazan and Win Den tel'Vosti bearing down on her from the opposite edge of the field.

"Scout!" The big voice bellowed from behind, booming with excitement. Val Con ground his teeth and kept walking; he had no wish to deal with Jason Carmody at this instant.

"Hey, Scout!" Jason insisted. "Over here, double-time! Got something to show you! Number one priority!"

That was final, then. Val Con sighed. A commander's priority outweighed any desire a man might have to protect his lady from the stresses of dealing with her kin.

He turned, and very nearly stared.

Jase grinned and dragged a sleeve across his forehead, leaving a streak of grime. His well-kept ponytail was in disarray, fine golden hairs pulled loose from the ribbon and standing out from his big head like an aura. His leathers were muddy and scuffed; there was a purpling bruise on one tan cheek, just above the beard-line; and his wide azure eyes were full of demonic glee.

"Look a sight, I'll wager," he said cheerfully. "Wasn't time to find my ball dress, though. This is hot, my son—got somebody you need to talk to!"

Val Con's heart stuttered. *Shan?* he thought, then nearly laughed.

Yes, he told himself, *very likely. As if Shan is so lacking in wits he'd endanger his ship and the a'nadelm's life by running an Yxtrang blockade.*

"You there, Scout?" Jason's eyes were sharp on him.

Val Con raised an eyebrow. "I am here, Commander. The question is: Where is this someone I must talk to?"

"Icehouse." The grin cracked free again, wild with pride. "Man, wait'll you—Hey, Captain Redhead!"

"Jase," Miri's voice was quiet, and a little husky from shouting practice commands. She smiled at Val Con and slid a comfortable arm around his waist.

"They're lookin' good out there, darlin'. When you figure on turning 'em loose to whip ass?"

Miri tipped her head and Val Con felt a sharpening in his own psyche, as if he was engaged in weighing values he recognized on some level past mere thought.

"Can take some heat, if you got it to share," Miri was telling Jason, calmly. "Ain't up to a pressure-cooker, but I figure to hold our own in a spat."

"Might have something to share, at that. Depends on what the Scout can get out of—"

"And what," demanded Emrith Tiazan arriving on Win Den tel'Vosti's arm, "is of such importance that Captain Robertson must need turn her back on me and walk away?"

There was an instant's silence.

"You're top brass, Jase," Miri muttered, and the big man started slightly before he bowed to the delm.

"Sorry, ma'am," he said, schooling his big voice to a polite boom. "I need the Scout and Captain Robertson to step along with me, Priority One."

tel'Vosti grinned, but Emrith Tiazan only glared, letting the silence stretch until it became a danger even Jason felt. Val Con shifted slightly, drawing the big man's eyes.

"It is possible," he murmured, "that Delm Erob will wish to survey this top priority, as well."

Jason looked doubtful, but produced another bow on the delm's behalf. "I'd be happy to have your assistance, ma'am—and General tel'Vosti's, too."

Erob inclined her head, her arm still twined with tel'Vosti's.

"Lead on, Commander," she ordered. "We are delighted to lend our—assistance."

Designed to withstand the rigors of quick-freeze, the vacuum of freeze-drying and, coincidentally, the detonation of a small bomb, Erob's back-up freeze-plant made an admirable prison.

The corporal on guard at the door offered the information that Doc Tien was still inside, guard-crew with her, all according to the commander's order.

Jason nodded and pointed to the monitor. "Take a look," he said. "It's the best I can tell you."

It was difficult to see anything but the size of the prisoner, with the medic and the guards all around. Still, Val Con felt his pulse quicken even as Miri turned to stare up at Jason.

"What'd you do?" she demanded. "Crack an Yxtrang across the head?"

He grinned. "Damned near broke my carbine. That brother's head is *hard.*"

"Yxtrang?" tel'Vosti squinted at the monitor. "You captured an Yxtrang? Alive? My dear Commander! You bring us hope."

Erob turned her head stiffly.

"Hope?" she snapped. She glared at Jason, for all the worlds like a strike-falcon baiting a bear. "What good is it, Commander? Shall we start a zoo?"

Jason laughed, short and sharp.

"Guess you could at that," he said, stroking his beard. "Put me and him in the same cage. He's just about my size, give or take a headache." He shook his head. "But his worth is what he knows and where he was. Found him up the hunting park. Alone."

tel'Vosti and Erob got very quiet. "So close?" Val Con murmured and Jason looked down at him, suddenly serious.

"Up on the east ridge," he said; "buncha hundred meters down from the top. Couple klicks out from where Kritoulkas is holding line—show you on the map." He grinned again and pointed at the monitor. "But what d'ya think, Scout? Ain't he a beauty?"

"He does seem to be indicative of his type." Val Con turned back to the screen, trying to see through a burly guardsman to the prisoner himself. "You say you hit him across the head?"

"From behind," Jason admitted, somewhat sheepishly. "He'd just got through sending a fongbear on its way and I fell on him like the mountain coming down. Seemed like a good idea, but, damn, then I had to carry him out!"

Miri laughed, eyes on the monitor. "How bad's he hurt?"

"Doc's checking. Once I found out I was in one piece I real quick sprayed him with a double-dose of Sleep-it from my medkit. Put his gear in the other room, there. 'Spect the scout'll want to see it."

"Will you?" Miri muttered.

Val Con sighed. "I anticipate the need. Jason seems to have surmised that a scout will speak Yxtrang."

"Oh." Miri blinked. "Have to rig up a talkie, I guess."

"Perhaps." Inside the freezer-bay, the medic had straightened, shut down her monitor and moved toward the door, shooing the guards out of her way like so many chickens. Val Con felt himself go cold as her patient was finally and fully revealed.

Something of his shock must have reached Miri through their lifemate link. She leaned close. "Boss? You OK?"

"OK—yes." He spun as the door opened, claiming the doctor's attention with a hand-wave.

"That man—is he whole?"

She shrugged, Terran-wise. "He'll do. Sleeping pretty sound." She glanced down at the med-comp. "If he's got reactions anywhere approximating a Terran of like mass, he ought to be out of it in forty minutes—an hour at the outside."

"Hour to look at his stuff," Jason said. "And to figure out how best to ask him." He paused and looked straight at Val Con. "You can talk to this guy OK, can't you, son?"

"Talk to it!" Emrith Tiazan repeated, somewhere between horror and fury. "Korval—are you able to speak to that thing?"

But Val Con was at the monitor now, studying the image of the man in the room beyond, thinner than his length predicted, stretched across a bed made of six hastily arranged packing crates, and covered with a standard merc pack-blanket. His short-cropped hair was light brown in color, the features of his face indistinct behind an intricate mask of tattoo.

"Korval." Erob again. He was mightily weary of Erob all at once, as he was weary of Jason and the war they had not yet engaged. This man here. This man . . .

"Korval!" Emrith Tiazan snapped, no doubt relying on the Command Mode to turn him. "I require response. Are you able to persuade that thing to speak to the point?"

It was a wrenching effort of will to turn away from the

monitor and the image of the sleeping giant. He came about slowly, feeling his face stiffen into unaccustomed lines, as it would, of course, following the tutelage of the old tapes. He felt the proper phrase rise to consciousness, and then to his lips.

Erob's face showed fear; tel'Vosti's disquiet. Jason actively goggled. Miri alone moved—to stand between himself and her delm, and to lay her hand upon his sleeve.

"Easy, boss."

The old learning let him loose, so that he smiled at her through the hunger of his need, and lay his other hand over hers.

"Forgive me," he said to Erob's startlement. "The Yxtrang language is difficult and in some ways uncouth. In certain matters, however, it is perfection itself."

He glanced over his shoulder for a last lingering sight of the screen.

"I am able to speak to this man," he told Erob softly. "Indeed, we spoke at some length when last we met."

She stiffened. "Do not trifle with me, Korval."

Val Con regarded her blandly. "I do not."

It was tel'Vosti who moved this time, to take the old lady's arm and very nearly shake it. "Let the boy be, Emrith! This is not the time to stare a dragon in the face."

Val Con turned to Jason. "I will inspect his equipment," he said, his eyes straying back to the monitor. "Do you give me a whetstone, and a length of good rope. I shall speak with him alone, when he wakes."

"Right!" said Jason. "Whatever you say."

Val Con nodded. "Exactly as I say." He glanced at Miri and smiled, suddenly and joyfully, into her worried eyes. "With my captain's permission, of course."

NIMBLEDRAKE

BETWEEN PLANETS

"That one," Liz snapped, certainty hitting her system like a jolt of Stim.

Beside her, Nova yos'Galan blinked, then fingered the controls, bringing the image into close-up.

"Look carefully, Angela Lizardi. You are certain?"

"Told you I'd know it if I saw it again," Liz said, shaking off the dregs of her drowse. "That's the one."

It wasn't much to look at, compared with some of the other Liaden clan sigils they'd scanned over the last couple hours, but made its point with a purity of line that Liz at least found—refreshing.

Nova yos'Galan had turned from her study of the screen and was looking at her out of wide violet eyes. "You are certain?"

Liz frowned. "How many times you want me to say so, Goldie?"

She had discovered rather early in their association that Nova yos'Galan did not care to be called "Goldie." She thus reserved the name for times of special aggravation, of which, unfortunately, there were many. The Liaden woman had a gift for setting a body all into angles.

This time, however, the nickname earned neither darkling

glance nor frown of disapproval. Instead, Nova turned back
to the computer display and fiddled the buttons on her armrest until the sigil was replaced with a screen full of Liaden
characters. She fiddled some more and the words dissolved.
When the clan badge was back on-screen once more, Nova
spoke, calmly and without inflection.

"That is the badge of Clan Erob."

Liz frowned again, trying to read something from the side
of her companion's face or the set of her shoulders, which
was about as useful as trying to read a meteor shield.

"If your friend held such a thing, she was of Erob, through
Line Tiazan. *Tee-AY-sahn*," Nova breathed and grimaced.
"Katalina *TAY-zin*. Pah!" She turned and looked at Liz once
more, eyes shielded now, hard as amethyst.

"Be—very—certain, Angela Lizardi."

"Think I'm playing with your affection? That's the design.
I'd know it if I was blind."

"Clan Erob," Nova said again, flat-voiced.

"If you say so. Got a problem, Goldie? What're they, the
Capulets?"

Puzzlement flickered in the depths of the violet eyes, and
was gone in the next instant. "Indeed, no. Clan Erob is none
other than our eldest ally. We were to have shared genes
again this generation, as I recall it."

"That so." Liz chewed on it a couple seconds. "Damned if
I can see why you're cooked, then. If Redhead and that
brother of yours are married—and I ain't believing *that* 'til I
got it from Redhead herself—but *if* they are, seems to me
you oughta be booking the band for the reception and pulling
together a guest list."

"Hah." The stiff golden face relaxed into what passed for
her smile. "But you see, I, too, entertain some . . . astonishment . . . at this lifemating. My brother Val Con, you understand, is not—biddable. It would require but a word in his ear
that he must marry to Erob and we should find him looking
in all directions, save that one."

Liz laughed. "Him and Redhead are well-matched, then.
And you and the rest of the family better stand back!"

"Well," Nova's smile deepened, actually touching the
depths of her eyes before she turned her attention back to the

screen. "Our search is made easy," she murmured, plying the buttons and shutting the search program down. "We to Lytaxin, Angela Lizardi, there to put our various questions to my brother and to Miri Robertson." She rose, shaking her golden head at the blank screen before glancing down to Liz, pale lips still curved in her slight smile.

"And to Delm Erob, most naturally."

"Sounds like a plan," Liz said and climbed to her feet, stretching tall. "You know how to get us to Lytaxin, I take it."

Nova bowed slightly. "Simplicity itself."

EROB'S HOLD

FREEZE-DRY PRISON

"This guy is a soldier?" Miri's voice held palpable unbelief.

Val Con looked up from his frowning inspection of the captive's pack.

"All Yxtrang are soldiers," he said, only half-attending what he said. "This one had been something more, once." He gestured with a mouse-nibbled ration bar. "He seems to have fallen on evil times."

Abruptly, he pitched the bar back into the pack and stood frowning into its depths. "Something's amiss."

Miri laughed. "Screwier than a hive of hurricanes," she agreed. "Take a look at this rifle."

He laid the pack down and went to where she had the bulky long-arm arranged across two packing crates. He knelt opposite and looked at her quizzically, but she only grinned and waved a hand. "All yours."

The rifle was clean and well oiled; to first and second glances a proper, soldierly weapon, though something about that nagged Val Con as he bent closer to inspect the firing mechanism and auto-circuitry. He checked, glanced up at Miri.

She nodded. "Looks like maybe him and the weapons-master wasn't on terms."

"So it does." He rocked back on his heels, brows pulled sharply together. "And no need for him to be carrying such a thing at all."

"Why not? Makes sense to take a rifle with you, if you're going for a stroll in enemy territory."

"It does indeed, for a soldier," Val Con said softly. "But not for a scout."

Miri blinked. "Scout?"

"Explorer, it would be rendered from Yxtrang. But—scout, yes."

She shifted carefully, drawing his eyes. "You said you know this guy?"

"Ah, no." His smile flickered, banishing all but a shadow of the frown. "Merely, we had spoken once, many years ago. I held captain's rank then—very young and very certain of immortality." He grinned. "Shan all but ordered me out of the scouts, when I told him the tale. I've rarely seen him so angry."

Miri looked at him carefully. "Which tale was that?"

"The one in which I caught an Yxtrang scout studying the same world I was conducting studies upon, snared him, spoke with him, and then let him go."

"Thought you should've cut his throat for him, is that it?"

"Thought I should have rather cut and run at the first indication that there were Yxtrang of any sort on-world." He smiled again. "Shan has a great desire for those of us under his care to behave with what he considers to be proper caution. But he sets so bad an example, cha'trez . . ."

She laughed and shook her head, pointing at the rifle, the pack with its load of defective gear. "Hell of a way to outfit a scout."

"I agree." The frown was back. "Even if he were sent as a decoy—an explorer might conceive of such a plan . . ."

"Let himself be captured?" Miri stared. "Yxtrang don't let themselves get captured, boss. You know that."

"Yes, but this one has had experience of being captured," Val Con said, "and is a scout besides. Though it would be rational to equip a decoy well, to bolster the fiction that here was a soldier upon some other mission."

"Think he's an escapee—a deserter?"

Val Con shook his head. "In that case, one would be certain to appropriate working weapons, good food—the edge on that survival knife is so dull he could only use it as a crowbar or an ice-chop!"

Miri sighed and came to her feet. "Puzzle, ain't it?" She glanced at her watch. "We're at twenty-five minutes."

"So." Val Con rose. "I'd best have these things with me."

"I don't like you going in there by yourself to talk to him," Miri said, suddenly not his partner, but his lover and his lifemate. "Take a guard."

He smiled and came close, touching her cheek with gentle fingers. "It will be well, Miri." He bent and kissed her forehead. "Besides, he's tied up."

Dream and memory danced for the pleasure of the Gods of Irony.

In the dream, he was caught, trussed like a rabbit and swinging from a tree, blade and pistol riding, remote as the Home Troop, in his belt.

In the dream, he roared abuse at his captor, who sat crosslegged on the moss below, absorbed in sharpening his knife. Memory provided an odor beside alien air, which was the scent of the oil the other applied now and then to the surface of the whetstone. The slide of blade along stone was comforting, a commonplace in a situation for which there was no analog.

The smell and the sound persisted, though the dream began to fray. The smell and the sound and the ropes, crossing snug over his chest, pinning his arms to his side, binding his ankles tight.

He opened his eyes.

Light stabbed, igniting a rocketing pain in his head, throwing reality momentarily awry, so that he snarled out of memory:

"Isn't that knife sharp yet?"

"The knife," answered the soft voice that had haunted his sleep these long, weary Cycles, "is sharp again, Ckrakec Yxtrang."

The sharpener lifted his head then, wild brown hair tumbling half into eyes like sharp green stones, and his face—the face—the face of his ruin, smooth and unchanged through the Cycles—though not quite. The right cheek now carried a mark very like a *nchaka,* or maturity scar.

"*You*!" He had meant to roar; instead a harsh whisper emerged as he tensed against the ropes.

The Liaden scout bowed from his cross-legged perch atop what seemed to be a packing crate. "I am honored that you recall me."

"Recall you!" The trade language failed him in that instant. Almost, breath failed him. Abruptly, he relaxed against the bonds and lay his head back, exposing his throat.

"If the knife is sharp," he growled in the Troop's own tongue, "use it."

The scout selected a strand of rope and tested the quality of the edge. Shaking his head, he took up the whetstone once more and resumed his sharpening.

"It would be more pleasant," he said, so softly it was a strain to hear him above the burr of stone stroking steel, "were we to talk."

"Talk." He twisted his head to stare, mouth curling into a sneer. "Still no taste for a soldier's work, Liaden?"

The unkempt head rose, bright eyes gleaming. "I see I have not made myself plain." He lay the whetstone by, and held the knife carelessly in one hand.

"The last time we spoke I was graceless," he said eventually in High Liaden. "I neglected to give you my name and rank. Nor did I request yours." He slid from the crate to the floor, blade still negligent in a frail hand.

"Shall we play the game out?" the Yxtrang demanded in Trade. "Though if you imagine that puny knife is enough to—" He hesitated because the little Liaden had moved silently out of his line of sight.

"Play the game out?" That soft, womanish voice, so compelling, unforgettable, once heard . . . The scout came back into sight. He brought the knife up, as if considering its ultimate merit, and brought it flashing down, suddenly held very business-like, indeed.

The Yxtrang stiffened, anticipating the pain as the blade sliced between his left arm and side, neatly parting the ropes.

"I am currently attached to the local defense force," the scout said in conversational Trade, as he moved south relative to the position of the Yxtrang's head. "A military necessity, as I am sure you understand. My name is Val Con yos'Phelium, Clan Korval, and I hold the rank of Scout Commander."

The knife flashed again, parting the ankle ropes. The scout nodded and jumped back to the top of his crate, folding his legs neatly under him.

"You are?" he asked in quiet Terran.

The Yxtrang lay unmoving, considering the knife, the scout's smallness, his own reach and the distance that lay between them.

"Your name and rank, sir?" The Liaden persisted, this time in Trade.

Cautiously he moved his legs, flexed arm and chest muscles against the loose bindings.

The scout sighed. "Conversation consists of dialog," he remarked in High Liaden and tipped his head to the left. "The request in your own language seems unnecessarily abrupt, though perhaps I judge it wrongly." He straightened.

"Name, rank, and troop!"

The Yxtrang snorted and sat up, putting his eyes on a level with the Liaden's. "Your accent stinks like a charnel-house."

"As well it might," the scout said calmly. "I meet very few people native to the tongue who are willing to converse with me. Your name and rank? No?" He reached behind and hauled a battered pack onto his lap.

"I find here that you are attached to the 14th Conquest Corps."

He said nothing and after a moment the scout worked the pack's fastening and rooted about inside, head and shoulders all but vanishing. He emerged eventually, held out the bulky Security-issue blade, and cocked an eyebrow.

"The 14th Conquest Corps equips troops shabbily, don't you think?" He waved it away, thinking of his own knife, that rode in his boot-top, that they had never taken from him, that had an edge to cut hullplate and—

"A knife is a knife, after all," the scout insisted. "I admit this one has seen ill days, but a few minutes' work will put it right. And it is surely of a size more fitting to yourself, Explorer, than to me." A moment passed . . . two.

"Take the damn thing!" the Liaden shouted in Troop tongue and thrust the knife forward.

Hounded, he took it, stared at it, and lay it down beside him. He should unsheathe it, he knew, and use the dull blade to skewer or to bludgeon the scout. It was his duty to report back to the Troop, to—

The scout was offering the whetstone.

"Your blade," he said, "needs care, Explorer."

"I am not an explorer!" That came out a proper roar, lancing his head with pain.

The little scout didn't flinch. "No? And yet I first found you behaving in a very scout-like manner, piloting a single-ship and making very curious studies. Surely you were an explorer then, at least?"

"No longer." The snarl startled stars across his back-eyes, and he winced, unsoldierly.

"You have been given medical attention," the scout murmured, "though it was predicted that your head would ache for a time after you woke."

"Medical attention? Why?" He leaned forward, shouting into the small, bland face. "Scout, are you mad? I am Yxtrang! You are Liaden! We are enemies, do you recall it? We are made to hunt and kill you!" He sat back, away from the face that neither flinched nor crumbled in terror.

"Occasionally," he continued, more quietly, "you kill us. But it is not done that you hit your enemy over the head with a rock and then call the medic to repair his wound."

"I did not hit you over the head with a rock, Explorer—"

"I am not an explorer! *Look* at me! Captured! *Captured like a cow for slaughter*! Twice to fall alive into Liaden hands! I am a failure, a weakness, and a shame! Rightly I am Nelirikk No-Troop!"

"Catch!" The command was Troop tongue. His hand flashed out—and he discovered he held the whetstone.

"What shall I do, Scout Commander?" he inquired with heavy sarcasm, "sharpen this blade so you may cut my throat? Or should I cut my own? That—"

"Would be a waste of talent," interrupted the scout. "I

have contempt for the 14th Conquest Corps, who put their insignia on such equipment as they give you—explorer, no-troop or common soldier!" He hurled the pack off his lap. Nelirikk caught it as it struck his chest.

"A canteen with worn filters, a knife so dull it's more bludgeon than blade—yes, you still have the one in your boot, and I see you cared for it—out-of-date ration packs, half-nibbled by mice; a fire-starter in danger of burning out on next use—"

"Surely, Commander," Nelirikk said with sudden weariness, "you know how it is to equip the expendables?"

There was a small silence. "Are explorers expendable, then?" the scout asked softly. "Are they so little valued that they might be sent out all but weaponless to chase bears in our park, with never a thought to the waste, should the bear prove superior today?"

"Explorers are not. No-Troops are."

"Ah." The scout sat quiet for a moment, as did Nelirikk, who wished he might lay back down and go to sleep against the pounding misery in his head.

"Here," the scout said abruptly; "this is also yours."

He opened his eyes and stared at the rifle in dawning horror.

"You're not going to let me go!"

"Take the rifle," the scout commanded. "It's heavy!"

He grabbed and sat holding the thing in one hand while he stared at the Liaden.

"I would not advise attempting to fire it," the little man said conversationally. "I am not certain if the firing mechanism or the chamber will go first. If the pin goes, of course, you are simply disappointed when you pull the trigger. But if the chamber blows, Explorer, I suspect you will be either blind or dead."

"Scout," he said, very carefully, "you are aware that I can smash you to jelly with this rifle, whether it is in condition to fire or not?"

"Certainly. But, before you do, there is another defect I would like to point out." The scout came to his feet upon the packing crate, and there was a sudden crystal gleam in his left hand, a flash and a pressure on the rifle—which had abruptly lost four inches of barrel.

Nelirikk looked at the severed segment, and then at the crystal knife in the scout's hand.

"I note this further defect," he said. "It is one I might not have discovered until it could not be remedied."

The scout nodded, crystal blade vanishing as he resumed his seat. "Precisely. Like the canteen, if you had come across bad water."

He snorted. "I am not going to drink bad water, Scout."

"No. You'll not die of bad water."

"What will I die of?" Nelirikk looked directly at his tiny enemy. "Answer me, Scout Commander—will you give me the honor of a firing squad? It is more than a no-troop deserves."

"Yes," said the scout softly. "I know."

There was another silence, then the scout spoke again. "But what befell you? Explorer to no-troop . . ."

"What befell me? *You* befell me! What else should happen to a soldier who survived the dishonor of capture?" Nelirikk rubbed the back of his neck, trying to finger away the worst of the headache.

"Security recommended execution. But the Command supposed I might yet have knowledge useful to the Troop, coward though I am." He looked back at the scout, sitting so attentive atop his crate.

"Ten dutiless Cycles, of eating after the *soldiers* had their fill, of speaking when spoken to, of being the loser's prize in games of skill between the captains! Ten cycles of scut-work and kicks and being banned from the piloting chambers—because you befell me! You should have cut my throat ten Cycles ago, Liaden. Be a soldier and do it now."

The scout was staring at him, wonder on his smooth-skinned face. "You *reported*," he breathed, so softly he might have been speaking to himself, except the words were Yxtrang, as was the shout that followed: "Gods damn you for a fool, man! Whatever prompted you to *report* it?"

Nelirikk stiffened. "What else should a soldier do?"

"Who am I to know what a soldier will do? But an explorer will use his brain and look first to his duty."

"You," Nelirikk suggested, with wide irony, "did not report."

"And be planet-bound for years, while my head was drained of every nuance of our encounter, and my abilities languished? I was trained as an explorer and discoverer of worlds—to do less than that work was to fail in my duty to my teachers."

The anger hit all at once—he saw it reflected in a sudden widening of the scout's bright eyes. The waste of it! The years of shame might never have been! He might have advanced the Troop to a dozen new worlds. He might have—

He took a breath and brought the scout back into focus, noting with something akin to approval the soldierly way in which the Liaden sat his post, eyes wary and hands ready—much good it might do him against Nelirikk's bulk and strength.

"You have endangered your teachers and your people," he said, "by failing to report. How if they settle that world we found together, while some of the Troop do the same?"

"My report indicated that I had identified at least one example of a potentially sapient race," the scout said; "and recommended the planet be studied again in a generation."

"You know that planet, Scout! There were no more sapient . . ." Nelirikk choked suddenly as the phrasing overtook him; gasped, "Me?"

"You," said the scout calmly. "I never considered but that you would do the same."

"Then that is the difference between us," Nelirikk said heavily. "For I only thought to do my duty, and report everything to the Troop." He looked up. "Kill me, Scout Commander."

The scout shook his head and the wild brown hair fell into his eyes. "As to that," he said, "I must speak with my captain and receive further orders." He unfolded his legs and dropped to the floor, soundless and graceful as a squirrel, passing just beyond Nelirikk's reach on his way to the door.

"Care for your blade, do," he said as he touched the button set into the door. "I will speak with my captain and return."

The door opened and the scout slipped through, leaving Nelirikk alone with his weapons.

The door rolled closed behind him, amber overhead glowing bright.

"Sealed," said the guard, and voices broke all around him, sudden and bewildering as a hailstorm.

In Liaden: Erob and tel'Vosti.

In Terran: Jason.

Variously:

"Well, what'd he say?"

"Is the information useful?"

"Are they going to attack through the park?"

"Well done, well done, excellent!"

"Shall we dispose of it now?"

Val Con gulped air, got his mental feet under him with wrenching effort and ran the Rainbow. He sorted the crowd and found Miri, silent and serious by the monitor, touched the song of her within his head and smiled into her eyes before glaring at the noisy rest and waving a hand for silence.

It came instantly, and he breathed a sigh of relief.

"The project requires time," he said in Trade, to avoid having to say it again. "Circumstances exist." He glanced over Erob's head to the towering Aus.

"Commander Carmody, have you plans regarding the upkeep of your prisoner?"

Jason laughed. "Upkeep? That's two steps ahead of me, son—I just thought you might get something useful out of him!"

"So I may," Val Con said. "However, he has not been well-cared-for by his troop of late. If I might—"

"Hell, bet he's hungry as a freeze-toad at ice-out! Boy that size's gotta eat as much as I do. Here . . ." He slapped a leg pocket; pulled out four ration-packs and tossed them over. After a moment, he unsnapped his canteen and held it out. "Best believe *these* filters are good."

Val Con bowed and heard Erob catch her breath, no doubt scandalized that one of Korval should acknowledge so deep a debt to a mere Terran. "My thanks, Commander. Shall I need to obtain your permission regarding any steps I might find it necessary—"

Jase waved a hand. "Do what needs done. You're a scout, ain't you?"

"Indeed," said Val Con softly; "I am a scout." He turned to Erob, amused to find tel'Vosti's arm firmly through his delm's, fingers curled unobtrusively around her wrist.

"Erob." He gave her full measure in the bow, made the sign of an equal requesting favor with his unladen hand.

"I see you, Korval."

"This prisoner was taken upon your lands. He is housed within your prison and lives at your pleasure. In recognition of these things, I request that I be allowed to deal with him— with this person Nelirikk—as my melant'i and the necessities of Korval dictate." He straightened and looked her full in the face. "On Jelaza Kazone."

Breath hissed out of her and tel'Vosti's fingers tightened about her wrist. "I require a fuller accounting of Korval's necessities," she said, as was her right in this.

Val Con bowed again. "I have former acquaintance with this Nelirikk. We met many years ago, when he was explorer and I scout captain. At that time, I dealt—inadequately— with him, and now wish to honorably correct an error in judgment."

"Honor? With that?" She flicked a glance at the monitor, which showed Nelirikk seated upon his makeshift cot, stoically sharpening the larger knife. "It is an animal, Korval."

Val Con sighed. "Erob, he is a man."

"And you would attempt Balance with it." She stared at him, at Jason, back at the Yxtrang. "So you feed it and allow it to sharpen its weapon. You think yourself able to take it, I assume. Mad your line and house may be, but I never heard that you were suicides."

He bowed ironically. "I am to take this as your agreement to uphold my necessities regarding this man?"

She was quiet a time longer, staring at the monitor until tel'Vosti shifted at her side. Her permission, when it came, was resigned. "Deal as you must, Korval. You will, in any case."

"My thanks, Erob. Korval is in your debt."

He turned back toward the door, rations and canteen in hand; saw Miri lounging by the monitor. "Hey, Cory," she said in Benish, which only they two among those assembled spoke. "You have a minute to talk?"

"Certainly." He grinned at her. "As many as you like."

"Good." She nodded, keeping to Benish. "Your intentions with this soldier are? I see no worry, here." She touched a finger to her temple. "Tell me the plan."

"Yes. This man is a treasure, cha'trez. It is imperative that we do not waste him."

"Hmm. But he talks like he thinks he's got no worth—talks like maybe he'll cut his own throat."

Val Con stiffened. "Miri. How do you know what he said?"

She jabbed a finger at the monitor. "Heard him."

"Yes," he said carefully. "But when he said those things, he was speaking Yxtrang."

"Yx—" Her eyes widened, finger rising once more to touch her temple. "You speak Yxtrang," she said, very carefully. "I don't speak Yxtrang."

"Not," he agreed with matching care, "so far as I know."

"Shit." She lapsed back into Terran. "Tell you what, boss: we gotta figure this thing out before somebody gets killed."

He flicked a glance at the monitor.

"Yeah, yeah. Necessity and all that. What's the back up? You want me in there, too?"

He heard the flat note of fear in her voice and in the internal song and reached to touch her cheek, scandalized old women be damned. "I may need to call upon you, cha'trez, my Captain. But at this moment, if you permit, Nelirikk and I have certain philosophies to discuss." He smiled and lay his finger lightly on her lips. "It will be well, Miri."

"You keep *saying* that," she complained, around the concern he felt almost as his own. "Just don't get yourself killed, OK?"

"OK," he said. The door cycled open and he stepped back into prison.

Putting the knife right soothed—and gave him time to think, to measure his weaknesses and his strengths.

The rifle . . . Nelirikk nearly spat.

Given a decent kit it could be restored; but he lacked the kit. He might also construct a small bomb from the compo-

nents that still functioned, if he had time. He doubted the
scout would be gone for more time than was required for the
knife, and there was certainly someone monitoring the small
scanner in the ceiling-corner.

A bomb, therefore, would be useless both as a surprise and
as a vehicle for escape, given the solid masonry all about.

The knife-edge was superb now, for the stone was of excellent quality. These were the sorts of things one looted for
on a Liaden world: the little things that worked better or were
more elegant.

It was odd that beings which the Command taught were
merely vermin should have the way of making such fine
things, Nelirikk thought suddenly. Similar objects, made by
Yxtrang hands, tended to be serviceable, but uninspired.

And an enemy had freely given this stone, that he might
bring his blade to an honorable edge!

An edge that could now easily pass entirely through something as thin and fragile as the scout.

Alas, throwing such a bulky blade would be inexact at
best, and it was folly to suppose the scout could thus be
taken by surprise. Worse, the scout carried a personal
weapon that sliced gun-steel like cheese. What it might do to
flesh and bone—

He thought about that.

It might be possible to goad the Scout Commander into
using the crystal blade. It might be possible, after all, to die a
hero's death, with no Yxtrang ever knowing that Nelirikk
No-Troop had failed yet again, that—

There was anger.

Nelirikk explored it, for anger sullies thinking.

When he thought of the scout, there was anger, distant and
indistinct, as if a cloudy remnant of those years of intensely
focused pain hung between them, obscuring what might be
truth.

When he thought of the rifle—

His heartbeat spiked, and he very nearly brought the blade
to his own throat as the shame of being given a useless
weapon broke across him.

Stupid. As always. With an effort, he calmed his thoughts
and considered the blade and the scout anew.

What did he know of Liadens, in truth? That they were people—sentient and self-aware—must be clear to the dullest of the Troop, no matter the Command's teachings. As people, then, following custom and system of their own devising . . . Was it conceivable that Liadens practiced some alien honor? Was it possible that this one left his enemy specifically alone, granting him honorable opportunity? The knife was very sharp: three rapid motions would solve many problems.

Nelirikk hefted the blade; sheathed it with a sigh. After a moment, he drew his grace blade from its snug boot top and used the whetstone on it.

Tending the blade was soothing. Perhaps the scout found it so, as well.

"I see you, Explorer."

Nelirikk looked up from his task, eyes narrow on the bag the little man carried.

"I see you, Scout."

Val Con nodded and resumed his former perch, settling the bag firmly in his lap. The Loop was disturbingly before his mind's eye, elucidating a 27 percent likelihood of an immediate attack, and an even more disturbing refusal to project an ultimate Chance of Mission Success or Chance of Personal Survival.

Light glinted from the blade Nelirikk was sharpening—a fine thing, as like the larger blade as a screwdriver was to the Clutch knife he wore in his sleeve.

He rummaged in the bag and tossed a food pack lightly toward the Yxtrang, who snatched it and the next comfortably out of the air, and sat holding them in his hand.

"Food?"

"Food," Val Con agreed. "Commander Carmody believes a soldier should be permitted to eat."

Cautiously, Nelirikk bent and returned his knife to its boot-sheath, expression unreadable behind the tattoos.

"Do eat," urged Val Con. "I suspect they may be better than the rations you were issued."

Nelirikk frowned at the Terran-lettered labels.

"You would eat this?"

Val Con laughed.

"It is not nearly as delicious as the rabbit one snares oneself, I admit. But the mercenaries buy their own food—surely they would not poison themselves. Most certainly not Commander Carmody, who gives this from his own day-kit."

He used his duty blade to open a ration pack while the Yxtrang sat watching.

"Shall we trade?" Val Con murmured, triggering the tiny heating element. "Are you concerned for the quality?"

Almost, it seemed that Nelirikk might laugh. He pointed toward Val Con's food.

"The explorer," he said, hesitantly, "is unfamiliar with local custom."

"Local custom is that hungry persons may eat. If you dislike what you have, you may have some of mine. There is water here, too, if you'll share the canteen. Or use your own, if you trust the filters."

"Eat," the Yxtrang repeated quietly. He opened the silver packet, discovered the tray and tray mechanism quickly, triggered it, stared again at the label.

"What food is this?"

Val Con glanced at the bright lettering. "Prime salmon. Excellent—though I hope you will not find it necessary for me to share it."

Nelirikk looked up sharply, wariness clearly visible through the facial decorations.

"No?"

Val Con laughed. "The food is good. But on my last mission the God of Quartermasters saw fit to supply my captain and myself with a year's rations of salmon and crackers—and nothing else!"

The Yxtrang sampled the fish carefully. In a moment he was eating with gusto.

"**Tell** me my death, Scout Commander."

They had finished eating and the small man had passed over the canteen. Together, they had gathered the remains of the food and put them in a recycle box, and now they looked at each other.

"How shall I die?" Nelirikk repeated, the Yxtrang words bittersweet in his mouth.

"I do not know," said the scout quietly, also in Yxtrang. "The orders I have are simply to do what must, of necessity and honor, be done."

"Honor?" The word seemed to hang overlong between them— he had not meant it as a challenge, in truth, but what could a captive-holding troop know of honor?

The Liaden shook his head; shifted on his seat.

"My curiosity and arrogance seem to have caused you much pain. I had never meant for a fellow seeker-of-worlds to suffer—certainly never as you have suffered. So, I seek to balance the evil I brought upon you."

Nelirikk stared, trying to grapple this concept into sense. The scout spoke of *personal* responsibility—*personal* retribution, personal action. The oddness of it made his abused head throb.

"Balance." He tasted the word for connotation—for implication.

He looked at the Liaden, sitting so solemn atop his crate, seeing no trace of humor, or malice, or deceit, or any attitude of attack. No attitude of defense.

Yet—questions of honor with *Liadens*? Those worthless enemies who had no respect, who—treated a man like a soldier, when the Troop had thrown him away.

"Balance," he said once more, and contrived a stiff, seated bow.

"Your ship, Scout Commander."

The green eyes were cutting sharp upon him. "Yes."

"The reason I am here," said Nelirikk, slowly, "is that during the strike on the landing field I showed your ship to the forward controller. A no-troop may not speak unless spoken to—" Nelirikk thought a moment of anger and glanced at the blade, which sat idle as he spoke equitably to an enemy.

"Despite the regulation, I gave warning that your ship was dangerous—that I had seen its like before. I told them to take it out—"

The Liaden had stiffened, face intent.

Nelirikk leaned an elbow on a knee, meeting those sharp eyes with puzzlement and some sadness.

"There is your balance, Scout. Freedom for freedom. For overstepping—for causing a general to seem a fool—I was sent to explore boundaries and map the importance of your ship's defense."

"It seems a balance for generals and units," the scout commented.

"Yes," agreed the Yxtrang. Then, thoughtfully: "Was there a junior officer onboard? Did you lose troops from this?"

"No, thank you. The ship—I could not return in the ferocity of the attack. The ship defended by—reaction."

"I saw it return fire to orbit," Nelirikk said, "but was told that it did not."

The Liaden nodded.

"Fired upon from orbit, it would return fire to orbit. The beam would be weaker, but enough to singe, I warrant."

"So." The Yxtrang's grin was savage. "Seven drop-jets and a strike on the battleship, at least. Your ship did you well, Scout Commander." He paused. "It was a ship to behold."

The Liaden acknowledged this with a sketched salute, smiling wanly.

"Did proper duty," agreed Val Con. "As you did. As I've done." He looked up sharply, waving a thin hand for emphasis.

"Does it strike you as a wasteful—even artificial—equation, Nelirikk Explorer, that doing proper duty tends to result in destruction?"

The question jolted—the more so because he had asked it of himself, as a thinking person must, while he had been explorer, and while he had been no-troop. His answer came a heartbeat later than it should have.

"The Troop survives! The Command survives!"

The Liaden moved his shoulders, expressive of some emotion Nelirikk could not name.

"Very true. Faceless and interchangeable, Command survives. I tell you that I, Val Con yos'Phelium, know about duty. Duty says you and I must fight, eh?" He brushed hair out of his face. "Duty demands that I attempt to kill the clos-

est peer I've met in several Standards. Duty demands blood
all too often—in this time, what does it demand of you,
Nelirikk?"

It was hard, that answer, but it was in him, blood and
bone. Any soldier would have answered the same.

"Duty demands that I call fire on your brave ship, Scout. It
demands that I kill you, given the opportunity."

"And then?" the Liaden insisted, *pushing* with mere
words! "What demands, after I die?"

"That I escape, back to my unit to—"

"To report and be shot!" shouted the scout.

Nelirikk bent his head in the Liaden way. "I might instead
be used as a target for knife practice."

The Liaden looked a bit wild-eyed.

"Do you wish to fight?" he demanded.

"Scout, I must!" Nelirikk looked to the blade.

"Is it true," asked the scout, very calmly, "that two men of
equal rank might fight for the higher position?"

"Yes," Nelirikk agreed, wondering at this change in topic.

"And that then, the winner commands the loser?"

"With the concurrence of the next above in the troopline,
yes."

"Ah." The Liaden slid abruptly down from his perch, head
tipped up to stare into Nelirikk's face.

"I propose," he said, "a contest." He turned his back,
walked to one end of the room and back, eyes brilliant. "I
propose that we fight—for duty's sake. We will fight as
equals—scout to explorer. If you should win, I will take your
orders. If I win, I will sponsor you to my captain for admittance to the troop—pledged to me and my line."

Nelirikk sat speechless, staring at the manic little man,
who grinned at his stupefaction. Fight a Liaden for troop position? Treat scout equal to explorer? Who would enforce a
win? The difficulties . . .

"*Are* you mad?" he asked slowly. "How could you hope to
win such a contest? I'm strong, fast, and weapon-wise—"

"Mad?" The scout's grin grew wider. "It is madness to
waste resources. It is madness to give in to the faceless. I will
represent you—Nelirikk Explorer—to my captain—should I
win. I swear it by Tree and Dragon! If you win—"

"If I win, Scout, you will likely be dead!"

The little man came forward, stopping just within Nelirikk's reach, face and eyes gone child-solemn. "Would you really waste so valuable a resource?"

Nelirikk stared, put his hand on the troop blade—and took it away again.

"I hope I do not waste resources," he said. "But where will you find a neutral here to serve as referee? How could we break?"

The scout waved a hand airily. "Technicality," he said. "Mere technicality. Do you agree in principle? If so, we will be able to devise details."

Nelirikk sighed, then slowly stood.

"It is better to do something than nothing. I know that you won't feed an enemy forever." He bowed, stiffly, but with good intent. "For duty and for balance. May you be strong for the Troop."

The Liaden returned the bow with fluid grace, then brought his fist to his shoulder in a proper salute.

"As you say," he agreed, and climbed back atop his crate. "Let us now consider technicalities."

Together, they pushed the storage crates in front of the door. On them went: a rifle, a pack, a long-knife, boots, another pair of boots, several more knives—including one sheathed in fine black suede, the handle of which gleamed like polished obsidian.

They stood, toe-to-toe and barefoot, scout and explorer.

The Yxtrang looked down on his toy-like opponent, a line from a camp-song echoing briefly in his head:

A soldier's opponent is more than might—
Little Jela was a demon to fight . . .

For clarity they went over the agreement, first the Liaden and then the Yxtrang, each speaking in the other's language to be sure there was no difficulty in translation.

"Thus shall it be," came the Liaden words from the Yxtrang: "should I prevail in this contest, I shall pursue my duty as I see it, you subordinate. Should the win be yours, I shall pledge myself and my services to you and your line until released."

"The win," said the Liaden in Troop tongue, "goes to the first able to count three on a vulnerable opponent; the loser yielding at once."

They backed away, then, each looking the room over, perhaps measuring the luck of this or that corner, or seeking an advantage of light, or filling their mind with a last living vision, each already distant from the world.

The timer on Val Con's watch beeped.

He moved forward slowly, accepting both the necessity for motion—from the L'apeleka stance, *Desiring Difficult Desires*—and the need for caution.

From the other side of the large room came the Yxtrang. The face behind the tattoos had gone distant: intention hidden deep within the eyes while the huge body came forward gently, gracefully, inevitably. Val Con noticed that the Yxtrang's feet, like his hands, seemed disproportionately delicate.

L'apeleka demanded the right elbow forward now; the Yxtrang answered by crouching a shade lower. Val Con pulled the arm in, saw his opponent's shoulder rise in proper reaction.

They were beginning the dance with caution: both testing responses or lack of, until at once they were in and close, arms in motion, knives the honest threat. Could-be threats were of this, that, or the other throw or kick, a punch hidden behind the placement of elbow or flick of wrist.

Nelirikk feinted, saw the feint ignored, the threat parried before execution.

Val Con's Loop evaluated the situation: a clear 43 percent Chance of Mission Success.

The Loop flicked away, lost in the sudden hugeness of the explorer, looming above, knife held so—

Val Con ducked, twisted—heard the hum of blade passing over-close to his ear, saw the big man recover a trifle slowly, used the heartbeat to barely touch an ankle with the blade—

And was past and behind, where he needed to be, but the

foot placement warned him and he whirled away just ahead
of the kick, Nelirikk grimacing with the effort it cost him to
keep balanced.

The wall was barely an arm's length from Val Con, forc-
ing him to dart in close again. He found the move in
L'apeleka: *The Blizzard Swirls.*

Hands, arms, legs, knees, feet blurred with the sequence—
he got a kick in on a solid thigh, a knifeless punch high on a
shoulder—and tried to dance away—too late!

The answering blow caught his shoulder, he spun with it,
tumbled, whipped around to find the Yxtrang in full charge,
leapt, kicked solidly at the face—and caught the ear as the
other's knife slashed his tough combat leather leggings.

Disengage.

The room was silent but for their breathing, and they
backed away, each searching for signs of damage. The
Yxtrang's ankle had a small spot of blood; his ear was dark
red. Val Con felt a slight sting; shrugged it out of consciousness—damage to his right leg was minor—no more than a
scratch.

Nelirikk adjusted his belt with a quick hand.

Val Con tried to move in; was held off by the other's long
reach. He moved left; found himself faced. Right—and again
the move was there, checking him, boxing him, trying—

Nelirikk was trying to get him into a corner, arms low and
spread.

Val Con feinted right, feinted left, went straight in for
half-a-step, then dove for the right arm, blade nipping out as
he tucked—rolled—and felt the force of the blow on the
floor behind him, gained his feet and whirled in time to see
the Yxtrang's blade bounce, once.

He was too slow: the knife was recovered.

Both were sweating now; the floor was slick with it and
with dripped blood, making a slip or misstep all too likely.

As if by common consent they moved downroom to a
drier patch of floor. It seemed neither wished to be on the
right side of uncertain footing.

CMS flashed behind Val Con's eyes: 41 percent.

He grimaced, and the Yxtrang started moving in, perhaps
taking it as a sign of despair.

Val Con drew back as if to throw the blade; Nelirikk glided casually away, adjusting his belt as he came back again, hands protecting face but leaving shoulders and thighs vulnerable. Val Con glanced at the unbladed hand—empty.

Three seconds! How many times had they already threatened each other with—

Val Con tried again to close; was fended away. Nelirikk lunged, Val Con twisted, avoided, skidded on dampness— snatched a moment to recover his balance.

A moment was too long—a heavy arm swung out, slamming him off his feet and into the wall. He bounced, rolled and came up, knife in hand, shoulder aching, but unbroken. There was blood on the floor from his leg.

This time he feinted a slip as the Yxtrang closed; wrapped himself around that massive knife arm and punched his blade into the upper shoulder.

Nelirikk grunted, shook—and Val Con was airborne again, flung loose like a hound from a bear. He came up and around as his opponent tossed his knife to the undamaged left hand and charged.

Val Con gave ground, saw the trap—

Nelirikk slipped on a smear of blood—and Val Con raced by, elbow lifting to fend off the descending blade—which was sharp, gods; a proper soldier's knife, fit for slashing leather, flesh, bone . . . The blood was quick. Hot.

CMS flashed; he ignored it. What did the Loop know about necessity?

He slipped.

The Yxtrang nearly fell on top of him: he scrambled away in time to avoid the lunge, jumped to his feet, wiped the blood off his arm, saw the depth of the cut, shuddered—and moved in.

Move in. Move in. Move in. He needed to be inside that long reach if he had to kill the Yxtrang, if neither would yield—

He ducked back, avoiding a fist. Saw the curiously graceful hand move toward belt and check as he feinted in.

So he charged. Straight at the huge man, blade ready to slice or cut and—

He skidded, lost his knife, slid behind the Yxtrang, who

snatched—and Val Con's good hand flashed out, snagged the ring of metal on his opponent's belt, and yanked.

Nelirikk saw the scout's knife on the floor, bent, grabbed—

But Val Con had it now: a thin strand of cutting wire as long as his arm. He hugged the giant's leg, pulled the wire loop hard—twisted, half-avoiding the hammer-blow of a huge fist—and hung on, *hung on* to the wire cord while oceans roared inside his ears and his vision went gray, ebbing toward black and Miri was there, terror sheeting her face, her hands overlaying his own on the wire . . .

The explorer went down. Val Con hung on grimly; clawed back to sense, pulled his knife to him with his bloody leg.

"One, two, three . . ." he gasped—let go the wire and came to his feet, as he must, knife in hand.

The Yxtrang lay half-sprawled on his side, knife held at throat-level, eyes distant. He sat up slowly, knife still high, eyes on Val Con's face. With his free hand he fingered the bloody loop around his legs, mouth tight.

Val Con stood back warily, wondering if he could dodge a thrown knife, or avoid a sudden desperate lunge.

Nelirikk explored the place where the wire lodged in his right leg. A spasm of pain crossed his face, eloquent despite the tattoo. Carefully, he turned the knife in his hand, holding it by the blade as if to throw, weighing its balance—

Then held it farther out, toward Val Con.

"I neglected to ask," he said in neutral Trade, "what language I should use when speaking to your captain."

Val Con sighed, slid his knife away, and accepted the offering. He cleaned it carefully against the sleeve of his fighting leathers, inspected it, and found its edge undamaged. He extended a hand to the Yxtrang, who hesitated before using the assistance to stand.

"You have accepted a brave challenge, Explorer," Val Con said in Yxtrang. "I must have the rest of the pledge before I may present you to my captain."

The big man half-lifted a fist to salute, caught the gesture, and made a ragged bow. "As you say." He paused a moment, either to recruit his resources or to puzzle out the most proper phrasing.

"I, Nelirikk . . . *I*, Nelirikk Explorer, pledge myself on Jela's honor to the person and line of Val Con yos'Phelium. My blood is yours, now and until my death. May your orders bring glory to us all."

Val Con bowed and held the heavy knife out across both palms.

"Your blade, Nelirikk Explorer. Wear it and use it as required, by my consent. The Tree and Dragon is now your shield also: I trust you will bring honor to us all."

Nelirikk took the blade in wonder.

"Can you walk?" Val Con asked him.

"If required, my leader."

Val Con shook his head. "Scout is sufficient for now, I believe. Do you rest while I go to bring my captain."

Miri whirled from the monitor as he came through the hatch, slamming her gun home with one hand and unclipping her belt-kit with the other. Behind her was Jason—and behind him were tel'Vosti and Erob.

"It is done." Val Con said. "Miri, you will need to—"

"Hold him, Jase."

Val Con stiffened; heard as if it had only now begun the song that was Miri within him—heard the terror and the beginning of the metamorphosis into anger. He sighed and leaned back into Jason's bulk, muscles shivering with reaction.

Miri slashed the ruined sleeve to expose the knife wound, sprayed it with antiseptic; reached for a pain bulb—

"No! Miri, you must talk to—"

She looked at him straight, gray eyes wild, and wiped the sweat from his face with an antiseptic cloth.

"You're mostly OK." Half question, half accusation.

"Yes. Some pain, some wounds that will heal, but—"

"What in hell were you trying to pull?" she yelled, terror abruptly sublimated into rage. "Next time you want yourself dead, try a step off a hundred meter cliff! Whatever gave you—"

She bent over the arm, still yelling, slipped for a moment into an argot that made even Jason cringe and slammed back into Terran for, "Jase—gimme a double staple patch outta your kit."

"Miri," Val Con said.

She swabbed his face again—hard; leaving the bitter taste of antiseptic in his mouth.

"Miri?"

"You ain't answered me, soldier! I wanna know where you got permission to pull such a damn fool stunt!"

"Necessity. Miri, please. It is done."

"Done is it?" she snorted, and knelt to get at his leg. "You look it."

"Attend me!" Val Con insisted, voice rising. He heard a faint pop as a sweat bubble broke in his ear.

She came up fast, eyes blazing. "Don't you lose your temper at me, you scruffy midget!"

For one searing moment, Val Con thought she might actually strike him, so exalted was her fury. Apparently Jason thought so, too, for he dropped his grip and stepped back.

Miri took a deep breath, hurled her free hand into the air and leaned close.

"So tell me, *partner*," she said, so sarcastically Jason retreated another step; "what's the plan? Huh? What'm I supposed to do now? What's the new gag? Yours all the way—so tell me about it."

The sarcasm hurt; his arm hurt and every other bit of him, too. Ridiculously, he regretted the warm solidity of Jason to lean against, and took a breath, pitching his voice for neutrality.

"Miri, my Captain, I request that you also give aid to the man inside this room, who is waiting to see if you will accept him as a recruit."

Her fear flared and his own anger melted. He reached to touch her cheek, which caress she allowed, shoulders losing some of the tension fury had lent.

"I said that I would sponsor him to you," he murmured. "Do me the honor of at least speaking with him before he bleeds to death."

She stared at him, anger and terror evaporating into wonder. "You want me to accept an *Yxtrang* as a recruit in a Terran-Liaden unit?"

"If the captain judges it wise," he said carefully.

She considered him out of wary gray eyes. "And if the captain thinks it's the worst idea she's heard since she left Surebleak?"

"That is the captain's right," he acknowledged. "But you will still wish to speak to this Nelirikk and show him some care, cha'trez."

"Why should I care a plugged bit what happens to him?"

"He is pledged to serve us, Line yos'Phelium," he explained. "There are—obligations. Such as seeing that one's servant has proper medical attention and does not needlessly suffer."

She flung her hand out toward the sealed hatch. "We *own* that?"

"Certainly not," said Val Con. "One cannot own a sentient being."

"Right." She closed her eyes. "Other people," she said, apparently to the room at large, "give their wives flowers."

She spun on her heel, eyes snapping open. "Open the door," she told the door-corporal and glanced back at Val Con and Jason. "The two of you got me into this; the two of you can tag along."

Nelirikk stood, awaiting the return of the scout. He dared not sit on one of the crates, for fear his wounded legs would fail when it came time to rise to the captain's honor. He had made scant effort to clean himself, for it was no disgrace, that a captain might see a soldier fresh from soldier's duty.

There had been a voice raised in the outerways; a murmured answer that must be the scout—and the raised voice once more, swearing, as he'd monitored from time to time from Terran ships.

If the raised voice were the captain, it would seem to register displeasure with the performance. It suddenly occurred to Nelirikk to wonder just how persuasive was the scout, and he worried somewhat, and shifted on his aching legs—

The door cycled open, admitting a procession.

The scout led, limping, with field dressings on arm and leg. Immediately behind was a Terran male who filled the doorway with his bulk—a full-sized soldier, dressed for war, yet looking like some scraggly farm-peasant, long-haired and bearded, without tattoos of rank or maturity-mark. Still, he moved with assurance; with command: A proper captain!

Behind came a tiny red-haired figment—an apprentice soldier, doubtless brought early from the creche in the emergency of the invasion—carrying what appeared to be a medical kit.

The scout paused, swept a bow and nearly slipped on the slick floor. The larger man turned his head to snap a command at the soldier in the doorway: "Get a mop and cleaners!"

"My Captain," the scout began, and Nelirikk turned his face more fully to the bearded man, thinking that it would not be so bad, to serve a captain at least of proper size . . .

"My Captain," the scout repeated, and bowed profoundly, head near touching his knees, as the figment continued forward, thumping the equipment she carried onto a nearby crate, striding past the big man and the small one, to stand wide legged directly before Nelirikk, matchstick arms folded across scant chest.

"Well?" she snapped, and Nelirikk's mouth opened in response to the command-voice before his mind recalled that it was not yet his place to speak. The scout it was that answered, properly—and most gently.

"Captain, this is the man I propose to add to the unit. Nelirikk Explorer, he is called; a thoughtful fighter and—"

The captain shifted; frowned. "Introduce me."

"Yes, Captain." The scout bowed obedience; Nelirikk brought himself to stiff attention, striving to ignore his injuries and the persistent buzzing in his ears, the while his mind raced to encompass a captain who was smaller even than the scout and—

"Explorer, attend! Here is Captain Miri Robertson, commanding Action Unit 1, Lytaxin Combined Forces! Captain, I bring you Recruit Candidate Nelirikk Explorer."

Nelirikk stared straight ahead, as proper, while the tiny creature unfolded her arms and walked almost casually around him, inspecting. From the corner of an eye, Nelirikk saw the large man grin, then go soldier-faced as the captain completed her circuit.

"Is this the man who was carrying that stupid rifle?" she demanded of the scout.

Nelirikk kept his countenance. The question was reasonable, after all; and the part of his sponsor to explain.

"Yes, Captain."

"Hmmmph." She walked behind him once more. "What in the hell is this?"

"I took it from his—"

"Can he talk?" snapped the captain.

"Yes, Captain." The scout effaced himself and the large man grinned into his beard.

"Explorer," the captain demanded his attention. "This thing you're tangled in. What is it?"

Nelirikk stared straight ahead, concentrating on the proper formation of the Terran words. "Captain. A *Shibjela*. If the captain pleases."

The scout stirred within Nelirikk's vision, eyes gone intent.

"Translate that," ordered the command-voice and the scout bit his lip.

"I . . . In Trade: Jela's Neck-jewel. Jela's Necklace, in High Liaden . . ." He paused, thumb rubbing over fingertips, as if he felt the texture of nuance and sense. "In Terran . . . perhaps Jela's Noose. Or—"

"Got it," the captain interrupted. She resumed her cross-armed stance directly in Nelirikk's line of sight. "Explorer. Do all Yxtrang carry one of these?"

Excellent! The captain thought quickly and to the point!

"No, Captain. My—the unit where I take my training pays homage to one of the original members. All who train there carry Shibjela. Other units have—"

"Other toys," she finished for him and barely turned her head.

"Jase."

"Captain Redhead?" The bearded man did not bow, though his expression showed clear respect.

"Got one of your toys?"

The big man grinned, stepped forward and produced an

oddly shaped piece of wood. It was perhaps a club, though it looked frail for such work; slightly edged, highly polished. Nelirikk's hand itched for it, to test balance and theory.

"Ever seen one of these?" the captain asked, walking to his left.

"No, Captain," he said, noting that the captain appeared to possess several names.

"Good. So we have some secret weapons, too." She was behind him again.

"This hurt?" she asked, and he felt a sear of pain where she touched him above the bleeding leg wound.

"Yes, Captain," he said, neutrally.

"Ought to. Looks pretty ugly. Can you fight?"

"Yes, Captain." He hesitated. "Now?"

"No!" She was before him again, head tipped back so he could see a grim face no larger than the palm of his hand, dominated by a pair of fierce gray eyes. "I mean—can you fight well? Ain't no slackers in my unit, you understand? My soldiers fight!"

"I can fight, Captain. I have many years of training. I use the autorifle, the—"

"Skip the sales pitch. How many languages you speak?"

"Yes, Captain," said Nelirikk, wondering—and then recalling that this was the captain who attached a scout to her command. "Languages: Yxtrang, Liaden, Trade, Terran, and Rishkak."

"Fine. You know how to take orders?"

"Yes, Captain."

"If I tell you to charge head on against armor and all you got is a rifle, will you?"

"Yes. Captain."

The gray eyes considered him blandly. "You really think you can take orders from somebody like me?"

He hesitated fractionally, began the proper answer—was cut off by a sharp wave of a child-like hand.

"You tell me what you think, Explorer. The truth, accazi?"

"Yes, Captain. It—occurs to the explorer that the captain is—very small."

Incredibly, she laughed. "Yeah? Well, it occurs to the captain that you're out of reason tall. If you can't take orders from me, I'll just hand you over to Commander Carmody and let him sort you out. I didn't go asking for another scout in this unit. Seems to me one's all the trouble I need." She blinked thoughtfully. "Might be easiest just to let you loose."

Nelirikk gulped. "Captain—"

"Dammit, Redhead!" Commander Carmody yelled, drowning every other sound in the room. "You can't do that! The stuff he knows? Why, darlin', the man's *beautiful*! We can't just be throwing him back in with some bunch o'rowdies who don't even keep the mice from the larder!"

"Great," she said expressionlessly. "You want him?"

"Now, now, my small, you know he's best off with you. Seems him and the scout there understand each other fine."

"That's what scares me," said the captain, with a noticeable lack of fear in either posture or face. She sighed and turned back to Nelirikk.

"All right, Beautiful, you had time to think it over. Which is it, me or Commander Carmody?"

He looked at the scout, who returned his gaze blandly; at Commander Carmody, who shrugged and put his hands behind his back; at the captain herself.

"The scout sponsors me to his captain, who has the wisdom to value the—resource of an explorer. I pledge to obey the captain's orders, if she will accept me into her troop."

"Hmmph. You know anything about first aid?"

"Yes, Captain."

"Good. Help Commander Carmody patch you up."

"Yes, Captain."

The bearded man came forward, med-box tucked under one arm. The captain went to the crate that had been the scout's seat and hoisted herself up.

"Explorer, you're gonna cause me lots of problems, you know that?"

"I had not considered, Captain. I—"

"Consider it! You got 'til this first aid stuff is done and then I want you to tell me what problems I might have with you and because of you—and how to fix them. Think hard, accazi?"

"Yes, Captain." Commander Carmody had set the box

aside and was on one knee behind him. Nelirikk felt him
touch the Shibjela and pick up the ring-end.

"All right, now, boyo. I expect this'll sting a mite."

His understanding of Terran was perhaps flawed, for the
quick jerk that pulled the cord from its nesting-place excited
an agony as exquisite as it was, mercifully, brief. He bit his
lip, soundless, and concentrated on remaining upright.

There was a slight hiss, a coldness, and then a numbness
on the wound, followed by the sound of his uniform leg parting. Resolutely, Nelirikk turned his thoughts to the problem
his captain had assigned.

"**Captain.** Study indicates that each small problem gener-
ated by recruiting an explorer to your troop comes from a
single, large problem."

The captain turned her attention from the Scout, with
whom she had been conversing in a language Nelirikk didn't
know, and frowned.

"That so?" she asked, but the question was apparently
rhetorical, as she commanded immediately: "Elucidate this
larger problem—and its solution."

"Captain." He brought fist to newly bandaged shoulder in
salute before he recollected such a gesture might well give
insult.

"The large problem is that the explorer is Yxtrang and the
troop you command is not. The solution . . ." Embarrassing it
was to have to give such an answer. Embarrassing and hardly
indicative of any value he might bring to her troop. Nelirikk
kept his face soldierly. "Captain, I conclude that there is no
solution. Biology is fact."

"Biology," she corrected, "is *a* fact." She came to her feet,
there on the packing crate, and crooked a finger. "Come
here."

He moved forward two steps and stopped as he sensed the
scout's increased tension.

"I said," the captain snapped, "come *here*."

"Yes, Captain." One eye wary on the scout, he came forward until his toes touched the crate she stood on. Even with
that added height, he looked down on her and had a moment

to consider the thick coil of hair wrapped tight 'round her head before she tipped her face up to him.

"What's all this stuff?" she demanded, tracing lines across her cheeks with a forefinger.

"Captain. *Vingtai*—marks of rank and . . . accomplishment. Done with a needle, to be permanent."

"Right. What's yours say?"

Nelirikk blinked, dared to flick a look at the scout and was answered by the quirk of a mobile eyebrow.

"Captain," he said respectfully, returning his gaze to her. "On the right—insignia of born-to Troop. The name is perhaps Jela's Guard Corps. In Terran I do not—"

She waved a hand. "Close enough. What about the left?"

"Captain. The left cheek marks me explorer. The double lines there show me—show me no-troop. These others . . . creche mark, apprentice troop, honors of marksmanship and piloting. This . . ." His hand rose and he ran his fingers lightly down the right cheek, feeling the old scar, nearly hidden by the layers of tattoo.

"This is *nchaka*," he said slowly. "When a soldier is done training and has his own weapons given, Sergeant of Arsenal bloods the grace-blade, to show the edge is sharp." He hesitated; glanced at the scout. "Point of information. If the captain pleases."

She waved a hand. "Go."

The word seemed to connote permission, rather than an order to leave, though literal translation—Nelirikk sighed. "Yes, Captain. History tells that *vingtai* were used by the first soldiers because it gave fear to Liadens."

"Gave fear—?" The frown cleared. "Right. If it stops 'em for a second and lets you get the first strike in, it's worth the effort. I guess."

She glanced over to Commander Carmody.

"Need us a medtech, on the bounce."

"All yours, darlin'," the big man said cheerfully and strode over to the door, shouting orders into the room beyond for someone or something called "Chen,"

"Tech'll be able to hack an erase program for the tattoos," the captain was telling the scout; "probably do a skin-tone, too. What about the hair? And—" She turned. "Can you grow a beard, Beautiful?"

Nelirikk stiffened. A beard? Did she think him a farmer? A merchant? A—Terran commander? Very nearly he let go another sigh. "Captain, it is that a soldier does not have a beard. It is part of discipline."

"Hmph. So, if you just ignored discipline for a couple days, would you start to grow a beard? Or are you like this one here?" She pointed at the scout, who lifted a brow, but remained silent.

"If discipline were ignored," Nelirikk said stiffly, "the explorer would begin to sprout hair on his face. With the captain's permission, it would then be very hard to read the *vingtai*."

"Not a worry," she assured him; "we're gonna get rid of all that facial decoration first off." She turned back to the scout, leaving Nelirikk gasping mentally. "How 'bout hair and beard? Anything we can do there?"

"Perhaps hormones and a shot of accelerant," the scout said softly. "He should spend the night in the 'doc in any case." He made a slight bow, slanting his eyes upward. "If the captain pleases."

"Big joke, huh? Just wait 'til—"

"Captain." Nelirikk had found his voice at last. She turned toward him.

"Yes."

"Captain, will you remove—" his hand went to his cheek, traced the familiar swirl of his Home Troop, touched the *nchaka*.

She frowned. "You said you wanted to soldier in my unit, didn't you?"

Nelirikk gulped. "Yes, Captain."

"And you said you wear those things to give fear to Liadens, right?"

"Yes, Captain."

"Well, my troop ain't giving fear to Liadens. My troop is aiming to give fear to Yxtrang, you got that?"

He stared, wrenched his mind toward thinking about Yxtrang as the enemy—and touched his maturity-mark once more.

"I understand, Captain."

She shifted on the crate and caught his eyes in a glance so fey he found he could not break it.

"You gonna be able to run this gag, Beautiful?" Her voice was comradely, though the Terran words confused.

As if she sensed his confusion, she asked again, in High Liaden: "Are you able to nurture the children of your actions, Nelirikk Explorer?"

He bowed. "I am held by my word to an—honorable opponent. It is understood that the troop failed in honor and sent me to find my death. I strive to do better for the children of my actions."

"Right." She was back in Terran. "When were you supposed to be picked up?"

"In six days, local midnight."

"OK, give the scout your ID, we'll take care of that detail. In the meantime, your orders are to cooperate with Chen, heal up, eat and rest. Have to spend a day or two in here, I think—" she glanced at the scout, who nodded thoughtfully.

"We'll get you a computer and a tech to show you the basics. The scout'll work up an outline for you to follow. *Information,* OK? And in your spare time, you can brush up on your Terran. Can't have you mistaking an order in the heat of things." She jumped down from the crate and stared up at him, a long way. "Questions?"

His head spun; he was suddenly as weary as if he had been fighting for days and sleep seemed very sweet. "No, Cap—" he began, then: "Yes, Captain. What will be my position in the troop?" Did they mean to keep him here in this cage, inputting data until he ran dry? Something in him refused to believe it of the scout, while all his life's accumulated experience clamored that it was the only rational use they might put him to.

"Position in the troop, is it?" She frowned. "You will be the captain's personal aide. You will report directly to the captain." Her eyes gleamed. "That OK by you?"

The captain's personal aide? Nelirikk blinked and looked to the scout, but was unable to read anything in that smooth face but a weariness as profound as his own.

"That is OK by me," he said, and tried not to see Commander Carmody's grin. "Thank you, Captain."

"Don't thank me yet," she said grimly and Commander Carmody laughed.

She turned away, the scout attentive at her elbow, then checked and turned back.

" 'Nother thing." She pointed at the Liaden. "You gave him an oath, swearing to protect him and his line, right?"

Nelirikk grabbed after his wavering attention. "Yes, Captain."

"Yes, Captain," she repeated and sighed. "You ask him what that *means*? You ask him if he's got triplets, or an aged father?"

Liaden clan structure was a complex social architecture. Nelirikk had studied it, as one studies everything available regarding an enemy, but had no confidence that his understanding approached actuality. He tried to keep the dismay he felt from reaching his face.

"No, Captain."

She sighed again. "Gonna learn the hard way, ain't you? Anything short of a direct order, if a Liaden asks you to do something, *get details,* accazi?"

"Yes, Captain."

"Fine. Now, the details you didn't get in this case include the fact that the scout and me are lifemates." She came a step forward, peering up into his face. "You savvy lifemates, Beautiful?"

"I—am not certain, Captain."

"Get certain. The broad outline is that him and me are one person. If I go down, the scout speaks with my voice. If the scout goes down—"

Something of his dawning distress must have shown after all, because she grinned and nodded her head.

"Tricky, right? Gotta watch him every minute." She glanced at the doorway, which was cycling open to admit a team of two, pulling a gurney, which supported a whole-body med-box, or autodoc, according to Terran. Nelirikk looked at the captain doubtfully: such things were reserved for generals . . .

"That's Chen," the captain said. "Gonna get cracking on

those cuts and erase the tattoos, all according to orders." She paused, tapped her cheek where his carried the *nchaka*.

"You don't worry about this one—man's scars are his own—but the tattoos make you look like an Yxtrang, when what you are is an Irregular. Can't have you gettin' shot by our side when Commander Carmody thinks you're so valuable, right, Jase?"

"Right you are, Captain Redhead! I think he'll look charming in a mustache, Chen."

"Do our best," the tech said easily as he approached Nelirikk with a hand-reader. "All right, son, roll up the sleeve, and let's see what you're made of."

Sighing, Nelirikk obeyed, and when he looked around again, he was alone with the techs.

EPLING STREET

The day was fine, the sun high, the air bright and bracing. Sheather filled his lungs appreciatively as he moved down the soft strip of *concrete* toward the living-place of Angela Lizardi, Senior Commander Retired, Lunatic Unit Inactive.

The T'carais, his brother Edger, did not accompany him on this mission. They had reasoned that two of the Clutch, walking together in an area where non-humans were not often found, would excite comment among the local population. Worse, the novelty of the sighting would doubtless sharpen memories. Dull remembrance was in the best interest of Clutch and human-kin, should one such as Herbert Alan Costello, the Juntavas buyer of secrets, find this place and begin his askings.

So did Sheather come alone to Angela Lizardi's home-place, bearing a message from T'carais to Elder and another, which was to be said to Miri Robertson and Val Con yos'Phelium, should the Elder deem it fitting that Sheather see and speak with those valued persons.

The numbers on the door-fronts counted this way: 352, 354, 356. The door that adorned the number named 358 was heavier than those other doors adorning other digits. This door was hewn of wood, not formed of plastic. This door was scarred and gnarled, beaten by weather. It stood before him with the aloof impartiality of an Elder, minding such duty as was its own, and which was far beyond the ken of a mere Seventh Shell.

Halted by the door, Sheather stood, great eyes dreaming on the scarred wood, accepting the awful dignity of the barrier. After a time, when it seemed right to do so, he lifted his hand and pressed a finger very gently against the glowing white button set in the portal's frame.

Beyond the scarred elder wood, music chimed, high and brief. Sheather waited.

After a while, it seemed right to press the button once more. Again, the music sounded.

The day was noticeably less bright when Sheather assayed the button for the third time. Music sounded, distant behind the door. Closer to hand, another music spoke.

"The lady gone away."

Carefully, for he was well aware of the fragility of even full-grown humans, Sheather turned. Carefully, he looked down.

A human eggling stood by his knee, face uptilted like a flower, brown eyes opened wide.

Humans thought Clutch big-voiced. Sheather made what effort he could, to shape his voice smaller.

"I am looking for Angela Lizardi, pretty eggling. Do you say she has left her home-place?"

The petal-pink skin rumpled as feathery brown eyebrows contracted.

"Lizzie-lady gone," she stated emphatically. "Momma say. I like Lizzie-lady."

"Your regard does you honor," Sheather said solemnly. "Do you know when Lizzie-lady left this place?"

The face puckered again, eyes misting in thought. Sheather stood respectfully, awaiting the outcome of thought.

"Dilly!" That voice was older, sharper. Sheather took his attention from the eggling and discovered a woman bearing down upon him, the child, and the door.

Straight to the eggling rushed the woman, bending to snatch her hand, then snapping upright with such force the child was jerked an inch or two off the soft concrete.

"How many times do I have to tell you not to talk to strangers?" the woman asked the child, her irritation and anger plain to Sheather's ears.

"The eggling did me a service," he said. The woman's eyes flicked to him and she went back a step, taking the child with her. "I am in possession of a message for Angela Lizardi and the eggling tells me she is away from home. Might you know the day upon which she is expected to return?"

The woman blinked, jerking the child close to her side. "Liz left sudden a couple days ago. Sent me a note to keep an eye on the place. We used to watch each other's places, back when I first come onto this street. Liz traveled more back then. Where she went this time or when she's coming back . . ." The woman shook her head, backing away another step. "She didn't say. None of my business. All she asked was to keep an eye on the place."

"I understand," Sheather stated, remembering to moderate his voice. "It is not my intention to call you from your duty. I am . . . sorry . . . not to have met Angela Lizardi at home. Perhaps I shall find her at home another day."

The woman frowned, thrusting the eggling as far behind her as possible while still maintaining a firm grip on her hand. "If I was you and I wanted to get a message to Liz, I'd go to Soldier's Hall and leave word there. Chances are she'll have given them someplace to find her."

"Thank you," said Sheather, inclining his head. "Your suggestion has merit."

"Glad I could help," the woman said and abruptly spun, snatched the eggling into her arms and dashed hastily down the walk.

Sheather paused to review his actions, but could identify nothing in his conversation or stance that might have suggested danger to the woman. Still, he conceded, where the safety of an eggling was the stake, it behooved an adult to be seven-times prudent.

Soldier's Hall, now. He felt he understood the location of that building, on the other side of the city. He would first go to his brother Edger and report these happenings outside the home-place of Angela Lizardi. Most especially would he report the Elder Door and the wise eggling. And then the two of them might walk out into the coolth of Lufkit's evening and seek Soldier's Hall together.

EROB'S HOLD

PRACTICE GROUNDS

Nelirikk emerged from the luxury of the autodoc healed, well-feeling and clean-faced, but for the *nchaka* and a startling bristle of silky brown hair sprouting between nose and mouth. The hair of his head had likewise sprouted from the soldier's crop he had worked so hard to maintain to a softly curling mop fully four fingers long.

As he scraped the stubble from his chin with the razor General Stores had provided, along with leather clothing such as he had seen others wearing, he studied this new face in the mirror.

The eyes—dark blue, surrounded by short, thick lashes—were as always, startling in the naked expanse of his face. The *nchaka*—that was comfort, though it was barely more than a beige thread in the unrelieved brown of exposed flesh. The beard, the self-same beard that had plagued his face for all of twenty-five Cycles, was a comfort. By the time he finished shaving, he thought he might recognize himself, were he to come upon a reflection unaware.

One Winston—a soldier old in war, as Nelirikk read him—arrived as he was finishing the breakfast that had been brought to him and for an hour it was drill—signals, emblems, insignia and call signs—until the old soldier announced himself satisfied.

"That's fine. You keep that hard to mind, now, hear me? Hate to have to shoot you 'cause you missed a call."

Mindful of his status as recruit, Nelirikk saluted as he had been shown. "Sir. I will not shame your teaching."

Winston laughed and waved a hand, already moving toward the door. "Hell, I ain't no 'sir,' boy. Just stay alive and keep Cap'n Redhead the same, and you done me all the honor I could want."

The door opened and Winston was gone; it stayed open to admit a technician and the scout. The technician pushed a gurney bearing a computer. The scout had a loop of cable over one shoulder.

"Explorer, I find you well?"

Nelirikk bowed, hand over heart, as he had seen the scout give to their captain, and answered in Terran, as he had been addressed.

"Scout, I am more well than I have been in many Cycles."

The little man nodded as the tech pushed the gurney against the wall, locked the wheels down and pulled out the keyboard.

"The med tech tells us that you were sadly undernourished. He took the liberty of injecting vitamins and supplemental nutrients." He smiled. "We are charged with 'feeding you up,' which directive I hope you see fit to take as an order."

He moved to the gurney. The tech took the cable, deftly made her connections and left with a nod to them both, uncoiling the cable as she went.

The door stayed open after she exited.

Nelirikk looked to the scout, but the scout was at the computer, touching the on-switch, nodding as the screen came live.

"I have constructed a program," he murmured, "as the captain directed. Attend me, if you please."

Nelirikk came forward and stood at the scout's right hand, marveling again at the other's seeming frailty. Yet he had fought like a soldier, winning through to his goal despite the logic that said he was too small to prevail.

One thin hand moved on the keypad. The screen flashed and Terran words formed.

"You will be given a question. Two consecutive returns signals an end to your answer. Should a point require clarification, you will be prompted. When all is made clear, you will be given another question." He looked up, green eyes bright.

"Questions and prompts are in Terran, to aid you in perfecting your grasp of that tongue. Should it be required, a touch of the query key, here, will bring up a rendering of the same question in Trade."

"I understand," Nelirikk said, around the chill in his belly. The man beside him tipped his head.

"Shall you honor your oath, Nelirikk Explorer?" he asked, of a sudden in the Liaden High Tongue. "Or is it that you believe I shall not honor mine?"

Nelirikk took a breath. "Scout, it will take many days to empty me entirely, no matter how clever your program."

"So it would," the scout said in brisk Terran. "However, the captain cannot spare you from your duty for many days. You are required to report to her at evening arms practice. In the meantime, this is your duty and I will leave you to it. After you have given me your recall code."

Nelirikk stood for a moment, then forced himself to move over to the place where his pack lay beside the shameful rifle. He had sworn, he reminded himself, as he reached inside and removed the recall beacon. He had sworn, and the Troop had sent him to die, which was the least of the Troop's sins against him.

Yet, it was as hard as anything he had done in his life, to pull the beacon out and lay it in the fragile hand of a man of the race of the enemy.

The scout received the beacon with a bow, green eyes solemn.

"Battle-duty, Explorer. I do not ask you to forgive it. I only say that I would not require it of you, for less than the lives which must be preserved."

The understanding of an arms-mate, from one who was no soldier? Nelirikk felt something in him ease, and he nodded in the Terran manner.

"I hear you. It is no shame, that a soldier fight as a soldier must." He drew a breath. "You will wish to know the place," he said, and rummaged in the pack once more for the captured map.

"Here," he said, unfolding it on the floor between them. The scout knelt down to see where his finger pointed, studied the area and nodded—nodded again as Nelirikk recited the procedure for sounding the recall.

"I shall contrive," he said, rising lightly to his meager height. "And now I shall leave you to your duty, and attend mine. I advise you—as a comrade—be on time to the captain."

A bow without flourish and he vanished through the open doorway. Nelirikk cinched the pack, picked up the useless rifle and walked over to that tempting portal. The small stone room beyond was empty, though there was doubtless a sentry outside the door in the right-hand wall. Still, a blow from the rifle would settle a sentry and gain him a working firearm.

The rifle was heavy in his hand. He had sworn, by Jela. And the Troop had sent him uselessly to die.

Nelirikk walked back inside the larger room, lay the rifle next to the pack and carried a packing crate over to the computer. He sat down, adjusted the height of keyboard and screen, read the first question, and began to type.

"OK," Miri told her troops. "Dismissed. Arms drill in an hour."

The vets she'd inherited—a couple 'falks, like Winston, who'd asked for the patrol, and a handful of others who had been separated from their units by the invasion—swung on out toward the mess tent like they'd just had a nap instead of a twenty mile hike. The greenies mooched out considerably slower, a couple walking like their feet hurt. Which, Miri conceded, they probably did.

In point of fact, her own back hurt from the unaccustomed weight of a full equipment pack, rifle and comm. But she stood tall until the last of the Irregulars was out of sight before sighing and reaching for the straps.

"Tired, cha'trez?" His voice was in her ear, his hands taking the weight of the pack as she eased it down.

"Tell you what it is," she said, as his hands settled on her shoulders, "I got soft."

"Ah," Val Con replied, comprehensively. His fingers were kneading gently, finding and smoothing the knots in her muscles, apparently by instinct. Miri sighed and bent her head forward. He rubbed the back of her neck.

"Gods, that's good. Don't get carried away, though. I wanna be alert when I introduce your pet Yxtrang to his unit."

"*Our* pet Yxtrang," he corrected, softly. She felt him shift balance, and then shivered with pleasure as he ran his tongue around the edge of her ear.

"Watch that stuff. I'm an officer."

"So am I." He nipped her earlobe lightly, hands pressing her waist.

Miri sighed, savoring the sensation a second longer, then slowly straightened. Val Con released her immediately, though she seemed to feel a moment of wistful lust, echoing and enforcing her own feelings, just before she turned to face him.

"Got more ways than a kitten, don'cha?" She smiled, reached out to touch his cheek, tracing the line of the scar.

"If the captain pleases."

"Big joke," she said mournfully, shaking her head. "Now, I think the new addition to the family is just as respectful as he oughta be. Do you good to watch how he carries on."

"I assure you, I intend to watch how he carries on very carefully, indeed."

She cocked her head. "Hey, you were the guy took his oath and sponsored him into the Irregulars. *Now* you got second thoughts?"

"Say rather that I do not dice with my lady's life. Nelirikk undertakes no easy thing here. To completely cut himself off from his people, his culture, his language? Worse, to give an oath of service and go to live among the enemy, the most of whom see him as an object to be vilified, hated, and feared?" He shook his head.

"Wishing only to honor his oath, yet he may fail of it."

Miri stared at him. "So you figure he'll crack quick?"

"I figure," Val Con said, taking her hand and beginning to walk slowly in the direction of the mess tent, "that the luck has favored us, in that Nelirikk has been so badly used by his people. I take him for a man who possesses a strong and innate sense of Balance, else he would never have allowed himself to be persuaded to that oath. If we are clever, and give him what he starves for—work, discipline, and respect—we may yet preserve him."

Miri chewed on that awhile as they continued their meander across the grass. "How come you're so interested in this guy? I know you said you owe him, but there's something more than that, ain't there?"

There was a small silence. "This *Jela* whom Nelirikk swears by—he of the neck-jewel?"

She nodded.

"One of the founders of Clan Korval was Cantra yos'Phelium's partner, a man named Jela, who had been a soldier. It is Jela's Tree that our clan watches over, in fulfillment of an oath he had from Cantra to keep it safe, should he fall. My study of Korval's Diaries inclines me to believe that Nelirikk's Jela is that identical soldier."

"Oh."

Diaries from a time before Terra had space. A soldier in the family who happened to have the same name as some Yxtrang war-leader. A tree which was paid the courtesy of a bow and a promise to recall it to its parent. Miri sighed to herself.

He believes every word of it, Robertson. Look at the man's pattern. He might be crazy, but he ain't lying.

"So what's that make you?" she asked, as they approached the mess tent. "Cousins?"

He smiled and squeezed her hand lightly. "More like students of the same master."

She let him see her sigh this time. "OK," she said. "We'll give the man his shot."

"Thank you, cha'trez," Val Con murmured, dropping her hand and allowing her to preceed him into the tent. "And remember, I will be watching."

•   •   •

The vets arrived on the field first, took their places and composed themselves to wait for the newbies to straggle in and sort themselves into lines.

A tall figure strode smartly across the field, straight up to where Miri stood near the situation board, Val Con at her back.

"Reporting for duty, Captain." Nelirikk snapped a sharp salute, now he had the merc way of it. Not only that, he was on time—not late, not early. *On time*.

Bland-faced, she took his salute, then walked around him as she had the first time, with him nothing but blood, sweat, and nerves and looking as much like a street brawler as a soldier.

Today, leathers gleaming and boots glowing, he was clearly a soldier. His utility belt held its pouch and the knife he had used in the fight with Val Con, enclosed in a battered but well-oiled sheath. He stood at attention like he meant it, eyes front while she completed her leisurely circuit.

He was big, but totally lacking the exuberant massiveness that characterized Jase Carmody. Nelirikk, Miri thought, lived private. His eyes might give him away. Maybe.

Without the tattoos, his face was ordinary: two eyes, a nose, a mouth, and a decidedly square jaw. The rapid-grown hair was sandy brown and wavy. The mustache was a sandy brown brush over the thin unsmiling mouth.

Circuit done, she crossed her arms and looked up at him.

"Explorer. Is your kit complete?"

"If the captain pleases. I have not a side arm."

"I see that. Anything else missing?"

"No, Captain."

"Enough ration-bars for your needs?"

"If the captain pleases. I am not informed of a mission. The kit and rations are more than adequate for general use."

Miri nodded. "Can you march in those boots today?"

"Yes, Captain."

"Could you march in them again tomorrow?"

"Yes, Captain."

What she did then was probably as stupid as anything Val Con'd done on behalf of this man, but she didn't question the right of it. A soldier who didn't have a sidearm was no soldier at all. Nelirikk, a pro, would know that, right down in his gut.

"Think you can work with the quartermaster?"

The tiniest flicker of surprise at the back of those careful blue eyes. "Yes, Captain."

"Good. After arms practice, you'll draw a sidearm and ammo."

"Yes, Captain."

"All right," Miri said, flicking a look over the field. The lines were formed now, soldiers at field rest. Time for class.

"Consider yourself on duty. And remember to draw extra protein and a second dessert at mess. Orders from the head med tech."

"Yes, Captain."

She marched forward, Nelirikk at her shoulder. Val Con took his usual place, a little off to the side of the main action, and stood there, bland-faced and perfectly calm. His pattern, when she looked at it, displayed some interesting tensions, but no real alarm. He was watching, like he'd said. Aware of the possibility of danger.

"All right, Irregulars," she called out over a field that was suddenly very quiet, indeed. "This is Beautiful. He's my aide and he'll be assisting in today's hand to hand drill. Squads count off by threes and—"

"That is an Yxtrang!"

Oh, hell, Miri thought, locating the miscreant. jin'Bardi. Of course it *would* be jin'Bardi. Man hadn't given her a minute's peace since he'd showed up at Erob's in the first wave of refugees from the city. Worst part was, when he put his mind to it, he could soldier.

"No chatter!" Reynolds, that was, a vet from Higdon's Howlers, and, like the rest of the vets, strawboss to a double-dozen newbies. jin'Bardi, predictably, ignored him.

"I say that thing is an Yxtrang, Captain! Do you deny it?"

Miri glared him down the field, which didn't do much good, jin'Bardi being a mean-tempered somebody, and answered, voice level and pitched to carry to the last soldiers on the field.

"I say this man is an Irregular, mister. Report for kitchen

duty after arms practice." She looked out over the quiet field. "Count off."

"And I say no!" jin'Bardi left his place and ran toward her. She felt Val Con shift—stopped him with a shoulder-twitch.

"At ease, Beautiful."

"That is not a man!" jin'Bardi yelled, voice echoing over the field. "And if you think that it is, you are not fit to lead this unit!"

You damn fool, Miri thought at jin'Bardi. The vets exchanged glances among themselves, and Winston took the lead.

"Now, see, among us real mercs, there's a tradition, kinda, where if somebody don't like the way the captain's leading, they can go hand-to-hand and whoever wins, their opinion wins, too. I ain't especially advising you to try that against Cap'n Redhead. What I'm advising for you is to take the fifty years kitchen patrol you just earned, and get back in line so's we can drill."

He paused and looked around the field, his gaze crossing Miri's for an instant. One eyelid flicked in a wink.

"I ain't got no problem with Beautiful joining up. Fact, I'm glad to have him. Can always tell a real soldier by the way he keeps himself, and shows proper respect to command."

The tension was easing out of the field—or it would have if jin'Bardi hadn't chosen that particular moment to sing out, loud and clear: "Fine, then! I challenge the captain here and now to hand-to-hand combat."

Miri sighed wearily, sensing rather than seeing Val Con drifting in from the sidelines. Beautiful stood at her back, at ease like she'd told him. She hoped.

"jin'Bardi, you got a deathwish?"

"Afraid to fight me, Captain?"

"In your dreams." Damn the man. Nothing for it, now. "Troops!" she shouted across the field. "Form a circle."

She unbuckled her belt and handed it to Beautiful, who slung it over his right shoulder, which, by a fascinating coincidence placed her side arm in position for a reasonably quick draw. He folded her battle-jacket carefully and placed it between his feet.

jin'Bardi stripped off his belt and jacket and looked around, but nobody was offering to hold them. He dumped the jacket onto the ground, belt on top.

The circle had formed to include Beautiful. Winston was on one side of him, Miri noticed. Reynolds was on the other. Val Con was on the far side of the circle, not quite directly opposite Beautiful. She hoped he had sense enough not to interfere with this one. There really wasn't any need for him to be concerned. She could take jin'Bardi hand-to-hand. The problem was going to be remembering not to kill him.

In the center of the circle, she turned to face jin'Bardi.

"Beautiful!" she called out. "Give the mark."

"Mark in three, Captain. One Captain. Two Captain. Three."

jin'Bardi came in fast, like she'd known he would, trying to startle her into a stumble. She sidestepped, got a foot around his ankle and a hand under his elbow and let him do most of the work of flipping himself onto his back.

He hit hard, but came up in a quick snarl of motion, and was heading back, low this time, and it wasn't until he was right on her that she saw the telltale gleam.

She twisted and at least he knew better than to lead with the knife. She countered with a move Val Con had taught her, dancing away, feinting in with a kick, tempting the knife.

And jin'Bardi, the idiot, took the bait.

It was quick, then. She slapped the knife away and gave him a ride over her shoulder, slamming him flat. The air went out of him with an audible *whoosh* and while he was seeing stars, she spun, grabbed the knife, and spun back, pinning his arms with her knees, and put the edge under his ear until she saw the first drop of blood and real fear in jin'Bardi's eyes.

"Give me one reason why I shouldn't cut your stupid throat!"

He stared up at her, and it was terror, now, and she kept the knife snug, wanting to be sure he was going to remember today's lesson for the rest of his life. No matter how short it was.

"If the captain pleases." The recruit's voice was near and respectful.

Now what? "Permission to speak."

"Thank you, Captain. This fighter shows potential of becoming a skilled soldier, with training."

Mithras, give me strength.

"You offering to take him on, Beautiful? Whip him into shape?"

"If the captain pleases. For the good of the troop."

jin'Bardi's eyes were showing a lot of white. His face was an interesting sort of greenish-gold color and wet with sweat. Miri leaned close, talking real quiet.

"I'm going to move the knife, jin'Bardi, and then I'm going to stand up and back away three paces. Then you're going to stand up and present yourself to Beautiful. Vary, and you're meat. Are we clear?"

"Clear, Captain," he managed, sounding pretty hoarse. He swallowed. "I yield," he added. High Liaden.

"You bet," she returned in Terran, and took the knife away.

She rose, backed away and stood holding the knife while he climbed painfully to his feet and walked over to where the big man stood between Winston and Reynolds, his face impassive.

jin'Bardi was shaking and he must've been hurting, but give him credit, he walked right up to Nelirikk and saluted.

Nelirikk didn't move. "It is proper discipline to thank the captain for a valuable lesson."

There was a moment of utter stillness from jin'Bardi. The circle waited. In her head, Val Con's pattern was cold, watchful, and stringently calm.

Slowly, jin'Bardi turned and bowed. "Thank you, Captain, for a valuable lesson."

"No problem," she said and looked up at Beautiful. "Take this guy to the medics and have them check him out, then report back here. Give my stuff to Winston."

"Yes, Captain." A salute. Her belt and jacket changed hands and Beautiful moved back from the circle. jin'Bardi, shoulders slumping, began to follow, was stopped by a raised palm.

"It is proper discipline," Beautiful stated, remorselessly unemotional, "to take leave of the captain."

Once again, jin'Bardi turned, made the effort and straightened his shoulders, snapped a salute. "Captain."

She nodded. The two of them moved away and the circle began to come apart. Miri walked forward.

As he came even with the situation board, jin'Bardi abruptly spun. "I want my knife back!"

Nelirikk stopped. "If the captain pleases," he coached, "may I have my weapon."

Miri stopped, feeling the weight of the thing in her hand, and something tickling at the edge of her mind. The balance was good . . .

"You want this?" she snapped.

"Yes," jin'Bardi snapped back and that quick the knife reversed itself and she threw.

The knife tumbled in the air, traveling fast, much too fast for jin'Bardi to have time to move. The blade passed so close to his cheek it seemed to glide over the skin, then buried itself deep in the situation board, a lock of his hair pinned tight.

"Say 'thank you, Captain,'" Nelirikk directed into the absolute stillness that followed the knife's *thunk*, "'for returning my weapon.'"

jin'Bardi licked his lips. "Thank you, Captain," he said faintly, "for returning my weapon."

After a moment, Nelirikk reached over and pulled the knife from the board. He offered it, hilt first, to the shaking Liaden.

"Soldier, your weapon. Inspect it for damage as we walk to the medical center."

Around her, she started to hear buzzes as the Irregulars shook themselves back into normal mode. Miri turned, caught Val Con's eye and decided she'd worry about where she'd learned how to throw a knife like that later.

"All right!" she shouted, over the growing noise. "Squads count off by three for hand-to-hand drill! Double-time!"

LIAD

DEPARTMENT OF INTERIOR
COMMAND HEADQUARTERS

The operative commissioned to discover what na-
ture of mishap had destroyed Tyl Von sig'Alda's ship, inno-
cently in orbit about the busy world of Waymart, had filed
her report.

Despite that this document directly contravened several
apparently known facts, Commander of Agents readily accepted the operative's assertion that no such ship had been in
orbit about Waymart during the span of days designated in
the search grid, nor had such a ship exploded upon the day,
hour, and nanosecond also named. The operative expressed
herself quite certain of these things.

Commander of Agents ordered the operative to her immediate superior for deep questioning under the drug, but it was
a formality. He believed her report, utterly. Oh, certainly, he
had the raw data received from the hidden transmitter upon
sig'Alda's ship, as well as his own excellent memory of
event. Mere facts.

And facts, as any Agent knows well, are open to manipulation.

Seated behind his desk in the room of chronometers, Commander of Agents indulged in fantasy.

Tyl Von sig'Alda, the fairy tale went, had not departed the

world of Vandar. Indeed, let it be that he had died there, during that brief period in which his ship had rested on world.

Val Con yos'Phelium, rogue Agent, having overpowered the man sent to return himself or his severed head to Headquarters, used the ship's key and lifted to orbit. There, he had not after all dawdled, but engaged himself in a fever of busyness, first seeking and then subverting the hidden beacon, the existence of which he would have easily deduced. That done, he had Jumped, but never, so Commander of Agents was willing to wager, for Waymart.

Or perhaps he had, as he was both subtle and intelligent.

In short, Commander of Agents concluded his fantasy, Val Con yos'Phelium could be anywhere in the galaxy, not excluding the hallway outside his Commander's door.

A peculiarly unnerving conceit, that.

It would all, of course, need to be checked.

With a feeling not unlike dread, Commander of Agents leaned forward and touched the switch that would summon his second to him.

A team of Agents, so he considered, in the few moments before that efficient person appeared. Certainly, a team of Agents to Vandar, to discover the whereabouts of Tyl Von sig'Alda, or the manner of his death. What else? How might they now discover a hint to Val Con yos'Phelium's thought, a clue that might point to his ultimate destination?

"You summoned me, Commander?" His second bowed and then stood silent.

Commander of Agents stirred, issued his orders regarding the team and the maximum priority mission they were to undertake. His second bowed. "There is something else?"

Where? Where might he go, whose clan, save one, was scattered to the Prime Points? What cause might move him more strongly? Balance? Or the safety of his kin? What reason might be read into random action? Which actions were deliberately random? Which only mimed chaos, with cold reason as the lodestone?

Where would he go, with all the galaxy to choose from?

"Dispatch a team to Jelaza Kazone," Commander of Agents said to his second. "I do not wish Anthora yos'Galan to depart her clanhouse just now. Contain her, first. If necessary, detain her."

His second bowed. It would be done.

"Also," Commander of Agents said, hearing himself with something akin to astonishment. "The raw data regarding the Terran female. Robertson. Have that sent to me here, Commander's Priority."

Again, his second bowed. "At once, Commander."

LIAD

JELAZA KAZONE

It was late when she closed the old book and re-
turned it to its place among its fellows. That done, she
stretched, hands high over her head, feet above the floor,
chair tipped nearly horizontal. For the count of ten, she held
the position, taut, every muscle straining. On eleven, she
went abruptly limp, breath exploding outward in a "hah!"
that echoed along the metal walls.

The chair snapped back to vertical and she laughed, using
one hand to push the wild tumble of dark hair up out of her
face. The other hand she held negligently downward, palm
out, fingers curled in silent summons at the comb that had
deserted its duty and now lay on the floor three feet beyond
her languid grasp.

Thus summoned, the comb flew to her hand. She used it to
anchor the hastily twisted knot of her hair, fingers lingering
along the satiny wood. This was a precious object—carved
by Daav yos'Phelium, Val Con's true-father, to adorn the
hair of his own dear lady. It had come to Anthora on her
halfling nameday, given by Val Con. Thus, the gift was
thrice precious and it was the ornament she wore most often.

She stretched again, somewhat less heroically and accompanied by a yawn, then gently came erect. Youngest of the

yos'Galans, she had inherited the full body of their Terran mother without the height necessary to satisfactorily complete the effect. Still, she was of Korval, and a pilot of the line, light on her feet and elegant in her bearing.

She turned now, spinning a graceful circle, and called aloud, "Lord Merlin? Come, sir. We walk and then we sleep."

Her voice came back from the metal walls, deep and nappy as velvet, with a ring that glittered off the edge of the ear and might, after all, have been the walls.

From somewhere down within the books came a "Mmer-wef!" and the thump of something solid striking carpet. A moment later, a rather large gray cat sauntered 'round the edge of a shelf and looked up at her out of round golden eyes.

Anthora smiled and moved toward the door, the cat flowing along at her ankle. He waited patiently while she worked the pressure-latch and followed her into the paneled hallway, then waited again while she canceled the lighting and sealed the library tight.

Duty done, the cat and the woman walked down the hallway and out into the inner garden.

The garden was lit by star-shine—well enough for one who knew the way. Anthora walked slowly, savoring the night air, cool with the scent of growing things. Down and 'round the path she walked, til she came to the center, the heart-place, of the garden, and here she left the path, and moved across the moss to lay her hand against Jelaza Kazone, Jela's Fulfillment, known to the World as Korval's Tree.

"Good evening, Elder," she murmured, and felt her palm grow warm, where it lay against the bark. She breathed deeply of the cool, minty scent and leaned back, settling her shoulders comfortably. At her feet, in a vee made by two shallow roots, Merlin tucked himself, front feet under his chest, golden eyes slits of satisfaction.

In the minty dark, Anthora closed her eyes. Purposefully, she filled her lungs with the scented air, Jelaza Kazone warming her back through the house tunic she wore. Slowly, as if of their own volition, her hands rose, palms vulnerable to the stars.

Anthora opened her Inner Eyes across the dazzle of the galaxy and in nightly ritual, began to count.

There, the cool flame that was Nova, blurred by the veiling of hyperspace. And, there—Shan, warm as a hug. Through him, less Seen than extrapolated, Anthora found Priscilla. And there—there was Cousin Pat Rin, aloof, as ever.

It was a foolish ritual in its way, there being no aid she might send to those so distant, should she find them in distress. She lived in no little dread, who was considered the heedless one, of the night she might count one frail candle missing and nothing she could do to recover the flame.

Still, she persisted, taking comfort where it was offered—and so far tonight she had counted four—Nova, Shan, Priscilla, Pat Rin—safe, for now, and treasured.

So, onward. She took another deliberately deep breath and cast her mind out once more. Val Con . . . She found him, his flame brilliant as before the Wrongness, which Anthora now knew was named the Department of Interior, and at his shoulder a bonfire, which was Miri-his-lifemate, whom Anthora had yet to embrace in a sister's welcome.

Well enough, six, and herself made seven. She brought her thought toward an easier goal, touched the children—Quin, Padi, Syl Vor, Mik and Shindi—and Great-aunt Kareen yos'Phelium, and Cousin Luken bel'Tarda, bright, all bright, in their safeplaces, then took deeper breath and flung her mind wider still.

She had first noted this one during her pregnancy with the twins. In that heightened state of power, it had been as plain to her as a comet on the horizon. Now, it was the glitter of a jeweled pinhead, sometimes sensed, sometimes seen, and sometimes lost entirely in the clamor of the worlds intervening. Tonight, she thought she would miss it, then caught a flash of its unique glitter, at the extreme edge of her ability to read.

There was no name to put to this tiny gem of flame, yet she welcomed it as she welcomed the flames of her named and known kin and dreaded its loss as nearly.

So then, of adults, counted and known, nine. Of children, the full complement of five. Clan Korval, numbering precisely fourteen, from the eldest to the youngest. The warmth at her back grew briefly warmer and Anthora smiled as she lowered her hands.

Fifteen, of course. One did not discount the Tree.

But even with the Tree, it did seem few—very few, indeed. No skill that lay to her hand would reveal the number of those who hunted them—but she guessed them to be far in excess of—fifteen.

She opened her eyes and stepped away from the Tree, but without the spring of joy the counting of her kin most usually gave her. Instead, she bade the Tree good evening in a tone that was nearly somber, and went softly across the mossy carpet to the paved path, where she paused and glanced back.

"Lord Merlin?"

The cat opened his eyes, stood, stretched and sauntered to her, stropping once against her leg before preceding her down the path, to the house and bed.

Quickly, he discovered the joy of having too much to do.

It was made quite clear that he was to be the captain's shadow and bodyguard, and to perhaps carry extra communication equipment if required. He was then a specialist attached to the captain by her order, outside the ordinary line of command.

There were times during the day when he was ordered to this place or that to return with a map or disk or perhaps a bottle of something, and there were times when he stood watch duty as was his right.

He knew, too, that he never stood watch alone—and that was understood as well.

At first, the scout was always within range, the Captain's Blade, as Nelirikk came to consider him, ready to slay any who might harm her. Gradually, the scout became less evident—was then missing entirely, sent here and there by the captain's word—or by the word of those others, of higher command.

He met with those others—Commander Carmody, who proved himself an astute and cunning officer, and an elderly Liaden who was made known to him as "General," a patriarch of the captain's clan—as well as seniors of mercenaries and house guard.

By Yxtrang standards they were woefully understaffed in the mid- and low-level officers, but truth known, they were fighters and not functionaries.

They asked him fact and opinion, numbers and names, battle plans and supply schemes. He told straightforward, and after a short time he understood they were not threatening when they asked "What makes you think that?" or "Why would that be the case?"

In short, they treated him as he had not been treated since his days of exploration: as if he had a mind as well as eyes. He spent more time with the AI computer: its questions were wonderfully complex, and his respect for the scout grew wider.

When he was not with the captain or in mess, he found it difficult not to be doing things. He studied as well as he could, spending hours in serious contemplation of colors and their meanings. And, on the midnight that the scout and half-a-dozen veteran soldiers awaited what transport the Yxtrang should send to retrieve one they would rather had died, he began his dedication gift to the troop.

The command of the combined Terran and Liaden forces headquartered here now knew much of what he knew, Nelirikk thought, as he carefully plied needle and thread. They knew and in the process of laying all before them, he had discovered truth. And in truth, after so many Cycles of bitterness, he found a certain peace.

The 14th Conquest Corps had quite liberally interpreted the orders it had received. He'd heard the rumor—and since none feared a no-troop, whose word was nothing but sound—he'd heard it in numerous places.

The 14th Conquest Corps had determined to treat the target of a long-planned multi-Corps invasion as a Target of Opportunity. It was a bold move, born of the intelligence that the target world was in upheaval. It was a move that—if successful—would advance the 14th to leadership over the 15th and 16th after too dismal a turn as back-up and support auxiliaries.

So, the 14th was reaching hard, straining for glory. Rather

than take one continent fully and await the 15th, it had gone for both of the large ones. The need, after all, was to own the planet when the other units arrived.

If the 14th merely fell short of its boldness—took one continent, but not both—the 15th would likely land troops and claim the victory for its own, relegating the 14th once again to back-up.

However, if the 14th were defeated . . .

Could such soldiers as he had seen here defeat the 14th Conquest Corps?

Nelirikk considered that, snipping and sewing in the night-time camp.

The Irregulars—his home troop—held a number of strengths: Its captain was war-wise and intelligent, neither over-bold nor underconfident. The scout was a strength, as the captain's near advisor, as trainer in hand-to-hand, and as fabricator of weird devices of surprising effectiveness. The unit contained perhaps twenty such as Winston, old in soldiering and canny in the field.

That many of the Irregulars were raw—was weakness. Their overall numbers were, also, a weakness, but balancing that was the accumulated experience of the senior officers and the fact that the Yxtrang general had not yet had time to secure more than a foothold on either continent as a base.

The 14th, Nelirikk considered, at last laying down his needle and stretching out on his cot, might well find itself with a war on its hands.

He woke abruptly, aware of some change too subtle to name, opened his eyes and saw the scout—a thin shadow against the dimness in his quarters—cross-legged and at ease on the locker at the foot of the cot.

The thrill of the discovery lay in its message. The scout was indeed *that* skilled. It was an honor to be aligned with such a man.

"I regret," Nelirikk said to the silent shadow, in Trade, for that was the language of the troop, "that my current position makes a salute awkward, Scout Commander."

"A salute is out of order in the present moment. I come

as—comrade, let us say—for your former comrades have proven themselves unworthy of the honor." The scout spoke his piece in Yxtrang.

Nelirikk felt a strange stir. Was this good news or bad? If the ambush had been successful then—

"I was within view of the site designated some time prior to the appointed hour. I remained twelve twelves of ticks beyond. There was no sound, Explorer. No sighting."

Shame was a rush of adrenaline that brought him upright on the cot. "By Jela, for a knife to cut their throats! They—"

"They used your drop-off as a recon run. I suspect they even now listen for radio reports to determine how far you might have come before being beset." This was in Terran. The captain had warned him of this—that he would need to "think lively" if he were to follow conversation between herself and the scout.

There was a moment of silence, then in Liaden came a sentence spoken as if it were Yxtrang, hard-edged and short.

"We speak now of Jela, whom you claim as near-clan."

Nelirikk went still, looking carefully at the shadowed scout.

"If I have offended, I would know why. Jela's Troop was always honorable."

"Indeed," the little man said quietly. "I am pleased to know that. For you should know that my clan is respected, my house among the oldest on Liad. We are generally accounted honorable, if misguided. The name of my house—and of the tree which stands over it—is Jelaza Kazone."

The Liaden words swept by and it took him a moment to register the under sounds. Running them past his inner ear once more, Nelirikk shook his head, Terran-wise.

"I cannot make whole what you tell me, Scout," he said, "other than your house name is similar to Jela's."

"No. Not an accident. Not merely similar. The house is Jelaza Kazone." There was a pause then, and a shift in language:

"In Terran it becomes 'Jela's fulfillment' or, perhaps, 'Jela's promise.'"

The language shifted again, without strain: "Trade might

have it as 'Jela's contract' or 'Jela's dream,' depending on the speaker and how they think of Korval."

The scout went back to Liaden, the sentence spoken with inexorable exactness: "As I say, Explorer-bound-to-Korval, my family, Clan Korval, is accounted honorable by many, and we of the blood still live in the house first-built by Jela's arms-partner and bed-mate, Cantra yos'Phelium. Our motto is *I Dare*."

The words echoed, found their match in the language of the Troop, and Nelirikk heard his own voice, chanting the campfire tale from his youth:

"And when Jela had faced this challenge, and made his dozen upon the day, a soldier called out from the ranks, 'How do you dare this, small soldier, when one rush could take you down?'

"Jela shrugged, and smiled, and with knife in sheath and empty hands shown all around, said, 'I dare because I must. Who will dare for me, if I dare not dare for myself?' "

Nelirikk sat quietly, recalling the fierceness of the struggle between himself and the scout—and the irony of it. That two of Jela's own should contend so! And who but the smallest should win? He laughed, softly, in the dark.

He sobered then, recalling things that the Troop did not know—or did not tell.

"Did Jela die on Liad, then?"

"Alas," said the scout, as sober as if the death had been yesterday. "Jela took one too many rear-guard, permitting his partner and her ship to escape. That, after all, was the essence of their agreement: he to guard the ship so the Tree might win through, she to guard the Tree, should he fall.

"She came away with his son-to-be-born and the very Tree that stands above my house. The tree here—Erob's large tree—is a seedling sent to seal the alliance between our two houses. And I must thank you for the Jela story, for it is not one we have in the Diaries."

"Diaries?" Nelirikk felt hunger lick through him. To read Jela's own words? "Jela's diaries?"

"Not precisely, though some of the log entries are surely in his hand. Jela's last years were spent with the space captain, my ancient grandmother. In her logs and diary she wrote down much wisdom, some her own and some his. The delms of Korval have kept the Diaries up, and study of them is part of each clanmember's education, so we do not forget that which must be recalled."

It was then that the scout offered treasure.

"Should we find ourselves able to leave here and return to Jelaza Kazone I will undertake to show what I may of Jela, if you like. The first diary entry of him, and the tree he carried out of a desert far, far away."

Seated as he was, Nelirikk contrived to bow. "A boon I would count it."

The scout inclined his head. "As it is in my power, Explorer."

There was not much to say then. Eventually, the scout stood, bowed formally and with meaning entirely too fine to be read properly in the available light, and slipped silently into the night.

DUTIFUL PASSAGE

IN JUMP

Primary operations had been moved to the reserve bridge. Priscilla, in charge of Second Team, was at station on the main—no, Shan corrected himself—on the trade bridge. He gritted his teeth and ran the board checks with a thoroughness they scarcely required, since it was the third check he'd initiated within the last half-hour.

The mood on the reserve bridge was of tension harnessed into purpose. The mood of the captain was of frantic worry degenerating into terror.

Shan closed his eyes, deliberately removing himself from board-drill and bridge, and ran the Healer's mental exercise for distance under duress and calmness under calamity.

He sighed once, centered in an unruffled crystalline pool, then opened his eyes again to the reserve bridge.

Or the "war bridge" as Uncle Daav had used to call it— most likely to tease Shan's father. Shan's recollection of Daav yos'Phelium was sparse, and memory's eyes had lately tried to translate the barely remembered features into Val Con's well-known and beloved face.

Val Con, who they were to meet at Lytaxin. Val Con, who would be delm—and quickly, it was to be hoped, so he might sort this mess they found themselves in and show the clan its enemy.

Val Con, who had supposedly killed a man to gain his spaceship, who had warned Shan away from "appalling danger" while the *Passage* was being rigged for death—

"We break Jump within the twelve, Captain," Ren Zel said quietly from second board, and Shan pushed all such thoughts away, even the growing fear that Val Con had not managed his murder, and was himself dead on some backworld—aye, and his lifemate buried with him.

"I have the mark," he told Ren Zel. "Prime to me, second string through four toggled in sequence. Courier boat thirteen is cleared to depart the instant we break—your call, pilot."

Ren Zel flashed a look over-full with dark surprise, then inclined his head. "Captain."

"Trade bridge standing by, Captain," Priscilla's voice was calm as always, but the corner of the screen that should have contained her image was gray, gray, Jump gray.

"Acknowledge," he murmured. "Reserve bridge is sequenced backup boards two through four. Trade bridge should stand ready to take fifth string—captain's bridge?"

"Monitoring, Captain." Seth was as matter-of-fact as if they'd been discussing routine shuttle maintenance. Or as if he didn't know that matters would be very bad indeed by the time control of the ship shunted to the captain's bridge.

Ten seconds to break-out, by the countdown at the bottom right of the screen . . . nine . . . eight . . . seven . . .

There was no room now for silly worries; no room for anything but the weary, familiar, bone-known drill while the ship gave one last gasp around them and the gray screens shattered into stars and an alarm went bong and . . .

"Courier, hold!" Ren Zel commanded and the collision warning howled as the main screen filled with the image of the tumbling abandoned weapons pod . . .

"All shields!" Shan called out even as his hands slapped the toggles.

The screen flashed, blurred—and the ship shook as the tremendous energy of the explosion bathed the *Passage* in radiation so fierce the shields flared.

"Air loss, Captain," Priscilla reported from the trade bridge. "Pod dock holed—emergency seals on."

"Get it!" Shan commanded, scanning the gauges, shifting a finger to touch another control. "Tower. Rusty, what do we have?"

"Ears," came the laconic reply; "but not many. You're carrying lots of stuff in the shield fields, Captain, and it's blocking most incoming . . ."

The main screen showed a throbbing blue-green shimmer with an occasional lightning-like flash. Shan flicked a glance at the filtering gauge and nearly gasped at the energy required to dim the scintillations to this near-blinding brightness.

"Mother attend us!" Priscilla cried. "Shan—"

"I see it." He flicked toggles, shunting computer time to the analysis board, which gobbled every nanosecond greedily—and offered up a schematic of the problem: The pod's energy and remaining ionized mass was caught between the shield layers, trapping the ship within a hollow sphere of deadly energy. If that searing plasma touched the *Passage*—

"Ren Zel, cycle the outer shield down to 200 kilogauss if you please. I'll take the inner up as high as I dare—and then you'll cut entire. On my mark."

"Yes, Captain."

"Mark."

"Two, Captain. One, Captain. Half. Quarter. Tenth—down!"

Shan nodded, though Ren Zel was too busy to see, and phased the inner shield up. The maneuver was chancy, placing the lighter coils of the meteor shields at risk—but that was minor for the moment—

He felt it then, as would the rest of the crew: the grate of a piercing headache as the magnetic and other fields phased in, coursed through the controlled shield and leaked into the ship.

Shan grimaced and cut back, watching the main screen as he did, seeing the filtering levels falling, falling . . .

"Engineering, magnetics check. All nonessential crew, magnetics check!" Priscilla's voice cracked over general inship as Shan brought the shields to a more reasonable level and the remains of the weapons pod blew into space like the gaseous nebular remnant of a supernova.

"Air report!"

"Under control, Captain. The pod bay took a direct strike from debris—a twelve centimeter hole and twenty centimeters of fracture."

Shan shuddered. Debris coming through an armored pod door with that much force—he could have lost a dozen people!

"We've got a temporary patch up," Priscilla continued. "We can replace that whole wall with a modular fix once we're—"

"Position report, Captain. Tactical report, Captain." Ren Zel's voice betrayed nothing, pitched exactly loud enough to override Priscilla's report.

"Tactical?" Shan asked.

"Tactical," Ren Zel affirmed. "There are warships all over this system . . ."

"Tower here! Shan, this feed—" snapped Rusty, quickly followed by Liaden-accented Trade: ". . . system is under attack by Yxtrang. Repeat, this system is under attack by Yxtrang. All shipping be warned. Flee and bring aid. This message by order of Erob."

"That's from a booster transmitter somewhere about six hours out," Rusty said. "I—"

"Bastards! Got you now! Ah-*hah*! We got you now!"

"No chatter!" Shan called out against Seth's bloodthirsty glee, and looked to Ren Zel, who was coolly accessing the military files available to his key.

"Hold a moment, pilot," he said quietly. "I have additional information here."

IDs blossomed across the long-screen as he shunted the auxiliary files available to the captain and first mate.

What Shan noticed first was the battleship, flanked by two cruisers.

The second thing he noticed were the swarm of smaller vessels, in-system strike-ships, clustered around the dreadnought like bees around a teel blossom.

The portion of his mind not engaged on the level of sight nudged him into awareness that the feed from the system beacon was still coming through, and that he was hearing— music. Heartbreakingly familiar music.

Val Con had made it to Erob.

It was Priscilla who noticed the other thing, and who said it quietly, on private line from her station to his.

"They've landed on Lytaxin, Shan."

Shan nodded and leaned back in the pilot's chair.

"So they have, Priscilla," he said, staring at the tactical screen, where the blockade was outlined, ship by deadly ship, cutting the *Dutiful Passage* off from Val Con—and from Korval's future.

He sighed.

"So they have."

The annunciator sounded as Shan began the calculations necessary for the final definition of the secondary equation. He called "Come!" without taking notice of the fact and dove deeper into the beguiling intricacies of vector-graphs, real-time movement, gravitational fluctuations, relative mass ratios, velocity transfer rate, and the potentiality of random speed shift.

A spiraling approach such as the *Passage* was currently committed to was impossibly complicated even without an Yxtrang armada between them and the target planet, he thought hazily, manipulating factors of seven. The math comp suggested applying a factor of 267 to shift potential and he OKed that with a finger-tap.

Not that the Yxtrang had taken any particular note of the battleship in their midst, after an initial flutter of radio exclamation. It was to be expected, however, that they were reserving their most serious displeasure for the *Passage*'s closest approach, and if one extrapolated a grav-flux rate directly proportional to the movement of the primary natural satellite . . .

Equation framed, the computer announced some little time later. Shan blinked at the screen.

"So you say." He sighed and leaned back, calling up a Healer's relaxation drill to chase away the ache in shoulders and back.

"Well," he said to the computer, tapping the *go* key. "If you think you've got it framed, let's see it, don't be shy."

"Captain?"

"Eh?" He glanced up, blinked the larger room into focus, and blinked again as he discovered the figure of his foster son, perched uneasily on the edge of one of the two visitor's chairs across the desk.

"Hello, Gordy. I didn't hear you come in, but I expect I must have let you in, mustn't I? Math does such very odd things to one's perceptions, don't you find?"

"Sometimes." Gordy's face was paler than usual and showing heretofore unsuspected lines. He pointed at Shan's computer. "I've been doing some math myself, if you've got a minute to check me."

Such seriousness. One should not have lines of grimness sharpening one's features at nineteen. Shan sighed and extended a long arm, saving the frame with a rapid series of keystrokes. He glanced up again.

"The name of your file is?"

"Murder."

Shan stared, ran a quick scan of that utterly serious emotive pattern and lifted both brows. "Auspicious."

The corners of Gordy's mouth tightened, in no way a smile, and he folded his hands tightly together on his knee. "Yessir."

Murder was a series of three interlocking equations, as deceptively simple as haiku. Shan's hands went cold on the keypad as he scanned them. He looked at Gordy, sitting so still he fairly quivered with strain.

"These are quite attractive. Would you mind awfully if I frame my own set?"

Some of the stress eased from the boy's eyes. "I was hoping you would."

"Fine. A few moments' grace, please. Get yourself something to drink, child—and bring me a glass of the red, if you will."

"Yes, Father." Melant'i shift—and of a sort one rarely had from Gordy, who was after all a halfling, and full of a great many useless notions regarding dignity. Shan returned his attention to the screen.

Fifteen minutes later, he sat back and picked up his glass, tasting the wine before he looked across at the waiting boy.

"I regret to say that your projections seem accurate in the extreme. My own calculations indicate explosive conditions reached eight nanoseconds before your model, but I suspect this is merely a reflection of the difference in our ages. Youth is ever optimistic."

Again, the tightening of the mouth, while the brown eyes shone with abrupt tears.

"I ran a sim," he said, voice grating huskily and then cracking. "Worst case, we lose *everybody*, Shan."

"Precisely why it's called worst case." He tipped back in his chair and had another sip of wine. "Don't look so ill, child. You've served warning. The patch on that thrice-damned pod is an unacceptable stress point. If we have to maneuver suddenly—if we have to maneuver and *fire* at the same time— poof! As you say, we lose everybody." He shrugged.

"Nothing for it but to go out and do a proper fix."

Gordy stared. "With all those Yxtrang out there?"

"Well," said Shan, with a casualness Priscilla would have known was all sham, "I don't expect they're going to be leaving soon, do you?"

"**You** are not going out there to repair that pod mount!"

Shan paused with the wine glass halfway to his lips, face etched in disbelief. "Your pardon, Priscilla? I cannot believe that I heard you correctly."

Black eyes flashed and her mouth tightened ominously. "You heard me."

"Well, if you will have it, I did." He moved to the bar and set the untasted glass next to the decanter of red before turning to her again, a frown on his face. "Need I remind you that I am captain of this vessel?"

"All the more reason for you to stay away and let someone else do it!" she cried, body taut as a harpstring, projecting passion with such force Shan's teeth ached.

He took a deep breath. "I suppose you have someone else in mind?" he inquired, keeping any hint of irony out of his voice.

Priscilla glared. "Yes, I do. Me."

"Oh, much better!" he approved, and the irony this time was impossible to leash.

He was warned by the flare of heat against his cheek, had time to think a thought and *reach* before the wine erupted from the goblet and, given direction by Priscilla's fury, smashed into a storm of blood-red droplets a whisker's breadth from his face.

"Oh dear," Shan said softly, looking down at the carpet. "We seem to have made a mess, Priscilla."

"A mess . . ." She was looking a trifle dazed, as well she might. The amount of finely tuned energy required to move a coherent volume of wine the specified distance with such rapidity and without breaking the goblet was certainly considerable. She closed her eyes and whispered something Shan thought sounded suspiciously like, "Mother grant me patience," before opening them again.

"Shan," she said carefully; "what is that?"

"That?" He caught the glimmer of what his construct must look like to her Inner Eyes and smiled.

"Oh, *that*! Well, I don't know how it should happen, Priscilla, but I became concerned that you might be going to dash a glass of wine into my face. Given the conviction, I thought it expedient to arrange for a shield of sorts. Pretty clever I thought it, too, especially on such short notice. But now I perceive that I should have arranged for something a bit more—encompassing—for here's the carpet, all spotted up and—"

"Damn the carpet! Shan—" Passion of a different sort broke and he found his eyes full even as hers spilled over and she was that quickly across the room, cupping his face in her hands.

"Shan, for sweet love's sake, don't go out there! Something—something *horrible*—will happen. I—"

Gently, he put his own hands up, running his fingers into her black curls and looking closely into her eyes. "A foretelling, Priscilla? Something that you *know* is true?"

His palms were wet with her tears. He saw the uncertainty in the back of her eyes before she shook her head. "I—I'm not sure." Passion flared once more. "Let me do it. The tests—"

"The tests show that you rate either excellent in manipulation and very good on speed or very good in manipulation and excellent in speed. The same tests show that the captain rates consistently excellent in both manipulation and speed. We have two Master pilots on this ship—the captain and the first mate. It's sensible to have one with the ship at all times. Since I out-test you on the repair module—just barely, I admit it!—and since speed and manipulative excellence are both very likely to be factors in making the needed repairs, I am the best choice." He sighed and dropped all shields, letting her see the truth in him.

"This is no act of heroism, I swear it to you. If Ren Zel, Seth, or Thrina were more able, the task would be theirs."

Priscilla's face was troubled. "But not mine," she murmured.

Truth was truth, and only truth was owed, between lifemates. "Only," he admitted, "under severest compulsion."

She stepped away from him, shaking her head. "You'd rather make me watch you die."

"But I have no intention of dying, Priscilla!" he cried, with counterfeit gaiety.

And felt her pain in his own heart, twisting like a sudden knife.

Outside repair was tedious, nerve-wracking work, in this case made more nerve-wracking by the interested presence of several Yxtrang warships. That the residents of the warships were more than a little vocal in their interest had early on moved Shan to cut his open beams to three: direct to the *Passage,* direct to Seth, and conference.

Seth was assigned as pointguard between Shan and the interested enemy, a task he undertook with a worrisome degree of enthusiasm. However, though two flights of insystem fighters had passed foolishly close to the edge of the *Passage*'s range during the last few hours of welding, sweating and swearing, Seth, the *Passage* and the Yxtrang had all managed to keep fingers from firing studs. Shan indiscriminately thanked every god and goddess he could think of for this rare display of moderation on all sides, and sweated even more in the heavy-duty suit, in an agony to finish before someone mislaid their common sense.

"I believe that's sealed," he murmured at too long last. "Ren Zel, check me, if you please. I don't really feel up to coming back outside tomorrow to patch the keyhole."

"Equations set and sim running, Captain." Ren Zel's smooth-toned and proper Liaden voice was as bracing as a cool breeze. "We have compliance to the one hundredth and fifth percentile, Captain."

Relief so exquisite it was almost pain. "Wonderful. Seth,

my sharpshooter, we're going back inside. Allow me, in the fullness of time, to buy you a glass of that reprehensible rotgut you drink."

"You're on—ah, hell, here we go again. Yxtrang flight-squad just inside eyes—screen eight. Must be flying school today."

"Let's hope it's not target practice, shall we?"

"They've been real polite so far," Seth commented. "I'll swing out and give you some room, Captain. The sooner I get a glass of rotgut in my hand, the happier I'm going to be."

"Spoken like a sane man, Mr. Johnson. Back off to vector sigma-eight-three, and I'll slide around to Bay Six."

"Gotcha. Changing vector—now."

"*Passage* note following vectors and track. Intend to inter-sect with Bay Six in—Seth! Screen four!"

Two of the Yxtrang craft had peeled out of formation, local velocity increasing to an insane level. Seth threw his own ves-sel into an evasive tumble that should have skated him toward the *Passage*'s well-protected belly and safety. Of a sort.

But Seth did not chose the life-saving maneuver. Instead, his tumble spun him *away* from the *Passage,* vectoring with the Yxtrang fighters.

One came after him, gun turrets tracking as they held the target despite the craft's maneuvering. The second fighter kept on—a straight, one would have said suicidal, run in to-ward the heart of the *Passage.* Toward Shan.

Multiple voices filled the void's radio frequencies. Shan's "Seth, return to ship!" was nearly overwhelmed by Priscilla's calm, "Safety interlocks off, full battle condition. On my mark, gunners."

Seth's voice broke into the end of Priscilla's instructions, on the dedicated beam between the lifeboats. "One family's enough. I'm on your man. They're after the lock."

It was all true in the tumbling way things happen in space; Seth's course had altered enough that his gun was tracking the lead enemy, the ship tracking him began to maneuver its way closer, and the lead Yxtrang was closing rapidly on both Shan and the lock he'd need to enter.

"Your screen six," came Priscilla's calm voice, this time tinged with an ice that made even Shan's blood run cold.

"This is the attack. Gunners, your mark. Three and Five spot Seth. Teams Four and Six spot the captain. Everyone else— standard defense."

Screen six showed a flight of five fighters whose meandering courses had suddenly become one.

The fighter tracking Shan veered away from the collision course, and Shan's reflexes brought him back toward the lock, and then away, away . . .

"Shan, we . . ."

"Can't risk an open lock. I'll loop around and see . . ."

"They're pairing up on you, Shan," came Seth's warning.

Shan felt a momentary touch of love so sweet and full it nearly overwhelmed him. Then he felt a wrenching he understood all too well; Priscilla had gone behind her strongest shields, as she must. As he must.

"Shan, close in on pod four!" Seth urged.

Shan cursed the little lifeboat: fighter it was not, despite the add-on guns. More massive than the fighters by dint of its planetary capability, it was never meant to fight a space battle.

He stabbed at the release button, flinging the valuable remote repair unit into space to gain a measure of response.

"Shan!"

Seth's scream came at the instant the first Yxtrang fired; then there was static and a missile to be dodged and another. Shan felt the g-forces pushing him sideways as the little craft answered helm and then the first Yxtrang ship was pieces in the void as Seth's elation echoed across the radio and the second Yxtrang was turning ever so quickly for another run at Shan.

Shan's screens glared bright as *Dutiful Passage* went to war.

The very first concern was the larger fighter flight; the two that were behind that, closing at high speed with some larger ships intermingled, would wait.

Priscilla ignored the screen that showed Shan's ship: he'd done as Seth suggested and closed in on the *Passage* as best he could. Her concern now was weapon-mix and security; it wouldn't do to show their full capability quite yet.

"Team Two," she said quietly into her mike. "Fire at will."

The ship's automatics cut in. She felt the minute tremble as the guns began their rapid fire and the ship compensated. It would be seconds before the Yxtrang crossed their path, and a good radar system might give them warning. Priscilla spoke to the mike again.

"Team Three, wide area coverage around Team Two's center. If you get a veer, target it in."

"Cluster incoming; looks serious." This from Ken Rik on the inner bridge.

Priscilla's attention snapped to screen three—several of the larger ships farther out had launched their weapons and were already dropping away from their escort of fighters. Too far for a missile shot. Still.

"Team One, your target is the hindmost of the midrange ships in Sector Three; your next target is next closest to us. You are cleared for two bursts each. At will."

Her eyes had already found the sight she wanted to see: Shan's boat close in to the *Passage,* firing an occasional burst toward something out of her sight.

The next screen showed it: Seth was still hanging away from the *Passage,* staying between Shan and the remaining fighter from the original attack group. He seemed to have earned some respect from the Yxtrang pilot.

A shudder went through the ship, followed by another.

"Team One. Bursts away, Priscilla," Vilobar's voice in her ear was calm. Perhaps he was calm. Inner senses stringently locked away, she chose to believe so.

The beams were a battleship's weapon. The beams—pulses actually—technically moved at just under the speed of light and carried with them a baleful mixture of particles, magnetic flux, and high speed atomic nuclei. She looked to her screens.

Unanticipated, Team One's bursts tore through the incoming cluster of missiles, and a few of the intervening fighters as well, leaving behind an awful shadow of explosions. A moment more, and the hindmost ship was incandescent fog.

Radio noise, already full of sputters and crackles from the first beam's passage through the Yxtrang, became a roar and hiss, and a second roaring followed as the second of the midrange ships followed its sister to vacuum.

"Fleas! Fleas!" Seth's voice was insistent in her ear. "Fleas!"

She slapped the switch, grabbed the screen and saw Seth's boat madly whirling and firing.

Watching, she thanked the Goddess for Seth, for his loyalty, and behind her Wall, among that which was locked away for this while, she feared—terribly—for his life.

For, in fighting to stay between Shan and the enemy, Seth had encountered a horde of the stealthy fleas—one-man ships barely more than a powered and hyper-armed space suit.

On visual she saw what she feared: his boat was dodging a dozen or more of the things, and though he had speed, they were a cloud around him, each firing and trying to attach weapons meant to mine a warship's hull.

"Seth!"

That was Shan, and now his boat was closing, firing, whirling, ramming.

"Twenty-three, Shan," Seth said. He might have been counting cargo pallets. Then, sharper—"I see their mother!"

The little boat whirled purposefully, the guns firing at a small dark spot in space as it picked up speed. Out, out, into the cloud of fleas and beyond. Away from the *Passage*.

"No!" Shan's voice was strong with Command. It made no difference.

The side of Seth's boat erupted. It spun, then—incredibly—straightened course, moving yet toward a nearly invisible spot against the stars.

"Damn," Seth said, and he was gasping. "Drinks are on me! Thirty-three." A pause. "Don't do anything stupid, Shan."

Then Seth's boat crumpled and exploded against the dark plastic mother ship of the Yxtrang fleas.

"Priscilla!" Shan's voice, high and hoarse.

"Teams Five and Three. Take it out." The ship shuddered and the bursts were away. The fleas' mother died in a flare of vapor.

"Priscilla, accelerate," Shan—no, *the captain* said into her ear. "There's a cloud of fleas closing on you."

His boat was spinning, moving, dodging, guns flaring—and each move taking him further and further from the *Passage*. From safety.

"Shan—"

"That is an order," he said, cold in command. "Accelerate!"

"Yes, Captain." Behind the Wall, she screamed and railed and rent her garments in anguish.

On the war bridge, she spoke quietly into her microphone, relaying the order to accelerate.

She had memorized this computer code seven Standards ago, offering at the same time a prayer to the Goddess, that she would never need to use it. Her fingers shook as she entered it now, but there was no shame in that. Neither the Goddess nor melant'i demanded fearlessness in the performance of duty, merely that duty was done.

The screen blanked as she entered the last digit, taking even the window at the bottom right corner, which elucidated the progress of lifeboat number four toward the planet surface. There was silence in the captain's office, as if the *Passage* were mulling over her request, and more than half-inclined to refuse it. Priscilla folded her cold hands together on the wooden desk, waiting.

The *Passage* made up its mind with a beep and a flash of letters on her screen.

DUTIFUL PASSAGE OFFICER ALTERATION ROUTINE.	
BEGIN RUN:	
RANK:	CAPTAIN
HISTORY:	SHAN YOS'GALAN, CLAN KORVAL
	ER THOM YOS'GALAN, CLAN KORVAL
	SAE ZAR YOS'GALAN, CLAN KORVAL
CANDIDATE:	PRISCILLA DELACROIX Y MENDOZA,
	CLAN KORVAL
HISTORY:	PET LIBRARIAN
	PILOT THIRD CLASS,
	TRAINING SECOND CLASS
	SECOND MATE
	PILOT SECOND CLASS,
	TRAINING FIRST CLASS
	FIRST MATE
	PILOT FIRST CLASS, TRAINING MASTER

ACCEPT: COMMUNICATIONS MODULE
                      EMERGENCY MODULE
                      LIBRARY MODULE
                      OVERRIDE MODULE
                      NAVIGATION MODULE
                      WEAPONS MODULE
                      MAIN COMP
ACCEPT: PRISCILLA DELACROIX Y MENDOZA,
                      CLAN KORVAL
RANK: CAPTAIN
ADJUSTMENT: CAPTAIN'S KEY FILE
ACCEPT
AUXILIARY INFORMATION: RANKS FIRST MATE, SECOND
MATE, THIRD MATE UNMANNED. HIGH RISK CONDITION
NOTED. OPTIMUM SOLUTION: APPOINT OFFICERS: FIRST
MATE, SECOND MATE, THIRD MATE.
MINIMUM SOLUTION TO UNACCEPTABLE RISK CONDITION:
APPOINT FIRST MATE.
END RUN

The screen blanked once more. Priscilla extended a hand that still showed a tendency to quiver and tapped in a retrieval request. A heartbeat later, Plan B lit her screen.

> *A changing array of safeplaces shall be maintained at all times, in the event of immediate, catastrophic threat to the Clan. There is no shame in strategic retreat. Even Jela sometimes ran from his enemies, the better to defeat them, tomorrow.*
> *Keep the children safe. Honor without love is stupidity.*
> *This by the hand of Cantra yos'Phelium, Captain and Delm, in the Third Year after Planetfall.*

The screen beeped, indicating the existence of an auxiliary file. Priscilla accessed it with the touch of a key.

This message was not nearly so ancient. In fact, it was mere weeks old, dispatched by Nova yos'Galan, Korval's first speaker in trust, to Shan yos'Galan, captain and thodelm.

Plan B is in effect. Assume our enemy omnipresent and dedicated to Korval's utter ruin. Contact no one, for we cannot know which alliances stand firm and which are rotted out from the core by the work of our enemy. Arm the Passage. Secure yourself. Repeat: Plan B is in effect.

Keep safe, brother.

Priscilla sat back in Shan's chair, staring at the screen. They had armed the *Passage*. They were, as far as conditions allowed, secure. The ban on radio contact was subject to captain's interpretation, given those same conditions. She touched another key, sealing the files once more. The diagram of Shan's descent to Lytaxin reappeared in the bottom right corner of the screen.

Eyes closed, she considered priorities.

The ship's priority, that there be at least one other in the command chain, should the captain fail, was best acted on at once. The radio . . . She reached out and flipped a toggle.

"Tower."

"Rusty, this is the captain," she said quietly.

There was a short, electric pause, then a respectful, almost somber, "Yes, ma'am."

"Please do me the favor," she continued, hearing her own voice take on Shan's speech pattern, "of constructing an anonymous message to the appropriate authorities regarding Lytaxin's situation."

"Yes, ma'am," he said again, then: "I'm assuming we don't want to give away our name or our location."

"That's exactly what we don't want, Rusty. Can you do it?"

"Take a little fiddling, but—yeah. I can do it. You want to review before implementation?"

"Please."

"Will do," he said, and his voice was brighter, as if the promise of a problem he was able to master had cheered him up. "Tower out."

"Thank you, Rusty. Captain out."

· · · ·

The screen on the side of the desk was live, displaying the current crew roster, but the decision had been made before ever she keyed in the request to see that document.

Priscilla sighed. Ten Standards she and Shan had captained the *Passage* between them. To name another to take the place she had made for herself, as duty demanded that she take Shan's rightful role was—not easy. Yet it must be done, for the safety of ship, crew, and kin. The temple had schooled her well in duty, before she had ever dreamed of Liad.

Priscilla closed her eyes and called up an old exercise—one of the first taught to novices in temple, honing her anxiety into purpose. She had barely opened her eyes again when the door chime sounded.

"Come," she said, and the door, obedient to the captain's voice, slid open.

"Acting Captain." He bowed respect from the center of the room and straightened, awaiting her notice.

She took a moment to consider him: A medium tall man, as Liadens measured height, skin an unblemished medium gold, hair and eyes a matching medium brown, neither beautiful nor ugly, not fat nor yet thin. He wore no rings of rank nor any more simple adornment. His shirt was plain and pale, his trousers dark, his boots comfortable and well tended.

He was a pilot of some note—first class verging on Master—and she knew him for a quick and incisive thinker. The information that he possessed humor would have startled many of his crewmates, but none of those would have said his judgment was unsound, or that his temperament was other than steady.

He was also inclined toward austerity, which was worrisome, Priscilla allowed, even when it was austerity applied to the best good of ship and crew.

From her seat behind the desk, she inclined her head and moved a hand toward the pair of visitor's chairs.

"I have a proposal to put before you, my friend," she said in mild, modeless Terran. "Will you sit and listen to me for a moment?"

"Gladly," he responded. His Terran was heavily accented, though his comprehension was excellent. He took the chair nearest the corner of the desk and folded his hands neatly upon his knee.

Priscilla closed her eyes briefly, opened them and considered Ren Zel's quiet face. She remained, perforce, behind her Wall, reduced to reading the emotions of others from the shifting clues of expression and bodyline. Like most Liadens, Ren Zel was a master at keeping his emotions well away from his face.

"An announcement will be made to the entire crew within the hour," she said, and took a breath, enough air, certainly, to force the few words out. "The ship has accepted me as captain."

Face smooth, Ren Zel inclined his head. "Has there been—word—of Captain yos'Galan?"

Priscilla shook her head, gesturing at her screen and the diagram describing the descent of lifeboat number four. "He will make planetfall within the next few hours. After the lifeboat is stable, we'll rig a punchbeam. For the moment, we—assume—that Captain yos'Galan is alive, but unavailable to us. Circumstances dictate that the ship be served by a full captain."

"Assume," Ren Zel said, voice expressing interest without judgment, which was only prudent from a man reared in a culture where a judgment expressed outside of one's proper area of concern might well result in honor-feud, Priscilla was free to ignore him, but she would have to stretch—and endanger her own melant'i—to read insult into his question.

"Assume," she repeated, and smiled with good intent, if limited success. "Understand that I am—shielded away. Without Healer skill. There are exercises I must soon undertake so that I may serve the ship as it must be served, but for the moment, I have no more knowledge of Captain yos'Galan's safety than what I can read from the tracking computer and from my own desires."

Something moved in the brown eyes. She thought it might have been pity. "I understand. Forgive me. I had not intended to cause you pain."

"You have a right to ask—to know. Shan is your captain, after all."

"Indeed, I owe him my life," Ren Zel murmured. "And yourself, as well."

In lieu of being able to pay Shan directly, Priscilla thought wryly and deliberately suppressed the shudder of anxiety. She lay her hands flat on the desktop and looked at him.

"Then perhaps you will find this proposal even more interesting," she said and tipped her head, seeing wariness at the back of his eyes.

"You know that we are short-handed, that we have been short-handed since the *Passage* became a full-scale battlewagon."

Ren Zel inclined his head. "And with the loss of Pilot Johnson and Captain yos'Galan we become less rich in resource."

"Exactly. In a ship—rich in resource—the second mate would move to first, third to second, and a third mate would be chosen by the captain."

"We do not have this luxury of personnel," he agreed. "We are at war."

She nodded. "The ship requires a first mate and the captain must decide who will serve the ship best. I propose yourself for first mate, unless you can think of a compelling reason why you shouldn't be."

Shock stripped his face naked. He sat—just sat—and stared at her for the space of three heartbeats. He closed his eyes then, and sat through two heartbeats more. He opened his eyes and they were distant, his face without expression. When he spoke, it was in High Liaden, in the mode called Outsider.

"The captain is reminded that one is clanless, with neither name nor kin nor melant'i to support one. The ship is best served by one who is alive."

"The captain recalls most vividly that you have been reft of your birthright," Priscilla said carefully, following him into Liaden, but only so far as Comrade mode. "The captain points out that your piloting license bears a name—Ren Zel dea'Judan. The captain fails of recalling a single instance of that name being dishonored in the several years of our association. The melant'i which you embody is pure. The ship can be no better served."

There were tears in the medium brown eyes and she dared not unshield, even to offer comfort. Instead, she sat and waited while he mastered himself, while he thought it through, and when he rose to bow acceptance.

"Captain, I am honored. I will serve willingly, with all my heart."

She stood from behind the desk and returned his bow, reaching into High Liaden for the ritual phrase spoken by a delm when accepting a new member into the clan.

"I see you, Ren Zel dea'Judan, First Mate. The ship rejoices."

Tears again, hidden by a hasty bow. "Captain."

She smiled slightly and shook her head. "First lesson," she said in Terran.

Quickly, he looked up, brown eyes bright. "Yes?"

"My name is Priscilla," she said, and held her hand out to him.

The crew, at battle stations, accepted her ascendancy to captain and Ren Zel's appointment as first mate with somber approval. She had detailed their mission: to take up defensive orbit about the planet and await the aid that surely must come in response to Rusty's carefully anonymous pinbeams.

"In the meantime," she said, "Captain yos'Galan's lifeboat has entered atmosphere. We will attempt to establish a dialog via laser packet when he comes to ground and we are sure his position is stable."

"Why not just use the radio?" That was Gordy, face tight, voice harsh with pain.

"The Yxtrang may ride our radio wave down to the planet surface and discover the location of an object we value," Ren Zel murmured, before she could frame a reply. "They have surely marked that one pod escaped the battle, and they must wonder after its worth. A laser burst is not so easy to follow, so we may shield Captain yos'Galan while informing him of our vigilance."

In the screen, Gordy nodded, jerkily. "I see. Thank you."

"Other questions?" Priscilla asked, and there were none, so she released them to their duties or their rest, then turned to Ren Zel.

"First Mate, the shift is yours."

He bowed, accepting the duty. Priscilla hesitated.

"Ren Zel."

He looked up.

"I—there are preparations that I must make," she said, slowly. "Preparations which are . . . of the dramliz. I will be in my cabin for the next few hours, but I will not be available to you." She bit her lip, and added that most dangerous of Terran phrases, "I'm sorry."

He moved his hand lightly, as if clearing the air of a faint wisp of smoke. "Necessity. I, to my duty. You, to yours."

She smiled, then. Almost she laughed. Practical Ren Zel.

"Of course. How could I have forgotten? Good shift, my friend."

"Good shift, Priscilla."

Self-healed, and whole once more, Priscilla drew a breath in trance slightly deeper than the one before. Her lips moved. The voice of her body whispered a word.

Weapons Hall leapt up around her, mile-thick walls breathing chill and fell purpose.

One did not seek this place lightly. Many—most—of those trained as Sintian Witches never had need to come here, though all were taught the way. It was the peculiar misfortune of those who had been born Moonhawk to know the way to Weapons Hall all too well.

Priscilla moved silently over the stone floor, her cloak pulled tight against the chill. At the end of the hall, she paused, frowning down at a blood-bright spot against the worn rock bench. Bending, she picked up a round wooden counter like those used in gaming houses, bright red in the center, but losing its paint along the rim. She smiled slightly and curled her fingers over the token, feeling it warm against her skin, and moved forward once more, to the long, weapon-hung wall.

The tale is that, for every art of healing, for every spell of joy a Witch masters, there is a weapon hung in the Hall, which is its dire opposite.

The tale is true.

Priscilla walked the long, weapon-thick wall. Three times, she put out her hand and when she lowered it, a portion of the wall stood bare. At the end of the Hall, weapons chosen, she closed her eyes and raised her arms and was gone from that place that was nowhere and nowhen.

In the bed she shared with Shan, Priscilla's body stirred. Breath and heartbeat quickened. Black eyes opened. Blinked.

She stretched, then, fully back in the body, and noticed that her right hand was clenched tight. Raising it, she carefully opened her fingers and looked in wonder at the round wooden counter, brave crimson enamel worn away around the rim.

To her newly wakened, battle-honed senses, the little token vibrated with power, with . . . presence. Carefully, she opened her thought to the artifact—and nearly cried aloud with wonder.

The wood was alive with Shan's presence.

She held it in her hand while she dressed, loath to surrender even so tenuous and strange a link with him. When she had wriggled, one-handed, into her shirt, she slid the token into her sleeve-pocket, taking care with the seal.

It wasn't until she had stamped into her boots and gone into the 'fresher to splash water on her face that it occurred to her to wonder what Shan might have found awaiting his hand, in the Witches' Hall of Weapons.

NIMBLEDRAKE

ENDING JUMP

Liz punched the third button from the top in the fourth column from the right, which probably said "tea" as plain as the nose on your face, if your nose happened to be Liaden. Since hers wasn't, she'd memorized which buttons Nova pressed to draw what kind of rations.

She fished the cup out of the dispenser and punched the button again, then walked both cups carefully down the narrow hallway to the piloting chamber. They were due to fall out of Jump pretty soon—a way stop, not Lytaxin itself.

Nova was at the board, which was where Nova mostly was, except for an odd hour of sleep, or a short stroll down to the canteen to draw tea or food—that she ate and drank while sitting watch over her board.

"Here you go, Goldie." Liz slid one cup into the holder in the arm of the pilot's chair, and, juggling the other cup, got herself into the cramped co-pilot's seat.

"My thanks," Nova said absently, busy with some figuring on a tiny work screen set off to the side of the main board.

"No problem," Liz said, anchoring her cup and pulling the webbing across. Not that Nova was likely to give them a thrill breaking Jump—she'd shown herself far too able a pilot for that. But, in Liz's experience, accidents did happen, and the ones who were prepared were the ones least likely to get hurt.

"Planning on making a long stop?" she asked. "Or just using the revolving door?"

Nova looked up, golden brows pulled tight. "Revolving—?" The frown cleared in the next instant. "Ah. I see. We shall pause long enough to hear the news, then move on. If the luck smiles, we will be dining with Erob twenty hours hence."

"Terrific," Liz said, without emphasis. She had a careful sip of her tea. "You got a pretty good handle on Terran," she said. "Haven't managed to really stump you yet."

"Were you trying?" Astonishingly, Nova looked amused. "But you might consider my handle to be not quite what it should be, when you learn that my mother was Terran."

Liz managed not to choke on her tea. "She was?"

"Indeed, and a scholar of linguistics besides." There was a muted chime in the cabin and Nova turned back to the screens.

"You will excuse me. We approach Jump end."

Liz settled her cup in the slot and eased back as well as she could in the chair, so of course they phased into normal space with no more happenstance than the usual snap of transition.

Nova was busy with the board. Liz picked up the plug she'd been given, as she thought, to keep her quiet during just such periods of pilot concentration, she slipped it in her ear, doodling with the one dial of the dozens decorating the board that she was allowed, even encouraged, to touch.

For a while there was nothing much. The usual traffic talk and between-ship chatter you'd get any time you broke system. Then there was something else. Liz froze, holding the setting steady, and pulled the plug out of her ear.

"Nova."

A flash of violet eyes none too pleased. Liz held out the earplug.

"Gotta hear this. Priority One. I picked it up on the shipping channel."

One slim hand moved, sideways to what it had been doing, slapped a toggle and the speaker came live.

"Repeat. All vessels shipping to or through Lytaxin space are warned that Clan Danut is invoking the war-impaired shipping clause of all contracts and will not carry, deliver, or receive goods bound for Lytaxin, based on reliable information. This by order of Delm Danut."

In the pilot's chair, Nova took a deep quiet breath. Liz looked at her.

"You know them?"

"Clan Danut," Nova said, still staring at the board. "They are a small clan; their principal warehouse is on planet here. If they were not certain, they would not speak." She moved then, hands dancing along the controls.

"We shall check another source, Commander Lizardi, for if one trader announces such news, another has information a little fresher!"

Liz watched as Nova's hands touched this comm-panel and that, heard what might have been a Liaden cuss word as a loud monotone note sounded, then saw hands busy again.

"It would be good of you to fetch more tea for me, and some of the board-biscuits—sixth key on the right side of the warmer."

Liz noted the half-cup of tea still locked to Nova's chair, but figured she could tell when she should be elsewhere for a moment.

As fast as Liz rushed for the vittles, whatever secrets the Liaden woman wanted hidden were still her own when she got back.

"Strap in this time, Commander," said Nova, hands busy on the board yet again. "We Jump as soon as our orientation and speed are correct."

"Whoa!" Liz started to reach out and get hold of a wrist, then thought better of it. "Where you putting out for?"

No answer.

"Answer me, Goldie, I got a right to know."

"Indeed you do," Nova said, her voice a calm and shocking counterpoint to her busy fingers. "We are going to Fendor, Angela Lizardi."

"Merc Headquarters?" She blinked. "What're you gonna do? Hire yourself an army?"

"If necessary. Jump phase in 20 seconds. Erob is Korval's

ally. We owe assistance in peril. And I have evidence from a
pinbeam bounce that my brother and his lifemate are on Lytaxin as we speak."

Nova turned her violet eyes to Liz. "The mercenaries will
have ways of determining if this rumor is true. Am I correct?"

Girl was too damn bright, Liz thought, and sighed.

"Yeah," she said, "they probably do."

"I thought so," said Nova, and the ship snapped into Jump.

LUFKIT

MERC HALL

There was a wonderful bustle of busyness, a splendid to and fro, not unlike to art. Not unlike at all, Edger considered, watching the hasty humans dart up and down the wide hallway. The art of which his youngest of brothers, Val Con yos'Phelium Scout, was a master.

He tarried by the door some noticeable time, by human counting, his brother Sheather at his side, absorbed in the spectacle.

Not all was hastiness within the hall. Here and there, at appropriate and artful intervals, were arranged islands of stillness: a counter, a computer, and a human sitting behind a table. It was these still islands which, in a soaring of art, inspired the most of the hastiness, Edger saw, noting with a connoisseur's eye the flow of tensions, light and human plain song between and among the stillnesses.

He could have tarried in contemplation yet some while, save that the introduction of himself and his brother into the fringes of the work did subtly alter the flow, and exerted compulsion upon one of the centers of stillness, requiring the human seated behind the table to rise and throw himself into the hasty human river. In a very short time, indeed, by Clutch standards, he emerged and engaged in that activity known as "salute."

"Sirs. I'm Sergeant Ystro Ban. Is there some assistance I can offer you?"

"I thank you, Sergeant Ystro Ban, and honor your inquiry. We come seeking a soldier and were told she might have left word of her whereabouts with kin at this hall."

The Sergeant's face knotted up most wonderfully and his eyebrows went up and down rapidly.

"Well, sir, we don't normally just give out the whereabouts of one soldier. If you like, you can leave a message for her here and I will personally make sure she gets it, when she reports in."

"I regret that our need is more pressing than that, Sergeant Ystro Ban," Edger said, and with no real astonishment then heard his brother Sheather's voice, questioning most mildly.

"I wonder, Sergeant Ystro Ban, is it always so bustling in your hall?"

"Huh?" He looked over his shoulder as if he had forgotten the bright, busy clatter in the course of their discourse together, then shook his head.

"Naw, this is something special. Got a blood war on our hands and everybody who can carry a gun is signing into the rescue team."

"Forgive me," Sheather said. "A blood war? What has gone forth?"

Sergeant Ystro Ban shrugged. "What it looks like is a Yxtrang invasion force came into Lytaxin system and set up housekeeping. Trouble is, there's mercs trapped on the planet, and we don't aim to let 'em fight this one without backup."

Edger exchanged a glance with his brother Sheather, who blinked solemnly and asked yet again.

"Which mercs are these, Ystro Ban, who are trapped upon Lytaxin?"

"'Bout half of the Gyrfalks, is what we heard here." He moved his head from side to side. "Word is Suzuki's on Fendor, which is fine by me. Wouldn't want to be on the same planet with Suzuki right now."

"It is these Gyrfalcons who are kin to our sister, Younger Brother?" Edger asked slowly.

"Brother, I believe they are."

"Ah." Edger turned his saucer eyes to Sergeant Ystro Ban. "Can you tell me if this hastiness we observe here will be replicated upon Fendor Mercenary Headquarters? And perhaps in other like halls?"

"Damn straight," said Ystro Ban.

"I understand you," said Edger and again sought the eyes of his brother, which were bright with the same thought, he would swear, that illuminated his own mind.

"I detect the hand of a great artist, Oh, my Brother," Edger said.

"I also," Sheather returned.

"And what more like our sister, that she should aid her kin in peril?"

"Nothing more," said Sheather.

"So." Edger turned back to the still and patient human and lifted a large three-fingered hand.

"I thank you for the gift of your time, and the jubilation of your news, Sergeant Ystro Ban. Do you go yourself to Lytaxin?"

"Couldn't keep me away with a battalion."

"I am gratified to hear it. Perhaps we may see you there. Come, Younger Brother, and reflect upon the depth of our brother's art, who inspires us to ever hastier action!"

ALTITUDE: 12 KILOMETERS

Habit almost killed him.

Shan flicked on the lifeboat's homer and directed its attention to Lytaxin Spaceport, his own attention more than half-occupied with keeping the clumsy little craft airborne and relatively upright while nursing the sadly-depleted fuel supply.

So far, he'd managed to avoid meeting anyone with a general grudge against Liadens and his goal was to come to ground before he did. The lifeboat's pitiful guns were all but exhausted and the thought of trying anything resembling evasive action against atmospheric fighter craft was enough to make his stomach knot.

Anxiously, he ran his eyes over the displays. Skies showed clear on screens one, two, three, and four. Good.

Screens five and six were something else again.

He had been at Lytaxin Spaceport no more than four Standards past. Then, it had been a bustling, mid-sized port, with half-a-dozen public yards and a sprinkling of private. There had been traffic, lights, and people—ships. Ships on hot-pads. Ships on cold-pads. Ships under repair and ships being hauled from one pad to another.

What remained was wreckage. Glass-edged pits marked

the places where ships had been caught unaware, murdered while they slept. The Port Tower was a bowed, half-melted framework of naked girders. The blastcrete streets had been bombed into gravel pathways, separated now and then by segments of fencing. Twisted metal was strewn haphazard and the blasted pathways gleamed where glass had run in rivers, and frozen again where it lay.

Destruction burned his eyes and his hands were moving across the board, ripping the lifecraft into another course entirely before his thinking mind fully realized his error.

The lifeboat bucked, responsive as a rock. Shan swore, briefly and with sincerity, flicked a glance at the falling fuel gauge and thence to the screens, which showed plain, placid sky all about.

More than a touch of the luck in that, he owned, and no more than he had traded for, should the screens suddenly show him the very Yxtrang fighter craft he wished so ardently to avoid.

But, if not the Port, where might he go on a planet riddled in war?

"To Erob, of course," he muttered, fighting the lifeboat's tendency to go upside down relative to planetary surface. "Do try not to be a slowtop, Shan."

If Erob were overrun by Yxtrang, scattered, murdered and no more? Shan sighed and glanced again at the fuel gauge.

"Why to Val Con, naturally enough. And pray the gods he's close by."

It was not wise, what he did next, and he was certain his teachers in Healer Hall would have counseled strongly against it. But there really was no choice, given the fuel gauge—riding in the red zone, now—the planetary maps the lifeboat did not carry and his own rather strong disinclination to die.

The little ship was steady for the moment. Shan gripped the edge of the console, closed his eyes and dropped his inner shield.

There was no time for finesse, no time to prepare himself properly. He brought Val Con's emotive template before his Inner Eyes and flung himself open, spinning out in a search that was far too wide, concentration centered on that unique pattern.

He found instead a vast and welcoming greenness, familiar from childhood, comforting as the touch of kin.

Shan took a breath and abandoned Val Con's template, listening for what the Tree might tell him.

It was not, of course, his own Elder Tree, but Erob did keep a seedling. Nor did Jelaza Kazone necessarily speak to those who served it, but it had ways of making itself and its desires known.

The Tree was not read as a Healer might read a fellow human. Rather, the Tree borrowed referents from one's own pattern, displaying them in sequence at once familiar and vegetative.

Thus, the message arranged itself within Shan's senses: Joy-Welcome. Joy-Welcome. Joy-Welcome. Spice-whiff and stem-snap, from a memory of breaking off a leaf. The taste of Tree-nut along his tongue. A second impression of leaf, and a sense of pushing, gently, away.

He was aware that his hands moved across the board and was helpless to stop them. After a short struggle, he did open his eyes and found the dials a blur, the fuel gauge half-gone in red. Within, the Tree touched one last memory—warm lips laid soft against his cheek—and withdrew. Shan slammed his Inner Wall into place, shook himself and looked to the screens.

Number three showed an Yxtrang fighter, growing rapidly larger.

The Tree's influence upon his body had produced a set of coordinates, residing now in the console's readout. Shan flicked a toggle and locked them, sparing a moment to hope the Tree possessed an adequate understanding of the limits of fuel and the action of gravity on an unpowered object.

The fighter loomed larger. Shan turned his attention to the guns.

Pop guns they were, though Seth had put his to good account, and badly drained besides. Shan's hands flashed over the board, shutting down auxiliary and non-essential systems, shunting the extra power to the guns. The energy level crawled upward, stabilized well below the ready line.

Shan chewed his lip, checked the board, checked the fighter—gods, *close*—checked the screens—and stopped breathing.

The Tree's coordinates were bringing him in on an encampment. He could discern tents, machinery, *soldiers* mistily in screen six. There was a standard, snapping bold in the wind below: an enormous white falcon stooping to its kill down a field of starless black.

Terrans. And no doubt close enough to the place the Tree had intended him to go. But not with an Yxtrang on his tail.

His hands moved again, dancing over the board, shutting down everything but air and the computers, sending every erg of energy to the guns and *still* they held below the line.

Shan flicked a glance at his pursuer, another at the camp and the surrounding terrain. He reached up and pulled the worksuit helmet over his head, hit the toggle with his chin and tasted canned air. His hands moved across the board, shutting down ship's life support, feeding the energy to the guns.

The gauge topped the line. And stopped.

Inside the helmet, Shan nodded and made one more adjustment on the board, draining what was now the topmost cannon, feeding everything he had into the belly gun.

Power surged in the single live cannon. He could have wished for more. He could have wished for both guns full primed and on-line. For that matter, he could have wished for a ship to equal the one that came against him, but time was short. He had what was needful.

Just.

He flicked a toggle, relieving the boat of its mindless adherence to the coords, and slowed, dropping a few artfully wobbled meters toward what appeared to be a canyon, or possibly a quarry, at the extreme edge of the encampment.

Behind him, the fighter took the bait.

The other pilot jammed on speed, guns swiveling. Shan waited, wobbling slightly lower—though not too low—toward that tempting rocky edifice. Waited until the fighter

was committed, until there was no possibility of a fly-by—
and no possibility of a miss.

Jaw locked, he whipped the thrusters, spending the dregs
of his fuel. Agonizingly slow, the lifeboat tumbled. The
fighter snarled by, the other pilot seeing the trap too late.
Shan hit the firing stud, and the single canon blared, hot and
bright and brief.

The fighter exploded, raining burning bits down into the
encampment's perimeter.

And lifeboat number four, guns and fuel utterly expended,
fell the few remaining meters to the planet's surface.

He opened the hatch into the wary faces of two soldiers—
one Terran, one Liaden—both holding rifles.

Quietly, he stood on the edge of the ramp, gauntleted
hands folded before him. He'd taken the helmet off, exposing
his face and sweat-stiffened hair; the land breeze was cool
against his cheeks. The sounds were bird sounds, and the
slight wind abrading leaf and grass.

It was the Terran who spoke first, sounding friendly despite the carbine she kept pointed at his chest.

"You OK, flyboy? Nasty fall you took there."

"Thank you, I'm perfectly fine," Shan assured her. And
smiled.

The flip maneuver had worked precisely as he had hoped.
The lifeboat had fallen about 12 meters, to land, right side up
relative to the ground and unharmed, on the rock apron at the
entrance to the quarry. The pilot had received a stern shaking
and would have bruises to show, but the space suit and crash
webbing had cushioned the worst. "Perfectly fine," stretched
the truth, given other conditions, but not nearly into fantasy.

The Terran nodded and turned to her mate.

"Call and let 'em know we're bringing him in."

He slung his rifle, pulled a remote from his belt and spoke.
"Quarry patrol. We have the pilot, safe. Will transport." He
brought the unit to his ear, listened with a frown, then
thumbed it off and hung it back on his belt.

"The sub-commander wishes to speak with him," he told
his partner.

"Right," she said and jerked her head at Shan. "OK, friend. Let's take a walk."

Eye on the rifle, Shan hesitated. The woman shifted, her demeanor abruptly less friendly. He held up his hands, gauntleted palms empty and unthreatening.

"I do beg your pardon! I have no wish to keep the sub-commander waiting, but the case is that I am separated from my ship and I have every reason to believe that an attempt at contact will be made, once it is recognized that my position is stable. I should be here to receive that message when it comes."

The woman shook her head. "Sorry, pal. Sub-Commander Kritoulkas wants you and we're under orders to bring you. Wouldn't care to have shoot you in the knee and carry you myself, but we can do it that way, if you insist."

Shan lowered his hands, taking a deep breath to push the sudden rush of distress down and away from the present moment.

"I would hardly wish to put you to so much trouble. By all means, take me to Sub-Commander Kritoulkas."

Sub-Commander Kritoulkas was a sour-faced woman with iron-gray hair and a prosthetic right hand. She glared at Shan where he stood bracketed by his two guards, sweaty and out-of-breath from his hike. Heavy-duty work suits are not made with strolls through the woods in mind.

"What else?" she asked, transferring her glare to the Terran soldier.

The woman saluted. "He did say he was separated from his ship, ma'am, and expecting a call."

Kritoulkas nodded. "Tell Comm to keep an ear out." She glanced at Shan.

"Anything we should say for you?"

He considered her blandly. "That I am safe and among friends."

"Think so, do you?" She looked back to the soldier. "Pass it, if the call comes. Dismissed."

The soldiers saluted and were gone, leaving him alone with the sub-commander's glare.

She sighed and braced a hip against her desk, folding her arms over her chest.

"OK, we'll take it from the top. Name and rank. If any."

"Shan yos'Galan, Clan Korval," he said. "Captain of the battleship *Dutiful Passage*."

"Battleship," she repeated and shook her head. "You don't look much like a soldier to me. Course, you don't look much like a Liaden to me, either." She shrugged. "Whatever. What're you doing here, Captain?"

"My ship took damage and I was separated during an Yxtrang attack that was launched during outside repair."

She nodded. "That's one. Take a step farther back and tell me the other one. Why is your battleship in this system?"

Shan sighed, shifting his shoulders inside the hot, heavy suit. He emphatically did not want any more questions from this abrupt, sour-faced woman. He wanted a shower. He wanted his lifemate, his ship, and the familiar routine of the trade route. None of which he was likely to receive in the near future, if ever again, though the shower might just be possible, if he were polite and answered the sub-commander's questions.

So.

"Family business. My clan is allied to Erob, and I have reason to believe that my brother is here."

"Yah? Name?"

"Val Con yos'Phelium." Shan watched her face closely, but saw no recognition there.

"Not somebody I come across. You sure he's here?"

"I am positive that he is here," Shan told her, the recollection of that painfully familiar music flowing from Erob's warning beacon vivid enough to raise tears. He blinked.

"Perhaps another name," he said to Kritoulkas' glare. "Miri Robertson?"

That meant something to her. She straightened, glare melting into astonishment. "Redhead? She's here, all right. Think she'll own you?"

"Yes," he said, by no means sure of it.

Sub-Commander Kritoulkas nodded.

"OK, Captain, here's what. Gonna have to pass you up-line anyhow, that being where we got folks who are real interested to hear about what things look like upstairs. We'll keep an ear on your 'boat down there and let your ship know you're among friends." Her mouth twisted a little at that. It might have been a smile.

"Meantime, we got a shift-change coming up in about four hours, which is about enough time for you to clean up, get something to eat and a catnap. Under guard, you understand, because I'm damned if I believe you're regular military and I ain't having you endanger my people."

A commander's natural concern was the welfare of her people. Shan's opinion of the sour-faced sub-commander rose slightly and he nodded.

"I understand entirely, ma'am. Thank you."

She snorted, and raised her voice, bawling for "Dustin!" A shortish Terran strode in from his post outside the tent and saluted.

"Yes, ma'am."

She jerked her thumb at Shan. "Take this guy to draw clothes and a couple sandwiches. Shower and time-out at the medic's station. Stick close and get him to the departure squad on time."

Dustin saluted again. "Yes, ma'am." He turned and nodded at Shan, face and eyes neutral. "OK, sir, let's go."

He turned toward the door, heard Kritoulkas clear her throat behind him.

"One more thing, Captain."

He looked at her over his shoulder and, incredibly, saw her grin.

"Damn good shooting, coming in."

Shan lay on the hard cot, head on a crinkling, antiseptic-scented pillow, and closed his eyes. He had showered, and put on the fighting leathers provided by the quartermaster. He had forced himself to eat one of the half-dozen sandwiches Dustin had pried out of the mess tent, and had drunk several cups of water. Now, more or less alone, if one discounted the guard at the cubicle's entrance, he prepared himself to enter trance.

He took a breath, and another, building the correct rhythm. The noises of the camp faded, his heartbeat slowed. When the time was proper, he slipped over into trance.

Healspace is formless, a void of warm frothing fog. There is nothing but fog within Healspace—until something more is required.

Warm within the formlessness, Shan spoke his own name. He smiled at the man who stepped out of the fog to join him, and extended a hand adorned with a purple ring to take a hand on which an identical stone flashed its facets against the fog. With the deft surety of a Master Healer, he opened a line of comfort between them.

The turmoil he confronted was acute: Grief, joy, guilt, fury, bereavement, horror, love, confusion, repugnance. My, my, what a muddle, to be sure, but after all, demanding nothing more taxing than a Sort and a touch of reweaving. His scan found no irredeemable catastrophe, no resonance which so imbalanced the personality matrix that forgetfulness must be imposed. The matter was not at all complicated, and work could go forward at once.

In Healspace, there is no time. There was the work, and the results of the work, Seen by Healer's Eyes. The work consumed the time that the work required. When it was done, Shan smiled at Shan, opened their arms and embraced into oneness.

Healed and at peace, he turned in the foggy nothingness of Healspace—and checked.

This place was not Healspace. Nor was it the medic's tent cubicle. This place was stone, strange and brooding: A vast stone cavern, or so he thought at first. Then he saw the weapons, hung orderly along the wall.

The weapons . . . shimmered, in their places, as if each held its present form by whim and might as easily be something, quite, else. He focused his attention on a particular sword, and felt it slip from edge to shield, from shield to explosive, from explosive to . . .

"Good moon to you."

The man's voice was beautiful. The man, seated on a stone bench to Shan's right, was lean and hawk-faced, the black braid of his hair vanishing into the tattered shadow of his cloak. A red counter moved in his long fingers, appearing, disappearing. Appearing. Gone.

"Good moon," Shan returned calmly, while with Healer's

senses he tried to Sort this place that was no more physical than Healspace, though it certainly was not Healspace. Nor had he ever met another in Healspace, save one he had called, or who had called him.

"Ah, but you haven't met another," the man in the cloak said, his fine black eyes glinting amusement. "I am you. Or you are me. Oh, my . . ." In his fingers the counter flashed and vanished. He smiled. "I can see language is not going to be useful in this conversation."

"I'm familiar with the concept, as it happens," Shan said, reaching out with Healer's senses to touch the other. He encountered a cool smoothness very like a Healer's protective Wall. "But we can hardly become all of myself if you are shielded away."

"Clever child. But as you say, this is not the sweet floating dream of a spellmist. This," he gestured, grandly, with one long, sun-darkened hand. A silver dagger appeared in that same hand. He considered it, shrugged and thrust it through his belt.

"This," he repeated, drawing the word out, "is Weapons Hall. You are here because you have found it necessary to be armed. Do tell me why."

Shan frowned, allowed himself to wonder if this after all was madness. Perhaps he was even now dying in the wreckage of the repair pod, his mind spinning a last, rich fantasy to disarm itself.

"Nothing so precipitate," the man in the cloak said softly. "As you well know. You are strong, hale and sane. That being so, I must again ask—why come here?"

"I don't know that I meant to come here," Shan told him. "It was necessary that I Heal myself, before I did damage. There is a war, you see, and the sub-commander is correct, damn her. I'm not a soldier. But the world is under attack. I must be able to fight. I must be able to—use all of my resources."

"And you trained as Soulweaver, the Mother be praised." The man tipped his head. "*When* are you? Captain of a ship that sails between the stars, and more than a touch of the Dragon in you. And your lady is a Moonhawk. I begin, I think, to see."

He stood, flinging the cloak behind his shoulders, revealing a shabby black tunic and patched black leggings.

"I—we—have been here no more than six times since Moonhawk showed me the way. We've never loved the place, nor sought it out of power-lust. Time, you understand, is not very orderly, but I do believe this is the only occasion upon which I met myself here." He beckoned and Shan went forward to take the strong, calloused hand.

"Shan is my name in your when?"

"Yes," he said, as they walked toward the shimmering wall of weaponry.

"In this when," the man lay his hand upon his breast, "your name is Lute. Let us arm me well."

The world looked different, even with his eyes closed.

The information that came through shuttered eyes somehow told him it was afternoon; it also told him that one wall of the tent where he'd been allowed rest-space was in shade.

His left arm was slightly warmer than his right—the sun was on that side of the tent.

There were sounds, each fraught with meaning: he could hear the quiet, regular step of someone walking a guard path; he could hear an occasional low mumble of voices, which meant that he was in an area where security was a concern.

Even the sounds he wasn't hearing meant something. He was alone in the tent, the med-tech having gone elsewhere for the moment.

He savored the information coming in, sorted it and milked it dry of meaning, while some back corner of his mind not engaged in this vital task was explaining very calmly that these things meant nothing to him. He was a master of trade, a Healer—a peaceable fellow, really, despite his place in the line direct of a clan descended of a smuggler, a soldier, and a schoolboy.

yos'Galan—the schoolboy's line—had always been respectable, though, in all fairness, the genes had been mixed across lines so often that it was difficult now to know where respectable yos'Galan began and pirate yos'Phelium ended.

Outside the tent, from the sunny left, came two sets of

quiet footsteps, accompanied by the low murmur of a woman's voice. He caught the word "backup" on the edge of hearing that seemed much sharper than usual, then the steps went beyond the tent and Shan realized he was ravenous.

He opened his eyes and sat up in one smooth motion. The cubicle was as he recalled it; the remaining sandwiches still wrapped under their cool-gel.

He made short work of them, feeding a hunger so great it was almost nausea, at the same time aware that he could always eat one of the ration bars tucked into his combat belt, if the sandwiches proved insufficient to his need.

As he ate, he considered. He was often hungry after a visit to Healspace—perhaps a two-sandwich hunger, he thought wryly, unwrapping the last of the food Dustin had wrangled from the mess tent. When he and Priscilla had traveled so far in spirit to talk to Val Con—both of them woke starving, having lost a tenth or more of their bodies' mass. Magic, Priscilla had said then. *Strong magic uses an immense amount of energy.*

So, Shan considered, polishing off the fifth sandwich with a sigh, Lute's Hall of Weapons must be very strong magic, indeed. He sat back on the cot and shook his head.

"Shan," he murmured, mindful of ears close by, "what in the blessed name of sanity have you gotten yourself into?"

He hadn't taken much from the Hall: a knife and a shield. Things that would serve any soldier well, Lute had said, then held out a thick manuscript. *Soldier Lore* was written across the face of its leather binding in the ornate characters of a language Shan was positive he didn't read.

"Behold, the most useful of all the weapons in the hall," Lute said with a flourish. "Take it."

Shan did, looking at his mentor—at himself—doubtfully. "It's rather heavy, if one is to be marching about. Which seems to be my next assignment."

"Nonsense," said Lute, "it's not heavy at all." When Shan looked again at his hand, the manuscript was gone.

It appeared that the lore of a good soldier was still with him; his bones felt steeped in it.

Shan shook his head and, in an instinct that was in no way his own, began to take inventory.

He had no gun, no sword, no distance weapons whatever in his belt or pouch. The blade he did have was neither a combat blade nor a bayonet, but part of a folding utility kit.

In an emergency, however, *Soldier Lore* informed him, a blade is a blade, so he inspected it carefully, oddly pleased with its quality and balance. He'd held worse and used it to good purpose—he shook his head, banishing the memory that was not his—It was *Val Con* who had the passion for sharp edges of all types; peaceable Shan was accurate enough with his pellet-gun, but he tended to rely on Healer skill as protection from harm.

Weapons check complete, Shan turned his mind to other details that required attention. He stood and walked out of the tent.

"Dustin?"

The startled guard's about-face nearly took Shan's mind off his purpose. The gun had come around—but not dangerously so.

"Sir. I thought you were gonna sleep till the cows came home."

"Are we expecting cows, Corporal? I didn't think . . ."

"Naw," the man waved the expression away with his free hand. "Just meant I was sure I'd have to rouse you when the time came. You've got another hour or so, if you wanna catch another snooze. Sir."

"I have slept, thank you. Is there a way I can check on the boat I came in on? It would be good to know if any messages have come through—or gone out."

"I don't think the sub-commander wants you just wandering around. Sir. It might be better if you'd just go on back inside and—"

Shan sighed inwardly. *Soldier Lore* noted that the corporal could be taken, if need be. He was measuring Shan's distance by soldier-speed, not by pilot speed.

Abruptly, a memory flashed of Cousin Luken bel'Tarda, as un-war-like a man as one could wish.

"All I ask," the gentle mannered merchant would say, as the child Shan tagged after him through acres of warehoused carpets, "is an honest advantage. When I have that, the other party is nearly always positive that my position is weak."

Shan tipped his head, deliberately meek, and reached out, oh, so gently, with Healer sense, inspiring Dustin with goodwill.

"Corporal," he said, voice and face all calm reasonableness. "I've spent the better part of a day inside my work suit inside a lifeboat. At least grant me a chance to walk around."

Corporal Dustin blinked and Shan moved closer, looking gravely into eyes the color of nutmeg. "I suggest you take me to the departure point," he murmured. "I should get a feel for my boots, if I'm going to have to march in them."

Dustin blinked again, glanced down at the boots the quartermaster had supplied. After a moment, he nodded.

"Yessir. We can move in that direction. Might happen we can at least take a glance toward that spitfire of yours when we go by."

Shan smiled and withdrew the tendril of goodwill. "Thank you, Dustin."

They had passed several sentries, but it became quickly apparent that Sub-Commander Kritoulkas did not believe in concentrating her people in one spot. Dustin directed him this way, that way, up a series of trails, all of which showed use, but none that were obviously more important than another.

Shan nodded to himself, pleased with the sub-commander's arrangements—and then, on the very edge of his sharpened hearing, caught a sound.

He listened, ignoring the sound of Dustin's boots scraping against stone: a familiar sound, common in ports and cities . . .

"Dustin," he said softly, "do we have heavy-lift rotor-craft on our side? Perhaps two or three of them?"

The corporal flicked him a startled look, stopped heavily and took his hard hat into his hand. He cocked his head to one side, listening—then snatched for his belt comm.

"Traffic," he said distinctly. "Possible copter noise, any ID?"

"Traffic," came the quick reply. "Ear's going on. Reports to Traffic Two, thank you."

Shan listened. The sound was distinct, now, though it was difficult to be sure of direction through the canopy of trees.

He thought of his late spiral worldward, the rotor noise growing in his ears. From what he recalled, the sounds were coming—

"From the coast," he said, abruptly. "At least two!"

Dustin looked at him seriously, nodded, and thumbed his Communit again. "Traffic Two, we have estimate of two plus rotors coming from the coast."

"Traffic Two acknowledges. The Ear says three, real low. Thanks, son." There was a slight burp then and the whisper of a new message from a dozen spots in the nearby woods.

"This is the Dealer, this is the Dealer. Shuffle the deck, please, and cut it three ways. Player names the game."

"Good ear, sir," Dustin nodded respectfully at him. "Best move with me. If we get separated—anyplace where there's a definite Y in the trail you'll find a dugout about ten meters in toward the empty side, long as you're inside the camp. Might need to hunt a bit. If there's crossing trails you should see a faint fifth trail—look on the opposite side of that."

Shan nodded, pleased again with the sub-commander.

By now the sound was a definite heavy chop. Coming in low. Fast and low.

At the first Y they came to Dustin took him straight ahead into the woods. The corporal ducked low beneath a branch, and disappeared. A moment later Shan found the dugout and dropped in beside him.

Shan felt the dugout slope deeper into the earth, could see where portions of the wall had been reinforced with local wood and branches. One of the cut branches, as tall as he and with a few gray-green leaves still clinging to it attracted his attention. He leaned against the branch. It flexed slightly, but felt sternly durable. His hand went around it comfortably . . .

"This is the Dealer, this is the Dealer. We've got a three-handed game of Stone Poker. Cards are on the table. Jacks are wild. Spectators will refrain from spitting."

Dustin nodded. "C'mon, sir. Jacks are wild means every available hand. Stone Poker means they're up toward the quarry somewhere—"

"My boat!"

"Yessir. Or maybe the Yxtrang wreck."

There was a roar overhead. Dustin ducked back into the dugout. Shan, peering upward through a gap in the trees, saw three black forms lifting into the sky—heading back toward the coast in a hurry.

"That refrain from spittin' stuff," Dustin said, easing out of the dugout. "That means no shooting til we get orders, sir."

Shan looked at him and held out his empty hand and his stick.

"Yessir, I know. Please follow me."

He began to do that, then realized that the sound of the re-treating rotors had changed somehow. He fell to his knees, found the gap in the sheltering branches—

The last of the copters was moving very slowly, almost hovering. Perhaps they had spotted someone or—

A figure appeared from the belly of the copter, sliding down a cable made visible by his motion. A second figure followed, and a third. Four . . .

There were eight of them on the ground, the last having dropped a good distance as the rotor began to move away.

"Sir?" Dustin had missed him and returned, sounding both relieved and annoyed. "Sir? You'll need to come this way—"

Shan stood, automatically brushing the dirt from leather-covered knees.

"Corporal, that last copter dropped eight soldiers over this way."

"I didn't see it," Dustin said doubtfully.

"I did. They must be on that rise over there. Slid down a rope in a hurry."

The comm burped and gave out a muffled chant.

"This is the Dealer. Side-bets are in order when you see cash. Repeat, side-bets are in order when you see cash."

Shan glanced at Dustin's worried face, eyebrows lifted in question.

"Sir, that means we can engage if we have to, local unit leader to decide." He grimaced. "Guess that's me."

He reached for the comm and thumbed the switch.

"Traffic Two, chance that eight slid down a straw near—"

He waved a beseeching hand. Shan nodded, pointed as best he could through the trees.

"Traffic Two, that's maybe eight down the straw near hill four."

There was a pause then, and Shan could feel the tension building in the man's emotive grid.

Finally, "This is Traffic. We have the straw report. Confirm visually, says The Dealer. Tell me go."

"Gone," said Dustin and tucked the communit in its holster, switch off.

Shan wished he'd had a chance to break the boots in. As it was, he'd have sore feet tonight. If the luck smiled, of course.

He also wished he had something more than a branch and a utility knife for weapons. He'd considered making a spear out of the stick—it was nearly his height and reasonably straight—but he didn't have the necessary time. So he carried it, hoping balefully that he now knew how to use a cudgel if he needed to.

The going was slow. They'd climbed down a hill and now were inching up a rocky slope sparsely studded with trees. Portions of the slope were nearly cliff, and it was Dustin's knowledge of the trails that kept Shan from taking several bad turns.

Halfway up the hill they heard muffled voices, speaking a language that Shan's sharpened hearing found unfamiliar. Dustin glanced back, signaling by tapping his ear and then waving an empty hand around the land.

Shan nodded, concentrated. After a moment, he pointed carefully to his left, but still uphill.

Ever more slowly they climbed, with Shan from time to time cringing at the amount of noise Corporal Dustin threw into the wind.

The alien voices wavered, lowered. Dustin looked back to him and Shan concentrated, heard not with ears this time, but with Healer sense: eight intent patterns, one lanced with red sparkings of pain. Shan swallowed and pointed for Dustin—to the left yet, but not nearly so far uphill.

At a crawl, they went on.

A few moments later Shan saw his first Yxtrang. And then his second, third, fourth, fifth, sixth and seventh. They stood alertly on the edge of a shaded pocket of bush and branches just above a near vertical rock drop.

Each carried weapons, some several. Shan recognized a sniper gun, four carbine equivalents, a heavy automatic weapon, and what looked like an anti-armor tube.

When his eyes got used to the light, Shan saw his eighth Yxtrang. That one was sitting down, in the dim pocket of bush, employed in fashioning a rough splint for his left leg. He stood, almost fell, and eased himself carefully back to the ground.

Voices again, as two of the standees leaned in toward the pocket, followed by a snarling phrase that might have been an order given.

One of the standees saluted, fist thumping to shoulder, then the seven whole Yxtrang dropped into trail crouch and moved off, melting quietly into the landscape.

Shan considered the remaining Yxtrang, who had readjusted the splint and was prying himself to his feet by using his rifle for a cane. It came to him, calmly, that a rifle was a far better weapon than a stick. He looked over to Dustin.

It took several moments to make the Corporal certain of what he wished to do, and more than a little exercise of his own will over the other man's to still the argument he saw leaping in the nutmeg eyes.

He moved slowly, silent over the rocks and twigs, and came up on the pocket of brush. He had a moment's vertigo, as he stared down the steep incline and he wished in that moment with all his heart to be back on the *Passage,* and never again be the man who had formulated—who would carry out—this plan.

He shook himself and crept forward a few more inches, making sure of his grip on stick and knife.

The Yxtrang looked up, surprised by the sudden, sure intrusion into his safe place, the trigger of his rifle-cane well away from any useful finger.

Shan moved, the cudgel swung in a knowing arc, slamming the hand that fumbled at the gun, taking the other man off balance, onto his injured leg. Shan closed, the cudgel rising quickly to catch the thrust of the Yxtrang's knife. The eyes that locked on his in the moment before the cudgel crushed the man's windpipe knew no pity, sought no quarter.

The Yxtrang's body went over the lip of the pocket, the knife still uselessly clutched in one hand.

Shan sighed once, short and sharp, and bent down to claim his rifle.

There had been two meetings—one, the scout and
captain alone in the privacy of the tent they shared, Nelirikk
standing guard at the entrance, as was his right and jealously
held duty.

That meeting, the first, had been a quiet thing, for all that
it danced through four separate languages, and at the end of
an hour they two had emerged and walked shoulder-and-
shoulder across the practice field, Nelirikk in his place as
rear-guard, until they came to the command tent.

The meeting there had not been so quiet.

Commander Carmody and aged General tel'Vosti—they
heard the captain out with the respect due her rank and battle
years. The elder female civilian—the delm of the House to
which the captain and the general belonged, and to whom
each owed differing degrees of allegiances in a pattern which
Nelirikk had not quite puzzled out—that was something else.

"You will send your lifemate alone into a nest of Yxtrang?"
she demanded, the Liaden High Tongue sounding like splin-
ters of glass.

"High melant'i, indeed, Lady yos'Phelium. But, tell me,
do, what you expect one man might accomplish against a
horde of ravening animals."

There was silence in the command tent for a moment and the old general looked no less grim than the Terran commander. Captain Miri Robertson sighed and shook her head.

"Couple points you're missing," she said, using Terran to counter the blade of the old lady's outrage. "First off, the man's a scout. He don't wanna be seen—you don't see him. Second, he's got a touch with an explosive that's really something special. Third thing is?" She looked at the old delm until that one stiffly inclined her head.

"Third thing is," the captain said then, "is it's his idea. I don't like it any better'n you do. Spent the last hour trying to talk him out of it. Won't give an inch. Stubborn, too, while we're airing his faults. But the fact of the matter is he's got a point. He's got a chance of getting in, creating serious damage, and getting back out alive. He's the only one we got that I know of has that chance, with the possible exception of Beautiful, here. If we don't stir Yxtrang around, keep 'em off balance and blow us up an ammo dump or two, we're all gonna be real sorry, real soon."

"Good soldier sense, from scout and captain," the General said. "Make your bow to the truth, Emrith."

She glared. "I have seen enough war to last me this lifetime and the next, Win Den. And I say to you that, dragon or scout, the only likely outcome of this lackwitted scheme is that he will die."

"Not necessarily," the scout murmured, and smiled when the delm's eyes crossed his. "I do hold—certain—skills, besides having the advantage of knowing my targets in advance. I may die, but I assure you that it is much more likely that I will come away whole, and return to stand at my lady's side."

Erob sniffed and used her chin to point at Nelirikk, where he stood guard inside the entrance.

"If that has an equal chance of creating mayhem and escaping, why not send it?"

The scout shook his head in the Terran manner and bowed lightly in the Liaden.

"Why so," he said, and to Nelirikk's ear the tone was almost teasing, "should the luck frown and I fall, I will have left my captain with a like weapon with which to continue the war."

"I'll OK it," Commander Carmody spoke then and nodded at the scout. "Draw what you need from stores, and mind! If you take that flitter, you bring it back, boyo. Am I clear?"

The scout bowed once more, eyes serious, though his mouth smiled. "You are clear, Jason. Thank you."

It was on the second day after the scout quit camp that Nelirikk was called to the command tent once more.

He went hurriedly, with a nod for the comm tech who had been testing his memory of call code and band protocol, and arrived to find commander, general, his own captain and the full complement of minor staff awaiting him.

"Sit down, Beautiful," the commander said, giving him the grace of his field-name, and with a wave that might have been an acknowledgment of Nelirikk's salute, or part of the order to be seated.

"Them big hummers of rotor craft," the captain said, without preamble. "What do they carry? Troops, equipment, special weapons? You got the floor."

It took him a moment to realize that he was not being offered a floor as his own, but the opportunity to speak.

"Captain. When well supplied, each can carry eight dozens of troops, or field artillery and four dozens. I have not the range of them since they may carry auxiliary fuel tanks instead of troops.

"They can be used well for forward supply, but are light on top and side armor. They are not attack aircraft and their gunners are but four. It is not unusual for them to drag-drop troops.

"Rumor is that the landing structure was designed for lighter work and is always under repair. Their crews think themselves far above the troops they ferry."

"Well, there's a bit of good news," Commander Carmody commented. "Too good to work as hard as they could for the ground guys."

"How many?" the captain demanded, intent. Nelirikk shook his head, Terran-wise.

"Each regiment has different numbers. I saw four pods of three at the base I was sent from."

"Fifteen hundred troops might thus be moved in a short-range rush, were everyone crammed to overload," said the general, looking up from the paper which was not filled with idle doodling, as Nelirikk had suspected, but a dense line of manual calculation.

"Gotcha." The commander nodded at tel'Vosti.

"Explorer," asked the general, "are they well supplied?"

"Sir. I do not know the mission. I cannot hazard to say."

"Good boy," the old soldier said unexpectedly. "Don't let us wish ourselves into troubles." He glanced speculatively around the table before he spoke again.

"Tell me, Explorer. If you were on the spot, and you knew there to be what might prove to be a courier boat for an opponent's battleship landed within range, what would you do?"

"Courier for a battleship?" The concept amazed. Yet the question was obviously serious. Nelirikk applied himself to the answer.

"If the general pleases. I would send one pod—three—well equipped soonest. A second pod would be fueled and ready for loading depending on need. I would also increase pressure everywhere that I could to disrupt . . ."

"Thank you," the general said, holding up a hand and nodding. "So would I."

Nelirikk sat a moment in uncomfortable silence as something was decided in several glances round the table.

"Yessir," Commander Carmody said, perhaps to himself. "When this little dust up is over, I'm gonna go up the park and find me that fongbear up there and pin a medal on his chest." He came to his feet and Nelirikk jumped up, snapping a salute, only to find that the other was bending over a kit belt.

The commander extracted something small from the belt and handed it to the captain, then turned to Nelirikk, a pistol in his hand.

"Beautiful, we're sending Redhead's Irregulars out in harm's way, and she refuses to budge without you."

The big man extended the pistol, butt first. Nelirikk understood that he was to take it, and did so, stunned by the purity of its balance, its perfect, deadly elegance. The grips were carved of wood, the metal a wondrous satiny . . .

"Took me the same way, first time I saw it," Captain Redhead said from his left. "But listen up, Beautiful—Commander Carmody ain't done yet."

Nelirikk snatched after his wandering wits, raised a hand to snap a salute and was waved into stillness. The commander pointed.

"That pretty belongs to Senior Commander Rialto and if anything happens to it—or to Captain Redhead—she'll give me hell. Bring them both back. That's an order."

His salute was waved away again and the commander held out another large hand.

"You'll want the ammo, too, boyo."

Some things, you didn't question.

Like when the man you'd married, thinking it was bad enough he was Liaden and thodelm in a House she'd figured out by now was one of the fifty called High—when the man you'd slit your own throat before you saw him hurt came to you the night he left for something that might not let him back alive and murmured, "Cha'trez, you must know this. I am Nadelm Korval, by lineage. You are nadelmae, by right of our mating. Should I fall, you must claim the Ring and as delm keep Korval safe."

You heard that, you just nodded, and pulled him close in the dark, and you didn't ask, *So, who do I claim this Ring from and why should they believe me?* and you didn't say, *What makes you so sure I'm gonna outlive you?* You just nodded, and held him and listened to his heart beat, strong and steady next to your ear, and then you kissed him and you let him go, the night swallowing him up, like he'd never been at all.

Likewise, Miri thought, looking down at the golden gyrfalcon in her palm, you didn't ask why Jase Carmody picked you for the hot seat, if he happened to find Nirvana, this war. You just took the token and didn't make a fuss, kept it close and hoped to every possible god of war and peace that you never had to show it.

Miri pinned the token to the lining of her sleeve, then sealed the battle jacket and looked up at her tall shadow.

He looked down at her, dark blue eyes alert, brown face expressionless. She'd gotten used to him, mostly, but there were times, like now, when she felt ice sweep down her backbone, remembering what this man was.

Going into battle with an Yxtrang at your back. Robertson, if I'd've known you were going to turn out a nut case I'd've left you on Klamath.

Miri sighed and straightened, giving her aide a grim smile.

"OK, Beautiful. Let's round 'em up and move 'em out."

They sat in what order they could in the back of a large farm truck bouncing its way along unpaved track. The captain had appointed of her troop three lieutenants, naming them properly First, Second, and Third, and she also appointed the sergeants. The under-officers then appointed the squads.

It was what one might expect of a unit put together of remnants and volunteers, moving in all haste toward its first blooding. Still.

The captain sat to his left, her eyes closed, though her grip against the catch-rope was not that of a sleeper. Nelirikk cleared his throat.

"Captain?"

The fierce gray eyes snapped open. "Yo."

"I have not had time to finish properly, but I have been working on something for the troop, if you allow."

She sat up straighter, looked into his face with a curious expression.

He reached among the hastily stowed supplies, and pulled a plain cloth sack from between several sealed containers of explosives.

"I had hoped to make it more complete, but glory comes upon us quickly . . ." he said, deftly fitting together the lengths of tubing.

Holding the staff in the crook of his elbow, he then took

the square of labored-over cloth from the bag, unfolding it as gently as he could in the crowded, lurching truck.

The captain stared, and for a moment he thought that he had offended, that she would reject his gift to the troop—

"That's some piece of work," she said, taking a portion of the flag in her hands. She looked up at him, feral eyes bright. "Your idea?"

"Captain. Yes. A gift for the unit for being permitted as a recruit. If it pleases."

The nickname of the unit, 1st Irregulars, was rendered in the trade language, as befit a troop made from as many different sources as theirs: bronze letters on a black stripe fully a third of the flag deep. The symbol—ah, that had been a hard night's thought!—a knife in silver with two sets of wings, one black, one white, set on a green field. One set of wings were dragon's wings, to honor Jela's arms-mate, who had founded the House of the scout. The blade was Jela's own symbol, of course; and the other set of wings was from the bird of the Gyrfalks.

"It pleases," the captain said amid the growing buzz of interest as others of the troop began to take notice.

"Hang it up," she said, then, and he did so, fastening it to the top of the distaff, where it hung, brave in its solitude, without yet the proper complement of captured enemy flags to adorn it.

"That's good," the captain said, softly. "That's real good, Beautiful. Turn it around now, so everybody can see." She came to her feet and jumped lightly onto the seat, one small hand on the catch-rope.

"All right, listen up! We still got us a bit of riding before we start our march, and we got one more important decision to make. First off, I want squads together."

In a remarkably short time and with only a little too much jostling, the squads formed themselves.

"OK!" called the captain. "Some of you close by saw what I have here. The rest of you take a good look at the unit's flag! Now you got a choice. You can go out there and fight and hope no one notices you. Or you can go out there and fight and let 'em know you're there. Which squads ain't in-

terested in carrying the unit flag into our first fight? Hold
your hands up and sing out!"

The close-packed squads were abruptly silent, sitting as
still as they could.

The captain let the silence stretch, then flashed a grin at
the assembled soldiers.

"Darn," she called out, "that's gonna make my job harder.
Be sure you understand that this is serious stuff. Which ever
squad carries this flag is gonna get a lot of heat. It'll be noisy
and it'll be for keeps. You'll have to run with it and protect
it, and, most important, you'll have to bring it back safe."

Nelirikk, holding the standard high, felt his heart lift. For
here, indeed, was a captain. On the spot, she created a competition, offering the flag. It was the preparedness check-and-
drill, with officers standing by to see what needed remedy,
what weapons were underprepared, which squad's knives
were out of place.

The truck cranked, lurched, and ground to a halt that shuddered every bone in the back. Nelirikk glimpsed forest
through the open hatch, with hills sloping away, and an over-
grown path too narrow to permit passage of the vehicle.

"All out!" the newly appointed sergeants bawled. "Fall
in!"

"Troop Beautiful." The captain spoke quietly under the
noise of evacuating the truck. "Please do the honor of marching the unit's flag down to squad three and turning it over to
their bearer."

He stared. After a moment, he remembered to breathe.
"Captain," he said, though it was not his place to remind a
captain, "I am not in the line of command."

She grinned at him. "Orders, Beautiful. And always remember—volunteering is its own reward."

FENDOR

MERCENARY HEADQUARTERS

The door guard looked first at Nova, taking in the leathers, the face, and the frown. The second look caught Liz, who nodded easy-like and lifted two fingers in casual salute. The guard nodded back.

"ID?"

"Lizardi," Liz said and obediently stared down the bore of the retina-reader. It beeped positive and the guard slung it back over her shoulder.

"Her?" A jerk of the head at Nova, standing silent and astonishingly patient at her side.

"She's with me."

"Recruit?" Palpable disbelief, there.

"Lookin' to hire."

The guard's face cleared. She nodded to Nova and touched a stud on her belt. The door behind her slid back along its track and she stepped aside to let them pass. "Cleared to Dispatch. Need a guide, Commander?"

"I remember the way, thanks," Liz said and stepped forward, Nova yos'Galan following a respectful two steps behind.

* * *

Fendor 'quarters doubled as Home and it was always hopping. This evening, the place was wall-to-wall with mercs, many with kits on their backs. Liz frowned. Something was up. Something *big* was up. She lagged half-a-second and let a crew of six pack-bearing techies get in front of her.

"Might be hard for you to hire," she muttered as Nova came abreast. "Looks like some big doings."

"Only lead me to Dispatch, Angela Lizardi. I anticipate no difficulty in hiring."

Liz snorted and lengthened her stride as much as conditions allowed. A couple minutes later, she took the right into Dispatch, which was crazier and more crowded than the main hall, and forged ahead toward the counter without bothering to make sure the Liaden woman was still with her.

She broke into the clear space before the counter and grinned in sudden delight.

"Hey, Roscoe!"

The square built little guy hogging the main screen looked up, bald head gleaming under the lights. Raisin-colored eyes scanned the crowd, pinned her. The enormous mustache—black like he was twenty instead of rising sixty—lifted in a grin.

"Lizzie! I known this one bring you out from hidin'! Come over an' tell me who you got."

She shook her head and walked over to him, reaching across the counter to grab both shoulders.

"What happened to your pigtail?" she asked, remembering the shiny, foot-long braid that had been his pride, even above the mustache. Roscoe pulled a long face.

"Ah, I sell it to buy a watch for m'wife, but you know what? Bitch leave me anyway." He laughed—a roar that belonged to a man twice his height—grabbed her forearms and squeezed—gently, because Roscoe was stronger than he looked. "Lizzie, you lookin' damnfine. I get relief in two hour. You stick aroun' an' we do a mattress test, eh? I book you in second wave." He dropped her arms and bent to the computer. "Tell me who you got."

"I don't have anyone," Liz said quietly.

"We wish to hire," Nova yos'Galan added from her side. Roscoe looked up, blinking his hard little eyes.

"You want to hire? You got to wait. Suzuki's hiring everything got a gun." He made a shooing motion with his hands. "Come back two, three day, we maybe got a couple 'prentices lef' for you to hire."

Nova shook her head. "My business is urgent and I will hire soldiers," she said, firm, but not with the blaze of temper Liz had expected. "Please let it be known that I will double the payout on Suzuki's contracts."

Roscoe stared at her for a beat of three before he looked over to Liz.

"Who the hell this?"

"I will pay," Nova stated, cutting Liz off before she could answer, "in cantra."

Roscoe pursed his lips. "She crazy?" he asked Liz.

"You could say."

"Fine." Roscoe looked back to Nova. "You crazy. You gotta hire. You pay in cantra. Nothin' I can do. You talk to Suzuki, cut you own deal. Then I make it OK wit' the 'puter. *Ichi?*"

"*Su bei,*" Nova said surprisingly. "Where may I find Suzuki?"

"You stay put. I bring her here. No way I miss this one." He grinned and flipped a toggle on the board. "Suzuki, you come front Dispatch," he said into the mike. "Somebody you gotta meet."

She had expected another such as Angela Lizardi—rangy, tough, and tall. But the woman for whom the crowd parted minutes later was no taller than herself, sturdy and efficient. Her hair was very short and very black. Her eyes were chips of blue ice, set at a slant in a composed, determined face.

Nova straightened, for if Val Con himself had named Angela Lizardi first speaker, then the woman who came now was surely a delm.

The woman stopped at the edge of the crowd with a nod.

"Liz," she said and her voice was quiet and clear. "We can use you."

"So Roscoe said," Angela Lizardi replied in her laconic way. "But I'm here with her." She jerked her head and Nova found herself caught by those slanting blue eyes.

The owner of the eyes bowed, not a generic, Terran, surrogate handshake bow, but something that recognizably approached the proper mode between strangers of unknown rank.

"Suzuki Rialto, Senior Commander, Gyrfalks Unit."

Nova bowed as between equals and saw interest move in the blue eyes. "Nova yos'Galan, Clan Korval," she returned. It was perhaps not best wise to give her true name within this crowd of unknowns, but one wished to deal honorably with honorable persons. She straightened.

"You may know us as Tree-and-Dragon Family."

The other woman's interest intensified. "Indeed, the unit has done business with Tree-and-Dragon in the past. What may I be honored to do for you, ma'am?"

Good. A person of integrity and quick wit. Nova inclined her head. "I have need of soldiers, Commander. Many soldiers, and at once. I am informed by this person here," she used her chin to point at Roscoe, "that you are hiring everything that has a gun. I submit that my need is at least as great as your own and ask that we work equally toward equal ground."

She heard Angela Lizardi snort, but did not deign to look at her. Suzuki Rialto's face betrayed slight interest, and a tinge of regret.

"It must of course pain me to deny Tree-and-Dragon Family this consideration," she said, most properly. "However, my need overrides every other conceivable need in this galaxy or the next. I am blunt with you, ma'am. You will forgive me when I say that I have people trapped upon a world under Yxtrang attack." She swept a small, square hand out, indicating the now-silent crowd.

"What you see here is a rescue force. You may outbid me—in fact, I don't doubt that you can. But I do not believe you will hire one soldier until we have rescued our own."

But Nova was staring at her, feeling a certain sense of wonder unfolding within her and tasting, *tasting* the tang of the luck, Korval's curse and Korval's blessing.

"Under Yxtrang attack?" she repeated, to gain the time she required to assimilate it and then shook her head as her mother had often done, not to express negation so much as baffled amaze.

"Commander Rialto, it may be we have a common goal."

Suzuki Rialto tipped her head. "Please explain."

"My brother is on that planet—local name Lytaxin. And the lifemate of my brother, as well."

"That's Redhead she's talking about there," Angela Lizardi put in and the other woman looked at her sharply.

"She says," Liz added. "I don't put much stock in that side, myself. Last I knew, she was calling him her partner." She pointed her finger and Nova raised an eyebrow. "Show Suzuki your picture there, Goldie."

She reached into her sleeve pocket for the folder, opened it and offered it to Suzuki Rialto, who took one quick look and laughed.

"Him? Last *I* saw them, she was as likely to kill him as kiss him."

Nova felt her lips twitch, all at once in sympathy with her new and unknown sister. "It is a common dilemma, when one deals closely with my brother," she said solemnly, closing the folder and slipping it away.

Suzuki grinned, then let the expression fade to one of calculation. "It seems our goal is the same, ma'am, as you have pointed out. I suggest that I am skilled in the hiring and outfitting of soldiers, as is Commander Lizardi. You are yourself perhaps skilled in an area where my expertise has currently fallen short."

Nova inclined her head politely, acknowledging the truth of the other woman's words and her own willingness to hear more.

"In what manner might I assist you toward attaining our common goal, Commander?"

The blue eyes met her straightly—the look of a delm, in truth.

"We need ships," said Suzuki Rialto.

Nova truly smiled, then, and bowed.

"As it happens, I can locate ships."

"I thought you could," Suzuki said gravely and offered her arm. "Let us retire and discuss particulars." She looked over to Miri Robertson's first speaker. "Liz? Are you in?"

"Couldn't keep me out with a battalion."

There had been opportunity to kill more Yxtrang, on the way from the pocket of brush to the quarry entrance. Dustin had accounted for two and Shan three—one of those a lucky shot into the impenetrable treetops, prompted by the very faintest of out-of-place leaf rustle.

But the quarry. The quarry was where the heavy action centered.

"Looks like they're after your boat, sir," Dustin whispered, as they crouched behind a conveniently placed boulder. The lifeboat was precisely where he had left it, upright in the entrance to the quarry, closer to the mercenaries' line than the Yxtrang.

"Indeed it does, Corporal, but why? It has no fuel. It has no weapons. It has a radio, but surely the Yxtrang have their own radios?"

Dustin looked at him oddly. "Hard to tell why 'trang'll do anything. Maybe they want it for a war prize. Important thing is, if they think it's worth arguing over, we gotta be sure they don't win the argument."

At the moment, it appeared that Sub-Commander Kritoulkas' regulars were holding their own in the argument. The Yxtrang liberally sprinkled throughout the trees opposite were actively involved in the dispute, but had made no push to advance their position. Shan sank a little lower behind the shielding boulder, thinking about that.

"Are we seeing a diversion, Corporal?" he asked finally. "Or are they waiting for friends?"

"Hard to say, sir." Dustin was moving, inching his rifle into position. Shan looked, saw the target, looked again and chose his own mark.

The argument continued, and all at once the Yxtrang began to move, pushing their line grimly forward. Behind them, deeper into the opposite wood, Shan's sharpened hearing registered the sound of heavy equipment, distinct even in the fury of the firefight. He flicked a look at Dustin.

"There's something big moving in the woods."

The corporal nodded, face pale except for the thread of blood down one cheek, where a chip off the boulder had cut him.

"I feel it," he said, mouth tightening. "Get ready to fall back, sir. They were waiting for the armor to catch up with them."

Around him, then, he felt a—withdrawing—as, one squad at a time, the mercenaries melted back from their positions. Across, the Yxtrang pushed forward, and the sound of the armor moving was thunder in the ground, rattling through his chest and into his head.

"Now," Dustin said. "Fall back." Shan nodded and heard the other man leave, even as he tried to recall if he had seen anything like anti-armor, in his brief and all-too-incomplete tour of the mercenary encampment.

Where, he wondered, *are they withdrawing to that will stand safe against a tank?*

A pellet struck his boulder, spraying his face with gravel. Shan ducked, found the range and fired. An Yxtrang soldier crumpled out from behind a bush that was too meager to shelter him and didn't move again.

He was alone on what had been the mercenary line, Shan realized, and about to be overrun by Yxtrang. Yet, why should he fall back, when the means to kill the oncoming tank was right here?

The lifeboat's coils still functioned, after all. It was but the work of a moment to set them to overload.

Decision taken, Shan began at last to move from cover to carefully chosen cover, angling toward the lifeboat.

Beautiful was two steps behind her, armed like an officer, and almost totally silent, which was more than she could say for the rest of the unit.

There'd been a kind of constant crunch as the Irregulars moved through the woods—nothing to be done about it at this point—and then a single distant boom, as if something really big had blown up.

That one was a puzzle. It wasn't the sound a shell made being fired, or the sound it made hitting something, usually. And it sure couldn't have been an ammo-dump because Miri knew Kritoulkas had been running mostly with carry-it-yourselves.

Her people did pretty good at not stopping when the guns started chattering.

There was a lot of gun noise she didn't recognize right off and that made her nervous, because if she didn't know the sound it was likely to be Yxtrang caliber stuff.

The battle-flag was about twenty steps ahead of her, wrapped tight around its staff. The squad that had it was moving out. Likely they thought they'd show up, unroll the flag, and scare Yxtrang back into space without a ship.

Not bloody likely.

The key here was going to be showing up at all. The Yxtrang, even if there were a lot of them, probably had their hands pretty full because Kritoulkas was bossing a near-pure Gyrfalks crew.

The communit in her pocket hadn't buzzed, which was good news—it meant Jase and the house guard were still holding a quiet fort. Be bad if the Irregulars didn't have a place to go home to, once the party was over.

She signaled a stop, waved her three lieutenants in. One of them hunted out this way, regular.

Beautiful was there, back to her. He was carrying his field pack and two extra ammo boxes for the automatic weapon carried by the flag-bearing unit, no complaint, no slowdown. At halt he'd dropped the boxes and instantly gone on alert.

Miri saw how he watched: lower level of trees, mid-level on rock-piles and such, eyes long enough on each spot to catch color or movement. The greenies either stared hard at one spot and waited for it to grow wings or swiveled their heads around so fast they'd get themselves whiplash.

She took her time deciding on the next phase of the march. The sounds were heavier to the west, which the local looie thought meant they were centered on an old quarry on the south side of the merc camp. That could be good if it meant Kritoulkas had the Yxtrang pinned down. The firing was getting pretty heavy . . .

She nodded, reluctantly broke the squads into two groups. The smaller group, four squads under the local, would take the uphill side. As they closed into the quarry they'd follow some path he knew.

Her main group of six squads would waltz right on down the main trail, trusting that the sub-commander was still holding up her end of the bargain with the mercs.

She felt eyes on her, turned to see Beautiful looking at her.

"What's up?"

"Nothing is up, Captain. No air cover. No sign of ambush in the trees. No listening devices."

Inwardly, Miri sighed. "I meant, what's bugging you? What should I know?"

"Captain, only the single large explosion. By now if there was artillery it would be in use. We have here one hundred. Probably the unit we will face has more."

"Great. Even odds."

She wasn't sure if he got the sarcasm; he simply nodded and asked permission for a drink from his canteen, since action might come upon them anytime.

The distant shooting went almost quiet for a moment or two and then became insistent and rushed.

She knew the sound of that—one side had managed to mass a bit of a charge. The heavy, nearly steady beat of a Paradis 88 made her suppose the Yxtrang were on the move against a well defended spot.

She waited while the lieutenants carried her news to the

sergeants, and then they moved on, the crunch of boots not nearly as loud as the growing noise of battle.

The four squads under the local lieutenant melted away as best they could. The main body continued ahead, with the sound of firing heavy and the acrid smell of battle permeating the air. Forward motion halted abruptly. Soldiers dropped, taking cover. Ahead, the woods were noisy, like whoever was there didn't care if they were heard.

Miri dropped, felt the presence that was Nelirikk, positioned like a bodyguard, protecting her back, while his height still allowed him to see beyond her.

The noise stopped as suddenly as it started, and then there was a more distant sound, as of confident marching. Miri began moving toward one of her lieutenants when the woods near her lead troops exploded with the sound of a Paradis 88.

The targets were up on the hill, and Miri could suddenly see the movement and hear the return fire of dozens of alien weapons. There was a whoosh, an explosion and scream— but by now it was clear which side was which and her lead troops opened live fire on an enemy for the first time.

It was obvious they'd stumbled into a flanking movement by the Yxtrang, one that the Paradis had been supposed to foil.

Now it was their turn, and she signaled her squads into a battle line, tried to straighten out a kink that could be dangerous. The folks on the hill hadn't been expecting quite so many people, apparently, but they were still willing to fight.

It was hard to tell, but it looked like there were more and more of the Yxtrang up on the hill, as if the whole damned bunch of them had tried an end around.

The Irregulars were returning fire, but the lead squad was in big trouble and likely to get cut off. The Yxtrang were concentrating fire there, and there were more of them on the hill, so many that it looked like a charge forming.

Miri pulled the whistle from her pocket, sounded the attention blast and the double-pulse of short pullback. The Irregular's firing dropped decidedly then as they all tried to worm backward five meters like they'd been taught.

"Beautiful, up there. A charge forming?" Miri yelled.

"Yes, Captain. I believe it likely."

"Tell that crew there to open up with their toy. Now!"

Nelirikk crawled to the crew with flag still wrapped tight, carrying the boxes of extra ammo to them, taking time to point out the most likely route down the hill . . .

There was something quite satisfying in the chatter of the Sternbach. True, it wasn't a Paradis 88, but it should do. She glanced back at the smoke-wreathed gun crew.

Shit. Now they were for it.

The gun crew sat behind their almost-shield of a downed log, the Irregular's battle-standard waving insults at the enemy.

Unexpectedly, up on the hillside, a spot of color showed, flapped—snapped to blood red.

Nelirikk was suddenly beside her, low to the ground, a very real grin on his face.

"Captain, we face Tactical Assault Twenty-Two. They are very famous for their attacks!"

She cussed but he didn't hear, for at that moment the woods screamed with Yxtrang rage and the charge began.

There wasn't time for finesse. Miri blew the command that released squads to sergeants. And when she turned to repeat the call in the other direction, she saw the Yxtrang behind them.

This charge was really aimed at the Sternbach—in fact both of them were. The unit was falling back on its own accord toward the flag; the Yxtrang were heading there, too.

A young trooper—one of the refugee volunteers—fell half a yard away, the side of his face gone. Miri dove, snatched up his rifle and fired into the oncoming mass while the Sternbach kept up its end of the conversation, and the Paradis—

An Yxtrang fell at her feet, dead, and the short sharp sound of a pistol going off behind her warned her to turn.

The pistol spoke again and there was a wounded Yxtrang flung by her. He started to rise, and she took him out, spinning into a forest of blades as the Yxtrang wave and the 1st Irregulars crashed together and merged.

Miri fired, dropped her man, found another target, and heard Nelirikk scream, "Yadak!"

She saw the blade flashing downward, killing-bright in a huge hand, swung the rifle up to catch it—

From behind and above, Nelirikk's arm swept out, into the blade, smashing it out of the Yxtrang's hand and Nelirikk's hands were around a throat, crushing, and he roared out, "Irregulars! Irregulars!"

The Sternbach chattered on and other voices took up the yell, "Irregulars!" and the flag stood over it all.

Nelirikk's arm was bandaged, but his care was for the flagstaff, whereon he hung—upside down—the flag of Tactical Assault Twenty-two.

Miri waited for yet more casualty reports, watching as the crew of the Sternbach fieldstripped it lovingly.

"Beautiful," she said finally. "What's yadak?"

"Captain." He was carefully looking more at the flag-project than at her. "Yadak was the field name of a dead man. It means nothing."

Miri nodded. She'd been afraid of that. "So you knew that guy. I'm sorry—"

He shrugged, discomforted by more than the wound, Miri thought.

"Yadak made many errors, Captain. He joined the 14th Conquest Corps. He came with them to this planet. He volunteered for Tactical Assault Twenty-two. And he attacked my captain with a machete while she stood command over a unit with Jela's insignia on its flag."

"You mean he shoulda known better?"

He took his time answering.

"Captain, Yadak and I both learned at Jela's feet. He left the home unit before I did, seeking action." He looked at her, blue eyes bleak.

"Yadak did not believe much in tradition. But, yes, Captain. He should have known better."

The position of lifeboat number four had been stable for some time. Ren Zel touched a switch on the main board.

"Tower." Rusty Morgenstern's voice was scratchy with fatigue.

"This is the command helm, Radio Tech," Ren Zel said, as gently as one might in the sometimes bewildering modelessness of Terran. "Please do the grace of directing a laser-packet beam to these coordinates—" The transfer was made from his screen to Rusty's with a keystroke. "Alert this station when a dialog has been established."

"Will do."

"Thank you," Ren Zel murmured, and hesitated a moment over the proper phrasing. "Do honor your rest-shift, Radio Tech. The ship depends upon your acuity."

There was a slight pause, followed by a sound that might have been a grudging chuckle. "Caught me, did you? I'll hit the sack as soon as we get Shan on the line. Tower out."

"Command helm out."

He returned to his duty. The watch-points reported nothing untoward. Apparently they had won a measure of respect from the Yxtrang in their first encounter.

Or the Yxtrang were biding their time.

Regardless, the *Passage* continued its spiral orbit toward Lytaxin. Ren Zel pulled up an auxiliary screen and began to calculate approach vectors, measuring this orbit against that, in terms of best defense of the world below . . .

At some point he became aware of a presence beside him and looked up to find Priscilla Mendoza standing quietly at his shoulder, her eyes on the watch screens.

"A quiet shift, First Mate?"

"A quiet shift, Captain. Lifeboat four has come to rest. The Tower is attempting to establish contact. The Yxtrang have been—circumspect."

"Well for the Yxtrang," she said, moving her eyes at last from the screens and smiling at him.

Ren Zel went cold, and in that instant she reached out to lay a hand on his shoulder—a sister's touch, warming, yet inexpressibly painful to one who was dead to three sisters of his blood.

"It's Weapons Hall," the woman before him was saying, her deep voice resonant; her black eyes brilliant and fierce. "I told you I had preparations to make. For the good of the ship."

"So you had." He cleared his throat. "One had not anticipated . . ."

She laughed, rich and full, drawing the eyes of the duty pilot in a quick flick over a shoulder before he returned to his board.

"No, how could you? I barely anticipated it myself, and I've been to Weapons Hall more times than I can count." Her eyes strayed again to the watch-screens, touched the corner that elucidated the position of lifeboat four, and moved on to the work screen.

"You're calculating defensive orbits. Good. We'll also want to bracket that battleship. Have you found anything like a defense system?"

"Debris," Ren Zel said, reaching to the board and bringing up the charts. "Ship's records indicate satellite defenses in orbits correlating to the orbits of clustered wreckage." He looked up into those brilliant black eyes. "The Yxtrang were thorough."

She nodded.

On the main board, the channel light glowed to life.

"Tower here."

Captain Mendoza leaned over his shoulder, extending a long arm for the switch.

"Hi, Rusty."

"Captain," the Radio Tech said seriously. "Wanted to let you know—there's no answer on that punchbeam."

Ren Zel held still, watching the side of her face, refusing to allow himself despair. For after all, there were many reasons why the laser-packet to lifeboat four might have gone unanswered, and not . . . all . . . of them were dire.

"I see," the captain said quietly. "Keep trying, in quarter-shift rotation. When the reply comes through, notify me immediately."

"Yes'm. Will do."

"Good," she said. "And, Rusty . . ."

"Ren Zel already read me the riot act," he interrupted. "I'm turning the Tower over to Tonee and Lina and getting me some shut-eye."

"Lina?" the captain repeated, blankly.

"Yes, Lina." The voice of the ship's librarian came briskly out of the speaker. "I speak Yxtrang, Priscilla."

"You do?"

"Certainly," Lina said, as if it were the most commonplace of talents. "Why not? The scouts gave the tapes. It would have been a poor use of the gift, to allow them to languish."

"Of course," the captain said seriously, but Ren Zel thought he saw the corner of her mouth twitch. "Carry on. Captain out."

"Tower out," Lina said. The line-light dimmed and the captain turned her brilliant eyes back to himself.

"Speaking of off-shifts—First Mate, I believe the shift passes."

He made to rise from the command chair, his eyes touching the screens once more. "Captain—" he began, and froze.

In watch-screen three—a blot of nothing where moments before the instruments had reported clean space.

"Fleas," he said, hand sweeping out for the all-ship. "All crew, attend! Fleas at three o'clock! Battle stations. Level red."

Beside him, he heard—no, he *felt*—a gasp, and his eyes leapt in some fey instinct to the corner where the coordinates for lifeboat four should be displayed—

And read instead the stark message from the tracking computer:

CONTACT LOST. LIFE POD UNIT FOUR OFF-GRID.

The explosion was—beyond his expectation.

When the ground stopped bucking, and after prudently giving it another few minutes to re-acquaint itself with a less volatile state of being, Shan sat up, sticks and gravel raining off his shoulders.

He had expected a . . . significant . . . result from overloading the lifeboat's coil circuits, and had taken care to put what he believed to be a sensible distance between himself and ground zero, dashing like a long-legged hare through the forest, stasis box under one arm, bulky Yxtrang rifle in the opposite hand, to drop at last behind a solid-looking boulder and bury his face in the mold.

He had not expected a force that would uproot trees around him, shattering boulders less stalwart than his chosen cover, and throwing cargo-holds of dirt and gravel high into the air.

In the aftermath of the shock came a silence so profound Shan wondered if he had been deafened. He stood, shaky, but keeping a good grip on the rifle, and wiped his face on the leather sleeve of his combat jacket. The silence was terrifying. The wreckage of downed limbs and exposed roots, bewildering. If the lifeboat's last duty had caused such damage here, what must the site of the blast be like?

"Really, Shan," he said, and it was a relief to hear his own voice, blurry and cracked as it was. "You might have killed someone."

Abruptly, he sat on the ground behind the boulder, jaw clamped against a sound that might with equal possibility be laughter or a scream. Automatically, he began an inventory.

The rifle was unharmed, the magazine full. The Yxtrang soldier's ammunition belt, too large for his waist, was slung from shoulder to hip, like a bandoleer. The Yxtrang's grace-blade, which Dustin had retrieved along with the belt, hung within easy snatch of his right hand.

Weapons counted and made certain of, he turned his attention to the stasis box. It was dented, the Tree-and-Dragon scratched, but the seal had held. He smiled when he saw that and lay his palm over the scratched insignia.

. . . more than a touch of the Dragon in you . . .

He shook his head sharply.

Priscilla, he thought, painfully, *is not going to take the news that the lifepod is off-grid with equanimity.* No more than he would, had their places been exchanged. Though it was to be hoped that his lifemate would have had more wit than to detonate a coil-driven vessel on a world-surface.

Sounds were beginning to nibble at the edge of the silence. Shan raised his head, listening, sorted out gunfire, some distance to the east.

Nodding, he came to his feet, picked up the precious box and the rifle and looked around him.

The fallen trees gave almost too much cover, the grounded branches were more hazard than assistance. So, he took a few moments to plot his course, from this rock, to that log, to that tree, to *that* one, and then to that large red rock, where he would plot the next stage of his travel.

He was in the midst of his third stage of travel toward the battle-sounds when his open Healer sense caught a familiar glimmer of pattern. He altered course and in a very short time was face to dirt-smeared face with Corporal Dustin.

"Sir." There was honest relief and not a little wariness in the nutmeg-colored eyes. "Thought we'd lost you."

"Only temporarily misplaced, for your sins," Shan said, slipping behind the corporal's sheltering log and settling the stasis box close.

"You near the big blast?" Dustin asked.

"I'm afraid I'm the one responsible for the big blast. If the coil circuits in a spacefaring vessel are simultaneously closed and set to charge at full, they will overload and catastrophically give up their energy in something just under five Standard minutes. I can do the math for you more precisely later, if you find you're interested."

"I'll just take your word for it," Dustin said. "Sir." He chewed his lip. "Shouldn't there be a safety trip, so you don't overload by accident?"

Shan looked at him. "There is."

"Right." Dustin sighed. "Yxtrang armor?"

"I'd wager a cantra, if I had one, that the Yxtrang armor is not going to be a problem, Corporal. They were stopping to inspect my boat as I fled . . . What's the situation here?"

"We're pretty scattered. Got seven, eight, within sight. 'Nother half-dozen down along the stream. Gin's got fifteen to the rear and hugging the hill."

Twenty-eight soldiers. *Seasoned* soldiers, Shan corrected himself. Soldiers who knew their business and operated like professionals. He looked at Dustin.

"We should consolidate, sweep in toward the quarry and secure the ground."

"Yessir." Dustin reached to his belt, pulled out the comm and flicked it on.

"Traffic Two, captain's gonna swing us back the way we come."

There was a moment of startled silence, then Sub-Commander Kritoulkas' voice came from the comm, very distinctly.

"Put the captain on."

Dustin handed the unit over. Shan found the talk button on the side and depressed it.

"Good evening, ma'am."

"You." Her tone was not cordial. "You happen to know anything about that lifeboat?"

"It seemed expedient to dispose of the object of the quarrel," Shan told her earnestly. "Especially as there was Yxtrang armor approaching."

"Great. Tell you what. Have Dustin move the crew—they know the drill. We're getting some help down from the house that'll make up the second hand. You stay pegged right where you are and wait for them. Keep the comm and tell me what you see. Can you do that, Captain?"

"Yes, ma'am."

"Then do it," she said, and the line went dead.

They flushed two pockets of Yxtrang on their way down toward the quarry. They took an anti-air tube from the first bunch and a couple more casualties from the second before Winston got close enough to lob in one of Val Con's home-made Grenade Surprises.

From the second bunch, then, they got two Irregulars dead, five of what Beautiful identified as Troopers Regular Field Long Arms, and the ammo belts that went with them. Miri sighed. The dead now numbered twenty, all greenies. The injured numbered slightly more, with five or six needing a 'doc pronto two hours ago.

The sweep went on, with the Irregulars and the bits of Kritoulkas' crew they picked up along the way hopefully pushing what Yxtrang were left down toward the quarry and into the second sweep line of seasoned mercs.

Some would get away, of course, running ahead of the closing jaws to regroup and—maybe—await pickup. The object wasn't to kill every Yxtrang in the park. The object was to secure the area to the old quarry and hold the line.

Miri scanned the terrain ahead. They ought to be coming up on the Eyes Kritoulkas had posted at the hinge-point pretty soon. When they hit that point, they'd swing south a little to close the loop, then squeeze back in toward the quarry.

"Captain," Beautiful said from behind her, but she'd already seen him—a lean figure in battle-leathers, ammo belt slung bad-ass style across his chest, a rifle—correction, an Officers Personal Duty Long Arm—held ready, but not threatening anybody.

It wasn't until she'd left the line and gone closer that she saw the white hair under the helmet, the winging eyebrows and the silver eyes she'd seen once before, in a dream that was true.

She stopped, pushing her own helmet up with a fingertip, saw him look first for the insignia, then back, for her face. He recognized her with a lift of white brows.

"Captain—Robertson?"

She sighed. "It'd have to be, wouldn't it? With the kind of luck I've got?" She ran her eyes over him again: dinged up helmet, filthy face, scuffed leathers and that damned bandoleer. And the rifle. Where the hell had he gotten that rifle?

"I haven't been having the best day myself," Val Con's brother told her in a voice that had probably been real pretty, fifteen bad frights ago. "I do think I ought to mention, however, that there is an Yxtrang standing behind you."

She turned her head enough to glimpse Beautiful out of the edge of her eye.

"Get used to him," she said. "His name's Nelirikk Explorer and he's sworn to Line yos'Phelium." She pointed. "Beautiful, this is the scout's brother, Shan yos'Galan."

"I give you good greeting, Shan yos'Galan," Nelirikk offered in High Liaden.

The silver eyes closed, as if maybe Val Con's brother had just gotten a bad headache. Not that Miri blamed him. His eyes opened and he inclined his head.

"I give you good greeting, Nelirikk Explorer, oath-bound to Korval." The eyes moved to her. "Where is Val Con," he asked, back in Terran. "By the way?"

She shook her head, briefly flicking her attention to the pattern of him inside her head: busy, concentrated, *intent*. Aware of danger, but not in trouble.

" 'Nother part of the woods. He's doing just fine, and he'll be real glad to see you, when we're all back in camp."

He held still a second, like maybe he was considering how much profit would come to her from lying to him. She didn't blame him for that, either, but waited until she had his nod before pointing at the comm on his belt.

"Kritoulkas says to pick you up for the sweep and leave Scotty here on comm-call," she told him, jerking her head to the Gyrfalk leaning heavily on the rough crutch.

He nodded again and pulled the unit free. Miri took it and handed it to Beautiful, who carried it over to Scotty and bent to help him settle into cover. The silver eyes followed him, face displaying a sort of wry resignation.

"You do get used to him, after a while," Miri said, and Val Con's brother looked back to her.

"I'm certain that one does," he said politely.

The worn red counter was in her hand, hot with Shan's presence. Shan's living presence. She was aware of it, and then not, as the demands of defense claimed her attention.

"Gun Teams Three and Five, fire at will."

The *Passage* shuddered. Her screen showed a brief blaze of clean space in the wake of the charge, filling as she watched with the mushy nothingness that was the fleas' signature.

Mother, how many can there be?

The red counter flashed in her fingers and there was a wrench and—*she stood high on her toes, craning over the cornstalks, staring down the blue sky to the ragged black horizon, and the wind of their coming was a furnace blast and where they passed, nothing was left alive . . .*

Her hand swept across the control board, struck one toggle: "Engineering, half-power to main engines, on my mark.

Mark." Another: "Piloting, on my mark accelerate ship's rotation to plus fifty percent." And a third: "All crew, strap down! Repeat. All crew, strap down!" She took a breath and touched the last toggle.

"Piloting, you have my mark."

The ship paused, gathered itself and began, slowly, to spin.

"Engineering, when we achieve plus fifty percent on spin, increase power to main engines to three-quarter."

"Engineering. Aye to three-quarter on plus fifty."

"Priscilla," the voice was very soft. "What do you?"

She turned toward Ren Zel, strapped in as ordered at the auxiliary board, caught the edge of his fear with that sense that wasn't Healer sense at all, but a far more frightening Sight, which was the burden of those who had been to the Hall.

She took a breath, banishing her knowledge of his secret terrors.

"The fleas," she said to his worried eyes. "Long-range weapons are useless. We could empty everything we have and still not stop them all. And we don't know how many have managed already to get inside the watch-points. If we increase ship's spin—"

He inclined his head. "Those which have not yet anchored themselves shall be thrown off and those who approach will have difficulty matching vector. As well as gravitational problems." He paused, frowning past her shoulder as the *Passage* tumbled around them.

"If the captain will allow me, there is another item of close-in defense which may be utilized."

She waved a hand for him to continue, saw the flash of the red counter along her fingers.

"The meteor shield. Should we adjust spin to opposite— matched as close as we are to a planetary gravity field, a charge will be built . . ."

. . . and the space between ship and shield would be filled with an effect not unlike an intense aurora. Which would fry everything in its field.

Priscilla looked at her first mate, past the properly expressionless Liaden face to the horror and the resolve within him.

"Necessity, Captain," he said, softly.

She nodded. "Necessity, First Mate." And touched the toggle for Piloting.

A halt was called when they reached the southernmost point of the sweep. Shan bent carefully, set the box between his feet, straightened, and closed his eyes. His bruises had stopped bothering him some time back, swallowed up in a weariness so vast that he considered it perfectly possible that he would fall asleep where he stood.

There were others on the march in worse shape than he— walking wounded. He could see the bloodred glimmerings of physical pain amid the larger matrix of the unit, as well as every conceivable shading of terror, stress, and anguish. Eyes closed, he shifted, thinking muzzily that he should do something about that. He was a Healer. People needed him.

He took a breath, ran a rapid exercise to energize himself—and saw the brilliant pattern of Val Con's lifemate very near at hand, attended by a massive calmness of mauve and mint.

Shan opened his eyes.

Val Con's lady was less than an arm's length away, the tattooless Yxtrang at her back. She was holding out a canteen.

"Thought you might could use a drink," she said. "Since you lost your own jug."

Water. The thought woke a torment of thirst. He took the canteen and put it to his lips. The water was warm, tasting faintly of plastic, and he savored it more than the most precious wine in yos'Galan's renowned cellar.

He allowed himself two exquisite swallows.

"Thank you," he said, offering the "jug" back to her.

She waved it away. "Keep it," she told him, the wave turned into a point at the scratched and dented stasis box. "What's in the keep-safe?"

He looked at her. "Seedlings."

"Seedlings," she repeated, expressionless, then nodded. "Beautiful here can carry that for you."

Shan froze. "I beg your pardon," he said carefully. "I may

not have made myself clear. This box holds half-a-dozen stasis-bound seedlings from Jelaza Kazone. It's my duty, as a pilot of Korval, to carry them to safety."

Val Con's lady held up a small hand. "I *said*," she repeated firmly, "Beautiful can carry the box for you."

It was, in any light, an order. She was Val Con's lifemate, and Nadelmae Korval could certainly order mere Thodelm yos'Galan as she chose in matters of Tree and clan. And in all good soldier-sense, the box was weighing him down, slowing him down, making him a less effective soldier. As commander of this particular military action she could just as easily order him to leave the box, as hand it over to . . . He looked up into Nelirikk Explorer's face, gathered himself for a deeper looking—and saw the big man bow his head.

"Be at ease, Shan yos'Galan," the Yxtrang said in High Liaden. "I am of Jela's own Troop. The seedlings of his Tree are safe with me."

"*Jela's* Troop?" Shan repeated.

Not possible, he thought first. *After all these years?*

If that isn't like Val Con's damnable luck, he thought second, with a touch of what he suspected was hysteria, *to pick up this particular Yxtrang, of all possible* —He snapped off that thought as a third occurred to him.

"Do forgive me if I raise a painful subject," he said to the Yxtrang, in Terran. "But I wonder if you had previous acquaintance of my brother. Perhaps eleven or twelve Standards ago?"

"Yes," Nelirikk said.

"And you've sworn yourself to his line?" Shan demanded. "I'd have rather thought you'd try to murder him."

"He tried," Miri Robertson broke in. "But the deal was that whoever came out winner in armed combat between the two of them would be boss, and Val Con won." She jerked her head. "Time to move out. Give Beautiful the safe."

He did as he was told, but it was with a definite pang that he saw the big hands close over the Dragon seal and lift the box away.

He was beyond weariness, into a state of hyperaware numbness, where every leaf-twitch abraded and the taste of emotions around him seared.

It was Healer sense that saved him.

The emotive grid was alien, dark with blood lust, dank with deep-held horrors. Shan felt it in the instant before the twig snapped under the force of the Yxtrang's charge.

There was no room to bring the rifle up, no time to go for the knife. The axe blade descending toward his head was black, light absorbing and wickedly sharp. Shan shouted—what, he had no idea—and *reached,* grabbing for the shield he had used to save him from Priscilla's wine-shower, a far-away lifetime ago.

The axe sang downward. Bounced. Broke.

The Yxtrang screamed rage and Shan *reached* again, into the dank undergrowth of horror, snatched up a squirming, squealing nightmare and threw it with every erg of his will into the Yxtrang's waking mind.

The scream this time was not rage. The Yxtrang threw away the axe haft. Hands clawing at his eyes, he whirled, crashing back the way he had come as gunfire exploded on all sides.

Shan sprang to the left, fell heavily behind a log, brought his rifle up and fired into the Yxtrang charge.

It was a quick, dirty fight, the Yxtrang being armed with nothing more than the standard long-arm and apparently without an officer to command them. The charge into the sweep line was ill conceived—or the last valiant act of desperate men. In either case, there were twenty of the enemy counted dead among the trees when the noise was finally over.

Shan sagged behind his cover, cheek on his arm, wondering, in a sort of foggy apathy, if he would be able to stand when the order came, much less walk.

Behind him, a leaf scraped leather and he rolled, rifle swinging up to target—

"Peace, Shan yos'Galan." Nelirikk Explorer dropped beside him, astonishingly quiet for so large a man. Feeling somewhat sheepish, Shan lowered the rifle.

"The captain sends to find if you are wounded."

Wounded? He tried to focus attention on his body, but gave the effort up after a moment with a frustrated shake of his head.

"Merely exhausted. I think. This is not the sort of outing I'm accustomed to."

Surprise showed on the big man's face. "No? But surely you have been a soldier?"

Shan sighed and dropped his head back on the ground, watching the other through half-closed eyes. "I have never been a soldier," he said, as clearly as his abused vocal chords would allow.

There was a short silence. "And yet you bring glory to the troop, for to capture that rifle was not easy. Unless you made your kill from afar?"

"From all too near," Shan assured him. "It must be noted, however, that the previous owner of the rifle was wounded. And I had a very stout stick."

"Stick." A grin cracked the impassive brown face. "Truly you are of Jela's get, and the scout's brother."

A whistle sounded: three short blasts, pause, one long.

Nelirikk stirred. "That is the call to move on. Stay vigilant a short time more, Shan yos'Galan. We are on the last leg of sweep. When we reach the quarry, there is rest."

The whistle sounded again: one short. Nelirikk grinned.

"My captain calls," he said, and vanished into the trees.

After a moment, Shan pushed to his feet, settled his helmet and stepped back into line.

BORDERING EROB'S HOLD

BEHIND ENEMY LINES

Thus far, Nelırıkk's information had been accurate in the extreme.

Val Con crouched in the slender concealment of an armored landcar's rear wheel-well and peered cautiously out. His time in the generator shed and in the ammunition cache had been well spent, and he flattered himself that his most recent efforts in the motor pool would not be found despicable.

As he worked his mischief, he counted—air transport, land transport, foodstuffs and stocked ammo. The count had confirmed Nelirikk's theory that the 14th Conquest Corps, in its stretch for glory, had perhaps over-reached itself.

And would soon be overextended more seriously still. Footsteps sounded, loud in the night. Val Con ducked farther back into his hiding place. Two sentries tramped by half-a-foot from his nose, eyes straight ahead, long-rifles resting on broad Yxtrang shoulders.

Val Con held his breath, exhaling very softly when finally they were past. His internal clock gave him two hours until the generator shed opened the evening's festivities. Time enough to create conditions productive of even more consternation before he removed to the flitter.

Carefully, using all of his senses, he checked the immediate area for watchers. Finding none, he eased out of the motor pool and melted into the shadows at the edge of the troop way.

Some minutes later he entered a barracks, ghosting down the cot-lined aisles. He paused here, there and briefly by the soldierly caches of battle gear at the base of each cot—silent, quick and unhesitant.

The luck was in it, that he encountered no wakeful trooper, though he was forced to freeze in place for a time his heightened senses demanded for hours when a long form shifted in its nest, muttering an irritable order to one Granch to have done and fire the damned thing.

The trooper subsided without coming to a sense of his true surroundings, and Val Con ghosted on, out of the barracks and into the night.

The communication center was his last call of the evening. Deliberately so, for anything he might contrive there would need to go forth quickly, and at an increased risk of his capture.

Val Con sank into the thin dark place between a water tank and a metal shed bearing the Yxtrang symbols for "Danger: High Voltage" and assessed the situation.

Communications Central was well lit and very busy, indeed. There were two sentries at the entrance and a constant hubbub of coming and going. Val Con frowned, noting the abundance of officer's markings on the scarified faces of those frequent arrivals and departures.

Something had happened. Something big had happened. He *knew* it.

He sank back in the shadow of the two buildings, watching the crowd come and go. He checked his internal clock. Fifty Standard minutes before the first explosion took the camp by surprise. Not enough time, good sense argued, to listen at Yxtrang doors in the hope of hearing something worthwhile.

And, yet—If the 15th had arrived?

He slid to the very edge of the shadows, held his breath, chose his path across the brightly lit roadway, and waited.

His patience was shortly rewarded by the simultaneous arrival of three agitated officers, whose jostling at the door distracted the sentries' attention just long enough for him to dart through the dangerous light and into the shadow behind the flimsy temp structure, where he followed the wires to his goal.

LIAD

JELAZA KAZONE

On the sunny eastern patio, Anthora yos'Galan looked up suddenly from her breakfast, and frowned as she scanned the empty lawns.

"Jeeves . . ." she murmured and the hulking robot standing near her chair replied, its voice proclaiming it a male of Terra's educated class.

"Working, Miss Anthora."

"I . . . believe . . . we may have company. Four individuals?"

"One to each compass point," yos'Galan's butler said smoothly. "Shall I deal with it?"

She was silent a moment, biting her lip and considering the patterns of the intruders. Coldness, imbalance, disharmony and ugliness—each so like the other that one nearly became persuaded they thought with one brain. But, no. She had seen the like of these before. The work of the Department of Interior was impossible to mistake, once seen.

"How did they get in?" she asked the robot.

"Accessing perimeter files. I have an anomaly, sixty-three seconds in duration, one-half hour ago. My apologies, Miss Anthora. They came through a particularly resistant section of perimeter. I see that stronger measures are called for, though one dislikes employing coercion."

She turned her head and blinked up at the featureless ball of its "head," momentarily diverted from the threat of potential assassins.

"Coercion? Jeeves, my brothers told me you were a war robot before they reclaimed you to be our butler. Surely you've practiced coercion in the past."

"One may be practiced in an art of survival without necessarily enjoying it," Jeeves commented, moving a pincher arm toward the teapot. "May I warm your cup?"

"Thank you," she said and held it out, silent until the tea was poured and the pot replaced.

"Tell me the truth, Jeeves. *Were* you a war robot?"

"I was many things, Miss Anthora. As befits the motivating force of an Independent Armed Military Module. Shall I deal with the interlopers on our lawn? It won't take but a moment."

Anthora sipped her tea, and extended her thought to the eastern pattern. Idly, experimentally, almost playfully, she exerted her will against the chill ugliness. And felt something move, deep within the construct imposed by the Department of Interior.

Anthora sipped again, shook her head, Terran style, and lazily set the teacup aside.

"No," she told the robot, "leave them. They won't be staying long."

Jason heard him out impassively, then got up and walked to the rear of the tent.

"Coffee, boyo? It's old, but the tea's older."

Val Con leaned back in the camp chair, weary, now that there was leisure. "Is there water?"

"That there is."

There was a slight clink and the sound of liquid running, then Jason settled again at the table, big hands curled around a steaming steel mug. Val Con raised his mug, closing his eyes and concentrating on the sweet feel of water along a parched throat.

Jason sighed, sudden in the silence.

"So, the 'trang're massing and they're facing this way. Not the best news we've had on the week, but not unexpected. Why else did you spend all that time with Erob's people, planting those little tokens of esteem around the grounds?"

Val Con opened his eyes. "It would be better, if they did not get this far."

"Can't argue with that," Jason conceded and raised the mug for a swallow of old coffee.

Val Con sipped at his water, and allowed himself for the

first time in days to touch the place where Miri's song lived within him.

For a moment, he simply beheld her essence. His eyes filled and he closed them, bringing all of his attention to her, asleep and distant as—

He opened his eyes and put the mug down so suddenly it thumped on the table.

"Fact of the matter is, 'trang general has his nose outta joint because Kritoulkas and Redhead just threw a bunch of his crack kiddies out on their ears," Jason said, possibly to himself. "Not only that, but they lost the prize, and a bit of their own armor, to boot." He shook his head. "Small wonder we're up for special attention." He raised the mug, drained it and set it aside.

"We're as ready hereabouts as we're likely to get," he said, suddenly brisk. "Next good thing to do is make sure we've done our best down the hill." He pushed back from the table and paused, eyes suddenly speculative.

"You'll want to be with Redhead for this next bit, will you, lad?"

Miri had been in battle while he was away from her side. She might have died—Val Con shook his head sharply and glared into Jason's face.

"I certainly want to be with her so we might usefully plan the best defense," he said, more curtly than he had perhaps intended.

Jason merely nodded and stood up. "We're both on the same wavelength. Meet me at the flitter in fifteen minutes and we'll go on down together. I'll just call over the Big House and let the general know he's in charge."

They were met by an improbably cheerful soldier with a newly healed gash on her chin. She ran a disinterested eye over Val Con and gave Jason a wide grin.

"Morning, Commander. You missed the party."

"That's right, Sandy, rub it in," Jason said mournfully. "I suppose I'm not taking it hard enough that you had such a good time t'other day when I was stuck up the hill with nothin' to do but watch the tyros train."

She laughed and turned, guiding them expertly through a series of interlocking trails.

As the lady's conversation was reserved for her commander, Val Con amused himself by identifying trenches and probable weapons caches, while he kept half an inner ear on the song that was Miri. She was very near now, he could tell from the flavor of the song. He discovered his heart was pounding, though the pace their guide had set was no more than brisk. Indeed, it was all he could do, not to leave his companions behind and run through the forest, into his life-mate's arms.

"Almost there," Sandy said, guiding them sharply right, then left, and abruptly there was a camp, and soldiers, and sky shielding strung over the whole.

The sentry went left without hesitation. Val Con, his attention on Miri's song, looked right, toward its emanation, hoping for a glimpse of copper braiding, or an edge of her face, but the way was filled with leather-clad strangers—

Val Con stumbled, heartbeat stalling. He found his feet instantly, heart slamming painfully into overaction. Breath returned with a shout.

"Shan!"

The white-haired man whipped around, pilot-fast, graceful in fighting leathers. His arms opened and Val Con hurtled into the embrace, hugging tight, his cheek against his brother's shoulder.

In that moment, he was a child again and Shan returning home at last from the long year of contract-marriage. He had been with his music tutor when he heard his brother's voice in the entry-hall and had leapt from the 'chora to fly down the stairway, into the ready embrace.

"Shan, *Shan . . .*"

"Hello, denubia."

Beloved voice and oh, gods, to hold his brother to him, to feel the heartbeat beneath his cheek and the lungs laboring so . . .

He eased his hold, leaning back in arms that seemed reluctant to lose him, raised eyes, and then shaking fingers to his brother's cheek.

"You're weeping."

Shan grinned, wavering. "So are you."

There was a sound quite close at hand, as possibly of a whetstone being drawn slowly down a blade: Jason Carmody clearing his throat.

"Take it you two know each other."

Val Con flicked a glance to Jason, noting the high color in those portions of the face not hidden by golden beard.

Blushing, he thought in astonishment. *We've embarrassed Jason Carmody, the man who has no shame.* Carefully, he went half a step back, releasing Shan with a reluctance that was echoed in his brother's withdrawal.

"Shan, this is Gyrfalks Junior Commander Jason Carmody, commanding the forces here." He lay his hand on the leather sleeve—*merciful gods, to once again touch kin*—gulped a breath and looked up into the big Terran's face.

"Jason, here is—here is my brother, Shan yos'Galan. Master Trader and—and . . ."

"And captain," Shan's voice smoothly covered his emotion, "of the battleship *Dutiful Passage,* in Lytaxin system. Perhaps, by now, in Lytaxin orbit."

The unnatural color was already leaving Jason's cheeks, though his eyes sharpened considerably.

"You don't say. Wouldn't be that you're the laddie brought that lifepod down into our quarry, would it?"

"Unfortunately, it would," Shan said soberly. "I do apologize, Commander, but there really was nothing for it. The pod was all but out of fuel. I had to come down somewhere."

"Well, and you're part of my reason for being here. We're bound for a bit of chat with Sub-Commander Kritoulkas and Captain Redhead, if you'd care to join us?"

Shan inclined his head and Val Con caught the flicker of a smile in his direction.

"I'd love to join you, Commander. You should be warned, however, that Sub-Commander Kritoulkas doesn't seem taken with me."

"Sub-Commander Kritoulkas," said Jason, turning to the left once again and motioning the patient sentry to move on, "isn't taken with most people. Count yourself approved though, laddie. After all, she let you live."

•   •   •

Val Con had changed, Shan thought, settling next to him round the sub-commander's hastily cobbled conference table.

He had thought so, when the two of them had spoken mind-to-mind and Val Con issued the orders that ended with four of the line direct on or near Lytaxin, and in peril of all their lives. Mind-to-mind speaking, however, had claimed more of his attention than he had supposed. The larger pattern had matched the Val Con he had known, and he hadn't leisure, then, to peruse its subtleties.

Now, as Commander Carmody spoke apart with Sub-Commander Kritoulkas while they awaited the arrival of Val Con's lifemate, he had leisure.

Damage. With Healer's eyes he traced a swath of devastation through memory, heart, and thought. That there had been enough of the essence of Val Con yos'Phelium left after the storm of destruction to effect a Healing was nothing short of miraculous.

For Healing there had been. Shan traced that, too, along the brutal path of ruin. Whole segments had been regrown, others were still in process. Still other segments had been patched, strengthened, and reintegrated into the whole—a whole that was recognizably and indisputably Val Con.

Only—different.

And just now beginning to show the colors of tension and distress.

Shan blinked, brought his brother's face into focus, and reached out to touch his hand.

"Val Con. What befell you?"

The mobile mouth tightened and Shan heard anguish and something that tasted of—shame?—along the edge of his Inner Ear, but the green eyes did not falter.

"The Department of Interior befell me." He took a hard breath. "I'm sorry, Shan."

Sorry? Shan shook his head, extending Healer's senses and once more tracing the scars, the damage, so very—much—damage.

"How?"

Val Con smiled, humorless. "You don't want to know."

"Then at least tell me—with intent?" But even as he asked, his inner eyes found the pattern, among the layers of scarring and repair. Not a Healer's touch, no. But the touch of someone very certain of his effects, who had inflicted his tortures with foreknowing thoroughness.

He blinked and looked again into his brother's eyes.

"Balance will be—difficult."

"Balance by Code," Val Con told him, "is not an option."

Shan nodded, seeing that resonate through the darkness of the man who was now his brother. Formerly, Val Con's pattern had—sparked, flaring here and there with excess energy and passion. This revised person showed no such exuberance, yet passion was not dead. Merely, it was—consolidated—a hot, bright glow from the deep center of him, from that place one might call his soul.

From that lambent center, from Val Con's very soul, leapt a construct of living opalescent flame, arching strongly and entirely out of that which was Val Con, to find its equal and apposite root—in the scintillate, stubborn essence that was Miri Robertson.

"Hey, boss." Her voice brought him out of a contemplation of that astonishing structure and into the world that was. She slid into the vacant seat at Val Con's left hand and nodded cordially to Shan, her Yxtrang taking up guard behind her—No, Shan corrected himself, behind *them*.

"Found your brother, I see."

"Cha'trez." Val Con's smile was so tender Shan felt his stomach wrench, even as he saw the flames of the lifemate bridge ripple and flow, back and forth, from soul to soul.

"Nelirikk." Val Con had turned in his seat to address the Yxtrang. "I find you well?"

"Very well, Scout. We have won glory for the Troop on the field, and gained two flags which hang subservient to our own."

Val Con lifted an eyebrow and looked to his lady. "Have we a battle standard, I wonder?"

She grinned at him. "Piece of quality merchandise, too. Cultivate a little respect and we'll show it to you, after the jaw's done."

"When am I not respectful?"

"You want the whole list, or will a summary do?"

"OK, here she is." Jason Carmody broke off his conversation with the sub-commander and the two of them approached the table. He grinned.

"Redhead. Kritoulkas tells me your bunch worked like pros."

She shook her head. "We did OK," she said seriously. "Lost a lot of people, though."

"Happens, when you're running with volunteers and tyros," Jason said, matching her seriousness. "Important thing is, you seen action and got the job done. They'll know what to expect next time, which is fine, because the scout's brought news of a bigger party coming our way. Seems you and Kritoulkas have earned yourselves some admirers."

"Not just that," Kritoulkas said in her sour way. "This last bunch of 'em were after the captain's lifeboat. Expect they might have thought he was sent from this battleship of his down to the house. House looks like a command post. Hell, a month ago, it was a command post."

Jason Carmody nodded and looked over to Shan. "Want to bring me up to speed on that?"

So, for the second time in as many days, Shan told the story of the sabotaged pod, the Yxtrang attack, and his unplanned arrival on the planet surface.

"And I find since that I've made a rather serious error, Commander. I honestly did think it was best for everyone to detonate the lifeboat and stop the Yxtrang armor. However, the lifeboat contained a working space-link radio, which Sub-Commander Kritoulkas tells me is something of a local rarity at the moment."

Jase nodded. " 'trang took out the satellite net first off. Standard operating procedure, according to Beautiful. We're gonna need to know what upstairs looked like, last you saw it. Grab you a computer outta—"

"That's done," Val Con's—*Miri*—spoke up. "Had him working on it soon as we pulled back here." She reached in her jacket pocket, removed a disk and passed it over. Jason grinned.

"One step ahead of me, which is what I should have expected, my small!" He looked back to Shan, who lifted his eyebrows.

"An outline of my ship's capabilities and strengths is also on the disk."

"Hah! Your idea?"

"It did seem the sort of information you might find helpful," Shan said and Jason grinned again.

"Gonna retire and let the crowd of you run the war. Call me when it's over."

"Might want to reconsider," Miri said, her shoulder nestled companionably against Val Con's. "My experience is that retirement's a good way to get yourself into more trouble than you know the name of."

Jase nodded. "I'll hold off a bit, then. Not any too fond of trouble, myself." He looked around the table, abruptly serious.

"Here's what, people. We're as ready up the house as stubbornness and the scout's ingenuity can make us. Kritoulkas and me're gonna walk the area when we're done here, to see if we're missing anything the 'trang might want. But we're at a bad disadvantage when it comes to air support and cover. As in, 'trang got it, and we don't." He looked at Shan.

"Think that ship of yours can provide any cover?"

"We carry one space-to-world gun," Shan said slowly. "Which is good for offense, but not particularly outstanding for defense. Besides that, we have no radio . . ."

"Don't give up so easy," Jase advised him. "Very possible that we'll capture us a 'trang radio for the scout to coax into honesty. You're right, though, son. Space-to-world weapon's nice to have on the side of the angels, but it's no substitute for good local air cover, which is what we don't have, Erob's force having gone West when 'trang bombed the fields, coming in."

Val Con stirred. "Air cover. But would a bombing run—several bombing runs—against Yxtrang strategic targets be of just as much utility?"

Jason shrugged. "Sure. While we're wishing for pie-in-the-sky we might as well wish for ice cream, too."

Val Con shook his head and leaned forward across the table. "There is nothing fantastic in such a bombing run, Jason. We have here—" he pointed to Shan, to Nelirikk, and touched himself lightly on the chest—"three pilots of Master quality. We have there"—a point off to the southwest—"many dozens of aircraft."

Jason stared. "Yxtrang aircraft."

"True enough. However, Nelirikk is in a unique position to coach my brother and me in the fine points of an Yxtrang board. I promise you, we are both able learners. And with three planes in the air, we might do real damage. With the luck beside us, we might just possibly convince the 14th Conquest Corps that the prudent course is strategic withdrawal."

"Hmm." Jason stroked his beard.

"Bad plan," Miri said flatly. Val Con turned his head, both eyebrows up.

"Miri, if it lifts, we can fly it. Neither Shan nor I has yet found his limit in piloting." He tipped his head. "Truth, Miri."

"I don't doubt it. But unless you're planning on a real spurt of growth in the next half-hour or so, it ain't gonna work."

"I don't under—"

"Simple." She cut him off and pushed her chair back, motioning him to stand up with her. "Beautiful, plant yourself there. Boss, you stand right here." When the two of them were side by side, she stepped back, arms crossed, and hitched a hip onto the edge of the table.

"If Beautiful is standard-issue, and from what we seen, he is, you're about a foot-and-a-half shy of make-weight."

Shan had to admit she had a point. One did not usually think of Val Con as small, but set against the Yxtrang, he appeared almost fragile. Viewed thus, it seemed even more fantastic that Val Con had fought hand-to-hand against this giant—and *prevailed,* as both Miri and Nelirikk insisted was true.

Miri shifted abruptly, leaning forward as if she had seen the steel overlay Val Con's pattern—which, Shan thought suddenly, she might well have.

"Ain't no use getting stubborn," she snapped. "Won't change the fact that *you're too little*! Cockpit made to hold Beautiful is gonna have stuff set outta your reach."

"If the captain pleases," the Yxtrang said quietly. "There is some variation in height among the Troop. Cockpits of fighter craft are somewhat adjustable. A pilot the size of the scout's brother can easily fly."

Miri nodded. "That's good. Any Yxtrang pilots measure down to the scout?"

Hesitation. "Captain. No. Occasionally an—undergrown— Troop survives to adulthood. But they are never pilots."

"Hah." Val Con lifted an eyebrow, catching his lifemate's eye. "*Scruffy midget?*"

Her mouth twitched. "Point is—"

"The point *is,*" Val Con interrupted, "that, if the cockpit can be made to accommodate Shan, then it can be adapted only a little more to accommodate me. We can certainly fabricate adaptations."

"Is that right, Beautiful?" Jason Carmody asked, across whatever might have been Miri's answer.

"Commander. I—I believe it possible."

"Then we go with it. Three in the sky, taking out the prime points, while the rest of us shred 'em on the ground. That should set 'em to re-thinking their position."

Sub-Commander Kritoulkas nodded. "You and Redhead want to walk the line with me now and get a feel for the situation while the pilots work out their differences? I got a feeling sooner's the way the smart money bets."

"Right you are." Jason loomed to his feet. "Meet us back here in a few hours, boyo," he said to Val Con. "We'll want to coordinate pretty close. Coming, Redhead?"

"In a sec." She waited until they were alone before pinning each with a glare in turn. Shan felt her will strike his and ring, like a blade off of hull plate.

"OK. The three of you work out the best way to run this gig. I understand you gotta take risks." She looked directly at Shan, which he hardly felt was fair. "What you ain't gotta take is *stupid* risks. Val Con."

"Captain."

She eyed him. "Figure your adaptations and test 'em out. When you've got things to where you think you can fly, I want you to think if you'd let Shan or Nelirikk or me fly with those arrangements. And if the answer comes up 'no,' I want you to back away from it, you hear me?"

"I hear you, Captain."

She shook her head. "For whatever that's worth." Once again, her eyes touched each of them in turn. "Nothing stupid, all right? It's an order."

"Captain," Nelirikk said. "We will bring glory to the Troop."

She sighed and slid from her perch on the edge of the table. "And here I thought you were listening to me."

Ship's archive provided latitude and longitude of Erob's clanhouse and Priscilla ordered the *Passage* into a synchronous mid-orbit above that location. It was the least they could do for Korval's ally, she thought.

The very least.

Since the successful repulsion of the flea attack, the Yxtrang had offered them no more harm, though Lina reported a lively interest in the *Passage,* its heading and possible mission, in the messages she monitored. It was Rusty's particular frustration that he had not yet been able to establish a link with the planet, while listening in on Yxtrang radio chatter remained absurdly easy.

As she approached the bridge to relieve Ren Zel, she considered the problem of communication. Erob possessed a pinbeam, but ship's archive indicated that the in-house had simply been a booster station, by which messages were sent to a satellite-based transmitter/receiver. The Yxtrang destruction of Lytaxin's satellite defense had also taken the pinbeam, which meant that a 'beam sent from the *Passage* to the address of Erob's receiving station would never find its mark.

But, Erob's *in-house* might still be capable of receiving, if there were some way to deduce an address. Ren Zel argued that a broadbeam call to any and all listeners imperiled more than it might aid, but she was beginning to reconsider that. If they were clever . . .

The door to the bridge slid open and she stepped through, nodding to Thrina and Vilobar, who were going off-shift.

They stopped for a moment, speaking to her with the warmth of old friends, but she read pity in them. That confused her for a moment until she recalled that, of course, they thought Shan was dead.

Silly friends. Shan wasn't dead. She would know if Shan were dead. Which she had told Gordy when he rushed to the bridge after the lifepod went off-grid. She saw him try to believe it and come half to terms with the fact that she would know. She could have helped him to full belief, but that would have required Healing and she didn't—quite—trust the edge of Healer sense that had been honed in the cold stone hall of weapons.

She made her way quietly to the command station and paused by Ren Zel's shoulder. He was a-hum with concentrated energy and she looked to the screens, seeking the reason.

"What is that?" she demanded, staring at the tangle of ships and IDs on his prime screen.

"I attempt to ascertain," he replied, without looking up. "They began releasing shuttle-craft about five hours ago, and now there are cutters, lighters, and work-boats away. Small craft, lightly armed; most have only meteor shielding; none, save the cutters, are planet-capable." He sat back and, most un-Ren Zel-like, ran a hand through his hair. "It makes no sense."

Priscilla frowned at the screen. The Yxtrang did indeed seem bent on sending as many poorly armed craft as possible into peril. Why? What gain? She felt something between her fingers, looked down, saw the red counter and idly walked it across her knuckles, her attention once again on *why*.

If the *Passage* were to pick off those defenseless craft one by one? The gain would be a measure of the range of her guns, as well as an understanding of the enemy: Would the *Passage* attack, waste power and supplies on pawns? Would a warrior chief, such as the commander of the Yxtrang battle-ship, trade materiel for that information?

No, she decided, the red counter warm in her palm. The trade was wrong—too many ships were fielded. His intent was otherwise.

Ren Zel's work screen showed a shifting, three-dimensional

pattern—Maincomp's view of the situation. Taken in whole, the pattern bore a relation to the *Passage's* own orbit, though it was obvious that they were in no peril from—

Priscilla froze, her eyes on Maincomp's pattern.

"Assume the current number of ships remains stable," she said, barely aware that she was speaking aloud. "Run calculations for six hours, twelve hours, twenty-four hours and display the results in sim."

Ren Zel's fingers were already moving across the board. The work screen blanked momentarily, then the simulation began.

The ships moved in strange ballet, revealing and hiding the Yxtrang battleship in coy display.

"Replay," Priscilla directed, "from the vantage of the battleship."

Once again, the ships danced, orbits intersected and diverged. Priscilla heard Ren Zel take a sharp breath.

"It opens. It closes," he murmured and Priscilla nodded.

"It's an eye. Those ships are shielding the battleship from us, and every"—she checked the sim—"every twenty-two hours, a path manifests in the shield-wall, from the battleship to the planet surface."

Ren Zel moved, demanding an elucidation of the point that passed beneath the Yxtrang battleship's position once every twenty-two world-hours, though she could have told him that—of course—it was Erob's clanhouse.

She leaned forward, reaching past him for the comm-switch.

"Tower, here."

"Rusty, I want you to send broadbeam to the planet surface, timed bursts thirty seconds in duration, three bursts over the next thirty minutes. The Tree-and-Dragon signature, if you please. Let's see who we wake up."

"Yes, ma'am." Keys clattered over the open line, then Rusty was back. "First burst away, Captain. Second and third on the timer."

"Thank you. Relay any reply to the command helm immediately."

"Will do. Tower out."

"Captain out." She flipped the switch and looked over to

her first mate, noting the weariness in him. Smiling, she touched his sleeve.

"The shift passes, friend. Get some sleep. The next few shifts may be very long."

The key was the start-up sequence.

Each pilot had fifty-five seconds to touch a prescribed series of keys, toggles, and pins, which simultaneously brought his fighter's various systems on-line, charged the engine and announced that the pilot was, indeed, of the Troop. Should the pilot miss or misplace a keystroke within the sequence, his plane would not only fail to start, but the defense computer would redirect the paths of two high voltage currents into the pilot's couch.

Encouraged toward excellence by Nelirikk's description of a failed sequence he had witnessed during his own training, neither Val Con nor Shan mislaid a stroke, from first run to last.

They moved from that to a generic description of an Elite Guard's personal armament—two to five hidden knives; a long arm with bullets carrying internal flechettes of pain-killer so a victim would not understand his wound, or fast-acting poison, or even hallucinogens; and an assortment of clubs, spikes, and such, and perhaps a hand gun as well—and a thorough lesson in the facial graphics of those most likely to be encountered one-on-one.

That done as thoroughly as might be on such short notice, Nelirikk had Shan go through the drill a dozen times more on the dummy board they had hastily constructed of scrap wood and one of Kritoulkas' conference chairs. When he pronounced himself satisfied with the performance, they set about modifying the "cockpit" to Val Con's dimensions.

The modifications included a broom handle, several shaped plastic grips, and a chock of wood to bring the brake pedal within reach of short legs. Val Con flew through the sequence, shaving time on each run, until Nelirikk called a halt.

"Scout, understand that if you fall below the allowed timing by a factor exceeding five, the defense computer assumes it has been subverted by an enemy robot and releases the electricity."

Strapped into the conference chair, Val Con sighed and pushed his hair out of his eyes. "Thank you. I will bear that in mind. Again?"

"Again," Nelirikk agreed. "Strive for fifty seconds."

And fifty seconds it was, perfectly done. Nelirikk nodded. "Enough."

Val Con unstrapped and came to his feet, leaning over the dummy to disengage his adaptations.

"And have you done as Captain Robertson commanded, brother?" Shan asked from behind him. "Have you considered whether you would allow her or myself or Nelirikk to fly with those mods?"

He knelt and pried the chock loose from the "brake pedal," then rose lightly and faced his brother.

"I have asked myself that question. And I must say that I would certainly never allow anyone who fell under my care to fly such a gerry-rig as we have here." He nodded toward the block of wood he held and look back to Shan, green eyes brilliant.

"Unless flying it held the best chance of their survival and the survival of kin."

"Necessity," the Yxtrang said surprisingly and Val Con nodded.

"Necessity."

"Necessity," Shan agreed. "I only wonder if your lady will see it."

"Ah." Val Con moved his shoulders. "My lady may not. But I expect that my captain will."

The channel light came on and Priscilla depressed the switch.

"Command helm."

"Captain, we got a reply from the broadbeam."

Such rapid reply could only mean a pinbeamed message. Priscilla smiled. *Good. We found Erob's in-house.*

"To my screen three, please, Rusty."

"Sent." The channel stayed open, which was odd. Priscilla looked to screen three.

"Pod seventy-seven?" she demanded, staring at the terse announcement that this unlikely entity was on-line. "Rusty, did you get a fix on the origin of this?"

"It's coming out of Erob's territory," he said and now she knew why he had left the line open. "Not the house. Mountain range toward the coast. Here."

Another window opened on her work screen, marking Pod 77's location on the planetary map. She upped the magnification, zooming in close, and called for place name display. The red counter was in her hand, alive with Shan's presence.

"Well," she said into the open channel. "Whatever it is, it lives on Dragon's Back Mountain." She sat back in the chair, feeling an electrical something, like a looming thunderstorm, stir the still ship air.

Dragon's Back Mountain. Priscilla drew a careful breath. Korval and Erob. Allies down the centuries. And a—pod?—situated on Dragon's Back Mountain. A gift, perhaps? Korval tended to protect its own interests closely, and Erob was seated upon an outworld, far from the homeworld's assistance, should it be attacked.

The counter blazed against her hand and she abruptly recalled yos'Galan's butler. A modified war robot, as Shan had told her, and, with its other duties, entrusted with the defense system surrounding Korval's valley.

Merciful Mother.

"Priscilla?" Rusty's voice carried concern. She shook her head, focused her thoughts.

"Yes. Rusty, do me the favor of sending to Pod seventy-seven in—in the code I will upload to you in a moment. Inquire into the state of its defenses."

"Defenses? Priscilla, how do we know it's not some wise-ass Yxtrang radio jockey, having himself a giggle?"

"We don't know that until it replies to us in our own code," she said, reaching to her board. Quickly, she ran her fingers over the sequence, accessing the captain's key file. She requested and received Korval's House code, uploading it to Rusty with a finger-tap.

"There. Send the message, please, Rusty. And wire the reply directly to me, whenever it comes in."

There was a momentary hesitation, then, "Will do. Tower out."

"Command helm out," she said absently, her fingers moving once again across the board, requesting information available to the Captain's Key, relative to Pod 77 or Dragon's Back Mountain, Lytaxin.

They were moving out this evening, bound for the quarry and points beyond. Meet Yxtrang before they knocked on the door, that was the gig. Surprise them, maybe. Buy time.

Time for the rest of the defense forces to man the serious talking points. Time for Val Con and Shan and Beautiful to steal the fighters and start their runs.

It was the planes that decided her on Erob's ruined airfield for the Irregular's hold-tight.

"No use stealing the damn things if you can't bring 'em home," she'd pointed out at the coordinating meeting. "We'll secure the airfield." She looked up and met Jase's eyes square across the table. "No problem."

He'd nodded after a second, and that was that. The only thing she had to do now was make good on her bet.

And not worry.

Walking toward her quarters to get her gear together and maybe grab an hour's nap, Miri snorted. It was funny how in the thick of things you never had time to worry. You dealt with whatever the gods of battle sent against you and mostly you weren't even scared.

Before and after—that was the time for nerves and terrors. Double, if you had a lifemate and a new brother and the man who'd guarded your back against his own laying their lives out in a cockamamie death-defying gamble.

She'd already come up with a dozen ways for them to die before they even got to the planes. Miri moved her head, shaking away the tally of possible destructions, but she couldn't shake away the knot in her gut or the cramp in her chest.

She turned right, nodded at the sentry and stepped into the dimness of her quarters.

Val Con got up from the edge of the cot, came two steps forward and opened his arms.

She flung forward, catching him in a hug as desperate as his own, thought to look at his pattern and felt the chill tingle of his fear in her blood even as she raised her head to meet a nearly savage kiss.

They made love like it was battle-practice, hard and silent and fierce, and when they were through, she held him tight against her still, one fist twisted in his hair.

"Damn you, don't die."

Warm breath exhaled into her ear. "I love you, too, Miri."

He pulled away and they straightened their clothes, found discarded weapons belts and buckled them into place. Val Con touched her cheek.

"I will meet you at Erob's airfield, tomorrow afternoon." He lay a finger across her lips and she felt a ripple of dark-edged humor go through him. "No problem, eh?" The finger lifted.

Miri smiled, though it was hard to see him through the tears.

"No problem."

Tactical Defense Pods 72 to 83 were retired from the Korval fleet with the building of the *Felicitous Passage,* two hundred fifty Standard years ago, according to the sealed file the Captain's Key had accessed.

Red counter gripped tight in her hand, Priscilla learned decommissioned Pods 72 through 76 had been donated to the scouts.

Pods 79 through 83 were used as live target fire in a series of defense exercises during a period of heightened Yxtrang activity.

Pod 77 . . . She scrolled down the file. Theonna yos'Phelium, delm, had bestowed Pod 77 upon Korval's staunch ally, Clan Erob. Then ordered the report Priscilla now perused sealed. She frowned, leaned back, and then touched the scroll key again, searching—there.

Pod 78, the last entry stated simply, *is on Moonstruck. Refer to Plan B.*

Her frown deepened. Refer to Plan B? But surely—The screen shimmered and a message box appeared in the bottom left corner, rapidly filling with text.

TACTICAL DEFENSE POD 77 ON-LINE.
WEAPONS CHECK.
INITIATE SCAN.
LONG GUN CHARGED.
SCAN CONCLUSION: MID-ORBIT HOSTILITIES.
INITIATING SECONDARY SCAN.
TARGETING COMPUTER ON-LINE.
TACTICAL COMPUTER ON-LINE.
SCAN CONCLUSION: INVASION CONDITIONS.
MANUAL OVERRIDE DISALLOWED.
ALL SYSTEMS ON-LINE.
ALL SYSTEMS ABLE.
AWAITING TARGET.

The scout's plan was simple: Steal three fighter-bomber craft from those grounded at Field Headquarters, lift and destroy planes, ammunition, armor, and similar other targets before they could be brought against the defenders.

It was a plan somewhat short on detail, but Nelirikk never doubted it would succeed, to the glory of captain and Troop. It was much too audacious to fail.

For this venture, Nelirikk had sacrificed the mustache and the unsoldierly hair, and stood once again in Yxtrang uniform, the officer to whom it had belonged having no further need. He had modified the rank-marks, so that he became an Adjutant of the Inspectors Office, and the scout's brother had with wonderful skill painted the appropriate *vingtai* on his face.

"Remember to clean this nonsense off once you're safely away," Shan said, standing back to admire his handiwork. "You do look fierce, if I say it myself. One might very easily mistake you for an Yxtrang."

This was a pleasantry, such as Nelirikk was coming to expect from the scout's brother, who was by no means as imbe-

cile as he sometimes spoke. Accordingly, he bared his teeth
in a grin, displaying the *vingtai* to best effect.

"Terrifying," Shan announced, his face betraying no noticeable terror. "I may swoon in fright."

"Why not sit down, instead?" the scout asked from the
doorway. "And allow Nelirikk to decorate you?"

"No need of that," Shan said, turning to put his brush by.
He turned back and Nelirikk gasped, hand slapping his
sidearm even as his brain told him that it was impossible that
a major of inspectors should be standing before him when
only a moment ago—

"*Hold*!" And that quickly it was the scout before him, face
full of danger, poised on the balls of his feet, having taken up
the position of shield to—

To who other than Shan yos'Galan?

Carefully, Nelirikk moved his hand from his gun. Carefully, he inclined his head.

"Forgive my error," he said in the full formality of the Liaden tongue. The scout settled, head cocked to a side.

"And yet it was not an error," he murmured in Terran.
"Your whole body screamed astonishment and alarm. You
went for the gun as defense. But, enlighten me—what did
you see?"

Shan cleared his throat. The scout spun on a heel to face
him.

"I suspect he may have seen an Inspector Major here
among us. At least, that was the impression I was trying to
convey." He looked up, silver eyes catching Nelirikk's gaze.
"I gather the illusion was convincing? How gratifying."

"Convincing," Nelirikk agreed, hoarsely. The scout shook
his head.

"I saw you turn to put the brush away," he said to his
brother. "I saw you turn back and Nelirikk reacting to threat.
There was no inspector major here."

"Ah." The silver eyes widened slightly. "Perhaps now?"

Nelirikk gulped, but this time managed to stand calm as
the major loomed over the scout, face pitiless behind the tattoos of rank and accomplishment.

The scout shrugged, read Nelirikk's face with a quick

green glance over the left shoulder, and looked back to the major.

"Nelirikk is convinced, in any case. I see only yourself."

Shan smiled and became once more a slim man of slightly less than middle height, slanting white eyebrows showing pretty against the smooth brown skin of his face.

"Recall that you were the only one of us who could curb Anthora when she was in a mood to have her way. It's doubtful that we'll meet with an Yxtrang of such discriminating will. And if we do," his mouth tightened. "If we do, I'm afraid I have other defenses."

"Do you?" The scout sighed. "These are new abilities, brother?"

Shan nodded. "I warn you that the explanation will be a thing devoid of sense. Though I am, of course, willing to try."

"Leave it for the present," said the scout, "if it's nonsense. When this is over, let us share a glass or two and tell each other fantastic stories."

"Done."

"Done," the scout echoed and stepped aside.

"So the two of you, fine-looking pilots, both, will proceed boldly across the field, pausing only to distribute explosives at likely looking Communications centers. You will then claim your planes and board. In the meantime, I will advance by a more circuitous route and stealthily steal my own. We will then proceed as discussed, each making at least one pass over the airfield before peeling off in his assigned direction. Questions?"

There were none. They had been through this before. And, after all, the plan was simple.

The scout nodded. "Good. It's time we were gone."

DUTIFUL PASSAGE

LYTAXIN ORBIT

In one hour, Standard, the Yxtrang Eye would be fully open, at once clearing a firing path from the battleship to Erob's House and placing the thickest layer of shielding ships between the battleship and the *Passage*.

Priscilla had run the math a dozen times in the last few hours, assigned the tactical comp to find the means by which the *Passage* could divert, prevent, or minimize the Yxtrang's beam.

The answer came back negative.

She had copied their situation files and downloaded them to Pod 77. What, if anything, that ancient non-sentient made of those facts, she had no idea. Subsequent efforts to engage it in dialog had met with no response. Perhaps it had simply stopped functioning.

Ren Zel, hastily briefed on his return to the bridge, stood silent, his eyes on the screen displaying the movement of the Yxtrang shield.

"No answer whatsoever?"

"Nothing," Priscilla said. "I wonder if I've offended it."

"Overloaded it, possibly," he returned, eyes still on the screen. "You say it is very old, and a defense logic. It would perhaps not be equipped to sift through such levels of data as the *Passage*—" He stopped and drew a slow, careful breath.

"Or perhaps it is."

Priscilla looked to the screen, saw the message window filling with words.

> TACTICAL DEFENSE POD 77 ON-LINE.
> DOWNLOAD DATA ANALYSIS COMPLETE.
> DEFENSE PLAN FORMULATED.
> PHASE ONE ENACTED.
> UPLOADING TO MOBILE UNIT TARGETING COMP.

Ren Zel flung forward, clearing a tertiary screen and accessing the targeting computer in three rapid keystrokes. Priscilla sat rapt, the red counter in her hand, watching the words form on the screen.

> ESTIMATED TIME UNTIL OFFENSIVE ACTION: 43 UNITS.
> SYNCHRONIZING MOBILE UNIT TARGETING COMP.

"It's uploaded settings for guns seven and nine," Ren Zel told her, fingers moving across the board, "and instructions to fire to those coordinates in forty Standard minutes."

> TACTICAL DEFENSE POD 77 ON STAND-BY, CONDITION
> ORANGE.

The words stopped and Priscilla stirred at last.

"Remove Pod seventy-seven's instructions from the targeting command queue, please, First Mate."

He spun his chair around, showing her a face which was entirely devoid of emotion.

"I cannot," he said quietly, and she read the effort he expended to hold to calmness. "The file is sealed."

"Sealed, is it?" She reached to her own board. "I'll pull them—"

Ren Zel cleared his throat.

"Forgive me. I should have said that the instructions and the coords are under the seal of Delm Korval."

"Under delm's seal?" Priscilla felt a thrill not unlike terror. Theonna yos'Phelium had left the power to implement delm's seal resident in the ancient defense pod. Theonna yos'Phelium had been a far-seeing delm, indeed.

Or a frothing madwoman.

Priscilla took a breath, felt the red counter warm in her hand and looked to Ren Zel.

"So, we can see it, but we can't change it." As she said that her witch sense told her it was true: some ancient Korval necessity now ruled their fate. "Fine. To my screen two, please. Let's at least find out what we've gotten ourselves into."

"**Uncle** Win Den!" Alys ran headlong out of the house as he was preparing to step into the flitter for an inspection of the outer ring defenses. He waited, remembering to frown.

"Well, niece? I thought you on duty at the core-comm."

"I was, Uncle. But there was a message . . ." she paused to gulp more air into her lungs. "A message on the telecoder—the old one, that never takes any messages?"

tel'Vosti froze, remembering late night fright stories told him by *his* uncle, too many years ago, and centering around that particular, always silent, telecoder.

"Go on," he urged Alys.

"Yes. The message says it's from the Planetary Defense Unit, and it—" her eyes lifted to his, baffled. "Uncle, it says that it's activated the meteor shielding over Erob Central Control."

LYTAXIN

WAR ZONE

Val Con melted away at the edge of the field, taking his bag of cockpit adaptations and another, similar to the one Nelirikk carried with him. His target was the comm shed at the south end of the field, which housed the back-up space-link. After setting the charges contained in the second bag, he would choose a plane and lift. The mark was one-half-hour.

Shan and Nelirikk walked openly across the field, Nelirikk bearing his bag of explosives, the scout's brother swaggering empty-handed, as befit the sort of officer he had found in Nelirikk's undermind. *Their* targets were the radar support shack and back-up communications.

The field was busy, but not overly so. They had arrived, so Nelirikk thought, in the trough between the first wave moving out and the second. Those who were abroad had duty to attend. No one paid attention to two officers arrogantly and unhurriedly about their own duty. They marched directly up to back-up comm, Shan waiting with cold impatience while Nelirikk deftly jimmied the lock, pushed the door open, stepped back and saluted smartly. In character, he ignored the salute and stamped into the shed, Nelirikk in his wake, swinging the door closed behind them.

"Do not touch that," he said, pointing at a green striped panel. "Alarm circuit." He had dropped his bag and fished out two of the scout's devices.

Shan took one of the explosives, moved to the left, seated it and armed it as his brother had shown him, while Nelirikk did his part of the work on the opposite side of the shed.

Two minutes later, they were once again striding across the busy field.

At radar support, the door was unlocked. Nelirikk paused, threw a worried glance toward his companion and was answered with a vicious glower from the inspector major.

Well enough, thought Nelirikk. *We do what we have come to do.* He thrust the door open and brought his fist up in salute. The major tramped by him with no acknowledgment, into the radar shed.

A tech jumped up from behind the board, his face displaying surprise that quickly became chagrin as he read their *vingtai.*

"Inspectors . . ." The salute was hasty, the face pale behind the tattoos that showed him a specialist, confirmed twice at combat radar, a volunteer who had achieved success in a difficult mission, originally of Ornjal's Tech Troop. "I was not told you were to be here. I—"

Shan frowned, and the tech gulped. Slowly, the gesture filled with such menace that Nelirikk felt his own heart stutter, the scout's brother pointed at the door.

"Inspector Major." The tech saluted. "I received no notice of your coming. Duty demands that I ask to see your passes."

"We have no time for that!" Nelirikk snarled, moving forward. "There have been security failures at several locations! We must check this facility and certify it! Out, and leave us to duty!"

Despite the sweat beading on his upper lip and the definite paleness of his face, the tech was not so easy to rout. He took a hard breath and met Nelirikk's eyes squarely.

"I need some ID, sir. You understand. I am required to . . ."

They had given the scout's brother perhaps thirty words of the Common Troop, without ever expecting he would have need of them.

"Fool!" he roared now, thrusting a hard hand under the tech's nose. "Papers, damn you!"

The tech jumped, saluted even more hastily, pulling his work orders, his day sheets, his meal cards, as the officer cursed him for a sluggard dog and seemed almost ready to strike him.

Shakily, the tech ordered his papers, offering them with yet another salute.

The scout's brother snatched them, looked them over contemptuously, with a special sneer for the coveted meal cards. Abruptly, he turned, shoved the offensive papers into Nelirikk's hands and stalked over to the screen bank.

"Troop!" barked Nelirikk. "Have you eyes?"

"Sir!" A shaky salute. "Yes, sir!"

"Good! Take them elsewhere if you ever wish to eat again!" He threw the papers and the tech caught them against his chest, his eyes on the meal cards Nelirikk still held in his hand.

"Yes, sir."

"Put yourself on half rations tonight," Nelirikk snapped, and pushed the cards into the tech's sweating face. "Dismissed!"

"Sir!" The tech saluted, threw a terrified glance at the major, who was now inspecting the lateral board, and all but ran from the shed.

Nelirikk pushed the door shut, dropped the sack and yanked it open.

"Quickly," he said, putting the bomb into the hands of the scout's brother. "We are off the mark."

Crouched in scant cover, Val Con waited while an officer dressed in what he had to believe was the original of the uniform Nelirikk had approximated for himself, face bearing *vingtai* eerily similar to Shan's artwork, performed what could only be an inspection.

Precious minutes ticked by and still the officer did not emerge from the comm shed.

Three minutes more, Val Con thought, belly down under a

cable lorry. *If he is not gone in three minutes, I will set the charges against the shed's exterior and trust in the luck.*

Chancy enough under the best of conditions, the luck being notoriously fickle. Yet, what else could be done? This whole mad venture sat on the knees of the luck, born of the desperate necessity of success. They must succeed in routing the Yxtrang. Must. The cost of failure was too terrible to contemplate.

The door to the shed opened and Val Con tucked his face into the crook of an arm, watching sidewise as the inspector and his aide marched to the waiting armored car, entered and were driven away.

Close on the mark, Commander, he told himself, checking the area carefully. *Be quick, now, and all's well.*

Finding the immediate environs suitably empty, he left his cover, ghosted to the shed and let himself inside.

The scout's brother was safe in his chosen craft. Nelirikk continued farther down the field, so that there should be some distance between the two of them on take-off.

From the corner of his eye, he saw an armored car make a wide turn and bear down on his position. There was no reason to assume that the driver of the vehicle was in any way interested in an adjutant inspector, but Nelirikk felt the newly shaved hairs lift on the back of his neck.

Taking care to betray no haste, he changed course, angling toward one of the newer, Raphix-class planes. The damned car came after and Nelirikk grit his teeth, marching on, soldierly, measuring the distance, if it came to a chase.

Behind him, the car accelerated. Over the engine's excitement, a voice shouted out in the language of the Troop, "You there! Halt for the Inspector Major!"

Nelirikk ran.

It was wonderful, Shan thought, what a little height did for one's perspective.

Snug in the cockpit of the quiescent Yxtrang fighter, trust-

ing his projected suggestion to any and all passersby that this
same cockpit was empty, he looked down the field of planes.

Some way down the field, lorries and refuellers were busy
preparing the next pod of planes. Shan made a note of that.

Closer to home, he spied the broad shoulders and soldierly
stride of Nelirikk Explorer, followed by an armored car bearing the Yxtrang graphic for "Inspection Office." Shan sat up,
trying to get a reading on the occupants of the car. His touch
fell short and he saw the car accelerate. Saw Nelirikk break
stride and bolt for the ladder of a plane.

It lacked five minutes of the mark.

Shan engaged the shock webbing, hands moving—though
he was careful not to be too quick—over the fighter's board.

Val Con was running too close to the mark. Delayed and delayed again by the movement of maintenance vehicles and
technical crews, he finally swung back, angling for the last of
three planes that sat in pristine isolation at the very edge of
the field.

It was chancy. The location was open, and the guards—
three guards, he counted—suggested that these craft were
meant to be flown by pilots of rank.

Chancy. He sank back into his sliver of shadow and tried
to weigh how chancy. The cause was not served, if he died
before he ever gained the air.

After all, he had promised Miri that he would meet her at
Erob's field this noon.

He smiled a little then, feeling the tension in his face. A
foolish promise on both sides, given what they both undertook. Still, she would expect him to exert himself to keep it.

A diversion was clearly required. If he could but entice the
guards a few steps away from their posts, he would have
Luken's oft-desired honest advantage that made a dash for
the nearest craft possible.

As if his thought ignited it, thunder roared across the field,
closely followed by a second boom, which was an air-to-
ground cannon being fired. A second engine roared into life
and the guards were running toward the sounds, rifles ready,

and Val Con threw thought away, gathered his bag and his breath and ran.

He didn't look for the guards. He looked at nothing but the ladder, convenient enough for one of Nelirikk's length, but requiring a leap at the end of his race, and with the bag to hamper him—

A pellet hit the ground a pace ahead, gravel bits exploding, and he jumped, grabbed the ladder, heard another shot, but he was climbing, and it was a third shot and a fourth. His hand slipped and he snatched a recovery, felt the bag slide and let it go, swarming up, up, and falling into the cockpit, the left leg numb beneath him, but he flung forward, slapped the switch and the bubble rose up and over, sealing him into safety with a click.

The engine roared to life and the plane began to move. Shan applied the brake, carefully, found the control for the cannon, crossed hairs on the armored car's position and pushed the firing stud.

The plane lurched under him, the armored car went up in a hail of metal, and he eased off the brake, letting the engine have its way as he saw the plane Nelirikk had chosen, with the Yx-trang numbers 32 on the tail, begin to creep forward. Nodding, he took the lead, relinquished the brake entirely and let the engines pull the plane down the runway, pushing her a little now, hauling back on the stick the instant he was able.

Climbing, he looked down, saw Nelirikk's plane leap off the field, and quite a commotion on the ground. A finger's width above the tree-tops, he leveled out and banked hard, sweeping back the way he had come, using the belly guns to kill the planes sitting weak and defenseless, pulled back on the stick at the end of his line, saw 32 flying neck-or-nothing, lashing the field into shrapnel.

It was now thirty-five minutes since they had separated and there was no third fighter in the air. Shan bit his lip, banked again, searching—and saw a plane rising, a sleek af-fair with the numbers 03 painted high on its proud tail. He grinned. Trust Val Con to steal himself a beauty.

For an instant it seemed to him that the pretty plane faltered, then it was climbing, arrow-bright, leveled and banked smoothly right, sweeping in low over the field, guns blaring.

All according to plan, Shan, he told himself, ridiculously relieved. *With a phrase or two varied. We're all safe in the air, for whatever that's worth. Go east, young man, and finish things up. After which, I promise, you may go mad.*

He pulled on the stick and made his turn, still climbing, east, in search of targets.

He'd been hit. The left leg, well above the knee. There was blood. A lot of blood. Not good.

There was also pain, now that he had seen the wound. He tried to shake it out of awareness, used the levers to shrink the cockpit to minimum, and discovered the shock webbing was too large for him, and then discovered that it didn't matter. He could not be webbed in and reach his instruments. Instead, he raised the pilot's couch to maximum and perched precariously on the edge. The pain . . .

The drill.

He stretched, took a breath and touched the first key, chanting the drill to focus his mind.

"Power check; external go. Internal, go. Clock set synchronize; clock reset to trip zero. Power on. External power stable. Internal stable. Release external cable."

He faltered, the pain chewing his thoughts. He ran the Rainbow, quickly, drawing the body away from the mind, continued to chant the drill.

"Drag brake on, mech brake on. Engine A start. Engine A positive, null thrust."

He was late on the mark. They would be worried, but he couldn't rush the drill, because . . .

Something would go wrong, if he rushed the drill.

"Engine B start. Engine B positive, null thrust. Clock check; timing positive. Annular pressure fifty percent, thrust positive. Scan positive. Weapon check; outboard cannon check."

There were soldiers, on the ground far below. They were running toward him. He looked up and there was a soldier there, too, at the top of the ladder, looking down at him through the dome.

"Remove fuse sixteen. Cap fuse sixteen. Pull pin seven."

There was a truck headed his way, he saw the cannon in its bed and hurtled through the last of the drill.

"Drag brake off, mech brake off, inlets open, full power, on."

He was moving, as the drill said he should, scattering soldiers as he gained speed. He looked up, saw the soldier still clinging to the dome, then forgot him as the speed built and off to the right a building exploded, brilliant orange smoke spreading rapidly in the whipping wind.

The speed was building quickly and the pressure felt good against him, except his leg . . . and it took him a moment to find the dial that told him the plane was going fast enough so he pulled back hard on the stick, and didn't notice when the soldier finally slid off the dome.

Climbing, he saw another plane circling, but it didn't fire, so he banked to the right, setting up for his run over the field, like they'd planned.

He saw another building blow up as he came in low—incandescence, then heavy black smoke, rapidly thinning. He triggered the cannons, saw planes and men die under him, then he was climbing again, and the other fighter was banking, heading east and he remembered that was the plan, too. Shan would go east. Nelirikk would go south. He would go west.

Accordingly, he banked to the right—"*Ah!*"

He held onto consciousness, the agony receded. Stretching for the dial, he upped the oxygen content in cabin, enough, he hoped, to keep him from getting sleepy. Not enough, quite, to make him drunk.

Filling his lungs with richer air, he stretched again to the board, and increased the cabin pressure, which would help reduce the bleeding.

This craft was a beauty, wonderfully stable. He took advantage of that to remove both hands from the controls and cut the rest of the leather away from the wound. Then he bandaged it as well as he could, taking care to make the wrappings tight.

WAR ZONE

"You will forgive me if I seem discourteous," Miri told the guy with the hatchet. "We are in train to engage the enemy and timing is vital. I suggest that you continue to the rear and remove your folk from active danger."

"Your concern does you credit," he replied, but not like he meant it. He gestured, showing her the rabble and the rakes, spears, pistols, pipes, knives and rocks that was the most of their gear.

"As you see, we are armed. We are prepared to fight. Forgive me if I notice that your troop is thin. We will bolster your numbers and increase the opportunity of success." His face was bleak, and not quite sane.

"We are before you now because we did fight, Captain, and we prevailed. All of us have dead in the city."

Last thing she needed, Miri thought. Buncha crazy civilians with no idea of discipline, half of them out on their feet and a short handful holding anything like useful weaponry.

She glared at the guy and he didn't flinch, there being something in the set of his mouth that reminded her, forcefully, of Val Con in his hell-or-high-water mode. She could move on without taking them, sure. But she couldn't stop them from following and making a mob scene on the field that would send discipline straight to hell and get needless numbers killed.

Damn it.

"Very well," she agreed, inclining her head at the angle that said she knew he had her over a barrel and she was letting him have his way, but not to push it.

"The sergeants will assign your people to existing squads. Understand me: you *will* follow the orders of the sergeants, from this moment until the enemy is defeated. In the meantime, I do not take children onto a battlefield."

She pointed at the nursery contingent—two dozen kids, none of them over eight or nine, guarded by three adults armed with hunting rifles, which were the closest thing to real weapons in the whole mob.

"Those will proceed, with their protectors, to the rear and beg grace of Erob."

"Captain, they will." He bowed then, deep and courtly, like she was doing him some kind of major favor, instead of inviting him to get massacred, and turned to relay her orders to the rabble.

"**Meteor** shield?" Emrith Tiazan looked at her kinsman, saw neither madness nor levity in his face, and asked, steadily, "What meteor shield?"

"The one that our instruments assure us is even now in place, covering an area with Korval's Tree as its center."

Korval's Tree sat in the front garden and well for them that it did, Erob thought, sighing sharply.

"It appears that the Planetary Defense Unit is concerned that the Tree may come under attack from space." She eyed tel'Vosti. "I must assume that its concern has at least one leg in reality?"

"I think we have no option, Emrith."

"So." She moved behind the desk, accessed the delm's archive and keyed in a search for "Planetary Defense Unit." The answer came quickly enough, and when she had read it she sighed again. Gift of Korval. Gods protect them all from Korval's gifts.

"Here is something to amuse, Win Den," she said,

scrolling to the end of the file. "In times when its attention is not diverted by the possibility of meteor strike, Planetary Defense Unit is none other than Dragon's Tooth, Korval's contract suite." She sat back, suddenly very tired indeed.

"The blood thins, Win Den. We should not have forgotten this."

"Peace dulls the senses," he said softly. "Give praise, Emrith, that Korval's Tooth has remained alive. Let us hope that it is also sharp."

Troops were moving, up from the south. Nelirikk identified the supply line, dropped the nose and used the cannon rather than squander the precious bombs nestled in the fighter's belly.

There was return fire on his second pass, and he spent a bomb to take out the anti-aircraft turret at the head of the column, then used the cannon again, killing a command vehicle before he was past it all and banking to the left, setting up for his final pass.

Two more bombs away from his hoard, and a foursome of land-armor destroyed. Nelirikk climbed and swung back to the course, well satisfied with his work thus far.

A storm was brewing and the rising wind was unexpectedly troublesome when the plane slowed in the aftermath of cannon fire. Shan held his altitude with brute force and swept back again, his cannon-fire concentrated on a line of slow-moving trucks.

The plane shuddered and lost forward speed rapidly. Shan gunned the engines and below him saw blossoms of flame as the ammo trucks exploded.

Pod 77's instruction to *Dutiful Passage*'s guns seven and nine was to fire a broad, low-level magnetic beam directly into the Yxtrang shield, intensity to remain constant for five Standard minutes, increasing to maximum for one-half minute and cutting out.

Priscilla shook her head, fingers building the equation in

screen two while Ren Zel fed data to Maincomp for simulation. A mag beam that low would deliver little more than a nudge to even the lightest of the shield boats. What possible defensive gain might accrue to such a—

Beside her, Ren Zel hissed, for all the worlds like an offended house cat. She gasped, startled out of her concentration, looked to the sim, and wondered at his restraint, that he had neither howled nor roared.

The mag beam fired, low and steady, off of gun seven for five Standard minutes into the mass of light craft, encountered in the third layer an extremely light pallet-skid. The beam pulsed, the skid—moved. In the fifth layer, the skid encountered a workboat and the pressure of its shielding coupled with the steady push of the beam started that craft moving as well.

The sim for gun nine showed a similar phenomenon, each beam finally pushing a cluster of ten small ships, toward the center of the Eye.

When the first of the defenseless boats hit the edge of the Eye, the power simultaneously pulsed to full. The boats, impelled by the beams, skittered into the firing zone, and—

"They won't stop the beam," Priscilla whispered. "They don't have enough shielding. It will go right through them."

"Not entirely," Ren Zel said. "The beam will lose energy as it passes through the obstacles and will strike the on-world target with somewhat less intensity."

She felt ill, even as she approved the Pod 77's tactics. A defense logic, indeed. Once the battleship's weakened beam struck through atmosphere, the ancient weapon would have a clear return shot.

"How many," Ren Zel asked quietly. "How many of those things are at large?" He inclined his head, acknowledging her place in the line direct of a clan not his own. "If it may be told."

"Two," Priscilla told him, and felt his relief as sharply as her own. "Only two. This one, and one other."

They'd been lucky. For one thing, Yxtrang hadn't been expecting them—not quite yet, anyhow. For another, they'd hadn't exactly been over-manned.

For a third thing, Miri thought as she waited for the last of the situation reports to come in, Yxtrang had thought they'd be going up against a professional fighting force.

What they got was the remaining Irregulars, whose ranks had been doubled and doubled again by the time they hit the airfield, by bands of desperate and vengeful civilians.

Miri wondered if the guy with the hatchet had managed to stay alive. Seemed like she owed the man an apology. *His* crew hadn't been rabble. She'd seen rabble, now.

The Irregulars launched the attack, hitting the Yxtrang mess tent with three rounds of mortar fire at half-through dinner. They'd followed up with an occupation of the ammo dump and turned the two captured field pieces against the disoriented Yxtrang.

It was the mob that attacked the remaining entrenched field piece in a wave. The soldiers there had faced knives, spears, rocks, and raw hatred. None had died easy, and there were an astonishing number of Yxtrang among the mass of corpses.

The last report came through and Miri sighed. Eleven Irregulars dead or missing. Hundreds of civilians, ditto. Yxtrang had spiked the fuel tanks with sand, damn their black hearts. She'd've done the same.

But, the airfield was theirs, theoretically, and a couple hundred meters in all directions, with a tenuous western connection.

Theory came in to it because the Yxtrang weren't being good losers. They hadn't thrown their guns away and run screaming from the field. They had retreated in as good order as possible, those who were left, and now they waited in the woods, maybe for dark, maybe for a dawn attack, but probably for reinforcements. Now and then, a couple would dance out onto the floor and throw a party favor, probing for weakness.

Miri, drawing on a stockpile of weaponry Yxtrang had forgotten to take with them when they vacated, called for occasional mortar fire to the south and east. To the west were the fringes of Kritoulkas' crew, and a couple pieces of modest merc armor.

She'd ordered the captured field artillery used for on-the-spot training—so far a quarter of the troop had been part of the drill. They were firing randomly on the valley trails most likely able to support incoming Yxtrang armor or supplies.

The civilians, with nothing nearby to murder, were in the way, milling around on the runway. That was no good. She called to one of her lieutenants to clear the field and a few minutes later a sergeant and a squad marched over to move the mob along.

Miri drank some water from her canteen and checked the time. Ought to be seeing planes, real soon. The wind was rising, and she could see heavy clouds on the horizon. Great. The piloting tapes Val Con had her learning weren't coy about the difficulties of flying in storms. The sooner she saw planes, the happier she'd be.

In fact . . . She tipped her head, frowning after the sound which might have been engine noise—but wasn't.

She listened with care. *Armor,* she decided. *Kritoulkas must've decided to advance herself a little while things're quie—*

She felt the rumble then, shouted, "Incoming!" and saw the Irregulars go for cover, and some of the brighter civilians.

Armor.

And it wasn't theirs.

He had used all his bombs, to the glory of the Troop and the mortification of the enemy. The 14th Conquest Corps had lost heavily this day, in arms, ammunition, equipment, and status.

They had lost pilots, too. Three of rank who rose against him had gone gloriously to duty's reward.

Nelirikk checked the fuel gauge, made one last mid-level pass over the wreckage and confusion that had been the 14th's southern stronghold, and set his course for Erob's airfield, where his captain and his arms-mates awaited him.

It was possible, Shan thought, that he had done lasting damage. Certainly, he'd played merry havoc with the heavy artillery, the armor, and the ammo.

And the planes.

Despite holding *Soldier Lore* deep in his bones, he was far too much Korval to kill ships without pain. Reason said that the ships of the enemy must be nullified.

But a pilot's heart wept for the pretties left dead or dying, never to know the sweet thrill of lift again.

The building storm was at his back as he came in toward the agreed-upon airfield and saw, with a gasp of relief, that the Irregulars' flag was flying.

In the woods, as he passed over, half-a-dozen armored vehicles, closing rapidly toward the field.

He banked sharply and saw the storm straight-on, a wall of boiling black cloud, lanced with lightning and topped with miles of blazing white thunderheads; then he dropped the nose, caught a tank in the crosshairs and pushed the firing stud.

First, there were no planes. Then, there were two, from opposite directions.

Miri watched the first come in ahead of the racing storm, saw it slow, drop, then swing back over the woods, and the noises it was making promised enemy.

"Mark that!" she yelled to the crews. "Get the mortar and both pieces on that heading. Rapid fire!"

The second plane circled the field once, waggled its wings a couple times, and then came in low, flared out neatly and touched down with barely a sound, coming around in a wide circle until its nose was pointing at the woods.

The pilot cut power, but a whine remained in the air as the hatch went up and Nelirikk, his face showing faint marks like daubs of paint, dropped to the ground, ran to her and saluted.

"Count three rounds in the nose cannon, my Captain. No fuel to fly with."

She took his salute, wondering how someone so ugly could look so good. "Can't help you with the fuel. We got armor gonna come outta those woods pretty soon. Can you aim the cannon while you're grounded?"

"Yes, Captain."

"Do it."

He bolted for his plane and it was time for the first one to come back in, too fast, to Miri's eye, touching down and flaming out in the same instant, rolling uncontrolled toward the far end of the field. It came to her that the pilot was dead, or bad hit, and she reached inside her head for the comfort of Val Con's pattern.

The last thing she remembered seeing was the bright orange 'chute popping out of the tail of the rolling plane, dragging its speed down to nothing.

The ship was on red alert, the crews responsible for guns seven and nine by the captain's order removed from their stations.

The timer in the corner of the main command screen counted to zero and faded. Targeting comp reported guns seven and nine on-line, magnetic beams, low.

Captain and first mate watched as actuality repeated simulation and the beams inexorably pushed defenseless ships into the maw of the Eye.

The Yxtrang battleship fired.

Shuttlecraft and workboats, pallet-skids and lighters, took the charge, expanded. And were gone.

"Beam energy leached by a factor of three, Captain," the first mate said quietly from his work screen. The captain nodded.

Targeting comp reported guns seven and nine off-line, targets destroyed.

The wind buffeted his ship. He corrected, nearly overcorrected. The horizon was higher than it should be, surely . . . ? A long reach to the board and that was corrected, too.

He was approaching his first strike zone, the airfield far behind. Below, the enemy moved. He found the supply column and came in low.

These were hardened soldiers, familiar with the sounds of battle. Few even looked up as air cover streaked over.

Val Con dropped the nose of the ship, brought video cross hairs to bear on the streaming troops, and fired his cannon.

The sound was a long low moan; the plane shuddered and lost forward speed rapidly. The slower it went, the more the local winds tore and tossed it.

The run took just seconds, the return a hard right bank and he gasped as the injured leg was pressed by acceleration.

Back again, flying low, nose down . . .

These *were* seasoned troops. There was return fire, but the anti-aircraft gun wasn't in position yet.

Val Con brought the crosshairs to bear once more, ignoring the figures running for cover, concentrating on his target.

This time he scored a direct hit, and the surprising blast lifted the plane and bounced him around in the oversized cockpit. He rescued himself with a snatch at the instrument panel, his vision black at the edges and the pain was a carnivore, eating him alive . . .

It was instinct, a snatch at life no less vital than his grip on the instrument panel.

He reached into that portion of himself that had been most abused by the Department, and flipped a certain toggle—on.

The pain did not fade, it was simply no longer relevant data. He was aware that he was wounded, that the wetness down his leg was blood, and he bent to tighten the wrappings, for it would be inefficient to die of blood loss before the mission was done.

Very distantly, there was song. The song comforted him, though he could not stop right now to listen. There were targets below him and the mission was imperative. If he failed, the song would die, and he would not allow that.

He had done with the moving troops and flown on, seeking other targets. He had tightened the wrapping on his leg again, and enriched the air supply. He cut a long strip of leather from his jacket and used that to tie himself, standing, against the board. The fuel gauge was fine. There were still many bombs in his belly.

He went over the field at mid-level, saw the shapes of space-worthy ships and knew he had found targets that merited his skill. He came back in, readying his guns, but they were alert here, they weren't a moving column that was vulnerable to air attack.

They fired missiles at him and he saw people on the ground, running for planes. He brought the nose down and fired at the planes, because it would be bad to have to fight them all in the air.

The rising missiles altered courses, seeking. Val Con saw one beside him, pacing him, it seemed. He veered toward it and it veered away. He laughed, veered toward it again, and watched it pull away.

Cannon-fire was not so coy. Bursts exploded just off his wing-tip and he banked right, braced hard against the board, and there was a song in his head and he wanted to listen, but he couldn't because there was an enemy plane coming against him and he had to uncap his wing cannon and fire.

He was nearly blinded by the explosion, felt his craft buffeted, heard the sound of metal shred bouncing off the high-strength skin.

Reflex took over and he banked sharply to the right, knowing that he shouldn't—sharply to the right, the leather tie held him up, and sharply to the right and now he was behind the plane that had been chasing him and if he pressed this switch again . . .

The cannon fire was pretty. He laughed at the explosion.

He'd gotten past the field, though, and he needed to kill the spaceships. He banked to the right, coming in low, and he'd always been good at this part. He knew how to almost touch the tops of the trees and he went over the big hump and remembered that he needed to have all the weapons live.

But the spaceships weren't sleeping anymore. One was awake and lifting, and people on the ground were shooting at him, two more missiles came by to look at him and veered off because the ship said he was an Yxtrang ace.

He fired his cannon at the rising target but he was too fast, and by it, and swept around to the right and pulled back on the stick because the target was climbing.

He needed to do something about that, he knew. This target—this target was *troop transport*. He couldn't let it get away and bring more soldiers down.

There was a song in his head. He'd heard it many times

before. He banked right and saw the target above him, and
pushed the power bar to full.

The target got slightly closer, but he knew it was faster
than he was and could fly higher. He fired his cannon, but it
didn't explode like the other targets.

It was hard to move with the power bar all the way up and
the leather strap was holding him tight while his mount
climbed directly under the target, but the target was getting
smaller.

There was a song in his head and he wanted to listen, but
the target had to be stopped. The sky was getting darker and
the target getting smaller and he couldn't go much higher because it was the wrong kind of ship—

He fired his nose cannon and his wing cannon and his missiles all at once. He fired and thought maybe he'd hit the target and then thought maybe he hadn't because it kept moving
and he couldn't go straight up anymore, anyway. His leg was
hurting and he was very tired.

He closed his eyes and sagged against the board.

He remembered then that the song was named Miri and
that he'd been very lucky to hear it.

Crub, what numbers of them were in the house rather than
in troop with his astonishing and admirable niece, or on the
grounds, had taken shelter in the deep cellars.

He had given warning, for whatever good that would do
them, to the defenders locked outside the shield, and relayed
an encoded situation report to Jason Carmody's last known
position, down by the quarry encampment.

Duty done, Win Den tel'Vosti sat behind his desk in the
back parlor that had become his war room, and waited for
what might occur.

"Uncle?" Alys stood poised on the threshold, looking
slightly rumpled in a tunic handed down from an older
cousin, the weapons belt pulled snug 'round her waist, gun
ready by her hand.

He sighed. "Child, you should be in the cellar with the
rest."

"But you aren't," she replied, irrefutably. "Why came you here?"

He sighed again, feeling very old, indeed, and as if all his years had taught him nothing.

"Because I am a general, child. Duty requires me to be at my station, in case there should be need."

"Oh." She came lightly across the room and leaned against his side, one arm across his shoulders. He put his arm around her waist, careful of the gun.

"What will happen, Uncle?"

"I don't know," he said softly. "Perhaps nothing." But even Alys was too old to believe that.

"Dragon's Tooth would not have awakened," she told him, "if it were nothing. Clan Korval is our ally."

Wisdom and folly in one short utterance, tel'Vosti thought. As if to be Korval's ally placed one in anything like safety. He hugged her lightly.

"That's so."

The lights went out. The computers went off-line.

There was sound: the scream of ten thousand fingernails drawn simultaneously down ten thousand slate boards, going on and on.

The air was filled with static and the room was very warm. Alys gasped and flinched, caught herself and stood quiveringly still against his side, her arm like a bar of lead across his shoulder.

The sound stopped.

The lights came up. The computers beeped and rebooted. The air was gentle, pleasantly cool against the skin.

Alys sighed and slumped a little. tel'Vosti remembered to breathe.

The intercom on the desk chimed. He leaned forward and touched the key.

"Yes?"

"Uncle, it's Kol Vus. There's another message on the old telecoder. Planetary Defense Unit says that the shield has deflected an energy bolt. Shield power is down, it says here, by fifty-five percent." There was a pause.

"Planetary Defense Unit advises us that the shielding will

not divert another strike. And then it says, 'Phase Two enabled, Phase Two confirmed, Phase Two in progress.'

Shan threw himself down the ladder and ran low across the field, pistol in hand, and flung to his belly next to the small leather-clad crumple.

His foray in the woods had stopped one Yxtrang tank, which left five more closing on the field. The Irregulars all seemed to be pointing in the right direction, the mortars and anti-armor guns in position. Nelirikk's plane, with the Yxtrang number 32 on the tail, was on standby power, which might well mean there were rounds left in the nose cannon. For the moment, the side of the airfield was as safe as any other position in the immediate vicinity, but it wasn't going to stay that way, and Miri . . .

She lay like one dead, face against the ground, the combat helmet askew, showing a bright gleam of hair.

That she was *not* dead or even wounded, he knew, though he barely knew what to make of the tangle of steel and fire that confounded his Inner Eyes.

The ground shook. A turret appeared at the end of the field, as the first of the Yxtrang armor cleared the trees. Shan came to his knees, pistol ready, heard the whine from Nelirikk's plane change pitch, and went down, covering Miri's body with his own.

Nelirikk's cannon roared, the ground steadied, Shan rocked back on his knees, holstered the pistol, gathered his brother's lifemate into his arms and ran.

She was so tired. Opening her eyes was too much effort. But she had to open her eyes, because . . .

Damned if she knew why.

It was warm. She was tired. So . . . very . . . tired. Better to sleep and not to care . . .

Because there had been three planes and only two had landed. She needed to open her eyes and look for the other one, the most important one, to be sure that it got home safe.

She demanded sight with all her will and heavy eyelids lifted. The world was a blur.

It took her a second to realize that was because she'd fallen across the instrument panel and her cheek was against one of the dials. She exerted more will, and got herself upright, helped by the strap around her waist, that anchored her to the board.

That was better. She could see the instruments, the fuel gauge, the altimeter—*how* high?—and the compass. And through the windscreen she could see—

A slow drifting. And that was wrong, she knew from the tapes he had made her learn. Wrong, because it meant—

The plane wasn't level.

Her hands were heavy, but she got one around the joystick, found the horizon meter and slowly pushed on the stick, watching the horizon line crawl down from almost vertical toward level.

The stick was hard to move. She tried to shift her weight to the left, to bring more push into play—and would have fallen if the strap hadn't held her.

Still, she managed to inch it down until the dial finally displayed a clear horizontal bisection, the blue-white of sky on the top, the black that meant ground on the bottom.

Now, from side to side out the window, there was a horizon, distant and level. It rotated slowly . . .

And that wasn't wrong or right, just a fact, until she knew where—and the compass heading showed that. She found the sun and realized she was flying in the wrong direction, bent to work the stick again, and below her was a boiling cauldron of gray and white and she jumped, the leg went, but the strap held her up and his voice was murmuring, distant and almost too soft to hear . . .

"Storm. Below."

She reached out to touch his pattern, but it wasn't there— no, it *was* there, but *around* her and, fading, somehow, its colors attenuating into mist, the interlockings beginning, slowly, to untwine.

She bit her lip. "You're dying. Val Con—"

"Fly. The. Plane."

•   •   •

The lifemate bridge swirled with energy and Shan could see Val Con's essence, very faint, and Miri's, much stronger—and an incomplete third that drew threads from each, spindle-dancing above, or below, or within the bridgework.

And he dared not touch any of it.

So he did what he could and sat guard over her body in the shell of what had been a hangar and eventually Nelirikk joined him there.

"The captain, I saw her fall." The blue eyes moved, registered the soft rise and fall of her breast and flicked up. "Not dead."

"Not dead," Shan agreed.

"The scout has not returned from his mission."

Shan nodded, his attention on the flow of the lifemate bridge. It had taken his father a full year to die of his lifemate's passing. But the connection between his parent's souls had been as slender as a thread of spider silk, compared to the conflagration that linked Val Con and Miri. If Val Con was dying . . .

"What ails the captain?" Nelirikk asked. Shan looked up.

"She's with the scout."

The blue eyes blinked, then Nelirikk nodded. "More armor comes. And soldiers."

Soldier Lore bestirred itself. "What's our situation?"

"We can prevail," stated another voice from the doorway, in rusty Trade. "With boldness."

A man strode forward—a Liaden male cradling an Yxtrang rifle in his arms like a child. A hatchet hung in a loop on his belt, stained red from edge to blunt.

Nelirikk rose to his towering height. The Liaden ignored him, walked past him and then stopped, looking down at Miri. After a moment, he turned and addressed himself to the Yxtrang.

"You fly for the captain? Eh? Kill enemy at her word?"

Nelirikk inclined his head. "Sir, I do."

"She allowed me and mine with her, on condition we obey the sergeants. The sergeant of my squad is dead and there are many others, who joined at the last, with no sergeant to order them, but who will fight with ferocity."

"You tell me this for a reason?" Nelirikk inquired and the man pulled his lips back from his teeth—a death's head grin.

"I tell you this because I desire you to lead us, Yxtrang-of-the-Captain."

"I do not—"

"My entire line is gone, damn you!" the Liaden shouted. "Will you take what I offer and use it well, or must my Balance fall short of my dead?"

A heartbeat of silence, no more. Nelirikk bowed.

"Soldier, I will lead you. For the glory of Troop and captain. Show me to your fighters."

She flew the plane, dropped the nose and brought it down into the clouds ruthlessly, remembering ships she'd never flown and emergencies she'd never experienced.

The sky was a long time gray; the buffeting and noise of the winds amazed her. The ship went subsonic with an odd fluttering and she had to fight the controls, stretching too far to reach—and then she was below the clouds.

There was green all around, and a river to her left. The clouds sweeping by obscured her vision momentarily and then tore away.

In the distance she could see the airfield, the Irregular's flag flying high.

Lightning flashed off the left wing and the plane lurched as thunder boomed through the metal walls.

She was closing on the airfield fast and the winds were making it difficult, tossing the plane like it was no more substantial than a butterfly. It was hard to see properly, to understand direction from this perspective.

Down and ahead—Yxtrang armor in the trees.

She looked to the board, saw she had bombs to spend. She checked on the situation through the windscreen.

And saw the Yxtrang fighter, closing fast from the right and behind.

She veered the plane, brought it right down on the deck, and saw Val Con's pattern all around her, overlaying everything in tired, fading color.

She knew what to do, stretched to the board and did it,

bringing the plane down, *down,* wingtips brushing the tree-tops, and the Yxtrang fighter was on her, but that wasn't important yet.

The Yxtrang on the ground had noticed her. She saw the turret on the anti-aircraft move, tracking, and she kept the speed steady, sweeping in low and insanely fast, waiting for it, waiting for it and the turret was on her and the plane behind had fired, but missed. She was directly over Yxtrang now, opened her belly and dropped the bombs, dumped what was left of her fuel and she was past and the other plane was still on her tail. The armor found its range and fired. Miri smacked the switch and the landing gear came down.

The fighter behind them blew up.

They were not soldiers, but they were fierce and willing, in their hatred, to take orders.

Accordingly, Nelirikk had them wait, in the cover at the near edge of the airfield. Wait, until the first plane flashed over, dumping fuel and the last of its bombs onto the heads of the enemy. Wait, until the anti-aircraft fired and destroyed the pursuer.

Then, with the enemy disordered and dismayed, he rose up, roared the battle cry—"Revenge!"—and led the rabble to war as the wind rose and thunder out-sounded the cannons.

The beam leapt up from the planet's surface, threaded the Yxtrang Eye and touched the battleship.

There was a flare, which would be the outer shields, Priscilla thought, and a second, which would be the inner.

She sighed and shook her head, for it had been a valiant effort, if ill-favored and—

That quickly the Yxtrang battleship broke and ran, accelerating, and rising—

"Position report, Captain."

Ren Zel's voice was level, betraying nothing. "Tactical report, Captain."

"Tactical?" Priscilla demanded and reached for her board, banishing the Eye and the battleship to a quarter screen, and

saw the break-in noise of a dozen ships, IDs blossoming—
Terran IDs. Terran troopships.

"Affiliation?"

"Tree-and-Dragon," Ren Zel said, as more ships phased
in-system. "Gyrfalk." He paused. "Juntavas."

"Juntavas," she repeated and looked over to him. He met
her eyes, blandly.

"Perhaps they consider the Yxtrang bad for commerce."

"I suppose that's possible." She looked back to her screen.
Something strange was happening close in by the Yxtrang
battleship. Space was behaving in a most unusual manner—
pulsing—and there seemed to be something phasing in, phasing out—in, out, in, out—

In.

Priscilla drew a breath, staring at the big asteroid, that was
behaving as no asteroid could.

"Priscilla!" Ren Zel said sharply and she put out a hand to
touch his sleeve.

"Clutch," she said, projecting calmness into his agitation.
"It's only a Clutch ship, friend. Captain yos'Galan's brother
is—adopted—of a Turtle."

"Yes," he said, taking a breath. "Of course."

Right rudder and some left aileron. Crab into the wind, but
not too much, and down two-thirds flaps to slow it. Keep the
nose down and almost level and pop those leading slats right
now to cut lift hard. Down flaps the rest of the way, don't
bounce. Main wheels down. Crush thrust reverse, slight
bounce, nose wheel down and guiding. The wind's up now
and we're getting off center, didn't correct the crabbing
enough and the rudder's fighting the wind hard and slam the
brakes now with that wounded leg—

The pain shot through her like jellyfish fire. She convulsed
where she lay, back arching, and Shan swung over, holding
her shoulders flat, reaching with Healer sense and then
pulling back because their patterns were united in a beautiful
alien arabesque, and Miri opened her eyes as the plane rolled
by them, too fast, even if—

"*Val Con!*"

She screamed herself back into the plane, and fell onto the stick, pushing it forward with the last of her strength. The leather tether cut into her and she should be sure, but she knew she couldn't move, no more, never again . . .

"Uncle," Alys said from the depth of the intercom. "Planetary Defense Unit says it's taking down the meteor shield, following a successful strike at the enemy's targeting computer."

tel'Vosti stared. Sighed.

"Thank you, niece."

"Yes. It also says that reinforcements have arrived."

LIAD

DEPARTMENT OF INTERIOR
COMMAND HEADQUARTERS

Of the four assigned to the detail at Jelaza Kazone, two were undergoing retraining. The report on the
Commander's screen indicated that one of those would quite
possibly re-attain his pre-catastrophe condition. The other
would not, in the informed opinion of the departmental senior overseeing the process, re-achieve his former level of
expertise. However, the senior remained sanguine concern-
ing that one's eventual effectiveness as a first-line operative.

Not so, Agent yo'Zeamin, whom the Commander's second had been obliged to dispatch in the antechamber of the
Commander's own office, nor Agent pel'Iso, fatally shot by
a Solcintra Port security guard during an ill-conceived attempt to steal a Jumpship.

From the two presently undergoing retraining came a tale
of horrific—nightmarish—event, alike in nothing save the
overmastering sense of personal doom. One reported a dis-
connection with the physical world coinciding with an overriding need to flee.

The second stated that his head had begun to pain him and
he had closed his eyes to ease the strain. When he opened his
eyes, he found himself standing on the outside of Jelaza Kazone's perimeter, near the place where he and the others had

crossed over the evening before. Disbelieving, he closed his eyes once more. And opened them to discover himself on the ridge that marked the boundary to Korval's Valley, with no memory of having walked there. He continued to function in this on-again, off-again manner until he was apprehended in Solcintra itself by a first-line operative, who took the precaution of locking him into a storeroom before placing the call to her cell-leader.

The most disturbing part of this unlikely occurrence, to the Commander's eye, was that the expert's report indicated the force in operation during the agent's lapses of perceptual sense was the raw will of the subordinated native personality.

It was this Agent whom the expert felt might be adequately retrained to basic operative. The Commander frowned, touched the button to activate the line to his second's desk.

"Commander?"

"Agent ven'Egut."

"Undergoing retraining, Commander."

"Yes. See to his termination. Unacceptable risk."

"Yes, Commander."

He cut the connection and swept the screen clear. Three Agents, lost to Korval. He would meditate upon the best answer to that. In the meanwhile, there was Agent yos'Phelium's pet Terran to consider.

A match program placing the gene-set known as Miri Robertson against the Book of Clans had yielded an—interesting—piece of data.

The genes of Miri Robertson closely matched the genes of Clan Erob, Korval's oldest ally.

This significantly altered the face of event—transforming an apparently chance meeting between yos'Phelium and a "Terran mercenary" into a bit of well-planned and long-standing subterfuge.

It also invested one place in all the wide galaxy with a reason for Val Con yos'Phelium's presence.

Commander of Agents touched the speaker-button once more. "I will have four full Agents of Change in the mid-level meeting room in twelve hours precisely. Commander's Priority.

"I will also have the history, decision point records, and current clan and strength particulars on the planet Lytaxin. I need full loyalty-compliance reports on any Agent ever on Lytaxin."

"Immediately, Commander," said his second. "Is there more?"

The Commander hesitated, considering three Agents wasted and likely a Korval dramliza responsible. Especial study was required there, with one mistake already laid to his account.

"Yes. I will have an overview of the current strengths of the various dramliz on planet, and a comparison of reputed powers. Also . . ." Here he hesitated. It would not do to disturb the balances quite yet. But, if Anthora yos'Galan were to call due a debt from another dramliza . . .

"Also please refer to me, for tomorrow's morning briefing, our contingency plans for dealing with the guilds and halls."

"That will be all for this moment," he concluded, and closed the line.

EROB'S CLAN HOUSE

The orders had come from the captain's own lips, and so, on the morning of the sixth day following the battle of the airfield, Nelirikk left the bunker-like infirmary beneath Erob's house and went out into the open air.

He marched with a steady step, eating one of the wonderful pastries the house cooks had brought to the captain's room. He wore a lieutenant's bar and captain's aide insignia, as well as the green scarf at his left shoulder—the troop-sign of The Irregulars—and a Tree-and-Dragon which the captain had very nearly been able to pin on him without assistance.

The orders. Orders. He was so pleased that she was able to give orders that he would have marched to every mountain-top on the planet for her.

"Get outta here," she'd rasped, pale against the pale pillows that supported her. "That's an order. Eat an extra dessert or two. That's an order. If you need something to do, go down the airfield and see what's cookin'. I don't want you back in this room before tomorrow unless you got a real good reason."

Her wounds were like unto a pilot's wounds. During those long hours of grief and waiting, when it was thought both would pass on to duty's reward, the Healer who was a star captain and a soldier had explained to him about wizards and the bond of lifemates. Yet, had not he seen the very real burns from the tie belts, the black eyes and pulled skin of high acceleration . . . Strange indeed were the lives of those who guarded Jela's Tree.

The world was strange now: Troops in good order patrolled, and while some looked on him warily, none barred his way. The air was good, the sun a pleasure, and he had elected to walk, as the captain's purpose had clearly been to insure his value to the troop and to preserve his health while she slowly regained her own.

The way he had chosen brought him to a ridge, and a view reminiscent of his not-so-long-ago vantage in the 14th Conquest Corps command shack when the courageous, silly plane had struck back with honorable intent against the Corps, and the scout's vessel had flung Jela's own challenge at the sky.

The valley was full of planes and ships of various sorts, for the mercenaries were taking no chance that the 15th would come to finish the campaign the 14th had started. There were missile units and fighters, and one odd small ship which he guessed to be the courier or personal vessel of a commander.

The blast crater where the scout's ship had been was already, and wisely, being recycled into a foundation for some new structure.

Was it a trick of his mind or was that not a scout ship dropping quickly into the valley?

His heart nearly crawled into his throat in admiration of those lines. One day, perhaps the captain would permit him inside such a vessel.

He finished the pastry in a gulp, watching as the scout ship set neatly down on the near edge of the field. In a moment he began to run.

There were three of them standing by the ship in casual uniform when he arrived: a woman and two men, all Liaden, all pilots by their stance and alertness, speaking with a soft Erob official. The official was pointing to a spot of trees and

Nelirikk heard, "Fighters . . . only defense left . . ." as he slowly approached the group.

The two men were surely of the elder pilots. One carried a cane, the other grew a mustache on his face, as if he were Terran. Both showed gray in their hair. Both were weeping openly, as the woman stood sober-faced and watchful.

Her eyes widened when she saw him, and she moved a hand, gently and with purpose. The men turned to face him, instantly alert to threat.

Nelirikk saluted.

The Liaden with the mustache—surely the first Nelirikk had seen—stood as if under great strain, face wet with his recent tears. The other man was both more at ease and more dangerous: his eyes quickly touched lieutenant's bar, scarf, Tree-and-Dragon, then lifted to Nelirikk's face.

Momentarily Nelirikk felt as he had when the captain had first walked round him. This one could take his life in a moment if need be. This one, by Jela—

"Nelirikk Explorer, Lieutenant First Lytaxin Irregulars," he stated in the Liaden High Tongue. "May I be of service, scouts?"

The three looked between themselves, and as one, they bowed, equal to equal as he had learned it. The Erob official took this as a good sign and removed herself quickly from the scene.

"Shadia Ne'Zame, Scout Lieutenant, First-In," the woman said, laying her hand over her heart. "Clonak ter'Meulen, Scout Commander," said the man with the most tears. "Forgive my display, Lieutenant. I have heard just now that my daughter died here."

The third looked him over very carefully, and drew from some inner pocket a hand on which gleamed a single, silvery ring. He opened his palm, displaying a pin which was the twin of the Tree-and-Dragon Nelirikk wore.

"I, too, serve Tree-and-Dragon, Nelirikk Explorer, and am at some pains to recall your name among our lists."

Nelirikk stood rooted, as if he faced the very scout, the scout who—

"I am recently recruited, sir. I am personal aide to Captain Miri Robertson, First Lytaxin Irregulars, who is lifemated to

Val Con yos'Phelium, Clan Korval. I serve Line yos'Phelium."

Gently, the scout lieutenant sighed. The man with the
mustache shook his head, Terran fashion, and looked pierc-
ingly at the man with the dragon in his hand.

"Clans revert to type, my friend. So here we have a true
Soldier and if that ship over there isn't a Juntavas courier—a
pirate, in plain speaking—I'll eat my coord book."

Ignoring his companion's speech, the nameless scout
bowed deeply.

"Sir," he said to Nelirikk, "I must put myself in your
hands and beg the grace of an introduction to your captain,
she who lifemated Val Con yos'Phelium, for I, too, am
pledged to line yos'Phelium. Where may she be found?"

"Sir, she is in the infirmary, recovering from wounds received in the recent glorious battle."

"Is she able to speak with me? Or perhaps her lifemate
might speak with me."

"The captain is now allowed visitors. I think it likely that
she would speak with scouts, although I cannot guarantee.
Her lifemate . . ."

He paused, recalling what had been brought out of the
Pilot Elite fighter.

There was sudden bleakness in the air, and the face he
looked down upon was very close to one he knew in its bland
intensity.

"Her lifemate, sir, is in the sealed autodoc. The medical
technicians expect he may be able to speak next week, and
perhaps in a month to walk."

The air warmed, the face before him all but smiled.

"Then I am persuaded you should take me to his lady with
all speed." And abruptly the shift came, from High Liaden
into the tongue of the Troop.

"Soldier, do your duty well, for your charge is a heavy
one." He bowed, and the language was again Liaden, in the
mode the scout's brother had taught him was called 'Comrade.'

"I am very pleased to see you, Nelirikk Explorer. My
name is Daav yos'Phelium."

ABOUT THE AUTHORS

Sharon Lee and Steve Miller live in the rolling hills of Central Maine. Born and raised in Baltimore, Maryland, in the early '50s, they met several times before taking the hint and formalizing the team, in 1979. They moved to Maine with cats, books, and music following the completion of *Carpe Diem,* their third novel.

Their short fiction, written both jointly and singly, has appeared or will appear in *Absolute Magnitude, Catfantastic, Such a Pretty Face, Dreams of Decadence, Fantasy Book,* and several former incarnations of *Amazing.* Meisha Merlin Publishing has or will be publishing four books set in the Liaden Universe: *Plan B, Partners in Necessity, Pilots Choice,* and *I Dare.*

Both Sharon and Steve have seen their nonfiction work and reviews published in a variety of newspapers and magazines. Steve is the founding curator of the University of Maryland's Kuhn Library Science Fiction Research Collection.

Sharon's interests include music, pine cone collecting, and seashores. Steve also enjoys music, plays chess, and collects cat whiskers. Both spend way too much time playing on the internet, and even have a website at:

www.korval.com